Praise for

Gift of the Shaper

BOOK ONE OF THE HIGHGLADE SERIES

"*Gift of the Shaper* is not mere fantasy, but reminiscent of classic mythology. Jennings explores the tension between opposing forces, an explanation of the origins of the world, fate and prophecy, supernatural and nonhuman characters, and the completion of a quest. Jennings is a true word artist."

—*San Francisco Book Review (5 stars)*

"A rollicking good read that is for the fantasy fiction lover in all of us. The book is packed full of adventure, action, suspense, and horror . . . The writing is akin to the classics of fantasy fiction from Tolkien and modern-day George R. R. Martin."

—*Seattle Book Review (4.5 stars)*

"Full of heart-pounding adventure, danger, and intrigue!"

—*Feathered Quill*

"A fun, entertaining debut novel that ends with a bang."

—*Reader Views*

"Wonderfully executed."

—*Manhattan Book Review*

Awaken
the Three

D. L. Jennings

Indigo River Publishing

3 West Garden Street, Ste. 718

Pensacola, FL 32502

www.indigoriverpublishing.com

Awaken the Three | D. L. Jennings, author

ISBN 978-1-950906-52-9 (paperback) | 978-1-950906-53-6 (ebook)

LCCN 2020931748

Edited by Earl Tillinghast and Regina Cornell

Cover and Interior design by Nikkita Kent

Cover Illustration by Ryan Goimarac

Cartography by Rachel Halmes

Author Photography by Vivian Vo

Special discounts are available on quantity purchases by corporations, associations, and others. For details, contact the publisher at the address above.

Orders by US trade bookstores and wholesalers: Please contact the publisher at the address above.

With Indigo River Publishing, you can always expect great books,

strong voices, and meaningful messages.

Most importantly, you'll always find **... words worth reading.**

They are lonely
While we sleep, lonelier
For lack of the traveller
Who is now a dream only.

—Edward Thomas, "Roads"

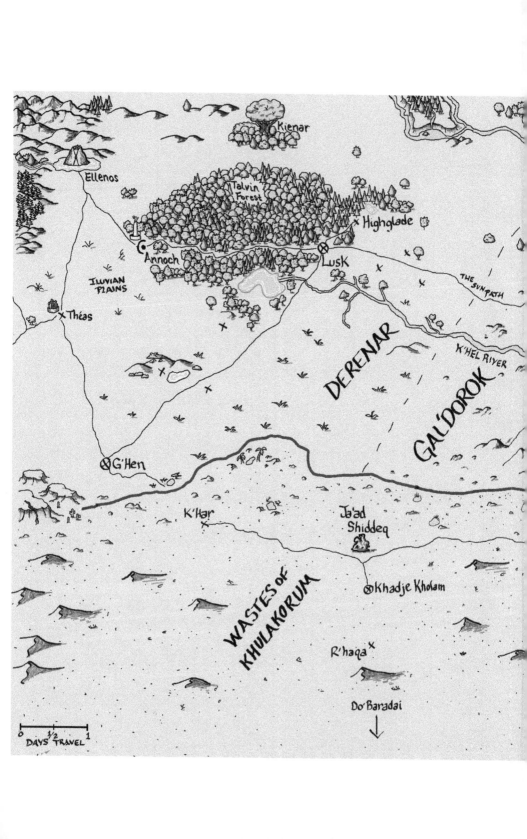

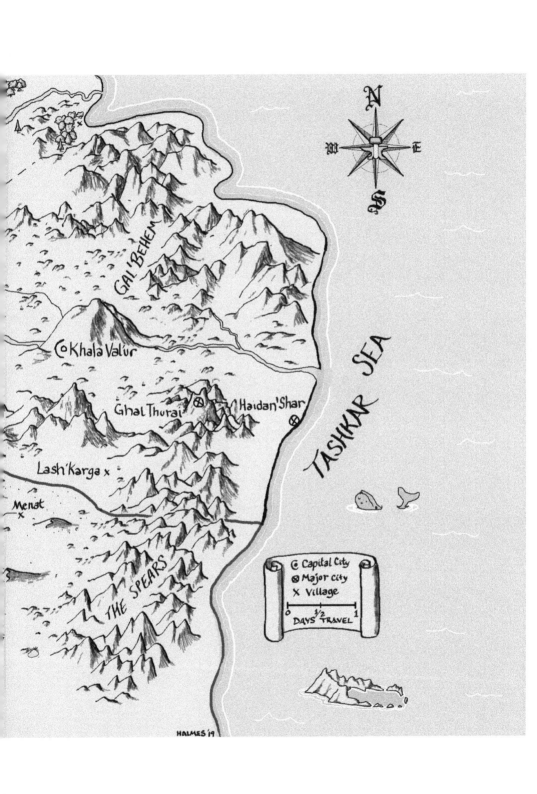

TABLE OF CONTENTS

Deep in the heart
Of old Do'baradai,
In the tumbling spine of the deep,
Wait the Holder, the Trav'ler,
And the Ghost of the Morn
For the one who shall make them complete.

'Neath rock, under stone,
And in darkness they sleep,
Still waiting to be but set free,
'Til judgment shall come
Upon pillars of black,
By the one who awakens the Three.

—Ancient Khôl prophecy,
from the book *The Night Sky and Its Names*

Prologue

Kunas, Master Khyth of Ghal Thurái, lit a lantern that pierced the darkness inside the doors of the mountain hall. Built far beneath the surface that had birthed the name "the Mouth of the Deep," it required a journey of some distance just to reach the entrance. Along with the treacherous paths that led to the outer gates, the city's depth was its true strength—a deterrent to thieves and invading armies alike. The black-hooded Servant of the Breaker checked his lantern and started down the long walkway, footsteps echoing in the abyss.

The sounds of the city below were not as loud today, with the Fist of Thurái having marched off who knows where under General Tennech, the Dagger of Derenar. But the men they'd left behind did a fine job of raising their own racket. They knew this was their chance to prove their worth to a city without a Fist.

As he approached the bottom of the deep stairway, the Master Khyth's footsteps slowed. A second set of doors stood before him, the entrance to the city.

Before he opened them, though, he hesitated. Barely discernible above the muted rumblings of the city below was something that gave him pause.

Was someone else there?

With a glance behind him, he held up his lantern. It creaked as it rocked back and forth, sending yellow light sliding up and down the rocky walls. He stood there for a moment before shaking his head and turning back to the blackened door that guarded the Mouth.

It was a door that took ten men just to open—ten men, or one Khyth with the power of Breaking. Kunas stared at the door, reached out with his power . . . and pulled.

The strain on his mind and body was immense, but filled him with a satisfaction that nothing else could, bending something to his will. The darkness around him filled with the groaning of iron as the door obeyed.

Kunas smiled.

Stepping inside, he raised a hand and reached out once again for the weight of the great door, compelling the iron to move; it listened. Slowly and heavily, the door dragged across the ground, finally coming to rest with a shudder that sealed away the city. Kunas dropped his hand and turned around.

Silence filled the caverns once again.

***

It had been many years since the city of Ghal Thurái had been left unprotected; in fact, until the Fist's most recent departure, no one could really remember the last time they'd left. The Fist of Thurái, a mainstay of Thurian strength, was as much a part of the city as the walls themselves. Yet even in its absence, the city was well protected: doors of iron, walls of earth; pillars of marble, gates of steel.

To the Thurians, their city was a fortress. It was their life. It was their hope.

To the Chovathi gathering beyond its cliffs, however, it was something else entirely: a wounded animal, lost and bleeding in the dark. An animal with no one to protect it from the destruction waiting beyond the walls.

An animal that would die like any other when the teeth of retribution closed down to tear it apart.

The struggle between the Traveler and the Holder of the Dead is older than the world itself, and the Ghost of the Morning is the eternal reminder of their sins. Her mark upon the world is everlasting, and her slumber just as deep.

—Excerpt from *The Night Sky and Its Names*, Author Unknown

From the private collection of Hedjetten Hota

Chapter 1

Khadje Kholam

Awaken the Three

Rathma

The sun was setting over the dunes of Khulakorum as Rathma doffed his hood, watching the colors retreat from atop his stone roof perch. His brown-and-black shemagh had been wrapped around his head and tied off, leaving nothing but his eyes exposed to the stinging sand and darkening dusk. Sparsely placed tents and huts made up most of the sprawling desert city, but closer to the center the city was denser and more built up, especially this close to the palace, where Rathma's eyes now fell.

Tonight was the night; there was no longer any room for doubt.

The tribal city of Khadje Kholam was one of the largest cities beyond the Wastes of Khulakorum thanks to its central location and trade routes between the other tribes, not to mention the palace that sat at the city's heart. A stronghold for the man who lived inside it, the palace had come to be much more than the stone it was built from—and held something more valuable than mere walls could contain.

A cursory pat of his body told Rathma that his sword, along with five daggers, was still concealed beneath his dark and loose-fitting tunic. The leather armor he wore beneath it would protect him only a little, a risk he had to take when dealing in stealth. On his forearms were leather bracers reinforced with steel that could deflect a sword swing or two, and into their undersides were slipped three thin, razor-sharp blades that could be thrown into an enemy's throat in a pinch. His dark, hooded cloak—a gift from his brother—came down past his knees, concealing the twin daggers strapped to his thighs, as well as a grappling hook and rope tied to his waist. Of all the weapons at his disposal, though, the last was the most dangerous in Rathma's hands: a recurve bow and a single quiver with twenty arrows. With shafts of wood and tips of sharpened steel, their true strength came in their reusability—a singularly important quality when hunting humans. And none did so better than Rathma.

A last-second mental inventory of his tools and weapons confirmed that his careful preparation would not be in vain. He went over the layout one last time to make sure he was ready for battle, mentally and physically.

A great stone wall formed the exterior of the compound that held the palace, a city within a city. The inside of the compound was large enough to hold a small army, and Rathma could barely make out the wall that enclosed the other side. There were four guard posts manned by one lookout apiece, one on each corner, watching the perimeter.

Beyond the wall were tents housing scores of sleeping soldiers loyal to Djozen Yelto—potential collateral if any of them awoke and decided to wander outside at the wrong time. And beyond those tents, in the very middle of the compound, was Djozen Yelto's palace, a small fortress in its own right.

Even without the walls surrounding it and the army of soldiers camped around it, the palace was not easily penetrated. It was protected by two armed guards in front of a reinforced steel door and topped with four more guards in a lookout tower.

What was on the other side of the steel door, though, Rathma could only guess: no one from outside the compound had been inside in over ten years. It was one of the reasons Yelto had remained in power this long.

Tonight, Rathma planned to change that. He dropped from his position on the stone roof, listening as the shadows fell.

Worship of the Holder of the Dead had spread quickly throughout the tribes, thanks in part to the influence of Djozen Yelto; Rathma planned to use that worship to his advantage. Every night at right around this time, the god's followers in Khadje Kholam would chant an invocation, turning their eyes to the sky—and away from the opening Rathma would need.

The guards on the wall raised their arms and eyes at last.

Do it, Rathma thought.

And as they started their chant, he moved.

The words that filled the air were as old as the stars in the sky that the Holder of the Dead commanded:

Ahmaan, Ahmaan, Ahmaan Ka.
Dobrak mahn ihmantu zjha
Mith te'kunde Lash'kun'a
Ahmaan, Ahmaan, Ahmaan Ka.

By the time the chanting stopped, Rathma had scaled the outer wall.

Perfect, he thought. The first part of the plan had gone off without a hitch.

On to the next.

He pulled himself up, came to a crouch, and leaned his back against the guard post that extended several feet above the wall on the southeast corner. Somewhere up there and out of view was the lookout, eyes on the dark and back turned to Rathma.

Rathma's fingers ran along the smooth edges of the stone as he found his grip. Raising himself slowly, his eyes cleared the surface. He saw the lookout's back come into view. In a silent, fluid motion, he pulled himself up and crouched.

Drawing his dagger and a breath, he lunged.

One hand reached to cover the man's mouth, while the other hand planted the dagger in his throat. Rathma squeezed, pulling the man back and onto the ground as they struggled; he would hold on as long as he must. The realization dawned darkly on him that, in doing so, he had become a sort of holder of the dead as well. He dropped the thought along with the man.

He looked around to see if his actions had raised an alarm. None was heard. The cloak from his brother hid him well in the moonless night, and his relentless training had quieted his movements. He was undetectable to all but the sharpest ears.

Rathma rolled the dead man off of him to find his eyes still wide with fright. Closing them with his fingertips, Rathma stood. *Looks like the Holder had his back turned as well*, he thought coldly as he pulled out his bow.

He had to reach the palace, but in order to do that, he had to deal with two other lookouts: one to his north and one to his west. After that, the last lookout on the northwest would be blind to his approach.

This next part was crucial—and dangerous.

A few hundred feet to his west, the next lookout was barely distinguishable against the darkness of the night, but Rathma could make out just enough of his shape to know where to aim. It was too much of a gamble to aim for the chest: the arrow could easily catch him in the shoulder, or miss his heart, or bury itself in his arm, allowing time to raise an alarm. The slightest sound could give him away.

No—he had to shoot for the head. He nocked an arrow, took aim, and held his breath. There were two archers in all of Khadje Kholam who could have made a shot like this, and they were Rathma and Rathma on a bad day.

His release made little more than a thrum in the still night air, and the arrow flew just as quietly. He held his breath for what seemed like an eternity as it sped after its mark. The thump he heard meant that it had found something, but he waited for a cry or a yell from the lookout to see just what. When none came, and the shadowy figure crumpled to the ground, Rathma finally exhaled.

One more to go.

The northeast lookout was the last he would need to dispatch. Rathma had already nocked an arrow in case the first one needed it, so he used it to aim at the lookout in the nearby post. He looked down the shaft of the arrow as he used it to track his target. Slowly, he pulled back and felt the tension in his bowstring. He held his breath . . . and released.

The well-fletched arrow did its job, as he watched yet another figure slump to the ground, another dead soldier in Yelto's employ. Turning his eyes to the north, Rathma looked upon the prize.

The tiered, windowless palace was three stories high and square, and the red clay roof tiles made the palace stand out against the golden sand of the desert that surrounded it. On top of the third tier stood a guard tower manned by four of Yelto's most trusted guards, one facing each cardinal direction. Rathma figured one of them held the key to the door below them that led inside.

Only one way to be sure, Rathma thought. He just hoped Kuu was holding up his end of the bargain.

He waited nervously, squinting to try to see a little better in the dark. The nearly moonless night was a liability as well as an advantage, a double-edged sword concealing him and his enemies alike.

But Rathma had his hand on the hilt.

When he heard a commotion from the north, he smiled. Kuu had done his job.

The four guards in the tower shouted in surprise, turning their eyes toward the noise—and their backs to Rathma.

Now, he thought.

He had already fastened the end of his grappling hook to the wall; pulling it taut, he approached the edge. He stepped off and rappelled down, lowering himself to the ground in two short leaps. He let the rope drop when he reached the bottom. Turning to face the palace, he hoped Kuu's distraction would be enough.

The bare dirt floor of the courtyard did little to cushion his steps as he ran, but he no longer cared about stealth. Now, his only concern was swiftness. He needed to cover a lot of ground while the guards' attention was elsewhere. Making his way past the rows of tents that lined the compound, he selected his path and never took his eyes off the guard tower at the top of Yelto's palace. Once he reached the palace, he would have to climb.

Approaching the great steel door, Rathma slowed to a walk. The stone that comprised the palace was different than that of the outer wall surrounding it, smooth and not easily scaled, but the eaves from the next tier provided just enough surface area to grab on to. Rathma took a running start at the wall, taking one step, two steps up it and going nearly horizontal as he climbed. Then, as his momentum was almost gone, he launched himself upward and back with just enough height to reach the eaves of the second story. He grabbed hold, nearly slipping off as his fingers found their grip on the hardened clay. He pulled himself up to his chest as his legs dangled beneath him and, finding himself steady, pulled himself onto the roof.

Only two more levels to go.

Rathma could hear the sounds of shouting from above him and knew Kuu was holding his own.

When his fingers found the top of the last tier, he pulled himself up slowly, just high enough to peek over the edge. He saw the four guards, only a few feet away, scanning frantically to the north for the source of the noise. They were dressed in long tan tunics that came down past their knees—long enough to protect them from the sweltering daytime sun, and light enough for them to breathe—over which they wore chainmail vests. Their open leather boots offered little more than protection from the heat of the desert floor, as they looked more like sandals than armor. Rathma knew right away what he should do.

He pulled himself up slowly and silently, lowering onto his belly as he rose over the edge of the red clay-tiled roof. Pushing himself to his knees, he donned his hood and reached for the twin daggers in their sheaths on his thighs.

Crouching, he crept closer. When he was within reach he surged forward, plunging a dagger into the foot of each of the two middle guards. They howled in pain, grabbing the attention of the two outer guards still looking for Kuu, who looked at their screaming counterparts to see what was wrong. They whirled around just in time for Rathma to smile at them. He raised his hands in surrender.

Then, in the blink of an eye, he bent his arms inward at the elbow, where his fingers found the ends of the long blades he had planted on the opposite forearm, drew them, and flung them out in a V before the guards could ask what he was doing there. Each blade hit its mark, landing right in their windpipes. Their hands went to their throats as they collapsed, choking on blood and steel.

Rathma moved forward and drew his shortsword. He ran it through the guard on his left by grabbing his arm and thrusting upward through his side, the one place the chainmail vest did not protect. Then he turned to face the only guard still upright, who had dropped to a knee to try to remove the dagger from his foot.

"Please," the guard said, putting out a hand and begging him to stop. "What do you want?"

"The key to Djozen Yelto's inner chambers," Rathma answered. "Where is it?"

With a shaky hand, the guard pointed to the one Rathma had just run through with his sword. "Th-There. It's on his belt."

Rathma kept his sword level and his eyes on the guard as he stooped to pat down the body in front of him. Hearing the jingle of a group of keys, he looked down to see about a half dozen, all of different shapes and colors, hanging from a key ring.

"Which one is it?" he asked as he unfastened the key ring from the belt loop.

Hearing no answer, he looked up to see his friend Kuu standing behind the guard with his dagger jutting out of the guard's back.

Rathma sighed. "Why did you do that?" he asked, wiping off his sword.

"He was going to kill you," Kuu answered. "You should thank me." He pulled out the dagger and kicked the body of the guard with his boot. Kuu's wavy black hair hung down to his chin, onto which the beginnings of a beard had sprouted. His emerald-green eyes stood out on his thin, dark face, which was capped with a big, crooked nose. He was skinny, and the meager leather armor he wore only accentuated that fact.

Holding up the ring of keys, Rathma sheathed his sword. "How will we know which one fits the door?"

"Try them all?" Kuu said with a shrug. "And will you take that thing off your face? I can barely hear you through it."

Rathma stood up with a sigh and undid the shemagh, shaking out his dark red hair to let it hang down past his ears. His eyes, the same shade of red as his hair, darted back and forth over the north courtyard where Kuu had fought his own way through. "What choice do we have? Come on."

Rathma walked south and leaped off, twisting to grab the edge of the story below him, then pushing off to drop backward to the ground. He heard Kuu muttering something about showing off as the thin thief grabbed on to the roof and lowered himself down, slowly.

Rathma had already been trying keys when Kuu dropped down beside him.

"That wasn't it either," Rathma grumbled as he slid another key off the ring and tossed it to the ground. "We might be here until morning."

Kuu was tapping him on the shoulder as he looked through the keys, trying to see which would be a good fit.

"Not now, Kuu. I think this might be it."

"But you may want to see this," his friend said as he spun him around.

"Well"—the key ring dropped to the ground as Rathma slowly reached for his sword—"you're wrong. I didn't want to see this."

D.L. Jennings

Standing in front of them were three men in long robes—dark blue with a white border—and one of them was holding a blazing torch above his head. Behind them, emerging from the tents, were perhaps twenty armored men brandishing knives and swords.

"So," the man with the torch began. "Do you think you can simply walk into the house of Djozen Yelto?" He had cloudy gray eyes and spoke with the accent of the western tribes. But neither of those things was what signified he was a Priest of the Holder; those two things alone would have been tolerable for Rathma.

It was the fact that the servants of the Holder of the Dead had their flesh from the neck up stripped away by some awful power, leaving their eyes permanently open and all of their facial muscles exposed. *That* was what disturbed Rathma more than anything.

"Ah," Rathma said. "We should have knocked."

"Take them," said the priest.

But as the swarm of men descended on the two young men from beyond the Wastes, in the blink of an eye, Rathma disappeared from sight.

Chapter 2

The Otherworld

Awaken the Three

D'kane

New and overwhelming power was coursing through D'kane, yet still he was trapped.

In the distance behind him, as tall as a mountain, was the lifeless husk of the former Breaker of the Dawn, from whom D'kane had drawn his power. He had the ancient god to thank for the surging and nearly incomprehensible strength inside of him, yes, but there was another ancient power with which he still had to contend.

A power that stood before him now, in defiance.

D'kane frowned. "What have you done?" he breathed. His eyes still stung from the earlier explosion of power.

"I've trapped us both here," she answered, "where your power will be useless."

The being before him, whose form was that of a young woman, was somehow different than the one D'kane had overpowered back in Derenar. Although her physical form was the same—blonde with blue eyes and a smallish figure covered by a worn white dress that had seen its fair share of scuffles—her presence had changed. Even her voice was different: it now commanded authority and made him uncomfortable. He had known that the woman had the blood of the Shaper flowing through her, but it was clear to him now that she indeed *was* the Shaper of Ages, not just the goddess's descendant.

"You're confined to the Otherworld," she continued, "like the Binder and I always intended."

Yes: this was the goddess who had crafted the Hammer and the Anvil of the Worldforge, the one whose power had trapped him here. Yet hers was not the only power D'kane felt. There was another power, somewhere, that seemed to be calling to him. Distant. Familiar. Faint. Tugging at him, as if some part of him had just woken up.

He regarded the Shaper with callous contempt. "Very well. I may not have the ability to leave this world, but I am under no obligation to give up trying. I will find a way."

The clashing of two titanic powers had already proven to be destructive, and D'kane wanted to find out just how destructive it could be.

He'd already destroyed two gods—what was one more?

Chapter 3

Kienar

Thornton

Thornton Woods knelt over the unconscious body of his sister as he struggled to reconcile what now lay in front of him. After Yasha had experienced the surge of power that came with the Breaking, her skin had blistered and cracked all over, looking like a piece of lumber that had been licked by too much flame. Her reddish-orange hair was just about the only thing that was familiar to Thornton as he stood up beneath the trees of Kienar. He knew that he had changed too, and he wasn't sure how the rest of the world would react. His eyes, once a simple dark brown, now swirled angrily with the power of the Otherworld, identifying him as Khyth to anyone who saw them. It was another thing he and his sister had in common now.

"We should be off," came a deep rumbling from behind.

Thornton turned to see Endar Half-Eye, commander of the Athrani Legion, with his massive sword resting casually over one shoulder. Beside him was Thuma, his second-in-command. Thuma was a big man in his own right, and a full-blooded Athrani, as was evidenced by his brown-on-brown eyes that marked him as being touched by the Otherworld.

"Ellenos awaits our return," Endar said with a grin, "and there is a great deal of celebrating to be done." The big half-eye—the product of a marriage between an Athrani father and a human mother—looked to the west, where the seat of the Athrani government lay. It was a few days' march for healthy men, longer for those recovering from fresh battle wounds.

"Ready the men, Thuma. I've gone without Ellenian ale for too long."

"Aye, Commander," Thuma said, saluting. The big Athrani turned to carry out his orders, disappearing into the sea of soldiers.

But Thornton was in no mood to celebrate, and the frown on his lips said as much. He had been torn from his childhood friend Miera in a situation he did not fully understand. From what he gathered, though, she was the goddess incarnate known as the Shaper of Ages, and she had sealed herself away in the Otherworld in order to prevent the Breaker of the Dawn from escaping. Thornton was hazy on the details; the world of the Khyth—of Breaking, and of their ancient feud with the Athrani—

was still very foreign to him. He scanned the faces of the men, a mixture of humans and Athrani, looking for one he recognized.

Specifically, he was looking for his father, Olson.

The big man would have been easy to spot: tall and muscular with a sturdy frame paid for by years of working over a blacksmith's forge, and a thick brown beard that matched the color of Thornton's own hair. So when he was unable to spot him among the men who were still steeped in their victory celebration, he began to worry.

The trees of Kienar, numerous and mighty, blocked out all but the most persistent rays of sunlight, blanketing the earth with jagged shadows. Thornton's eyes had grown accustomed to the darkness, though, and they continued the search for his father. As they wandered, they fell upon a regal black figure who was exchanging emphatic words with someone he could not see. As he approached, Thornton saw that it was in fact *two* black figures: Kethras and Ynara, children of the forest of Kienar, who stood in apparent opposition to each other.

"I will not leave you, Ynara. This forest is just as much my home as it is yours," Kethras growled. His voice was deep and rough, booming like a landslide.

Thornton had only seen the two Kienari argue once before, and it was a frightening sight to behold. Taller than him by almost two feet, Kethras and Ynara looked the way hunters were meant to look: sleek and sinewy, with movements as quick as they were strong. The fine black fur that covered their bodies served to make them nearly invisible in the shadows, with only the flashing of their sharp teeth to give them away as they talked.

"It is not your choice, brother," Ynara said calmly. Her voice, while softer than Kethras's, had a sharp quality to it that always reminded Thornton of a carving knife being dragged across a block of wood. "You know just as well as I do that one of us must leave. And now that the mantle of Binder has been passed to me, it is I who must remain."

Thornton thought he could hear a sadness in her firm words. He approached as Kethras drooped his wiry shoulders in defeat. The two Kienari turned toward him when they heard him approach.

"Has your sister woken yet?" Ynara asked, peering from behind the taller figure of her brother. Her great black eyes and cat-like face made her look threatening even as she smiled.

"No," Thornton answered. He was still getting used to hearing people call Yasha his sister, a fact that he had only recently discovered. "Endar already suggested tying her to a horse so we can leave . . . I don't know how serious he was." He looked back at the commander of the Athrani Legion, who was making sure all of his men were prepared to make for home, stopping occasionally to shoot suspicious glances at the young Khyth woman sleeping beneath the trees.

"Give it time and she will awaken," Ynara answered. "She has been through a great deal, and we all owe her much."

Thornton nodded as Kethras turned to him, looking solemn as ever. The tall Kienari wore a quiver on his back, empty from having fired off all his arrows in defense of the forest.

"If she does not awaken soon," Kethras said, "you and I can take turns carrying her."

Thornton was surprised at his words—not because he was offering to carry a Khyth, but because he would apparently be coming along. He studied the dark face of the Kienari before finding the words to respond. "You're coming with us?" he asked. "To Ellenos?"

Kethras looked to his sister before nodding an affirmation. "I am," he rumbled. The words sounded forced. "Ynara insists. I must speak to the High Keeper."

And though he wouldn't have let the Kienari catch on, Thornton felt relief at the revelation. He didn't like being carted away by the Athrani army, but if he would have Kethras to talk to, he felt that he could at least tolerate it. It was comforting to have a familiar face around—even if it was covered in fur. The thought made him smile to himself, but it faded just as quickly as he remembered why he had come over in the first place.

"Ynara," Thornton began, "I can't find my father anywhere. Endar said the last time he saw him was when he sent him to Naknamu." He indicated the Old One, the tallest tree in the forest. "Have you seen him?"

Ynara frowned as she glanced at Kethras, almost too quickly for Thornton to see. But not quickly enough.

"What?" Thornton asked. "What is it?"

"Your father," Ynara said, "is in the Otherworld."

The words stung, robbing Thornton of breath. *The Otherworld.* He'd already lost one person he cared for to the clutches of the ethereal plane; he hadn't been prepared to lose two. "But Miera had you seal it when she sent us back," he protested. "Why didn't she send him through too?" Thornton furrowed his brow as he looked for answers in the faces of the two Kienari. It was no use, though; their expressions offered nothing.

Ynara reached out her great branch of an arm and rested it on Thornton's shoulder. "That is for the Shaper to know, young one. I cannot say."

Her words did nothing to comfort Thornton as he shrugged off the hand with a scowl. He looked again at the tree where he had found himself earlier after being jettisoned from the Otherworld by a selfless Miera. The reminder that both his father and his closest friend were somewhere on the other side only served to upset him even more. He almost spoke his displeasure aloud but thought better of it. He knew Ynara had sealed off the bridge to the Otherworld, just as Miera had asked, but now that he knew his father was over there too, he began to wonder just how sturdy the seal was. He felt the weight of the white-ash-handled hammer that hung from his back—the hammer that had somehow been the key to opening and closing the gate. The same hammer he had held since he was a child. The hammer that seemed to be pulling on him in a way he had not felt before.

Before he could give it more thought, though, Ynara spoke up.

"You must not dwell on it. The greatest danger to all life, the Breaker of the Dawn, is no longer a threat to us thanks to Miera. And thanks to your father," she said. The words hung in the air. "Miera wouldn't have been able to do what she did without his help."

The surface of the old tree, Naknamu, was rough and dark, and gave almost no indication of being as old as people said it was. Supposedly it was old even when mankind was young. Thornton rubbed his eyes before looking it over again. Its great branches shot out in all directions, and the leaves were broader than most men's hands. If nothing else, Naknamu was sturdy, a testament to the hardiness of the Kienari who guarded its branches.

Thornton pushed his thoughts away for the time being. As he did, Kethras nodded in the direction of his sister.

"Look," he said. "She stirs."

Thornton whirled around to see Yasha moving, which was more than she had done since they had found themselves forced out of the Otherworld. She started to sit up but fell back to the ground beneath her own weight. *She's still too weak*, Thornton thought. He hurried over to help her.

"Don't move too much," he said as he came close. "Ynara says you're still weak."

"Who?" Yasha asked. Her swirling green eyes looked at Thornton, then past him to the trees that surrounded them. "Where are we?" she asked weakly. "The last thing I remember . . ."

Realizing that unconsciousness had deprived her of quite a bit, Thornton knelt down and put a hand on her shoulder. "Don't worry, you're safe. We're in Kienar with friends." He looked up to see Kethras approaching. "You remember Kethras, don't you?"

Yasha looked up and down the slim frame of the Kienari as recognition filled her eyes. "Of course," she said. "How could I forget someone that scared me half to death the first time we met?"

"In my defense, I'd never met a Khyth that didn't try to kill me." Kethras took a knee to look her in the eye, baring his teeth in what Thornton had grown to recognize as a smile. He offered a strong black hand to her as Thornton did the same, helping Yasha gently to her feet.

As the young Khyth woman brushed herself off, bits of dirt and leaves fell from the gray robes of an apprentice. She stopped when she looked up, having just seen where she actually was. Her eyes went wide as she stared in awe at the immense forest that surrounded them. "So this is Kienar," she said in a hushed tone. "It's . . . amazing."

From what Yasha had said about her life before, Thornton knew this might be one of the first times she had ever seen a forest. The black mountain walls that comprised the Sunken City of Khala Val'ur let in no sunlight, and the only life beneath them was the humans and the Khyth who called the city home. Thornton watched as his sister admired the living forest around them.

"If she can stand, she can ride," came the voice of Endar. The tall half-eye was walking toward them, sword still in hand, unarmored from the waist up. His salt-and-pepper hair framed a strong jaw that made his sharp green eyes stand out even more, especially the left one, which rested on a red background that indicated his maternal Athrani heritage. Thornton still hadn't worked out just how Athrani heredity worked, but he was hoping to learn more when they eventually made their way to their capital city.

Ynara chimed in. "If she must ride, then I have just the mount." The younger Kienari approached holding the reins of a small brown mare that Thornton immediately recognized.

"Matilda!" He laughed. "What are you doing here?" He ran his fingers through the dark brown mane of the animal he'd known for years, as she shook her head happily. Matty had been hauling Miera's flower cart to and from the city of Lusk for as long as Thornton could remember. She was old, trusty, and apparently happy to be in a place filled with delicious grass.

"She was a gracious traveling companion," Ynara said, handing Thornton the reins. "She's seen more of Derenar and Gal'dorok than most horses her age ever will."

The explanation was good enough for Thornton, who was smiling again at the sight of another familiar furry face. The reunion was almost enough to push aside thoughts of his father.

Almost.

"Then we should get moving," Endar said. "Sh'thanna will be waiting—and wanting a full report when we arrive." He turned to his second-in-command, saying over his shoulder, "Thuma, make sure the men are ready to march. The quicker we get there, the better."

Thornton finished scratching Matilda behind the ears. Looking at Yasha, he asked, "Have you ridden before?"

The red-haired Khyth nodded. "Every apprentice is taught to ride from a young age; General Tennech insisted."

"Then I'll help you up."

Thornton reached out his hand to his sister, laughing to himself when he thought about it: she was the one who had first told him about his heritage. Now, *he* was going to be the one telling her about hers, and the fact that they were brother and sister. She had been kind enough to break it to him gently; the least he could do for her was the same.

Yasha took his hand and placed a foot in the stirrup of Matty's saddle, letting her robes ride up to her knees as she draped her legs on either side. Thornton could tell right away that she was a seasoned rider: she looked almost as comfortable in the saddle as on her feet. He looked ahead, where the bulk of the Athrani Legion were finishing their preparations.

The metallic clatter of swords and chainmail filled the forest as the army gathered up the last of the war-fighting supplies to fall into formation and begin the march home. Endar, seated atop his war horse, raised his sword to signify the beginning of the march, piercing the air with a booming shout that set thousands of armored feet into coordinated motion.

"To Ellenos!" the big man shouted.

With a glance up to Yasha, Thornton said, "I guess that's our cue."

She looked a little stunned by the commotion, but nodded despite it all. A tap of her heels on Matty's sides spurred her onward, in line behind the might of the legion. Thornton walked beside her, missing his own horse, Jericho, who was stabled safely back in Annoch. *Probably feasting on oats and carrots*, he thought with a smile. Though he wasn't fond of riding, he realized that this was the first time he'd ever been away from the sturdy old workhorse. His smile waned and his shoulders sagged a bit at the notion. *Just one more thing to miss*, he thought.

Kethras walked on the other side of Yasha—the Kienari's own long legs doing a better job of carrying him than any horse ever could—and seemed to be saying a silent goodbye to his forest as they left.

There will be a right time to ask him about everything, Thornton reasoned. He hoped he would know just when it was. He was so consumed with this hope that, as they rode away, he barely felt the hammer as it pulled on him again.

D.L. Jennings

Ynara

As Ynara watched the armored procession streaming out of her forest, she let her eyes fall upon her brother, Kethras, leaving the protection of the trees. It hurt to make him go, but it had to be done.

She had always been closer to him than any of their other brothers and sisters, and she finally knew how their Mother had felt when she'd sent them away to find Thornton. It was her responsibility, she knew, but knowing never changed anything; it only spread out the pain over a longer period of time.

Looking up at Naknamu, she remembered what the ancient tree was like when she was young, all those thousands of years ago. She knew its branches well, and they seemed to bend toward her now in a loving embrace. It made the pain of separation at least a little more bearable.

She was its protector now; she was the forest. She was the Binder of Worlds.

And one day, she knew, she would also be the Last Kienari.

Chapter 4

Ellenos

Lilyana

"Lily, wake up."

No answer.

The words were sweet and gentle. They were her mother's words—Coraline, daughter of Eidaline.

"Lilyana Coros. I'm not telling you again."

Full name. She meant it. A little less gentle, but it didn't detract from the lovely contralto of Cora's voice.

"Yes, Mother."

Lily's own words came out barely above a whisper as she pulled the patchwork blanket over her head to steal just a few more seconds of darkness. If she had known it was the last time she would hear that voice, Lily would have kept the covers over her face just to hear her speak again. She would have treasured it. She would have savored it.

She would have . . .

She would have . . .

It didn't matter. All that mattered now was *her.*

***

Lily fought off her sleepiness with a yawn and walked over to where her mother was finishing brushing her hair.

"Where are we going today?" she asked.

Coraline was looking in the polished silver mirror at the reflection of her and her daughter, two women separated by about twenty years and not much else.

"Well, aren't we eager?" Coraline said with a laugh. She moved over and patted the worn cushion on her seat. "Why don't we fix you up and I'll tell you."

Lily sat down and looked up into the eyes of her mother, framed by high cheekbones that made them stand out even more. She had trouble describing her mother's face as anything but perfect, but Coraline's soft jawline and delicate lips made more than a few men stop in their tracks and stare. Her looks were her most valuable asset, and she had no qualms about using them. She took care of the way she looked, accentuating her feminine qualities and making sure that the men who saw her liked what they were seeing—liked it enough to pay good money for it.

The underbelly of Athrani society was not publicly acknowledged, but it was very real. They liked to think of themselves as better than their human and Khyth counterparts, but they weren't—they were just better at hiding it. Her mother was certainly good at hiding it from Lily, and it wasn't until much later that Lily would even connect the dots as to how she really made her money.

Darling, Coraline was always saying, *you pay attention to those women with the fine clothing. That will be you someday.*

Her mother took the dark wooden brush to Lily's hair and hummed softly as she ran it through. The melody was plain and bright; the tune, comforting.

Lying 'neath the falling rain
Scattered under stars,
She rides the wind to heart's content
Til he returns again.

The loveliness of Coraline's brown-on-blue eyes and long brown hair was surpassed only by her voice.

"I like that song, Mother. What is it?"

"Just something that your grandmother used to sing to me when I was a girl," she answered.

It was a simple little tune, but her mother's soothing voice did wonders to it.

"What does it mean?" Lily asked.

"Oh, I don't know," Coraline said as she kissed her girl on the head. "But I always thought it was my mother's way of telling me how she missed my father."

Awaken the Three

She leaned in close to Lily and whispered, "Now hurry up and get your dress. The blue one."

Lily's eyes lit up, and she raced to the wooden chest in the corner of the room. She opened it and didn't have to look far: her favorite dress, the blue one with white frills, was nestled neatly near the top of the chest.

She pulled it on over her head with a smile. Tonight would be unforgettable.

Chapter 5

Gal'dorok

Awaken the Three

Duna

Duna Cullain had marched the armies of Gal'dorok halfway across Derenar by the time she even considered resting. In just a matter of days, they had almost made their way back to Khala Val'ur, city of the Khyth.

The peaks of the Great Serpent, Gal'behem, were visible on the horizon.

Not much longer now, she thought with relief.

She looked back over the men—a mixture of the Fist of Ghal Thurái and the warriors of Khala Val'ur—and finally saw just how many they had lost in the Battle for the Tree. They were a thin, weakened force. *Pathetic*, she thought. *Beaten by a smattering of Athrani and a few dozen Kienari. Truly pathetic.*

The next realization came slowly and heavily: they were her army now.

Wherever Tennech had run off to, she knew he would not be coming back; she had heard how the Khyth dealt with failure. The general must have known he was as good as dead if he ever showed his face in Khala Val'ur again. And after Commander Durakas's brains had become acquainted with a Kienari arrow—and shortly thereafter, the forest floor—she was now the highest-ranking military officer in both Khala Val'ur and Ghal Thurái.

The highest in all of Gal'dorok, in fact.

The epiphany dried out her throat and left her tongue feeling thick and numb. She frowned.

Duna's thin blonde hair hung down over a pair of green eyes that were spaced just too far apart, she knew, and her wide forehead left little room for the rest of her face to grow. She conceded that she wasn't much to look at, but if anything, this fact was what had driven her to success; she had thrown herself at her work because throwing herself at men had proven to be a waste of time, energy, and self-esteem. Though the men around her had no interest in her sexually, they held nothing back from her politically, wasting no time with deceit. They treated her like one of their own. Commander Durakas had seen this, and her fearless attitude, and had decided to take her under his wing.

Only now, that wing had been torn off and left on the floor of Kienar, and she was going to have to figure out how to fly on her own.

The sounds of hoof beats behind her jarred Duna back to reality. She was surprised when she looked around to find that her army had come to a stop. She whirled back around on her mount and shouted, "What is the meaning of this? I gave no order to stop!"

A bigger man toward the front of the formation spoke up. "F-Forgive us, Lady Cullain, but look"—he pointed over her shoulder, to a point far off in the distance—"there."

She turned and strained her eyes in the darkness. Far beyond the reaches of Khala Val'ur, beyond the spine of Gal'behem, was the mountain fortress of Ghal Thurái.

Only now there was no fortress.

Flames and an empty horizon filled the space that should have been Ghal Thurái. Great plumes of smoke curled their way up into the night sky as they reached for the stars, like gray fingers.

"What is it?" one man called out.

"What does it mean?" cried another.

"Quiet!" Duna shouted as she turned around to face her men. "We will know soon enough. But our debt is to Khala Val'ur, and we must make our way there or face the wrath of High Khyth Yetz." The mere mention of the name made more than a few men shiver, but just as many were steadfast in their resolve.

"It's a sign from the Breaker," someone shouted. "We're needed in Ghal Thurái!"

Murmurs of agreement sliced their way through the rumblings of the army, growing increasingly dissonant. Those from Khala Val'ur wanted nothing more than to return home. But those from the Mouth of the Deep saw what could only be their once-great city in flames.

"Lady Cullain, let us return to the Mouth!" one man near the front begged. "The Khyth can wait. And for all we know, there may not be much time left."

Duna narrowed her eyes as she thought. *Whatever happened in Ghal Thurái was recent. If there was ever a chance to stop what is happening in the city, that chance is now.*

She looked back to the faces of her men.

Tired, ragged, exhausted. Determined.

"Then we will continue on to the Mouth," she said. "I will answer personally for our . . . diversion." As she spoke the words aloud, she pictured the face of the most feared man in all of Khala Val'ur and shivered. Yetz would not be pleased with their lateness—but he also didn't know what he didn't know. And if she kept it a secret from him, Duna reasoned, he never had to find out.

A click of her heels on her mount spurred it forward.

She only hoped that she was right.

Chapter 6

The Wastes of Khulakorum

Awaken the Three

Rathma

It hurt every single time.

Rathma could already feel the headache that always followed his jumps through reality, but he couldn't afford to give it a second thought; he knew he wasn't in the clear just yet.

Rathma could hear growled obscenities coming from inside the courtyard; Kuu wasn't born with the gift of farstepping like Rathma was.

"I'm sorry, Kuu!" he managed to shout through the pain. "You know where I'll be!"

He had to keep going.

"Just stick to the plan," he said to himself through gritted teeth.

The jagged slabs of rock that made up the outside of the compound were mostly obscured by the darkness, but the flicker of torches waving around them cast shiftless and wandering shadows, and one of those shadows—Rathma—was moving quickly away.

But even as he moved away from the compound, he knew that his friend was more than capable of taking care of himself. Kuu had a few skills that even Rathma envied. But, for now, he was on the run.

***

Djozen Yelto's men, while certainly fast and determined, were not born with the gift of farstepping, and therefore were simply no match for Rathma. In fact, as long as he could see to where he was farstepping, Rathma could blink in and out of the landscape with nothing more than a thought—a thought which was always followed by violent nausea. But he simply had to put enough space between himself and Yelto's men until he was sure that he would be safe. He had no choice: he would have to do it again.

Each time Rathma farstepped, it took a toll on him physically, but in this situation it didn't matter how much.

Taking a breath, Rathma tried to calm himself. He had no idea how his older brother was able to farstep so easily; it had always been a struggle for him. With a grimace, he looked at a point far off in the distance and braced himself again. He closed his eyes and focused.

Now! he thought, doing what only a Farstepper could do: moving through the air like lightning. He reappeared once again, a great distance away . . . and collapsed.

***

Rathma had no idea how long he had been out for, but the throbbing in his head told him that it was a while.

Never again, he swore to himself.

The "gift" that everyone called farstepping was a cruel joke wrapped in a hex dipped in a curse. It was no wonder that most chose not to pursue it at all. But others, only a handful that Rathma knew of, embraced it. His grandfather had told him about a Farstepper who was even able to travel to the Otherworld itself, staying there for days at a time. When he emerged (so the stories went) no time had passed at all. But that was neither here nor there: it was most likely Grandfather exaggerating—or the end result of someone trying to impress a girl. Rathma had always brushed it off as nonsense.

But one thing was for sure: his own brother was one of the most gifted Farsteppers that Rathma had ever heard of. Which was why, when he left their desert at the age of eighteen, everyone in the tribe had been devastated.

Lying on his side, Rathma pulled tight the cloak that his brother had given him. He shivered in the air of the cold desert night and fought off the headache that threatened to overpower him. "Dammit, why did you have to leave me here?" He coughed. In the far distance he could see the torch lights of the servants of the Holder, searching the area in vain for some sign of the Farstepper.

"Perhaps he knew that you would never amount to anything," scoffed a deep voice from behind.

Rathma didn't have to see its owner to know he was in trouble.

It was a voice he'd heard boom orders to the followers of the Holder, once at the beginning of the day, and once again at the end. A voice that belonged to a man who sought to rule the Wastes at any cost.

A voice that conjured such hatred that Rathma would do anything to overthrow it.

Rathma rolled over to see, grinning down at him, the last man he expected outside of Djozen Yelto's stronghold. The same man who had somehow managed to follow him across the impossible expanse of desert between him and the fortress.

"Yelto," Rathma croaked.

"In the flesh."

Dressed from head to toe in the finest silks that money could buy, Djozen Yelto looked like a man who always got what he wanted. He was heavy and bald, with skin the color of the dark desert sand, and was known to truly care for only two things in this world: himself and the prize that hung from his neck.

Years ago, Yelto had traveled south to Do'baradai and had returned clutching a strange dagger, followed fiercely by the Priests of the Holder. What happened in that old, crumbling ruin of a city was a secret only Yelto knew, but his rapid rise to power soon after was seen as no coincidence by the tribes. He wore the dagger around his neck as a reminder of this rise—among other things.

But everything Yelto did was just a grab for power, and Rathma knew it. Even the appointing of his own successor to the position of chief of the eastern tribes had been done out of ambition. And now that he had subjugated and proclaimed himself chief of the central tribes as well, he was frighteningly close to making truth out of rumors and whispers—uniting the tribes under one banner: his.

Rathma retched again, the taste of fear now mingling with the nausea of farstepping. "Well, you found me. Now what?" he asked.

"Now you stand trial," Yelto answered. "You and that Wolfwalker friend of yours. For treason." He grabbed Rathma by the rough material that made up his cloak's collar and pulled him up, whirling him around to look him in the eye. With a grin wider than the slice of moon above, he added, "And I doubt the sentencing will be light."

Rathma frowned. They'd caught him and Kuu. That definitely wasn't part of the plan.

No matter, he thought. He was caught now, and there was no getting away. Yelto had his hands firmly on him, and the pure iron shackles that were wrapped around Rathma's wrists meant that he wouldn't be farstepping his way out of it.

No, Rathma thought. *This is the end. Might as well face it like a man. That's the way Jinda would have done it.*

If he couldn't master farstepping like his big brother could, he could at least try to live—and die—in a way that would make him proud.

Rathma Yhun frowned as he clenched his jaw, looking defiantly at the lights ahead, and began the long walk back as a prisoner of Djozen Yelto.

Chapter 7

Derenar

Awaken the Three

Thornton

The Athrani Legion marched over the plains and hills that lay between the Forest of Kienar and their home, the capital city of Ellenos. They had been moving slowly with Endar Half-Eye leading the way, but Thornton noticed that their pace had quickened as they drew closer to their destination. He thought he would probably have done the same if they were marching toward Highglade. Allowing himself some mental respite, he thought about the first time he'd left the village on his own.

His father had been reluctant to let him go into Lusk by himself, but Thornton was persistent in his pleading, and the big blacksmith had finally relented. *You go straight there and come straight back,* he remembered his father saying. He was standing there, big arms crossed over a barrel chest, looking and sounding as hard as steel. *No dawdling.*

Of course, that had been the plan all along: to come straight home. It was just nice to get a small taste of freedom, even if it was only for the day. His horse, Jericho, was much younger back then, a spry version of the aging workhorse that was waiting for him back in Annoch. And his father's beard had been only a fraction of the face-filling monstrosity that Olson was known for.

But at the end of the day, when Thornton and Jericho were pointed back toward Highglade, they had both felt themselves moving faster. It wasn't anything that Thornton had consciously decided, but he found himself riding slightly harder, Jericho's legs pounding slightly faster, when they had rounded the trail that led into the small, wooded village they called home.

So Thornton had to admit that he was not surprised when the footfalls of the Athrani soldiers were getting closer and closer together.

Yasha, riding beside him, seemed to notice this as well.

"We must be nearly there," she said, turning her head. "I know we're riding in with them, but I can't help feeling nervous."

Thornton looked up at her, seated upon Matilda, and did not have to ask why she felt that way. She wore the hood of her gray robes over her head, doing the best she could to conceal a face scarred with power, a consequence of the energy she had unwittingly released in the Otherworld. But unlike some of the Khyth that Thornton had seen whose skin had been similarly charred, Yasha's skin was a soft, muted gray that nearly matched her robes. Against her swirling green eyes, it almost made her look beautiful. But both of them knew her robes would not be enough to hide who she was—*what* she was—from the eyes of the Athrani living in Ellenos.

"We'll stay close to Endar when we get there," Thornton said. "He can vouch for us. I know he will." His words were meant to be encouraging to his sister, but he wasn't so sure if even he believed them. He barely knew the Athrani half-eye, and he knew of his intentions even less. In the back of his mind, he was almost afraid of being thrown into a jail cell upon their arrival. After all, both he and Yasha were Khyth, and the blood feud that existed between the Khyth and the Athrani was older than he could comprehend.

"You come with the protection of Kienar," Kethras said, surprising Thornton; he'd been silent for most of the journey and he'd almost forgotten he was there. "You will be safe."

Standing a whole head above Yasha—despite his being on foot and her being on horseback—Kethras's words carried well.

Yasha still had a worried look on her face. "If you say so," she replied.

Thornton and Yasha were Khyth, it was true, but neither of them had chosen to be. That was another matter entirely, however, and Thornton hoped the citizens of Ellenos would at least be understanding. Whether they would be, or whether they would choose to lock them up in a dungeon, they would find out soon.

***

The Athrani Legion came to a halt on the edge of a sprawling body of water.

"There she is," Endar said from the front of the legion. The big man had a hand to his forehead to shield himself from the rays of the setting sun. "She certainly is a sight for sore eyes."

The murmurs of agreement that rippled through the army were punctuated with excited shouts of celebration.

The legion had come home.

The old stories say that Asha Imha-khet was beautiful, so beautiful that she captured the eye of not one but two gods. Yet, as beautiful as Asha Imha-khet was, she was equally prideful. Pleased with attention and unwilling to make a choice, she had no desire to choose between the two gods, so she did not. She loved them both in secret, never telling the other. And that was to be their undoing—all three of them.

—Excerpt from *The Night Sky and Its Names*

Chapter 8

Khadje Kholam

Awaken the Three

Rathma

Djozen Yelto tightened his grip on Rathma as they neared the gray walls of the sprawling compound. Built to keep outsiders out just as much as to keep its residents in, the walls were an effective deterrent to roving nomads and to those, like him, who were followers of the Traveler.

Rathma said a silent prayer as they approached, knowing he would soon be passing out of the Traveler's reach and into the clutches of the worshippers of the Holder of the Dead—then, if the trial went how he guessed it would, to the Holder himself.

Darkness had taken hold of the desert; the air around them had cooled, inviting its night dwellers to once again make their way to the surface. The desert wolves, kings in their own right, were free to roam about with no fear of the sun bearing down on them. Rathma hoped the ones he saw skulking around were friends of Kuu.

"I'm surprised you didn't just send someone after me," he said casually to Yelto. "The mighty Djozen Yelto leaving the protection of his walls . . . I never thought I'd see the day."

The words brought a grin to the face of the fat eastern tribesman. "And risk you getting away?" chuckled Yelto. "No, my boy. This was a noose that the hangman himself must tie. It was simply too risky to entrust to someone else."

The crackling of the dozens of torches planted high on the wall was the only other sound that accompanied their soft footfalls in the sand.

***

Rathma pulled his cloak tighter around him. In the desert, the temperature swings between night and day were not for the weak, and he was eternally grateful that Jinda had left him such a useful gift. It was just a shame that it would most likely be burned along with him and Kuu.

As they approached the walled fortress, he recognized the robes worn by the Priests of the Holder. He could see the blue and the white long before he could see their skeletal faces, still haunted by tendons and muscles. It made them look like burn victims close to death.

Those unblinking eyes, Rathma thought. *They look so dead. So lifeless*. He shivered at the sight.

"I am pleased you have returned," said one of the robed figures. His words, directed at Rathma, were raspy and sharp, like the voice of a serpent. "As is the Holder."

"How go things here, Priest?" asked Yelto. He did not use his name because Priests of the Holder had no names; they gave up their identities when they entered into servitude. It was one of the reasons for their disfigurement: everyone was equal in the sight of the Holder, and none showed that more than the nameless, faceless Priests of the Holder.

"We have secured the Wolfwalker inside, as you asked. He was . . . difficult." If a skeleton could frown, Rathma thought he was seeing it now.

"I do not doubt that," Yelto answered. "The southerners spend their whole lives ducking death. I did not expect it to be easy."

They stood outside a great metal gate that separated the interior of the compound from the endless burning desert. Rathma knew it was well guarded on the inside, which was why he'd chosen to avoid it entirely when he planned his earlier entrance. To be passing through it now came as an unwelcome twist of fate.

Yelto barked an order that sent the gate rumbling open, churning upward on chains that were connected to a wheel manned by four sentries. When it lifted, Rathma's breath nearly left him.

In the middle of the compound, surrounded by no fewer than fifty of Yelto's men, was a cage big enough to hold a wolf. But inside was no wolf, as Kuu's older brothers were always saying. A pathetic-looking gray desert fox was lying on its side, eyes closed, with a long gash running down its rib cage. Its mouth was muzzled, and its left hind leg was chained to the thick iron bars that lined the cage.

"Kuu!" Rathma shouted. Turning to Yelto, he growled through clenched teeth, "What have you done to him?"

The fat Djozen raised his hands in mock distress. "Only what was necessary. If he wasn't so intent on escape, we wouldn't have had to deal with him so harshly. You heard the priest: the boy was a handful."

Rathma yanked at his own restraints while looking Djozen Yelto in the eyes. "If you've killed him, I swear by the Traveler . . ." He swallowed his words and tried to replace his anger with rational thought. "He had no part in this plan. Set him free."

Yelto laughed. "That will be for the tribunal to decide. Now"—he gave Rathma a shove—"inside."

Chapter 9

Ellenos

Awaken the Three

Thornton

Thornton had seen more of Derenar in the last few weeks than he had in his entire life, but nothing could prepare him for the sight before him: the entrance to the mighty city of Ellenos, First City of the Athrani.

Outside the city walls, higher than the surrounding countryside by many hundreds of feet, was an enormous steel structure. Its base was situated in an expansive body of water that stretched out like the biggest moat he'd ever seen. The "wheel" that everyone seemed so relieved to see didn't look like much of a wheel, despite its name; it was mostly steel beams that crossed as they climbed upward, with smooth white brick that dug into a grass-covered mountain beside it. But even more perplexing was the fact that Thornton could not see the city. *Why did Endar seem so excited to see this?*

"I don't understand," he said as he scratched his thick brown hair. "Where is Ellenos?"

Endar laughed so heartily that Thornton was afraid he might rupture something. "Up there!" he said as he pointed.

Thornton followed Endar's finger to the top of the wheel, where the end of a long, straight canal was flowing into the center of a mass of great green hills. Ellenos, it appeared, was built into a caldera, with the sides of the mountain serving as natural walls surrounding the city.

"Then how do we get to it?" Thornton asked.

Turning in his saddle to look at him, Endar smiled. "We ride."

The half-eye took off the purple cloak that was draped around his shoulders and handed it to a pikeman who was standing beside him. The pikeman fastened it to the end of his weapon, raised it high into the air, and began waving it back and forth.

As he did, Thornton felt a rumbling below him. "What—" he started to say, but his words were caught in his throat as he witnessed a marvel of Athrani Shaping. The very water in the lake in front of them started turning into stone, forming a bridge that stretched from the shore, where the army stood, to the base of the so-called Wheel of Ellenos.

"But first we walk," Endar said without looking back. His heels did the talking, and his horse, who trotted forward and onto the stony bridge, did the walking.

Thornton and Yasha stood in awe as the soldiers of the legion streamed past them and onto the bridge. Thousands upon thousands of men, Athrani and human alike, made their way onto the platform, which until only moments ago had been water.

"Are you going to stand there gawking all day," Endar shouted back to them, "or are you going to get on?"

Thornton and Yasha exchanged glances, finally deciding to follow the rest of the men. Kethras walked hesitantly behind them.

"I guess the worst that could happen is that we drown," Thornton said, grinning sheepishly. No one was amused.

The bridge they walked across ended at an enormous platform with great steel beams on both ends. Following the beams up, Thornton saw that they crisscrossed in the middle, halfway up the gargantuan steel wheel, and looked to be attached to a second platform on the top that mirrored their own.

Just as the two of them planted their feet firmly on the platform, Thornton felt a rumbling again.

"The Athrani are particularly proud of this next part," Endar said.

Thornton looked over the edge of the platform and saw that it was lifting off the ground. Craning his neck upward, he saw the corresponding platform above them starting to come down in a reciprocal, circular arc. With his eyes as wide as the steel floor they stood on, Thornton watched as the world below them fell away.

"H-How . . . How . . . ?" he stammered.

"How does it work?" Endar said, finishing the sentence for him. He pointed at the platform that was beginning to come down on the other end of the mighty wheel. "In a word: water. The canal at the top fills up with enough of it to create a counterweight. When it's full enough, the wheel begins to turn. After that, it's a simple matter of weight distribution and balance/counter-balance."

Despite Endar's use of the word *simple*, Thornton thought it was anything but. He looked off the platform to watch the trees below him shrink from sight, and his head was spinning faster than the wheel as he tried to comprehend it all. He'd never seen anything like it, never imagined something like it could even exist, as his blacksmith brain focused on the enormous gears in the center of the wheel that seemed to be responsible for their movement.

"Believe it or not," Endar said as he leaned in close, "the wheel was a man's idea. A human man. It's a part of Ellenian history that the Athrani won't tell you. Oh, sure, they built the thing," he said with a wave of his hand. "And it's hard to say if something this massive could have been created without the use of Shaping. But Athrani minds don't work like that. It would have taken them another thousand years to come up with the design."

On the edge of the mass of men and Athrani, Thornton was acutely aware of his insignificance as they moved through the air on a ton of steel. He watched the plains disappear as they blended into a singular green mass, dwarfed by the side of the mountain they slowly scaled. When they had nearly reached the top, their starting point looked like one great stretch of green, and Thornton realized just how far they had marched—and how high they had climbed—by the fact that he could take in the whole countryside with a glance.

The great wheel suddenly shuddered to a stop, opening into a canal that led into the city. As Thornton's eyes followed the watery road, they fell on a sight that he almost believed he was dreaming instead of seeing: a city draped in gold with forking towers and sky-scraping buildings that he could hardly believe were real. The low-lying clouds that blanketed the city made it seem like a waking dream, and the fingers of fog weaving in and out of the towering houses and buildings provided the most amazing backdrop for the sunset that was working its way through the city as the legion came ashore.

Waiting for them, just off the edge of the platform, was an enormous wooden ship that was bigger than some of the buildings Thornton had seen in Annoch. It had windows carved all around it, and Thornton counted at least five levels. There was a wooden ramp at the bottom that the men of the legion used to start filing onto the ship.

"Now, to get you to the High Keeper," Endar said as he started toward the transport. He looked at Thornton and Yasha, and smiled. "I hope she's in an understanding mood."

Thornton felt unease creeping back into his throat as they moved slowly down the waterway. *Moods are like the weather*, his father used to say. *Mostly unpredictable and oftentimes dangerous.*

Looking out past the city lined with gold and fog, he took a deep breath.

I just hope we can ride out the storm.

Chapter 10

Ghal Thurái

Awaken the Three

Duna

The Fist of Ghal Thurái was legendary, respected throughout Gal'dorok and feared just as widely. They had earned their reputation in blood and steel, and were among the greatest fighting forces ever commanded. So when Duna Cullain had marched them from the brink of defeat in Kienar to the foothills of the Great Serpent, Gal'behem, she had most certainly expected more of a welcome than the one she got— the one she got was barely a welcome at all.

In fact, the only one there to welcome them was the last person she preferred to see: Kunas, Master Khyth of Ghal Thurái. The shoulders and hood of his black robe were painted orange by the flames above, pouring out of the cliffs of the Mouth of the Deep and bringing unwelcome light to a smoke-darkened sky.

Duna looked at the Master Khyth and noticed that he was not his usual defiant self. She wasn't quite sure, but she thought she was seeing weakness. Helplessness.

Even . . . fear?

"So, the mighty Fist returns," Kunas rasped, and the sound made Duna cringe. Those Khyth who had undergone the Breaking all seemed to have this quality in common: the essence of their voice was stripped away, leaving only a ragged whisper that was as unsettling as it was powerful. "Yet it does not feel like a victory march."

"It is not," Duna said with a frown. "We suffered a great many losses in Kienar."

"What losses, Lady Cullain?" the Khyth asked, narrowing his eyes and peering around her to examine the army. "And where is the commander?"

"Losses comparable to what appears to have happened here," Duna replied. "And you are looking at her."

Kunas stopped, puzzled, looking back at her. "I do not understand."

"Then listen well," she responded coolly, keeping eye contact with the Khyth. "Tennech has fled, and Commander Durakas has been slain. That leaves me as the highest-ranking officer in Gal'dorok—and, consequently, as general."

The Khyth flinched. "Then," he said, bowing slightly, "you have my apologies, General Cullain."

Bowing and apologizing, Duna thought suspiciously. Both were extremely out of character for Kunas, who considered himself above reproach and authority. And technically, being selected by none other than High Khyth Yetz, he was both.

It made her uneasy.

"Think nothing of it," she said with a dismissive wave.

She tore her eyes off the black-robed Khyth before her and let them wander over the winding road that led to her city. She traced the path upward to the entrance: once a beautiful marble masterpiece and testament to Thurian craftsmanship, it was now a heap of collapsed, smoking rubble. Guard towers that had been carved into the side of the mountain were now abandoned and crumbling. The city was in ruins, and no one had seen it coming.

She glanced back at Kunas.

Or maybe someone did.

There had been a sizable defensive force here when the Fist left. Whoever did this had known its defenses would be down.

Whoever did this had had a plan.

"Tell me what happened here," Duna finally said. She did not let her eyes leave the smoke from her city.

"It was the Chovathi, Lady—" He caught himself. "General Cullain. Swarms of them. They came from beneath the earth, from the rocks, from all around. They were upon us in no time."

"When?"

"No more than a day ago. We were caught unaware and undefended. It was as if they knew when we would be at our weakest, primed to strike at the perfect moment. And," he added, "they were organized. Working together. It was a concentrated attack unlike any I've ever seen from them."

Looking back up to the ruined exterior of Ghal Thurái, she caught glimpses of Chovathi scouts skulking about, in and out of the rocks that

made up the mountain city. It was entirely unlike the Chovathi to orga-
nize together in the way that Kunas was saying.

"A clan, then," Duna said flatly. She rolled the thoughts around in
her head. "Perhaps more than one."

If they could take over a city like Ghal Thurái in a matter of days . . .

"General," Kunas said, interrupting her thoughts. "The city is lost."

Duna nodded absently.

"But," he went on, "perhaps it does not have to remain so."

She turned to the Master Khyth. "What are you suggesting?"

"That we seek help from the east."

"The east?" Duna repeated despondently. "You mean . . . ?"

"Haidan Shar."

Duna frowned at the words. *Haidan Shar*, she thought. *I had hoped it
would not come to this.*

A rich coastal city built on the cliffs overlooking the Tashkar Sea, the
city called the Gem of the East had based its economy on fishing, but
had boomed into a bustling and wealthy power when gold and other precious metals were discovered in the caves and rocks nearby. Soon it was
attracting merchants from all over Gal'dorok—sometimes even as far as
Derenar—at a much faster pace than even the capital of Khala Val'ur
could keep up with. They were self-sustaining, and not overtly hostile to
the other cities of Gal'dorok.

Yet Haidan Shar had one thing that Khala Val'ur did not: a hu-
man-run government. While Khyth were tolerated in the city, their role
in its rule was completely different than in Khala Val'ur or Ghal Thurái.
This resulted in an uneasy peace between them. Haidan Shar was a
human city in every sense of the word. When the Sunken City of Khala
Val'ur had called for aid in the march to Kienar, the Gem of the East had
remained silent. Perhaps now that the Chovathi had shown themselves
to be a greater threat to just passing travelers, though, they would help.

But there was still another reason why Duna did not want to enlist
the help of Haidan Shar. The thought brought her hand to the dagger
she'd had on that night. She might have to finally reveal its secret, one
she'd been keeping for decades now.

"We have always had a . . . *complicated* relationship with the Sharians," she started. "Yet we have never had a reason to be united until now." She turned to Kunas. "We cannot take back our city alone."

Kunas nodded. "I agree."

Her eyes went back to the rubble. They would have to begin reconstitution immediately. "Are there any survivors?"

"Yes, General," he answered. "They have fled to Khala Val'ur."

"How many?"

"A few thousand. Mostly women and children who were able to escape through the back tunnels while the Chovathi swarmed." He paused and looked back at their burning city. "The others . . . fought bravely."

Duna clenched her jaw. It was the Thurian way to die gloriously in battle, she knew, but sometimes she wished that the warrior ethos didn't flow so strongly through the veins of every man beneath the Mouth. Who knows how much time it bought the survivors? If they had started their retreat earlier instead of seeking that glorious death, it might have left her with a battle-ready force to take back the city. But now she wondered if even the combined might of Gal'dorok could overcome an entrenched Chovathi force at all. Especially one that was organized.

"Eowen," she called out to the messenger. "Come here. I have a task for you."

The blond man appeared before her and kneeled. "Yes, General," he said.

"I need you to make your way to Haidan Shar," she replied. "Explain to them what has happened here. Appeal to their humanity if you must, but emphasize the gravity of the situation."

Eowen nodded as he rose.

Duna looked back to her burning, crumbling city, and as the skyward-dancing flames leapt off the mountains that once stood so proud, she was only certain of this: she would finish the work that the Dagger of Derenar had begun.

She would wipe the Chovathi from the face of the earth.

"And Eowen," she called after the messenger as he started his journey to the east. "Tell my sister I said hello."

Chapter 11

Ellenos

Awaken the Three

Thornton

As much as his eyes were on the city of Ellenos, Thornton could feel the eyes of the Athrani on him.

When the legion had reached the top of the wheel, they had unloaded onto a waiting ship that would take them into the city. Now, floating down the canal on a vessel of unimaginable weight, Thornton could feel that same weight pressing down on him and his sister. He watched as Yasha pulled her hood tighter over her head in a futile attempt to conceal her appearance. She flashed him a look that communicated just how alienated she felt, and Thornton suddenly knew what it meant to feel different. He knew how Kethras must have felt in Annoch—or anywhere that humans outnumbered Kienari—and looked to see if the staring from the Athrani was having any effect. If it was, Kethras certainly didn't show it. His great black eyes were unblinking, focused on surveying the city ahead. Hands folded behind his back, the son of the forest stood unmoving, an inky black oak tree rooted in the hull of the Athrani transport.

Something about Kethras's calm demeanor gave Thornton comfort as he looked back to his sister, Yasha, and again to the shore. They had been moving through the water for some time now, and Thornton guessed they were headed into the city's center. Everything about the First City was impressive to him, and he wasted no time taking it all in.

He'd noticed a number of canals that intersected the one they were floating down—some perpendicular, some coming at sharp angles—no doubt used to get quickly from one end of the city to the other. Some of them had smaller vessels floating down them, holding just a handful of people; most of them would wave at the huge transport as they passed. A great purple flag planted at the top of their own ship bore a golden outline of an eye with six lines radiating out of it, three on top and three on the bottom, which Thornton thought looked like eyelashes. He figured it to be the banner of Endar, and it was most likely what people recognized when they would wave at them.

Another thing that intrigued him about the city was that Athrani buildings were so much different than human buildings. Thornton thought it was most likely due to the fact that they weren't so much constructed as they were *Shaped* into being. They seemed to have been carved from a single source, like statues of marble and gold that towered toward the sky. And they were so close together, too! That had always been something that stood out to him in Lusk, and even Annoch: that there was almost no space between one building and another. In his small village of Highglade, people had entire fields to themselves. But in the cities, where the population was astoundingly large, there was simply no room for that kind of privacy. That was abundantly clear here in Ellenos, where sometimes it looked as though several dissimilar buildings were all part of one massive structure.

But one thing was obvious to Thornton as he gawked at the buildings they floated past: Ellenos was stunning. The word *majestic* echoed in his mind, and he thought that he had finally found somewhere worthy of the description. The rolling hills and valleys that made up the landscape of the city were perfectly incorporated into its construction. Even the light of the setting sun seemed to have been part of the city's layout as it sank below the surrounding mountains to usher in the dusk, bleeding together the shadows that stretched off the Ellenian buildings.

"She's impressive to behold, isn't she?"

The words startled Thornton as he realized just how entranced he was at the sight of the First City. He turned around to see Endar grinning at him, once again draped in the purple cape that marked him as commander of the Athrani Legion. Coming out of his trance, Thornton stammered a yes.

"She's the only home I've ever known," the big half-eye said. Clasping his hands and putting his forearms on the edge of the ship, he leaned over to share the view. "Sometimes I feel like that spoils me."

Thornton looked away from the commander and back to the fantastically made structures. Some of them looked like houses, others he recognized as inns, but many of the larger structures were entirely foreign to him. "I can see why," Thornton admitted. "I've never seen anything like it."

Yasha piped up. "If you've ever seen the depths of Khala Val'ur, you'd know just how good you have it."

Since undergoing the Breaking, Yasha's once-soft voice had taken on an ethereal quality that Thornton thought sounded like an echo trailing just behind her words. She was still soft-spoken, but the change in her voice commanded something when she talked, something that was enough to make Endar jump.

"So she does speak!" the commander exclaimed, turning to marvel at the girl from the Sunken City. Pressing his back into the wooden railing that formed the edge of the deck, he looked her up and down before speaking again. "Tell me: What is Khala Val'ur like?" His arms were crossed over his gold breastplate as he stared at her inquisitively. "I've never had the pleasure."

Yasha squirmed a little and looked away. "It's dark," she said. "And cold. The inside of the city never sees the light of day, so a huge fire is kept going to take the place of the sun. It's a poor substitute," she scoffed.

"I would imagine," Endar said, taking in a lungful of air.

"It's nothing like this," Yasha continued, looking off the bow. "The Khyth are very calculated. Everything is linear, and everything serves a purpose." She shifted her gaze to some hills in the distance that looked as if someone had planted a tree in them that had grown into a cluster of buildings. "I mean, they moved the *mountains themselves* to build the city," she said with a sweep of her arms. "If they don't think something belongs somewhere, they'll smash it and make room for something that does."

Endar nodded. "You'll find that the Athrani are quite different."

Thornton was already looking past his sister when he felt the ship begin to slow. "What's happening?" he asked Endar.

The huge half-eye grinned as he looked out beyond the helm. "We've arrived."

***

Despite the beauty of the city that had surrounded them since they'd set foot inside it, Thornton suddenly felt cold and afraid. He looked at the face of his sister and saw that same nervousness reflected in her eyes. But one look at Kethras, stoic and tall, reminded him that his black-furred friend would do anything to protect him. He'd seen it in the forests of Kienar, and on the road from Lusk when the two Kienari had first made their presence known. Kethras had only just met him and Miera that night, but had been willing to die for them—and to kill for them.

Endar seemed to sense the unease that had penetrated the deck like a fog, and placed his hand on Thornton's shoulder. "Relax, blacksmith," he said. "The Keeper is wise and just. You've nothing to fear."

The words did little to ease Thornton's twisting stomach. He was still an enemy—to them—in the heart of their capital.

"Besides," Endar added in a hushed voice, "I'm told that you're friends with the Shaper. That carries some weight around here."

A smile cracked Thornton's lips as he thought of Miera again. *Funny how she's helping even when she isn't here to see it*, he thought. His shoulders relaxed as the ship began to dock, and Thornton found his thoughts wandering off to the Otherworld, to the last place he had seen Miera before she . . .

Before . . . He shook his head to try to jar the thought loose. It was no good to him. He wasn't sure if there was any way he could get to her now, but he promised himself that he would never stop trying to find one, no matter how dangerous it might be.

And, judging by the whispers of the men as they had marched across Derenar, it was *very* dangerous.

Chapter 12

The Wastes of Khulakorum

Awaken the Three

Sera

The last few days—weeks?—had been a blur. Sera's chest ached, her head pounded, and her mouth was dry. Working her fingers up to the mostly healed wound on her shoulder, just above her heart, she felt the edges of a newborn scar that had come from the tip of an Athrani spear. Tennech told her that she'd nearly been killed, and in the ensuing darkness of sleep and recovery, she sometimes thought that might have been the better option.

Hovering on the brink of death is not an easy feat, and Sera was finding out why. She had lost a lot of blood on the ground beneath the Tree, where the force from the blow and the initial shock had rendered her unconscious—and where she very likely would have bled to death if Tennech hadn't dragged her away and patched her up. She had just been lying there helpless on the ground, slowly dying, while the flow of battle rushed on around her. But after being taken from the forest, and being asleep for most of it, her body was allowed to start the recovery process.

She had spent more time unconscious than awake, but that trend was slowly starting to reverse itself. Her bouts of wakefulness were becoming the norm as the darkness and the dreams returned to their rightful place: under her control. Sleep was no longer something that forced itself upon her; now it was at her beck and call. Like the movement in her left arm and shoulder, control over her consciousness was gradually returning.

She heard the sounds of quiet talking just as the pain in her shoulder forced her eyes open. As she sat up and looked around, she saw to whom the voices belonged: General Tennech, with his back to her, was talking with Captains Hullis and Dhrostain. Hullis, the tall blond Thurian, noticed she was awake and gestured toward her.

Tennech turned his head, and the semblance of a smile tugged at the corners of his mustachioed mouth. Sera blinked a few times to make sure she wasn't seeing things, but the sight made her think delirium had set in again: Tennech was not wearing his armor, and was dressed in clothes befitting an emissary or a high-ranking government official. The other two men still wore most of their armor, with the exception of their heavy breastplates. The general turned to her and walked over.

"Good, you're awake," he said. "We were waiting for you before we made the final leg of the journey."

Sera glanced around; she didn't recognize their surroundings. They seemed to be in some sort of oasis, with long stretches of desert surrounding them on all sides. There were perhaps a dozen tall trees that provided shade, and a deep pool of water that was responsible for the vibrant green in a sea of dead brown. If she had to guess, all of this meant that they were in or near the Wastes of Khulakorum. Nowhere else that she knew of matched this description, and nowhere else had a desert so large that it could take up an entire field of view.

"Of course," Sera said as the general drew near. "Where . . . Where are we?"

"At the edge of the Wastes," he answered, looking back over his shoulder to the men from Ghal Thurái. "By my calculation—and the captains agree—the tribal city of Khadje Kholam should be about half a day's walk to the southeast. If you're feeling up to it, we can leave now to arrive at sunup."

Sera stood up and swept her hands through her long brown hair, collecting it and pulling it down to rest in front of her left shoulder. Before her, the colors of dusk were starting to make their way across the sky, and she realized that she had been sleeping for much longer than she'd intended. *Maybe I haven't fully recovered after all*, she thought.

Her eyes scanned the rest of her surroundings as she tried to get her bearings. As she did, she saw two reasons why they had made it this far: the Gwarái.

The two great masses of black were sleeping in the shade, and Sera wondered how the Thurian captains had managed to get something so big to cooperate. The Gwarái wore leather reins that were fastened to their long, thick necks. Other than that, though, the four-legged monstrosities should have been free to do what they wanted—one tends not to argue with anything so large. Sera was still not fully used to being around the two towering creatures; their countless dark scales over a long reptilian body made even the largest warhorse look tiny. But they had gotten them this far, so she had no reason to complain. Any other pack animal would have had immense difficulty making a journey this far in a reasonable amount of time.

The thought triggered a memory. She started looking around frantically, scanning the trees and desert floor. Tennech must have noticed her eyes darting back and forth because he moved closer to her, asking, "What is it? What's wrong?"

"Ruen," she answered. "Where is Ruen?"

Tennech put a hand on Sera's shoulder, and the blood froze in her veins. She barely registered the next words from the general's mouth.

"There was no other way to get you here," he began. "I had to have one of the Gwarái carry you."

"Where is he?" she demanded. "Tell me where my horse is."

The words seemed to catch the general off guard, and he moved his hand away from her shoulder. "He's safe, Sera. Don't worry." He was putting his hands up in a calming motion, but it looked to Sera more like a defensive posture. "He was in no shape to make the trip, so I sold him to—"

"You *what?*"

"I sold him," he said, raising his voice to match hers, "to help offset some of the costs." He was looking her right in the eye. "We both know that horse was on his last legs. It's a wonder we got anything for him at all."

Sera was seething. "You had no right! He was my only possession." Her brown-on-blue eyes were awash with rage, and she briefly, very briefly, pictured his death.

Tennech put a stop to it quickly. "Remember your place, child," he said coldly. "You came to me with nothing. I took you in, I fed you, I clothed you. I gave you everything." The words were as sharp as they were true.

Her anger, a crackling fire, had not been snuffed out—merely redirected. "Fine," she said, turning back to the blanket on the ground that formed her makeshift bed. She gathered it up, loudly and forcefully sheathed her blades, and made for the two captains. Walking right by them, she said, "Let's go," to no one in particular.

Hullis and Dhrostain shrugged and looked to Tennech for confirmation. When the general nodded his consent, the two Thurians cautiously awakened the sleeping giants and pointed them away from the sinking sun.

Sera, despite having no idea where they were going, was fine with leading the way. She'd dodged death once already.

Let it try again, she thought bitterly.

Chapter 13

Haidan Shar

Awaken the Three

Benjin

He's going to be so mad, thought Benj as he raced down the stairs. He was already late and would have no time to give the horses their feed. He shouted something half apologetic to the stables as he passed, determining to give the animals double rations when he made it back.

If he made it back.

Captain Jahaz was not easy on him when he was late. Last time, he had nearly split his skull wide open and Benj had spent the better part of a week recovering. And his mother hadn't had any sympathy for him either. She'd simply said, "I told you to be early. Early is on time, and on time is late." Benj hated it when she said that, but he hated it even more when she was right.

The muddy road from the Flats seemed extra filthy today as Benj was already starting to feel the bruises he would surely get from Jahaz. His feet hit the paved road that led to the castle, and he looked at the rising sun. He cursed again under his breath and dug deep to find the strength to keep running. As armiger to Captain Jahaz, Benj was practically expected to be filthy; a little more sweat on his dirty brown tunic and pants would not even be looked at twice.

Approaching the castle, he nodded a curt greeting to the two guards standing at the bridge that led inside.

"Jahaz will have your hide," said one as Benj raced by. The other guard chuckled in agreement. Benj didn't bother with a reply—he knew it was true.

The guards motioned to the ones manning the wall, who began to lift the gate just enough so Benj could slip through.

"Hurry through, Master Benj," came a mocking shout from above. It was followed by a chorus of laughter from the rest of the guards.

At least I'm good for something, thought Benj. *The guards sure love me.*

He raced through the courtyard and up through passages and staircases too many to count. When Haidan Shar was first built, none of this had been here; it was a later addition that only came with the vast influx of wealth from the precious minerals that surrounded the great city. The Gem of the East, as it was called now, had started out as little more than a gravel pit. But as traders from far away began to hear the stories of the gems in the east, gems that would eventually become the city's namesake, the Sharians realized that they could very quickly have a war on their hands over the riches. *Their* riches. Riches that should stay theirs, no matter how many corpses they would have to bury them under.

So the masons had built, the smithies had smithed, and, in the blink of an eye as armies measure time, Haidan Shar went from a quiet fishing town by the sea to a sprawling fortress worthy of royalty. And, only a few years before Benj had been born, that is just what Haidan Shar found itself with.

"Yes, Your Grace," came a voice from up ahead. "But he needs his arms to carry my sword and feed the horses. Perhaps a few broken ribs will instead serve to remind him to be on time."

It was Jahaz's voice, and he was addressing the queen.

Benj felt sick.

He'd come to a halt outside the great wooden door of the king's war room, but couldn't work up the courage to go inside. Captain Jahaz was in there, along with the rest of the War Council, and Benj knew how loud the door was. There was no way to sneak in. They already knew he was late.

He took a breath and pushed it open. It groaned exactly as loud as he had hoped it wouldn't. He couldn't see the twenty-two pairs of eyes staring daggers at him as he walked in, but he knew he would have seen them if he'd opened his own.

"How nice of you to join us," Jahaz said coldly. His dark brown eyes seemed to be boring into his skin.

Benj didn't breathe. It was protocol for an armiger to be there, at his master's beck and call, any time he might be needed. This was one of those times.

"We'll talk about your tardiness later," Jahaz continued. "Come."

Benj opened his eyes and let out the breath he'd been holding in, knowing in the back of his mind that future breaths might not come as easily or pain-free. "Yes, Captain," he said quietly.

Walking over to where the captain was standing, he took his place by his side. The eleven captains were standing with their armigers and looking at the queen, seated on her throne, looking more relaxed than she usually did in the war room. She smiled.

Standing next to the throne was a blond man whom Benj didn't recognize.

The queen spoke. "Now that we are all here," she said as Benj cringed, "please continue, Eowen."

"General Duna Cullain wishes to form an alliance between the armies of Khala Val'ur, Ghal Thurái, and Haidan Shar, united under one banner for the first time in history against the Chovathi menace which threatens us all."

A smirk worked its way onto the queen's face. Then the smirk started spreading, first to a grin and then into laughter.

"Your Grace," Eowen stammered, looking confused, "I do not understand why you laugh at this proposal."

"Not at the proposal," the queen said with more than a hint of amusement. She leaned forward on her throne, eyebrows arched in curiosity. "I laugh because somehow my sister Duna has become a general without my help."

Chapter 14

Ellenos

Awaken the Three

Thornton

Thornton was one of the last souls to leave the ship, and he couldn't stop staring at the perfectly smooth, blue-hued marble structure in the distance. It was pyramid-shaped, with a grand entrance facing south made up of four towering granite columns, spirals of gold snaking up them. The columns supported a white marble slab that served no purpose save one: opulence. The polished quality of the whole structure reminded him of the eyes of a Khyth: cloudy and nebulous, as if the stone itself were alive.

Gesturing toward it, he asked Endar, "Is that where we're going?"

The big half-eye was the last to disembark. "It is," he answered.

"So that's where the Keeper . . . lives?"

Endar's chuckle was just loud enough for Thornton to hear. "That's the Temple of the Shaper, if that's what you're asking. Just like the one in Annoch. Only this one has no Anvil."

Thornton considered this. "Then why have a temple?" he asked.

Endar's footsteps come to a halt behind him. Turning around, Thornton saw the half-eye looking down his nose at him, eyebrows raised in surprise.

"I'll advise you not to repeat that question. But to satisfy your curiosity, I'll answer it here." He was scratching the salt-and-pepper scruff on his chin that had grown in the last few days. "It serves as the throne room for Sh'thanna, High Keeper of Ellenos, and as a constant reminder to all Athrani that we owe everything we are, and everything we have, to the Shaper of Ages. We wouldn't be who we are without Her Gift. Even a half-eye like me."

Thornton hung his head. "I'm sorry. I didn't mean any offense by it."

Endar waved it off. "Nonsense," he said. "No harm done. You're not one of us, so you couldn't have known."

Thornton flinched at Endar's words. They stung, even though Thornton was sure Endar hadn't meant them to. *Not one of us.* Never had that been more obvious than now. Even the eyes looking back at him in his reflection in the water seemed strange.

He looked around for Kethras and Yasha, suddenly feeling the need to be surrounded by something—anything—familiar. Fortunately for him, the two of them stood out like mud on a wedding dress: a tall, slender Kienari and a gray-robed Khyth, afloat in a sea of Athrani. They couldn't lose him if they tried.

Yasha had her hood pulled tightly over her face and was following closely behind Kethras, looking like a child chasing after a walking tree. Her long red hair peeked out and stood sharply against the ashen skin that marked her as a Khyth of the Breaking—something she had spent most of her life despising. But now there was nothing she could do to reverse the stigma that came with the power in the form of her charred and ravaged exterior.

Thornton could see the Ellenians sharing whispers with each other, no doubt about the outsiders who had inexplicably made their way into the heart of the First City. He weaved his way through the men of the legion to catch up with them as, all around him, Athrani life buzzed about frantically.

The cobblestone road they were traveling on ran north–south, from the dock from which they'd come to the grand entrance of the Temple of the Shaper, and Thornton's eyes followed it down. Rows and rows of shops were set up in the open air along the road, and it looked like a bazaar had made its home around the temple. Cloths of every color that Thornton could think of lined the tops of the shops, and they seemed to do so in an organized fashion: purple meant fresh fruit; red meant weapons; black was armor; gold seemed to signify spices or perfumes; orange, books and scrolls. He couldn't determine the purpose of the blue since it appeared to be attractive women just standing around. There were a handful of other colors, too, whose purpose he couldn't discern, but there weren't nearly as many of them compared to the vast number of roadside shops in the market. He turned his head from left to right to take in the whole scene and realized that the heart of the city was much, much bigger than he'd imagined.

The citizens of Ellenos were almost entirely Athrani, but they were as diverse as Thornton remembered the citizens of Annoch being: Some dressed in fine clothes or robes; others, in little more than rags. Some had long white hair; others had short, dark hair. Most were tall; others were smaller. A few were fat; most were modestly built. And the different-colored eyes he saw were almost as varied. Behind the normal eye color that every human had was a second color that was the hallmark of the Athrani people, signifying their link with the Otherworld and their status as Shapers. The colors differed from person to person, and Thornton couldn't tell if they even stayed the same within a family. *Though they make for some vibrant backgrounds*, he thought.

The sounds of merchants pitching their wares filled the air, even at dusk. Thornton saw a few of the Athrani shopkeepers come outside, and, waving their hands around as he'd seen a few Shapers do, they seemed to make fire out of thin air. And, from what he understood of Athrani Shaping, that was actually what they were doing. He quickened his pace over to Yasha, who was staring at the throngs of shops and people, and took her arm.

She was walking behind Kethras, who seemed to be navigating the masses of Athrani fairly well. In a voice barely above a whisper, she said, "I never knew what I was missing, living in the cold blackness of Khala Val'ur."

"I know what you mean," Thornton answered. "I always thought of Lusk as a big city when I was growing up. And then I saw Annoch." He paused. "This place puts them both to shame."

Just as he was finishing his sentence, he heard Yasha cry out and felt her arm tear away from his. Turning around, he saw her tumbling to the ground. A tall, green-robed Athrani was scowling at her.

"Watch where you're going, *Khyth*." The Athrani spat out the last word with a scowl as he towered over her. "Your kind isn't welcome here."

Thornton moved to shield her with his body, and he heard a low growl come from Kethras's direction, followed by the unmistakable sound of steel sliding across leather as the Kienari freed his dagger.

"Apologize to the lady," Kethras warned, "or you'll see just how easily Athrani blood can be spilled." He was holding his knife with the hilt facing up, postured to slash the blade across the Ellenian's face. His elbows were out; knees slightly bent. Thornton guessed that few people living had ever seen a Kienari in such a stance.

The Athrani began to move his hands in an incantation to the Shaper of Ages, and Thornton felt the air around them spark with power; but Endar would not have it.

"Stop!" the great half-eye bellowed, stepping in front of Kethras. "Stop this at once. They're with me." He gestured for them to lower their weapons. Looking back and forth at them, he said, "No more blood needs to be shed. Too much of it still covers the ground in Kienar."

The green-robed Athrani made a face as if he were sucking on a lemon, and began to back away. "Strange bedfellows you find yourself with these days, half-eye. If consorting with the Khyth is the price of our victory at the Tree, I wonder if it was worth the effort."

Thornton watched the Athrani fade into the crowd as Endar placed his hand on the hilt of Kethras's still-readied dagger. Lowering it, he spoke in quiet tones. "I'm sorry for the actions and words of my countrymen," the half-eye said, offering a hand to Yasha, who was still on the ground. "The Athrani are not known for their open-mindedness." Pointing to his one eye that spoke of his mixed heritage, he added, "Trust me."

Yasha got up and dusted herself off. "It's fine," she said. "I didn't expect this to be easy." She pulled off her hood, shaking out her wild red hair as it tumbled down. "And I guess there's no point in trying to hide anymore."

"There never was," Endar said with a smile. "Now, come. We've nearly arrived."

Shaken from the encounter but thankful that their destination was close, Thornton continued the walk to the temple behind the legion.

***

Kethras moved with an air of suspicion as he followed the Athrani Legion toward the entrance of the temple. His big black eyes looked sunken and hollow against his black fur, but Thornton knew they were taking in everything, even things he himself couldn't see. He was glancing back and forth among the merchants in the market, the way a predator scans for prey. It made Thornton nervous.

Suddenly, Kethras narrowed his eyes and turned to look at Thornton and Yasha. "Quickly," he said to them. "Inside."

Thornton looked around, thinking another Athrani was looking for trouble. "Why? What's wrong?" His mild annoyance came out in his voice, as he was quietly hoping to take in the sights of the city for just a bit longer.

"It is difficult to explain," Kethras said, "but I don't want to take any chances. Stay close."

Thornton didn't hesitate. He felt his palms start to sweat as he followed the tall Kienari toward the temple. He trusted Kethras's instincts, but he knew it himself too: something was off; he could feel it. And from the corner of his eye, thought he could see it—what looked to be the faint figure of a woman. But when he turned to see what it was, the figure disappeared from sight.

Almost as if it had never been there at all.

Grabbing tighter the arm of his sister, Thornton found himself moving into a second Temple of the Shaper, a towering construct that existed more or less for the glory of the being he knew simply as his childhood friend Miera. It was open to all, but represented someone who was now cut off from the rest of the world.

The irony was not lost on him.

The old stories say that Lash'kun Yho was the younger twin of Ahmaan Ka. They also say that being younger was the only way in which Lash'kun Yho came second to his older brother: he was smarter, stronger, and faster than Ahmaan Ka, and he took every opportunity to prove it. The two of them fought like brothers, competing in every way: wrestling with each other, racing and chasing each other, hunting longer and running faster, trying so hard to prove that one was better. But their competition was always for pride—always, that is, until Asha Imha-khet.

—Excerpt from *The Night Sky and Its Names*

Chapter 15

Khadje Kholam

Awaken the Three

Rathma

Rathma relaxed a little when he could see that Kuu was still breathing—as much as he could relax in irons, surrounded by enemies.

Before leaving him to the soldiers, Djozen Yelto had marched Rathma into the middle of the compound where the caged gray fox was sleeping, and Rathma watched as its rib cage drifted slowly up and down.

All around them were soldiers in Yelto's employ, and Rathma knew they weren't going anywhere. Most of them had a curved, short sword at their side. The ones who did not wear swords wore spears instead, with a small dagger strapped to a thigh. All of them wore tan tunics with chainmail underneath. The shemaghs they used to cover their noses and mouths during the day were pulled down loosely around their necks, forming cloth triangles that pointed at their belts. Most of the soldiers were quiet, but Rathma could hear a few of them exchanging whispers that more or less confirmed what he was thinking: that their trial would be quick and unfair. But what they were more intrigued by was that Djozen Yelto himself had left the compound to track them down.

Rathma felt the wooden end of a spear catch him in the back as a guard behind him said, "Move."

Rathma gave the guard a cold look but did as he was told. He held his shackled hands in front of him as they walked, and they appeared to be headed for the entrance of Yelto's chambers. In front of them, holding a torch above his disfigured face, was a Priest of the Holder whose empty eyes were staring right at Rathma. The muscles on the priest's face twitched and tightened, and Rathma felt the bile creep up in his throat as he realized the priest was smiling.

"Don't worry, child," the priest hissed. "The Holder will take you soon." Turning to the guard, he pointed inside as the thick metal door to Yelto's chambers was opened. "Take him in and chain him up, then bring in the other one."

"Yes, Priest," answered the guard. His voice sounded shaky, and Rathma could tell that the skeletal figure made him nervous too.

Crossing the threshold, Rathma could see why the Djozen hardly ever left: the interior was lavish, spacious, and carefully adorned, displaying all the wealth and power that a man of Djozen Yelto's lofty position would have. Large, colorful rugs were laid throughout the chamber, which was nearly as large as the courtyard outside. Candleholders made of gold lined the walls, and thin reddish-pink marble columns, one every ten feet, provided support for the ceiling and created an aisle down the middle.

The centerpiece of the chamber, though, surrounded on each side by two huge columns, was the throne. Elegant in its simplicity, the high-backed gold-covered chair stood eight feet tall, with a thick lavender cushion providing the perfect spot to rest Yelto's better-looking half. He was sitting on it now, surrounded by three bare-chested women, with another one sitting in his lap, sharing whispers and laughs with the fat Djozen. The smell of their flowery perfume caressed Rathma as he walked closer and almost made him forget the trouble he was in.

Yelto looked up as the guard brought him in, waving off the women and giving a playful slap on the bottom to the one who had been on his lap. "Ah, good," he said as he waved the guard in. "Bring him in." In his other hand was a silver goblet that spilled wine as he moved it. He watched the women with a hungry grin as they scampered away.

The guard grabbed Rathma's arm tightly and walked him front and center before the big man. "Kneel," the guard said as he forced him down by his head.

A metal ring on the ground had a thick chain connected to it, which the guard had used to hook on to Rathma's shackles, effectively locking him in place. He could stand up, but the chain was short and allowed almost no movement; he would have to bend forward if he didn't want to remain kneeling.

Forced into bowing before Djozen Yelto. Rathma scowled. *I'd rather kneel,* he thought as he did just that. He settled onto the floor and looked up defiantly to the man on the throne. "Let's get this over with," he said.

"Anxious, are we?" Yelto said as he took a sip of wine. "You Yhun boys always want everything now, now, now." He wiped his mouth with a long silk sleeve and set the goblet on the arm of his throne. "Well, you're on my schedule now. Look around," he said with an elaborate sweep of his arm. "You're in my world, boy."

Rathma didn't have to look around to know he was right.

Awaken the Three

It had been almost ten years since Yelto had returned from Do'baradai. His rule began when he deposed the western tribes' Hedjetten—the one man to whom all the western tribal chiefs answered—and took his place as their new Hedjetten. The only true rule of law in the tribes was the rule of might, and Yelto certainly had that.

After he had conquered the West, Yelto turned his eyes to the East, and to the Hedjetten who ruled its tribes. When word of the fate of the western tribes reached their ears, the eastern tribes conceded to Yelto's rule with surprisingly little resistance, and in doing so had made him the first Djozen: a man who ruled over two Hedjetti. Yelto had now done what no man before him had thought possible: he had begun to unite the tribes.

This all, of course, had been made possible by the help of the Priests of the Holder, who enabled the coup and had helped ease the transition of power. "The Holder's will," they had called it, and no one had argued otherwise. *Just like sheep*, Rathma thought. *Maybe stupider.* All that was left was for Yelto to assimilate the southern tribes and he could call himself ruler of all the lands beyond the Wastes.

That, of course, was easier said than done.

Behind him, Rathma heard the sound of footsteps. This time, though, he heard two pairs. Turning around, he saw who was responsible for them: led by two guards, with a muzzle over his mouth and a collar made of thin chain links attached to a rope, was Kuu.

Even as a fox, Kuu's emerald eyes stood out. They looked out of place in a body that was lined with gray fur, but even Kuu's older brothers—strong Wolfwalkers by any measure—couldn't change the color of their eyes following a transformation. It was the biggest giveaway when looking at them: a wolf or fox with human eyes meant that they were born with two legs, but chose to walk on four.

The guards walked him over to where Rathma was kneeling and tied him to the same metal ring on the floor. When the rope was secure, one of the guards removed the muzzle and Kuu shook his head, clearly happy to be free of it.

"Good to see you again, Kuu," Rathma said, smiling weakly. "I would have hoped you'd gotten away, though."

Beside him, the small gray fox began to change.

His front paws swelled and spread, while his hind legs grew thicker and more pronounced. Then his entire body seemed to lengthen and thin, like an earthworm being pulled by both ends. His gray fur retracted into his body, revealing Kuu's light brown skin and dark hair that had been hiding underneath. His nose, crooked and big, hadn't changed much.

"I almost made it," Kuu said with a grimace. The rope was tight around his thin neck and he pulled at it, trying to loosen it a bit. Lucky for him, it seemed the guards were not the best at knot tying and he was able make some room to breathe. The rope that hung from his body as he stood up was the only thing he wore.

Rathma was used to that, but what he wasn't used to was the large scar running down his side, the gash Rathma had seen when Kuu was still a fox. Beside it were several more puncture wounds that hadn't been evident before either.

Noticing Rathma's eyes on them, Kuu waved it off. "Lucky shot," he said.

Rathma was skeptical: it was more than just a lucky shot—it was a couple of them.

Before he could say something, though, Yelto slammed his hand down on the arm of the throne.

"Someone get this boy some cover," the Djozen growled. Pointing to a guard standing near the entrance, he said, "You. Find wherever this . . . *animal* shed his clothes and put them back on him. I won't have him tainting the decency of this court."

Kuu swung the rope around in his hand. "What's the matter, Yelto? Intimidated?"

Rathma elbowed his friend in the ribs before he got them sentenced even faster. "Quiet, Kuu. Stop playing with that."

Djozen Yelto said nothing as he took a long drink from his wine, looking down his nose at the two boys before him. The sound of hurried footsteps echoed throughout the stony hall as a short, squat guard charged his way into the chamber room with a pile of clothes in his hands that apparently belonged to Kuu.

"We have them here, Excellence," said the guard as he stepped in front of the boys, obscuring Kuu from Yelto's line of sight.

"You're too kind," said Kuu. While he dressed, Yelto turned his attention back to Rathma.

"Might I ask," the Djozen began, "what you planned to do once you got inside this chamber, using the key you took off the body of my guard?"

"You might ask," Kuu said as he poked his head out from around the guard. "But we might not answer."

Rathma almost laughed, but managed to keep his composure by biting his lip and looking at the ground instead of Djozen Yelto.

"It doesn't matter," Yelto said dismissively. "I know very well what you intended." He tapped his fingers a few times on the side of the throne while resting his jaw on the palm of his other hand. "Any fool with half a brain could see by the weapons you were carrying that you planned to kill me." He let the words sink in. "And do you know what they call that? The assassination of your leader?"

The next voice to answer was neither Rathma's nor Kuu's.

"Treason, O Great One," it said.

Rathma cringed when he heard the serpentine voice; it was a Priest of the Holder.

The slow sound of footsteps echoed off the walls as the priest walked in, punctuated by the hollow sound of his wooden staff striking the ground.

Step . . . Step . . . Knock.

Rathma stared straight ahead at Yelto, hoping not to see that horrid, skeletal face again.

Step . . . Step . . . Knock.

Even the thought of his jaw muscles expanding and contracting was enough to make him choke.

Step . . .

Step . . .

Knock.

The footsteps came to a halt just behind the two boys, and the hairs on Rathma's neck stood up.

"Correct," Yelto said. His voice was a powerful baritone, made even stronger by the acoustic quality of the vast stone hall. "Treason."

Looking at him now, towering over them in his throne, Rathma could understand why western tribes had acknowledged Yelto as their leader: big, heavy, and strong, the great man's size was enough to cow even the bravest of men. And it did not stop there.

A by-product of his wealth, Yelto's size also proved his power. He ate what he wanted whenever he wanted, drank almost hourly, and had his every desire met here in the confines of his palatial throne room—or his bedroom, if he wanted privacy. The last bit of hard work he'd done was wiping the blood from the blade he had used to cut Hedjetten Hota's throat, the very blade that now hung around his own neck as a reminder to all who saw it: peasant or ruler, Yelto would dispose of you if it fit his plan.

And right now, Rathma and Kuu most certainly fit his plan.

"And what does the Holder of the Dead say about treason, Priest?" Yelto asked with a sly grin, tracing the hilt of his dagger with a finger.

"That it is the worst of all crimes, and must be punished as such."

"And the penalty for treason?"

"Death." The word was cold and unforgiving. "They shall have the flesh stripped from their faces to be laid bare before the Holder of the Dead. Then they will be cleansed with fire, and shall stand in judgment before Ahmaan Ka for the sins which they have committed."

The guards were right, Rathma thought. *Quick and unfair.*

They weren't even afforded the chance to defend themselves—not like it would have mattered if they had been; Djozen Yelto would see them flayed, maybe even using his own dagger to do it, and the "trial" that had just taken place was the best way to ensure that.

"Throw them in a cage until morning," Yelto said to a nearby guard, with a dismissive wave of his hand. "And bring me more wine."

"Yes, O Great One," answered the guard with a bow of his head. He hurried over to where Rathma and Kuu were standing and unhooked the chains that held them to the floor. He was anything but gentle as he secured a good length of chain to them and made sure they weren't going anywhere unless he directed it. "Out with you," the guard said with a jab to their backs.

Rathma complied—as if he had a choice—and looked back one last time at Djozen Yelto. He could do nothing but shake his head at how casually Yelto had handled the whole thing. *Amazing*, he thought. *He's just condemned two men to die and he acts as if he's ordering breakfast.*

But that wasn't what bothered him the most.

What bothered him, more than anything, was the smirk that spread subtly, almost invisibly, over Kuu's face as they were being led to their deaths.

Chapter 16

Ellenos,
Temple of the Shaper

Thornton

When Thornton walked into the temple, he was struck by how familiar it felt; its halls were vast and seemed to resonate with power. It reminded him of Annoch's temple, where he'd first been told that Miera was the Shaper of Ages reborn, how her spirit passed down from mother to daughter in an endless, unbroken line of ascension. He wondered if there was similar power here, and thought of the hammer strapped to his back. He remembered watching it burn blue when it had come in contact with the Anvil of the Worldforge. So far, it appeared that nothing in this temple would cause it to do so, but the memory still made him tense. It was the last thing he had seen before the half-eye Dailus had torn it from him.

Only a few dozen men had been chosen to address the High Keeper of Ellenos. Endar had been the one to call them out by name, sending the rest of the legion home. Granted, those not chosen were happy to be able to break off and see their families again (and there would inevitably be a boom in the Ellenian population about nine months from now), but it was a great honor to be called into the presence of High Keeper Sh'thanna. Thornton wasn't sure why; he had met Sh'thanna's counterpart, Aldryd, in Annoch, and no one was lining up to see *him*. Thornton supposed he would just wait to see what all the fuss was about.

***

Walking slightly behind Endar, with his sister to his left and Kethras on the right, Thornton's breath nearly caught in his throat when they came into the throne room that made up the temple where Sh'thanna was Keeper. The inside was absolutely gigantic. The sloping walls of the pyramid had huge moon-windows carved into the sides that allowed the glow from the night sky to stream in and bathe the throne room in light. Everything around them had a bluish hue to it, owed to the marble that made up the temple, and there was hardly a spot on the walls or floor that wasn't covered with some ornate weaving or tapestry.

And sitting on the throne was a woman who was every bit as regal as her chamber.

Endar knelt before her and bowed his head. "High Keeper Sh'thanna," he said. The metallic sound of moving armor filled the chamber as the rest of his men did the same, taking one knee and placing two fingers on their left shoulders in a salute. "It is an honor."

Thornton looked at the High Keeper on her throne and realized that, if she was anywhere near Aldryd's age, she looked marvelous. Small streaks of gray ran through her light blonde hair, which she wore pulled back in elegant braids. Her piercing blue-on-blue eyes seemed to be taking in everything in the room, and the look on her face told Thornton that she was aware of everything that happened in her sphere of influence. She held a long wooden staff in her right hand, the purpose of which Thornton couldn't make out, but it looked ceremonial in nature. Plain and white, it was topped with a circle that had three metal rings: one at the top, middle, and bottom. And the purple and gold robe she wore was flowing and elegant, with wide sleeves that nearly touched the ground as she sat.

"Rise, Endar, son of Olis," the Keeper replied from her throne. She extended a hand, palm upward, and gestured for them to stand. "You have certainly earned it," she said with a smile. Her eyes went to Thornton and his companions. "Now, please, introduce your friends to me."

The warmth of the words made Thornton relax a bit. She did remind him of Aldryd after all—kind and compassionate—and he hoped his intuition was right.

"Of course, High Keeper," Endar said. He motioned for Kethras to step forward, and the tall Kienari bowed his head. "This is Kethras, of Kienar. He and his sister Ynara were crucial in turning the tide against the Khyth, and his ferocity in battle is like none I have ever seen."

Sh'thanna looked him up and down with raised eyebrows. "I am honored, Son of the Forest," she said with a dip of her head. "This is my first time meeting one of your kind, though I have heard stories about you since I was a girl."

Kethras bowed deeply and gracefully. "I am humbled to be welcomed so warmly into a city of men," he said. With a nearly unnoticeable glance around, he added, "And Athrani."

The Keeper smiled. "The pleasure is ours. Judging by Endar's description of how you aided my men, I am the one who should be thanking you." She turned to Thornton. "And you must be the Highglader I've heard so much about."

Thornton, unsure of what to do, dipped his head and placed his hand over his left shoulder in an awkward salute. "Yes, High Keeper," he answered. "Uh, Thornton, son of Olson"—he coughed—"blacksmith of Highglade?" The end of his sentence curled up, making it sound like a question. He'd never been in front of someone where everyone acted as formally as they were now, but he was fairly sure he had done it right. He wasn't exactly used to dealing with royalty, or whatever Sh'thanna was.

"Pleased to meet you, Thornton, son of Olson," the Keeper said with a smile. "I gather that you are the one who wields the Hammer."

Hushed whispers swirled around Thornton, who, feeling the weight of Hammer of the Worldforge on his back, slid it out from its holder and grasped it vertically just below the solid black head. Its intricate and ancient engravings on a handle carved from white ash intimated the power that it held and, likewise, the power of the one who held it. The throne room was as silent as a tomb as everyone in attendance suddenly had their attention snatched up by one of the very artifacts of creation.

The Keeper's eyes went from Thornton to the Hammer and back to Thornton.

"How is it," she began, breaking the spell of silence that the Hammer had woven, "that you came to wield it?" Her words were pointed, but genuinely inquisitive. "The stories say that no Khyth may use the Hammer."

Thornton flinched, as he was still not used to being referred to as that—*Khyth*.

"I . . . do not know, Keeper Sh'thanna," Thornton said with a shrug. "Maybe the stories are wrong."

He slid his hammer back into its leather carrier and saw that his answer clearly did not satisfy the Keeper. "It belonged to my father," he went on, "and he passed it to me when I was old enough to swing it. I never knew that I was, well, *what I was* until the Hammer was taken from me. That was when"—he looked to Yasha, who nodded reassuringly—"I found out I was Khyth."

He took a breath, searching for the right words. "It's hard to explain, but I think the Hammer chose me somehow, like it was a part of *me* that was missing."

The High Keeper raised her eyebrows. "That, I can believe. The Hammer of the Worldforge is a powerful thing, and it would not surprise me in the least to know that it is capable of attaching itself to something or someone." She paused, tilting her head slightly. "Even a Khyth. But I must say," she went on, "I never would have thought I'd have one standing before me in the Temple of the Shaper." She seemed amused, a slight smile curling its way onto her lips as she leaned forward. "But I'm told by Aldryd that you are friends with Her."

Thornton gave her a quizzical look. "You mean Miera?" Sh'thanna raised an eyebrow, but Thornton kept going. "I mean, uh, yes, Keeper. That's right. I've known the Shaper since she was small." He added a bow at the end, hoping it would smooth things over.

The Keeper looked over at Endar, smiled, then looked back to Thornton. "Please, tell me what she's like."

Thornton had to think about it for a moment and realized that, in all the time he'd spent trying not to think of Miera, he missed her. He'd been pushing away the thoughts of her after she had sealed the Otherworld so that he'd almost forgotten about the part of his heart where she lived.

"She's kind," he started, "and thoughtful, but not afraid to be stern. She's definitely headstrong, and she'll disagree with you if she hears you say it"—Kethras laughed at this—"but most of all, she's selfless. She almost never thinks of herself. I think it's what I like most about her."

Sh'thanna closed her eyes as if she was concentrating very deeply on something. "Yes," she said without opening her eyes. "That sounds like her." She took a deep breath and looked at Thornton again. "Her mother would be pleased," she said with a weak smile.

Thornton nodded, thinking nothing of the words. Sh'thanna, peering behind him, said, "And what do we have here?" She was looking at Yasha.

Endar spoke up: "Ah, this is—" But before he could finish, Yasha stepped forward and introduced herself.

"Elyasha, Khyth of the Breaking," she said defiantly. "Of Khala Val'ur." She took a knee in a genuflection so graceful that even Thornton was surprised. With a bowed head, she said, "At your service, Keeper."

A murmur went through the halls of the temple as the Athrani guards on either side of Sh'thanna shifted uncomfortably. They each had a sword in hand, and Thornton was sure that they could handle themselves against any threat, but the fact that one girl made them nervous was enough for him to take a second look at his sister.

"Forgive me, Elyasha," the Keeper began, "but it is highly unusual to have a Khyth of the Breaking this deep in the heart of Ellenos. In fact, it is the first time in my lifetime that it has ever happened." She looked reassuringly to the guards, and silence once again filled the throne room. "But if you have the trust of my best commander," she said with a glance toward Endar, "then you have mine as well."

Yasha relaxed visibly, and so did Thornton.

"And," the Keeper went on, "I understand it was you who brought the traitor Dailus to us. Is that correct?"

"Yes," Yasha said softly.

Thornton knew that she had disobeyed her master by taking the half-eye Dailus to Annoch. She had done so at great risk to herself: she could never return to her home of Khala Val'ur, and there was no guarantee that she would be welcomed by anyone outside of it.

"Dailus had just surrendered the Hammer of the Worldforge to D'kane when they turned on him and tried to have him killed," Yasha said. "They ordered me to bury him, but I saw my chance to escape, and I took it." She had no hint of emotion on her face as she locked eyes with the Keeper.

"And for that you have my thanks," Sh'thanna said. "Now. Since you were a witness to the crime—as were you, Thornton—you will take part in the sentencing." She tapped her staff on the floor twice, and its echo filled the room.

There was a bit of commotion over Thornton's shoulder, and he turned around to see just what. *Sentencing—what is she talking about?* he wondered.

Right as the thought finished floating through his head, Thornton felt his anger rising as none other than Dailus, traitor to the Athrani, was marched into the chamber in chains.

It was Ahmaan Ka who struck first. They say that he was jealous of Lash'kun Yho, who seemed to be winning the heart of Asha Imha-khet. So he did what any jealous lover would do: he struck down Lash'kun Yho in a fit of rage.

But a god is not so easily killed. Their body is only a vessel, yet even a vessel needs a spirit. And so it was that Lash'kun Yho's spirit traveled to the Land of the Dead, but not before tearing out the spirit of his twin brother and taking it with him. That was when Ahmaan Ka became what he is now, and forever will be . . .

the Holder of the Dead.

—Excerpt from *The Night Sky and Its Names*

Chapter 17

Khadje Kholam

Awaken the Three

Rathma

Rathma awoke to banging on his iron cage.

"Time to wake up," came the gruff voice of the guard. He was running his sword back and forth over the metal bars, producing a clatter that made Rathma's teeth hurt.

"I'm up, I'm up," Rathma groaned. He had barely slept during the night in the confinement of the cold cage, and was almost glad that he would be let out of it soon despite knowing where it would lead him. He rubbed his eyes, ringed with weariness, and looked around for Kuu.

The light-brown stone that made up the floor and the walls was different than the stone he had seen in Yelto's throne room. It looked rougher, less refined. He had tried to pay attention when the guards brought him in, but most of the walk had been down a spiraling staircase that led them rather deep underground. It was cooler than the main chamber upstairs, bordering on cold, relative to the desert heat, but there was not much else to it. There was a table and a chair by the wooden door that led upstairs, and a handful of iron cages scattered throughout the underground chamber. Rathma's own cage was in relatively good condition, but most of the others were rusted and worn. Shackles hung from the walls, and a single cell with ceiling-to-floor metal bars took up the rest of the space. It was clearly intended for short-term holding, and that suited Rathma just fine. He didn't intend to stay long.

Just as he thought he might be down there alone, a familiar voice came from down the hall.

"Can't we sleep just a little longer?" Kuu whined.

"Quiet, dog," the guard answered sharply. Turning back to Rathma, he bent down to unlock his cage. "Soon you'll have all the rest you can handle."

"Did you hear that, Rathma?" Kuu piped up. "I think he's trying to scare us. Ooh, I'm shaking."

Kuu was almost never serious, Rathma knew, but this morning he was in rare form.

"If you don't stop yapping," the guard growled, "I'll make you wish you had." He was fastening the chains in place on Rathma's wrists before letting him out. He looked annoyed, and his movements were quick and abrupt. "Come on," he said as he gave the chains a jerk. "Over here."

The front of the cage fell open and Rathma tumbled out. The guard picked him up and walked him over to the wall where a pair of shackles were hanging, fastening the shackles to the chains around Rathma's wrists.

The last thing Rathma saw was the guard putting a blindfold over him. "Hey," he said as he struggled against it. "What's this for?"

"So you can't see," the guard answered in a mocking tone. Rathma felt the cloth tighten as the guard wrenched the knot. "No more talking."

He felt him check the chains one more time by giving them a quick tug. Then the sound of footsteps faded away as Rathma once again found himself alone.

He moved his head around, trying to find some way to disturb the dark cloth that obscured his vision, but it was too thick and well placed. *No such luck*, he thought.

Since he couldn't see, he would have to rely on his other senses in order to get a fuller picture of his surroundings. His fingers met the stone of the wall, rough and cold, and he dragged them over its dry surface to find the shackles that held him to the wall. They were cold too, colder than the stone they were attached to, and thick. Most likely made of iron. Kuu was somewhere off to his left, he could hear him giving the guard a hard time, and the door leading upstairs was in front of him to the right. As far as he could tell, there was just the one guard. He strained to listen for any other voices, any other noises—breathing, talking, anything.

Besides the other two souls in the room, it sounded as though they were alone.

Over the sounds of the guard struggling with Kuu, Rathma thought about all the careful planning that had gone into this, but also all the unknowns they had to deal with. Like what was inside Yelto's chambers? How many guards were posted inside? Were there any exits? Any entrances? All were variables he just couldn't answer without putting eyes on the inner chamber; Yelto's men were too loyal and too smart to give away information about it to outsiders.

The two of them had planned for what they could and determined that waiting any longer was too much of a gamble. Yelto had sealed himself away for too long, and, like a dog who is fed by hand, he had grown fat and complacent.

But we hadn't planned on the priest being there, Rathma thought. *And at night, no less.* That had certainly changed things. A voice in the back of his mind said that if they had known he would be there that night, they might have abandoned the plan altogether.

Not like it mattered now.

Kuu's cage slammed shut.

"Let's go," Rathma heard from behind him as the clank of a key sounded just above his head, undoing the shackles that held him to the wall. He smelled the leather of the guard's vest behind him, and the faint odor of perspiration. He felt a hand clasp his shoulder and another in his back, pushing him toward the door that led upstairs. The door whined open on its well-worn hinges, and Rathma felt the heavy, warm air from the stairwell tumble in past him. It would be a long, dark trip to the site of the execution. And, as one braces for a blow from an incoming fist, Rathma tensed under the inevitability of his own death march.

They walked in silence up the stairs, and Rathma could almost feel their twisting ascent up the stone stairwell. The air got warmer and warmer as they reached the top, until it was the temperature he had grown to know in Khulakorum: just heavy enough to make the sweat come burrowing out, and unforgiving enough to make it stick. The door in front of them clicked open.

"Just taking this one out to the front gate," said the voice behind him. It was lower and sounded different. Strained.

"Right on time," answered a second voice in front, off to the right. "Where's the other one?"

"Bringing him up next," came the grunted reply.

"Is he still in his cage?"

"Sure is."

"We can send a man down to get him, then."

Rathma felt the hand on his shoulder tense.

"No need," the guard behind him said. "I'll come back for him."

"It's no trouble." Off to the side, Rathma heard, "Yujai, go fetch the Wolfwalker."

Then he felt himself being pushed again. "Move," the guard whispered.

Why is he whispering? Rathma wondered. He shrugged it off, suddenly finding himself moving at a hurried pace—not quite a jog, but certainly a brisk walk.

Their two pairs of footsteps echoed through the chamber room, occasionally muffled by walking over one of the many rugs or animal pelts that decorated it.

"Taking this one outside," the guard behind him said to someone in front of them. "The Wolfwalker should be up shortly."

"Oh," came the response. The voice sounded thick and slow, and Rathma thought that his head most likely was, too. "Okay," he lumbered.

From in front came the sound of shifting armor as the heavy iron door to the courtyard was opened, and sunlight streamed in. Even from under his blindfold, Rathma could see a difference in the darkness, which brightened around him as if Lash'kun Yho himself were brushing away the night. Then Rathma felt the blindfold loosen, and the guard's hands frantically grabbed at his shackles. A sudden commotion came from behind them, from the stairwell leading to their holding cells, as shouts of confusion filled the air.

"It's him!" one voice bellowed. "It's the Wolfwalker!"

By now Rathma had managed to shake loose his blindfold, and he looked down to see Kuu, dressed in the uniform of the guard who had been watching them, working the key to his shackles and dropping them to the ground.

"Go," Kuu said, his face grave. "Get out of here. This time, I know what to expect." His face was covered by the shemagh, but Rathma knew his eyes. "My brothers are out there waiting."

"But—"

"Go!" Kuu demanded. "Find your brother. Find Jinda. Tell him that we need the Vessel." With that, Kuu pulled down his shemagh, unsheathed his sword, and started to buy Rathma some time. "Don't make me regret this."

Chapter 18

Ellenos,
Temple of the Shaper

Awaken the Three

Thornton

Dailus the half-eye was wearing night-black robes ("the traitor's mark," Thornton heard them called) and was hunched over as he walked. Two guards flanked him, spears to his back, and one led from the front by a chain around Dailus's neck.

"Go on," said a guard through clenched teeth, smashing the butt of his spear into his back. "You don't even deserve a trial," he spat.

Dailus's long white hair jostled under his hood as he lurched from the blow, but he kept silent. His blue eyes—one filled with a ring of gold—were stoic and empty.

Seeing Dailus made Thornton's pulse quicken, and his fists flexed instinctively. He felt his old anger for the half-eye begin bubbling up again. He would have taken a swing at him right then and there, if not for something catching his eye.

Or, rather, some*one*.

When the guards pulled off their helmets, standing before him, with dark skin and long, dark hair to match, was someone he knew.

"Alysana?" Thornton asked, baffled. He had not seen the G'henni serving girl since Annoch, where, dressed in the simple garb of a servant, she had helped him find the Temple of the Shaper. What Thornton saw before him now, though, was almost a completely different woman.

She was certainly not dressed like a servant either.

"High Keeper Sh'thanna," the dark-haired woman said. She shot Thornton a quick look of recognition and moved her hand as if to say, *Not now.* "We received your message."

Sh'thanna answered with a smile. "Thank you for bringing him all the way from Annoch." Her words were not loud, but they carried well. "How is your sister?"

"Mordha is well," Alysana answered with a bow of her head. "Keeper Aldryd sends his regards."

The name brought a smile to Sh'thanna's lips. "I would rather he had come himself, but I understand that these are uncertain times. But since he could not be here, I am pleased to see that you are instead."

124

Thornton looked back and forth between the High Keeper and Alysana, slowly piecing things together. He knew that Dailus had been held in Annoch with Alysana's sister, Mordha, who was second-in-command of the guard. But Alysana should not have been asked to escort Dailus when Mordha was more than capable. When Thornton had left, Alysana hadn't even been part of the Guard of Annoch; in fact, she'd never even mentioned it. But here she was, dressed in their armor and escorting a prisoner as if she'd been born to do it.

How is this possible? Thornton wondered. *Why was she put in charge of bringing Dailus here? And why would the High Keeper have requested her by name?*

Sh'thanna took a step down from her throne. The High Keeper's feet found the maroon carpet that extended from the throne to the entrance of the temple, and she began to walk toward Dailus.

"I've heard of your crimes," Sh'thanna said, addressing the half-eye directly. Her smooth face gave no indication of her age, and her lips, light pink, gathered themselves in a frown. Thornton was surprised to see her looking up at Dailus, as Sh'thanna barely reached his shoulders. She was not exactly short, but she looked it next to the lanky Dailus. Yet it did not detract from the power she exuded as she uttered the next words.

"Treason," Sh'thanna said powerfully, clasping her hands behind her back. "What say you to these charges?"

Dailus stood silently, looking somewhere in the distance with a glazed look in his eyes. Thornton noticed that he had a few bruises on his face, no doubt from some of the guards in Annoch who had taken their anger out on him, but otherwise looked healthy. His black robes did well to hide his thin figure, but made his gaunt face and light eyes stand out.

"Have you nothing to say?" the Keeper asked, anger mingling with her words.

"No, Keeper," Dailus answered. His voice was soft and sad, and nothing like the voice Thornton remembered. It was the voice of a man who had lost everything.

"Good. A traitor deserves no defense." She stretched out her arms in a proclamation. "Dailus of Ellenos, son of Jecko," she said in a loud voice. "For the crime of treason against your people and against your goddess, I find you guilty, in the Temple of the Shaper and in the sight of my people." She pounded her staff once on the ground. "You are hereby sentenced to die in a manner that fits your crime."

Thornton was stunned. He wouldn't even have time to take out his anger on the half-eye.

In a graceful motion, with her robes flowing, Sh'thanna turned around, climbed the three stairs back up to her throne, and sat down again. "Alysana," she said with a dismissive wave, "have him escorted to his cell. We will carry out justice at dawn."

The G'henni nodded and gave a jerk of the chain around Dailus's neck. "Move," Alysana said, and Dailus complied. The four of them walked toward the rear of the throne room and disappeared around a corner of blue marble.

Still in stunned silence, Thornton looked questioningly from Yasha to Sh'thanna.

The High Keeper was the first to break the silence.

"You were both witnesses to Dailus's crime, which could have doomed us all. If he had not done what he did, perhaps we would not be talking right now; but if we had failed in our response, we *certainly* would not be." She looked away in disappointment. "I knew his father, Jecko; he was a good man and always had the interest of his people in mind." Sighing, she added, "Dailus, unfortunately, is nothing like him."

The throne room was once again steeped in silence as Sh'thanna looked up at the faces of her people and to the faces of those around them.

"But your being here is more than just a victory for the Athrani people," she said. "You are a symbol for victory at the Tree, a champion of the Shaper—and justice." She looked away and up to the moon-windows. "And tomorrow we will see that justice carried out. I should like you three to be there."

Thornton and Yasha nodded in return, but Kethras did not move. The Keeper looked back to them as if waiting for an answer.

"Athrani justice is not Kienari justice," Kethras answered. "But if the High Keeper wishes it, I will be there."

Sh'thanna nodded in approval. "So be it." She turned to the commander of the legion. "Endar, I want to thank you once again for answering the call of the Keeper of Annoch. Your swift action and valiant efforts in battle proved to be the difference between destruction and salvation."

Endar looked flustered but brushed it off with all the grace of a bear swatting at honeybees. "Nonsense, Keeper. It was my honor to serve." His purple cloak hung off his back as he bowed.

"You may go, Commander. You and your men have my thanks."

Endar came up from his bow and gave Sh'thanna a nod, turning and leading his men out of the temple. As they left, the clamor of armor followed them down the halls.

"Thornton, Elyasha, and Kethras," the Keeper said, "you three have my blessing and protection while you are here in the First City. What you did for us at the Battle for the Tree is beyond recompense. Should you have need of anything while you are here, simply ask and it will be given."

Before Thornton could answer, however, the echoed sound of footsteps preceded a familiar face coming back into view. From the rear of the building, Alysana emerged once again and approached the Keeper's throne. She bowed, turning to look at Kethras and Yasha in turn. They shared quizzical glances as the G'henni turned to face the Keeper again. The resolute look on her face punctuated the words that followed, surprising everyone, including the High Keeper.

"I am sorry to interrupt, High Keeper, but the prisoner has spoken."

The aged Athrani's face was blank. "What is it, young one?" she asked. "What has he said?"

Alysana gave a look of worry, glancing from the High Keeper to Thornton.

"He requests . . .

"He requests to speak to Thornton."

Asha Imha-khet, the Ghost of the Morning. For failing to choose between the two gods, Ahmaan Ka and Lash'kun Yho, and for inciting their jealousy, she was given to neither in the end. Her spirit was denied entrance to the Otherworld, as well as to Khel-hârad, Land of the Dead. She is eternally bound here, to this earth, in the hours between darkness and light, forever caught between waking and sleep.

—Excerpt from *The Night Sky and Its Names*

Chapter 19

Khadje Kholam

Awaken the Three

Kuu

Kuu woke up in the tiny iron cage, with his ribs still hurting from the night before. One of Yelto's men—with a great eye at night, apparently—had managed to land an arrow or two in his side. Good timing on the guard's part, as Kuu was just about to break free of the compound. Any longer and he would have had to find an excuse to be caught. Rathma could have kept going, the Farstepper didn't play a part in this part of the plan, but it felt good to have the company.

He winced as he took a breath that sent a bolt of pain through his ribs, brushing it off knowing the sensation would pass. It was part of what made him so reckless and fearless, thinking and feeling he was invincible: every time he changed shape, his wounds would heal. It taught him to deal with much worse pain than this.

He looked around the underground room that the guards had thrown them in after their "trial," and saw that it was still dark. The torches that had been lit when they were dragged down had been extinguished after he and Rathma were thrown in their cages. He was at the end of a rather long hall, with a wooden table and chair on the opposite side for the guard to sit at. It was empty now, but depending on how much longer it was until daybreak, Kuu knew it would soon be occupied. He reached inside his thin vest to the hidden pocket sewn into the fabric. A smile spread over his face when he felt the keys that were still secreted inside. The guard hadn't even noticed that Kuu had taken them. He didn't know how much time he would have before they came to take him and Rathma, so he took advantage of being conscious and alone.

He started to quietly unlock the shackles around his wrists; he would have to leave them on for when the guard came to take him out of his cage, but he would loosen them for now. Once the guard got close he could toss them off and—hopefully—overpower him. It would only work if there was one guard, though; any more and Kuu might not be fast enough. If an alarm was raised, it would mean the end of their carefully planned infiltration of Yelto's compound. Getting captured had been the one way to find out exactly what was on the inside, and it had worked like a charm. Kuu had seen what he needed to and made mental notes of it, although their real goal was still locked away somewhere else.

D.L. Jennings

Yelto must be keeping her somewhere even more protected, Kuu thought. But there was no time for that now; his brothers would come up with something.

The only thing left to do now was escape.

He looked up and down the hallway and then back to the bars on his cage. *Easier said than done,* he thought. *Of course Rathma left this part to me.*

He heard the door open. Kuu watched as a guard stepped in with a single torch, using it to light the others in the hall. No other guards came in behind him.

Alone, thought Kuu. *So far so good.*

The guard walked out of sight, toward Rathma's cage, and started making a racket that could have raised the dead. He was trying to wake them, Kuu knew, and he was not being gentle about it.

Kuu shouted, "Can't we sleep just a little longer?" As he did, he slipped the key back into his vest in case he needed it later. *Never hurts to be ready for anything,* he thought.

The guard barked an indignant reply, followed by a metal clank, telling Kuu that Rathma's cage was open. His own cage would come next, he figured. He definitely needed to be ready.

Turning the corner, the guard came back into view. He was wearing a sword at his side, and a leather breastplate that was ubiquitous among Yelto's men. *Those could come in handy,* Kuu thought slyly. He would need to make himself look helpless so the guard wouldn't suspect anything. A couple of snarky remarks usually did the trick.

Kuu flung a few expletives his way, as well as insulting his parents— always a great target, and relatively easy in Khôl. By the time the guard got to him, he was sufficiently worked up.

"That's enough out of you, dog," the man said in a sharp tone.

Kuu had his hands behind his back in a feigned display of submission. "But I wasn't done!" he said with mock regret.

"I'm going to enjoy watching them flay you."

The guard looked inside the cage at Kuu's hands behind his back, double-checking the shackles around his wrists, and let open the cage just as Kuu freed his own wrists from their bonds.

"Sorry to disappoint you, then," Kuu said. As quickly as he could, he reached up and grabbed the guard by the collar and pulled, causing a collision between his face and the metal bars lining the cage. *That should do it,* Kuu thought. When the guard didn't immediately collapse, Kuu gave him a strange look and thought he might have been losing his touch. "Your face is tougher than it looks," he admitted, and smashed the guard's face on the cage again. The second collision did the trick and the guard slumped to the ground.

Kuu climbed out and looked around. The small hallway had just one torch in it, but the rest of the underground room was well lit by other sources of light. He hadn't heard any other guards come down, and hoped his ears hadn't deceived him. He reached down and started to undo the guard's armor. "Lucky for me they didn't send a fat one," Kuu said as he slid the breastplate on. He took his sandals, sword, and shemagh, leaving the thin but muscular man mostly bare, and rolled him into the cage where he himself had just spent the night.

Closing and locking the cage, Kuu tossed the key up and snatched it from the air as he walked toward the entrance of the room. As he got closer, he saw his red-haired friend, blindfolded and shackled to the wall, groping around, searching for Holder knows what. Kuu snickered at how clumsy and helpless Rathma looked, and wanted nothing more than to savor the moment. He watched the Farstepper, who probably thought no one was watching, looking like a helpless coyote cub that had lost its pack and its eyesight.

I could at least have some fun before we leave.

Coming up behind Rathma, Kuu grabbed him and, in a deep voice, said, "Let's go."

He thought for sure that Rathma would catch on right away, but his fake guard voice had apparently been better than he expected. Rathma moved forward with no resistance, and Kuu suppressed a snicker as they walked.

He reached out and opened the wooden door in front of them that led into the hallway. He took a breath. This next part would not be easy.

***

"Don't make me regret this," Kuu said to Rathma.

Turning as he took out his sword, Kuu moved with the grace and precision of a practiced thief, swiftly covering the distance between him and a handful of guards. They were caught up in the confusion, and Kuu used that to his advantage.

"He went that way!" he yelled, pointing in the opposite direction. There were four of them, and the gears were turning slowly in their heads. One of them had half drawn his own sword, and the other three looked as if they should consider it. Before they could, Kuu was on them.

"Ha, gotcha," Kuu said as he sent his sword through the open side of one guard's armor. He watched the eyes of a second one grow large as the alarm registered; but there was no time for it to fully take root, as Kuu had already grabbed the dagger that was sheathed at his thigh and driven it up, into the man's jaw. He ducked a punch from the third guard, who was placing his hand on his own sword. A quick twist from Kuu and a sword to the belly of the fourth guard left the two men facing each other.

"Sorry to leave like this," Kuu started, dropping his sword to the ground with a clang. "But dying would be pretty inconvenient for me." He stepped backward and reached inside himself, where the power he had yet to fully master was waiting for him.

It was hot, like grabbing a piece of metal that had been baking in the sun, and soon a sensation spread over him as though he were pulling on a coat made of searing hot needles. He felt his legs lengthen and contort as the rest of his body went through the tumultuous process of becoming something else.

Inside his body, he could feel his bones breaking and resetting as his skeleton did what it needed to in order to make the transformation. Part of that process was what would heal any wounds that he had previously picked up. His skin would change, and his muscles, too; but the pain that came with it all was very real.

Despite all the practice he had changing while moving, the process wasn't easy. He had leaped into the air so he could use the momentum to carry him forward toward the door leading from Djozen Yelto's chambers to the courtyard outside. Just as his arms became legs, he touched the ground. His shoulders had broken and reformed themselves, slightly more forward, just below their normal position on his body, allowing for the reduced flexibility but increased speed that came with his four-legged gait. The tail that popped out behind him, which he still hadn't really found a good use for, wagged itself into being as he fled through the open door.

His eyesight was sharper as a wolf (a fox, technically, but he was still working on changing into larger animals like his brothers could). For now, though, he settled for the diminutive form that was still relatively easy for him to change into. He was so much quicker than he ever was on two legs, and he found himself flying through the courtyard, ducking through the open legs of surprised guards and weaving his way closer to freedom.

Shouts of "Grab him!" filled the air, but Kuu had no intention of being caught this time. If foxes could smile, Kuu would have done so; instead, he simply let his tongue hang out the side of his mouth as he ran, speeding over the sand and making his way toward the hidden outcropping in the desert that he and his brothers called home.

As he did, two towering and great black figures made their way toward Djozen Yelto's stronghold, with what looked to be four human riders flanking them. His timing, it appeared, was flawless as always. Tongue wagging, he fled, arrow-like, across the desert sand.

Chapter 20

Ellenos,
Temple of the Shaper

Awaken the Three

Thornton

"Absolutely not," Thornton said. His frown was deeper than the brown of his shirt, one dirtied by years spent in front of a forge, the soot and sweat making their marks. "I have nothing to say to him, and I don't want to hear anything he has to say to me."

Yasha was standing beside him and showed no emotion on her face. As far as Thornton could tell, she had no stake in whether Dailus went or stayed. Which is why, when she spoke up, it surprised him.

"I think you should at least go down there," Yasha said.

Thornton was shocked. "You of all people."

Yasha flinched at the words, but her expression did not change. "He's locked up"—she blinked—"and awaiting execution." She stood with her arms crossed, looking every bit the defiant Khyth apprentice Thornton knew her to be. "What if he has something important to say? This could be our last chance to hear it."

Thornton considered her words carefully. He thought about Miera and his father in the Otherworld. If there was the smallest chance that Dailus knew something about either of them, he supposed it would be worth listening to him. He turned to Kethras. "What do you think?"

The dark-eyed Kienari stood in silence, flicking his tail and touching a wiry finger to his lips in thought. "I suppose, if he is locked up," he said, "it would not hurt to listen."

Taking the Hammer off his back and placing it at the feet of the High Keeper, Thornton said, "I'm leaving this here, then." Looking at Alysana, he said, "Take me to him. My friends are coming too. Let's go."

The G'henni nodded, and said, "This way."

***

Alysana led the three of them toward the back of the throne room, where a small doorway led down a dimly lit hall with sprawling, purple-curtained walls. About halfway down the hall was an unremarkable brick archway that opened into a stone staircase that tapered from sight.

"He's down there," Alysana said.

136

Thornton stared at her for a moment. "You're not coming?"

"No. Anything that Dailus has to say is between you and him, and I have no business listening to it." She held out her hand for Thornton to proceed. With a smile she added, "Just don't let him out."

Thornton shook his head, bewildered, and looked into the darkness. After taking a moment, he said, "Kethras, . . . why don't you lead."

The Kienari did not hesitate, and Thornton watched him slip by him and into the blackness that cloaked him so well. Yasha followed, and Thornton brought up the rear.

He did not relish having to speak to the traitorous half-eye. *But what could I say that could make things any worse?* he reasoned. He followed the sounds of footsteps into the dark hallway leading to Dailus's prison.

Chapter 21

Khala Val'ur

Awaken the Three

Duna

Duna had never cared to see the inside of Khala Val'ur before, and she had never regretted it. But now, standing under the never-ending blackness of rock that encased the underground city, she was beginning to question that decision. She had been met by a pair of low-ranking guards who were her escort to see High Khyth Yetz, and they had taken her into the vast interior that the city was known for. It was like nothing she'd ever seen before, and its enormity made her feel very small as she looked into its depths.

All of this hidden underground, she thought, *yet still bigger than Ghal Thurái.*

The Sunken City of Khala Val'ur was a burgeoning city, and its painstakingly designed streets and layout all had an order to them. When she first laid eyes on them, she had actually gasped. She was not expecting such an expanse below the surface—and it was *absolutely* expansive.

The "entrance" to the city was a tunnel that connected the world below to the one above; and at the bottom of this tunnel was the beginning of a long, spiraling rock staircase that looked as though it had been carved right out of the walls that made up the city. *No doubt done with Breaking,* Duna thought. Her eyes traced the path that went clear to the other side, and she noticed that the stairs ran the circumference of the city two whole times. It was like a staircase on the inside of a watch tower, only thousands of times more massive. Scanning the inside of the city from her vantage point at the top, she saw how truly great the city was.

And in the center, blazing and bright, was the ever-glowing fire that lit the city.

"That's where you'll be going," said the guard, bearded and stocky, as he pointed at the conflagration. "High Khyth Yetz will be waiting."

Duna had never met Yetz before, but she was sure there was a reason his own people feared him. The fact that General Tennech would abandon his army and flee the city, essentially exiling himself, rather than face the consequences of his failure to High Khyth Yetz was not lost on her. She wondered how much of the blame would be shifted to her.

***

The men of the Fist of Thurái had followed their Valurian counterparts into the barracks of the Sunken City. There, they would wait until Duna came back to retrieve them, but she knew it would be more than just a temporary situation. With Ghal Thurái in flames, they were now soldiers without a city. And, as their leader, Duna was now the general of the armies of Gal'dorok. Labels had no meaning anymore: Thurian, Valurian—they all now marched under the banner of the Hand.

"Through here," the bearded soldier said.

After their long trek to the bottom of the city, Duna was almost relieved that their destination was in sight. They had been walking for what seemed like an eternity, and the spire that housed the High Khyth was now almost within reach.

The houses they passed were increasingly elaborate and well protected: metal gates in front with impenetrable doors and locks that looked to be just as much for show as for function. And in the center of all of it, the center of the city itself, waited Yetz.

***

As they approached, the guards were silent and seemed nervous, perhaps even fearful. They stood well clear of Duna as she approached the ornate door with a single knocker in the middle.

Despite knowing what the Khyth were capable of, Duna was not afraid. She knew they respected power more than anything, and Duna commanded power. She had looked power in the eye and stood her ground. She was ready.

She approached the door and grabbed the brass handle of the knocker.

Bang! Bang! Bang!

The knocker rang out like thunder as it struck. The sound hung in her ears as she waited for a response.

Then, beyond the door, she heard a low voice that gave her chills.

"Ah, Duna. You have arrived," it said. Reminding her of Kunas, it had a dead quality to it that was shared by all of those who had undergone the Breaking: somehow hollow, like a piece of it was missing—or had been removed. "How unfortunate."

Duna swallowed. Hard.

Chapter 22

Ellenos,
Temple of the Shaper

Awaken the Three

Elyasha

The corridor that led to Dailus's cell was dark, but Yasha had little trouble navigating it. Ever since she had brought about her own Breaking, she noticed that she had become more sensitive to light and to sound. Her skin pulsed with the newfound power that had a slow, dull burning to it. It gave her body an ashen coloration that reminded her of potter's clay, and made her reddish-orange hair stand out that much more in contrast. She was already self-conscious of her looks, and this last change had certainly done her no favors.

She felt different inside, looked different on the outside, and knew that whatever power she had awakened in herself had changed her—*was changing* her.

She frowned as she stared into the dark.

"Yasha," Thornton said from behind her. He cleared his throat, and the sound echoed slightly off the stone walls around them.

"Huh?"

"I asked if you were okay," he said. "You've, uh, stopped in the middle of the stairway."

She had been deeper inside her own head than she realized. "Sorry," she answered as she started down the stairs after Kethras. "I'm just distracted."

The three of them were walking down a cold brick stairwell that was unlit, save for the torches that burned at the bottom. When Yasha began to wonder why there were no other torches on the way down, she realized that an Athrani Shaper could simply call flames from the air; they had no need for torches here in the heart of the temple.

"Down here," Kethras said from a dozen steps in front of her. He looked back at her, and Thornton stepped into the light as Yasha followed. The scene before her gave her a start.

Dailus, in his black robes, sat cross-legged on the ground in an unremarkable Athrani prison cell made of ceiling-to-floor bars and simple stone. His arms were spread out parallel to the floor, and Yasha could see that his wrists ended at the walls of his cell. It looked as if someone had lopped off his hands and he was holding the ends of his wrists against the wall. Then she looked closer and realized that wasn't the case at all: the Athrani guards, in order to render his Shaping useless, had encased his hands in stone.

It seemed cruel to Yasha, but also entirely necessary. This was no ordinary prisoner.

When Yasha first entered the room, Dailus's head had been bowed so that his long, light hair concealed his face; but Yasha's surprise at seeing him had made her gasp, and she suddenly found herself looking right into the blue eyes of the Athrani half-eye.

"I wondered how long it was going to be," Dailus said. His voice was quiet, but something about it made Yasha uneasy. "They tell me you're the one who saved me. Elyasha, is it?"

Maybe it was the memory of seeing him run through by Captain Dhrostain's sword, or the fact that she knew he was a traitor. Or maybe just seeing him was enough to remind her of her former master, D'kane, the man who had usurped the Breaker.

Regardless of what it was, she didn't like it.

"It is Elyasha, isn't it?" he asked again.

Yasha couldn't bring herself to answer. She simply stared at the black-robed Athrani in front of her, letting the whole situation sink in. *Here sits a man who betrayed his own people*, she thought. Yet he looked like a man who had gained nothing and had nothing left to show for it.

She looked at his hands, or at least where they should have been, and blinked.

Dailus seemed to read the confusion on her face and gave her a weak smile. "Effective, isn't it?" he said with a nod of his head, indicating his hands. "Cut off from using Shaping, while being immobilized at the same time." He tugged at the wall as if to prove his words, and let out a sigh. "The Athrani certainly know how to make a prison."

"Good," came the answer from behind, startling her.

It was Thornton, who had stepped forward into the torch-lit room. Backlit by the two flames behind him on the wall, the blacksmith's swirling brown eyes looked menacing as they stood out against his shadowed face.

"You can rot in here for all I care."

Dailus was silent as he looked up at Thornton, who had crossed his arms in defiance. Yasha had never thought of Thornton as intimidating on account of his cheerful disposition, but he had certainly crossed that threshold now. He stood stone-faced before the traitorous half-eye, and for a moment Yasha saw flashes of Olson in the young man.

"I can't atone for what I did," Dailus said slowly, his head lowered. "But I can try to undo some of the harm I caused."

"Harm?" Thornton snapped. "You could have killed me! You could have gotten us all killed! I can't believe you would help someone like D'kane after knowing what he wanted."

Yasha watched the half-eye flinch, and she knew the words had cut him deeply. Unconsciously, she eyed the spot where Dhrostain had run him through with his sword.

"I know," Dailus answered. "It was . . . foolish. Irrational. I thought that if I helped him, I could finally find somewhere I belonged." He looked up with pleading eyes. "I'm sorry."

He looked, and sounded, like he meant it.

Thornton scoffed and turned his head away, arms still folded protectively in front of him.

In the intervening silence, Kethras stepped forward from the shadows.

"Alysana said you wanted to speak with us," he said from behind Thornton. Despite having been the first one in the room, it seemed that the Kienari had gone unnoticed to Dailus, who looked surprised to hear him. "So speak."

Dailus squinted in Kethras's direction, as if trying to make him out. The tall Kienari was barely an outline in front of the torches, with two dancing shadows flickering before him. Only the illuminated edges of his fine black fur were visible in the light, making it seem as though a void had walked into the room and made itself known.

"Very well," Dailus said to the walls of his prison. "I will make it short and simple." He looked back out at their faces. "With the Shaper locked away in the Otherworld, it is no longer possible to move between worlds by using Her blood, but that does not mean it is impossible.

There exists in this world a being capable of moving between our world and Khel-hârad."

Thornton looked puzzled. "Khel-hârad?" he repeated. "The Land of the Dead?"

Dailus nodded.

Thornton furrowed his brow, looking from Dailus to Yasha, then back to Dailus. "What good will that do? Miera is in the Otherworld."

"There are two reasons," Dailus said slowly. "One: the only way to enter the Otherworld is now through Khel-hârad."

Thornton looked impatient. "And two?"

"And . . . two . . . ," Dailus began. He seemed to be searching for words. "Thornton, there is no easy way to say this." The half-eye looked right at him when he spoke.

"Then just say it," Thornton said through clenched teeth.

"Thornton"—he paused— "your father . . . is dead."

Chapter 23

The Wastes of Khulakorum

Awaken the Three

Sera

Sera walked behind the towering Gwarái as they moved through the outskirts of the desert city. They'd been walking for a while, and, despite the creatures' enormity, the denizens of the desert looked at them with little more than passing curiosity.

But, seeing a large compound up ahead, she felt like that could soon change.

Rocky gray walls were manned by several sentries who seemed to be in disarray as they shouted back and forth to each other, pointing and scrambling about chaotically. On the edge of her vision, retreating from the compound and over the sands, was a streak of gray that seemed to be the cause of the chaos.

She couldn't make out what the guards were shouting, but she saw another figure moving northward, a man wearing a dark tunic, who seemed to be in a hurry as well.

From behind her, Tennech said, "It appears we have arrived at an interesting time."

The two Thurians, Hullis and Dhrostain, had dismounted from the Gwarái and were flanking the general.

"That's all that we seem to have anymore," said Dhrostain. He was scratching his dark black beard, which was the only hair on his head. He looked up to the taller blond captain and said, "I'm sure it's your fault, somehow."

Hullis gave the short man a skeptical smirk.

Tennech stepped forward. "Let me do the talking," he said with a dismissive wave. "And remember what we discussed."

The general had styled his close-cropped, graying hair in a way that made him look dignified, which his fine clothes certainly matched. Sera could scarcely remember the last time she had seen him without his armor; it was like looking at a different person. It if had not been for the long mustache that framed his mouth, she might not have recognized him at all.

"You're in charge," Hullis conceded. The blond Thurian captain was still wearing his armor and, walking with Dhrostain behind the general, looked more like a bodyguard than a soldier. He kept one hand on the hilt of his sword and his eyes dutifully forward.

The four of them walked to a north-facing entrance of the compound where two agitated-looking guards were standing. They held long spears and were dressed in tan tunics that hung loosely around them, ideal wear in the desert heat.

"Greetings," Tennech said. He was raising his hands as he walked, in a clear display that he was unarmed. The guards did nothing but scowl and draw their spears closer to themselves. "We have traveled far, and seek food and shelter," the general continued. "Will we find that here?"

"Nuku indzjhi?" the first guard said. "Utiwaka? Way Djozen Yelto jipawa?"

Tennech spoke through the side of his mouth to the Thurians: "Wonderful. Do either of you speak Khôl?"

"I picked up a little when I was in Lash Karghá," Dhrostain said.

"Very well, then. You do the talking."

Dhrostain grunted and addressed the guard. "Khala Val'ura wa," he said haltingly. "Malakha jip. Mek'dju hho?"

The guards looked at him strangely, then burst out laughing.

"What did you say?" Tennech asked.

"I asked if they had any beer," the Thurian said plainly.

One of the guards, a muscular man with coarse black hair, turned and went inside the compound. Tennech watched where he was going while the other guard eyed him suspiciously. Moments later, the guard was back. He pointed at Tennech and Sera, saying, "Du'irikha. Ghaman kemmu'ka dzebiya'ha," and motioned for them to follow.

Tennech looked at Dhrostain, who simply shrugged. Frowning, the general looked again at the guard and had started moving toward him when the dark-haired man put up his hand to stop him. He grunted and pointed at Sera.

"I think he wants you to follow too," Dhrostain said to her.

"I don't like this," Sera said flatly, crossing her arms over her chest.

The other guard postured angrily and whacked Sera with the wooden end of his spear.

"It would appear we have no choice," Tennech said.

"Du'irikha!" the first guard repeated.

"Yes, I caught that the first time," Tennech said, his hands still in the air. "Sera," he said with a turn of his head. "Listen to the man."

Sera was holding on to the scowl that had worked its way across her face, but managed to suppress her rage at being welcomed to Khadje Kholam by the butt of a spear. She made a mental note of what the guard looked like and put it away for future use.

"Fine," she said, and raised her hands as well. "But I still don't like it."

***

Sera walked behind Tennech, who in turn followed the guard. The three of them were inside a high-walled compound that contained a large number of tents and other sorts of living quarters. Looking around, she could see the remnants of several cook fires that were still smoldering, as well as an increasing number of men coming outside who looked as if they had just woken up. By the time she finished looking around the rather large compound, they had reached a great metal door.

The guard put out his hand to motion them to a stop, leaning his spear against the rocky wall. Beginning with Tennech, he checked the two of them for weapons. Despite Sera's objections, the guard was very thorough with his search of her. Appearing satisfied, he picked up his spear again and knocked loudly by using the butt like a battering ram.

"Effective," Tennech said dryly as the door swung open. The two Valurians followed their escort inside, into an interior that made High Khyth Yetz's quarters seem plain. Sera hadn't seen such opulence since Ellenos. And, even then, the decorum of the First City had been ostensibly for the glory of the Shaper. This interior, this palace, was for the glory of the one who lived inside it, and nothing else.

Whoever had decorated it thought very highly of him- or herself.

The uneasy feeling in her stomach rolled around and spread its arms.

They were barely past the door when they heard a voice.

"My men tell me you speak a foreign tongue," it said. It was low and thick, and lined with the rough tones of the tribal accents from beyond the Wastes. "Where are you from? Haidan Shar? Théas?" His voice echoed throughout the spacious chamber that was filled with precious metals and animal skins.

"Neither," Tennech answered. "Khala Val'ur is where we call home."

He and Sera were peering into the dimly lit hallway that led into a vast throne room.

"Ah, Valurians!" the voice boomed. "Come in, come in. And forgive my men. They are cautious due to recent events. But I assure you: you are welcome in my house."

Tennech looked at Sera and tapped on his own chest, indicating that it would be he who would do the talking. She nodded and followed his lead.

Walking in, she saw to whom the voice belonged.

Seated upon a gaudy throne of gold was an overweight man dressed in silks and jewelry that made even the ostentatious smuggler Ghaja Rus look like a pauper. He had dark black hair that was pulled back in a ponytail, and his skin was a shade of brown that reminded Sera of tree bark: healthy and strong.

"And whom do I have the pleasure of addressing?" Tennech asked. The general's voice projected more than normal, causing Sera to think he was trying to sound impressive.

"Djozen Yelto, Ruler of the Sands, Servant of Ahmaan Ka, and Uniter of the Tribes of Khadje Kholam," the fat man said. It was a verbose title, and Sera knew right away that her guess had been spot on: this man thought *very* highly of himself.

Tennech bowed with a flourish when the two of them found themselves standing near the edge of some small steps leading to the throne. The steps were broad and flat, made of a smooth and polished stone resembling marble, and were mostly covered by a dark brown rug that Sera was sure had been alive at some point.

"I am Aldis Tennech, of Khala Val'ur," he answered, "Dagger of Derenar and the Caller of Gwarái. I have come to you with an offer."

Awaken the Three

Djozen Yelto shifted in his seat. He eyed Sera and then the general, and stroked his chin. He spread his hands and said, "Then tell me what it is you bring to me."

Without hesitation Tennech answered, "I have come to offer you the next Shaper of Ages."

Chapter 24

Ellenos,
Temple of the Shaper

Awaken the Three

Thornton

At first it didn't even register. Thornton just stood there feeling his jaw slacken as he looked at Dailus, safe and imprisoned behind the iron bars of his cage.

Then the words hit him like violent waves breaking on the shore: one after another, after another—forceful and unrelenting.

". . . dead."

(Crash!)

"Your father is dead."

(Crash!)

Nausea crept up in Thornton's stomach as he felt his knees weaken.

"No," he whispered. "You're lying." He didn't believe the words even as they escaped, but it felt good to say them out loud. He looked up at the half-eye and felt renewed rage build in his chest. "You're lying!" he shouted.

He grabbed at the metal bars that separated Dailus from freedom and shook them desperately. "You're lying!" he screamed again.

The half-eye was silent. He broke eye contact and stared at the floor, looking as useless as Thornton's own attempts to shake the iron bars.

Useless, that is, until he felt the bars began to bend.

"Thornton," Yasha said with sudden alarm in her voice. "Stop."

Small bits of rock worked themselves loose from the ceiling, falling to the ground in an earthy cascade of dust. The prison around them seemed to groan as if it, too, were feeling the pain of Olson's death. The bars creaked and twisted in place.

"Thornton," Yasha repeated.

But Thornton couldn't hear her. He wouldn't hear her, wouldn't hear any of it; he was cut off and numb, cocooned in a shell of his own fury, and unable to feel anything else. The bitterness and rage that surrounded him had blossomed from deep inside, cutting off the rest of the world as it rose. He felt a burning in his body, as though his blood had caught fire.

"Thornton!" Yasha screamed. The panic in her voice had changed to fear. "Stop! You're going to kill us!"

The words reached his ears, but Thornton's focus was elsewhere. Deep in his mind, he reached for his anger and grabbed hold.

The fact that Dailus had been the one to tell him of his father's death—the man who could be held most responsible for it—made Thornton shake with anger.

Dailus.

Traitor.

The one who had stolen the Hammer was now heaping news of his father's death onto him like a shovelful of hot coals. The concept didn't even seem real. His father, larger than life, should never have been taken from this world without having a say in it.

Thornton reached out and embraced his anger as he felt his blood burn hotter and hotter. The world around him had almost ceased to be, but a strong, firm hand on his shoulder suddenly brought him back.

Thornton.

He gasped like a swimmer coming to the surface after being held below the waves.

Thornton!

It was the voice of Kethras, rough and deep, yet . . . soothing.

Thornton slumped to the ground. The prison ceased its trembling, and the iron bars were quiet again.

Then came the almost-inaudible whisper of Dailus the half-eye.

"You had to learn eventually." The words were quiet, not forceful.

In his haze, Thornton felt Yasha's hands under his armpits as she tried to help him to his feet. "I think you've said enough. Let's get him out of here and get him some rest."

Thornton felt a second pair of hands on him, and he suddenly found himself standing again. His head was swimming and his thoughts were cloudy; but as he staggered to the stairs that led up to the throne room, helped along by his friends, he heard Dailus speak once again.

"You can bring him back," he said. "And the Three can help."

Awaken the Three

Dailus

The Ellenian prison cell was dark when it came to him again.

Dailus, the voice said. It burned behind his eyes like a red-hot spear being pressed into his flesh. *Have you done what I asked?*

Dailus shivered despite the sensation of heat that enveloped him. "I did. I told them what you said." He grabbed the sides of his head and doubled over. "Ah!" A sudden, intense rush of pain leapt through him.

Good. The rasping voice was coming from all over, echoing inside Dailus, but Dailus knew he was the only one who could hear it. *If you do what I say, you will live.*

"No," Dailus gasped. "I don't want to. Just . . . Just let me die."

Searing laughter tumbled through the recesses of Dailus's mind. *Only when you've outgrown your usefulness to me. Until then, you are mine to do with as I please.* Dailus felt another shot of pain flood his mind, and he cried out again. It felt as if someone were pounding a sculptor's chisel into the back of his skull. "I remember! Stop! Please!" he begged. "I'm yours to command."

The words dripped out of him like spittle. "Just . . . stop."

He would say anything to make the pain stop. Do anything. He would take the Hammer again if he had to.

He would take a life. Anything, *anything* to make it stop.

He felt the burning embers die down and knew that he was alone again. Shivering, he felt the pain-wrought tears course down his cheeks as he wished for death. This had all been too much for him to handle, and he wasn't sure just how much further he could go.

But, for now, he had to find some way to awaken the Three—or at least make sure that Thornton did.

Chapter 25

The Wastes of Khulakorum

Awaken the Three

Kuu

As Kuu raced over the sand, he looked back at the shrinking stronghold of Djozen Yelto's, which was becoming no more than a speck on the horizon. He still had a good bit of ground to cover before he got home, so for the time being he continued to wear his vulpine hide.

His small gray body was well suited to the desert terrain and even more efficient at retaining water than his human body was. That, combined with the fact that he was light and quick, meant he could cover more ground quicker with less of a toll on his body. If he had to, he could have kept running all night.

But, as it stood, he had only a few more miles to cover before he would reach his family's stronghold. As Yelto's fortress disappeared behind him, he caught the familiar scent of home before it came into view. He was close.

He slowed to a trot as he covered the last stretch of desert between him and his family. Looking around at the sparse vegetation that existed this deep in the desert, he wondered whose idea it had been to settle here in the first place and wished he could give him a piece of his mind. The ground was mostly hard dirt as far as the eye could see, cracked from the lack of moisture and dotted by the squat, bulbous ykesha bushes with their hard, skeletal branches.

To live here was to conserve water, and to waste it was to die. Nothing in this desert was ill-suited to survive.

Finally, when he got close enough, Kuu started his transformation back to the form into which he had been born. As his bones cracked and shifted with their realignment, his sharp green eyes rolled back into his head as he tried to block out the pain. It was never easy.

Standing up and stretching his tall, fleshy body, Kuu spotted the false door that led to his family's keep. He steadfastly insisted they call it a hideout, but his brothers just weren't ready to make that leap. Dusting off the wicker handle, he pulled it open to reveal the darkness below. He got his footing on the rope ladder and climbed down.

"Is that you, Kuu?" he heard from inside. It was the voice of Sivulu, his oldest brother.

"Yeah, Siv, it's me," Kuu answered. He had just put his feet on the hardened dirt floor when he heard Siv sheathe a dagger. *Always vigilant*, thought Kuu.

"So?" Siv asked from the darkness. "Any luck? Did it work?"

The underground keep was spacious and clean, and its location under the desert floor ensured that it was cool enough to make for comfortable living. Kuu's brothers liked it dark, but would occasionally keep a lamp or two lit. Just as Kuu stepped into the large, circular common room, he saw a spark and then fire.

The small flame lit up Kuu's emerald eyes, and he saw the familiar form of his older brother sitting in a wicker chair with a small cushion on it. Sivulu's shaggy black hair matched his beard and capped a rugged face that women made no secret of finding attractive. Leaning back in the chair and clasping his hands behind his head, Siv looked at Kuu expectantly.

"Well?" his brother asked.

"I saw what I needed to," Kuu answered. "I know how we can get in and out, and now I know how many men there are." He looked around the room. The four beds lay low to the ground, and the hand-made furniture that decorated the room was simple in design and function. They did not live lavishly, by any means. "Where are Aurik and Kaurik?"

"They should be back soon," Siv answered. He leaned back a little farther in the chair, which creaked under his weight. "They're out recruiting."

"Good," Kuu replied. "We're going to need more bodies than we thought. Yelto's chambers house about fifty men, and—"

Siv held up his hand. "Save it for when the twins get here."

Kuu scratched his head. "Well, here's the thing, Siv . . ."

His big brother frowned. "What is it?"

"There were Priests of the Holder with them."

Sivulu took a breath and leaned forward in his chair, putting a hand to his face and rubbing his eyes with frustration. The soft lamplight made the wrinkles in his forehead more pronounced as he scrunched up his face. "Then we have to move soon," he said as he stood up and looked down at Kuu, standing just a few inches taller than him.

"I know," Kuu said despondently.

"Don't worry," Siv said as he clapped a hand on Kuu's shoulder. "The plan will work. I promise."

Kuu managed a meager smile and hoped his brother was right. They were staking their lives on it.

Chapter 26

Ellenos,
Temple of the Shaper

Awaken the Three

Elyasha

Yasha recognized the use of Khyth Breaking when she saw it, and Thornton had most certainly done just that upon learning of Olson's death. What alarmed her was not that he *had* done it, but the ease with which he did—and with no training whatsoever. Until just a little while ago, he hadn't even known of his Khyth heritage, yet here he was, bending iron and moving stone as if he'd been doing it for years.

Yasha knew she had to get Thornton away from Dailus before he did any further damage—either of them—and was quick to get the Highglader out of there. She scowled at the thought of the Athrani half-eye imprisoned below them as she dragged Thornton, with the help of Kethras, back toward Sh'thanna's throne room, where the Hammer stood just where they had left it. Coming around the corner, Yasha heard Alysana talking with the High Keeper before they came into view. When they did, the G'henni was the first to see them. She stopped mid-sentence and directed the Keeper's attention to their approach. Looks of concern washed over the two women's faces when they saw Thornton's state, the High Keeper being the first to speak.

"What happened?" she demanded as she rose from her throne. "Was this Dailus's doing?"

Yasha contorted her face as she searched for an answer. "Yes," she said. "And no." The answer only served to transform the looks of concern into looks of confusion from the women before her.

Kethras stepped forward to speak.

"Thornton has just learned of his father's death," said the Kienari as he helped stabilize Thornton, "and did not take it well."

The High Keeper frowned. "I'm sorry," she said. "Perhaps some rest will do him good." She motioned for one of her guards to come over. "Help Master Woods to one of the guest rooms."

The guard approached, and bowed slightly, bringing his fist to his shoulder. "I shall see to it, High Keeper," he said.

"Oh," Yasha called out, pointing to Thornton's hammer. "Bring that with you. If he wakes up and it's missing, you might not like what comes next."

The guard looked worried as he retrieved the hammer. He picked it up by the worn white-ash handle, admired it briefly, and went back to assisting a woozy Thornton toward the other side of the throne room.

As she watched the two of them leave, Yasha wondered just what was happening inside Thornton. She knew that the kind of power he had just displayed would leave any Khyth apprentice reeling, but she also knew it shouldn't have been possible for him to tap into it at all, not on the scale that he had.

She determined that, after he got some rest, she would try to help him understand who he was and what he was now capable of, mostly so nothing like that ever happened again.

He probably wants nothing to do with it, she thought. But she would at least bring it up. At the very least he could learn to control it.

"Keeper," Kethras said as the two men disappeared from sight, "there is a matter which I have come before you to discuss, and another matter that Dailus mentioned; I believe them to be one and the same." He was bent at the waist with one long arm extended before him in genuflection.

He looks so regal, Yasha thought. *Like he was born for this.*

His elegant manner must have taken the Keeper by surprise, as she shifted in her seat and blinked her blue-on-blue eyes, taking a moment to think before answering.

"Certainly," Sh'thanna replied. "What is it?"

"We would seek the help of the Three."

A frown crept onto the lips of the High Keeper. She stood abruptly and clapped her hands. "Guards, leave us," she announced to the room.

Her words resounded off the blue-hued walls as her guards and advisors exited quietly, leaving Kethras, Yasha, and Alysana alone with the High Keeper. Taking her staff in hand, she leaned on it slightly as she descended the wide stone steps to the throne room floor. It sang out each time it struck with a clack, like tiny lightning strikes, the only sound in the big, empty chamber.

She looked her guests in the eye, pausing on each as though trying to bore into their souls. After a time, and seemingly satisfied with whatever it was that she found, she spoke.

"The Three are dangerous, and the Holder of the Dead, even more so," the High Keeper said in a low whisper. "Tell me why you would seek them out."

Kethras exchanged a glance with Yasha. "We fear that the Shaper is in danger," he answered. "And that the power of the Breaker may be too great."

"Nonsense," the High Keeper said.

"While her sacrifice was noble," Kethras went on, undeterred, "and well intentioned, there are those of us who fear that it may have been . . . ill-conceived." He paused for a moment, hesitating. "The Binder of Worlds is among those who share this fear."

Yasha's eyes opened wide at this revelation. *If the Binder is worried, maybe there really is a reason to be afraid.*

Kethras went on. "The Binder believes that, given enough time, the Breaker could overpower and corrupt the Shaper, making her sacrifice—and everything we fought for—for naught."

"And you truly believe that the Three are the answer?"

Kethras nodded grimly.

The High Keeper shook her head slowly. "Then the cure may be worse than the disease."

Yasha wanted to ask what the High Keeper meant by this, but she held her tongue; the old Athrani did not look like she was done talking. She turned her back to them and looked above the throne, where an old but well-preserved tapestry hung. There were many elements to it, most of which Yasha could not make sense of, but two dark figures at the top stood out very clearly against a larger white one that looked to be a woman.

Pointing to one figure, she said, "Ahmaan Ka, as he was called then, was an ancient and jealous god who served the Shaper long, long ago, along with his brother, Lash'kun Yho," she said, sweeping her hand across to indicate the second figure. "But, as those with power so often do, Ahmaan Ka found himself asking why he should serve another when he was so capable of seizing power for himself." She steadied herself on her staff and lowered her eyes and her voice. "So he rebelled."

"Rebelled?" Yasha whispered. "How?"

"He began to take the souls of the dead for himself, using them to fuel his power, while keeping his actions hidden from the Shaper. His mistake was not in taking power," she said as she raised a finger, "but in thinking that the Shaper would not notice." Sh'thanna turned her head so that the edges of a troubled smile could be seen on her face. "But she did notice. And she punished him severely for it." She faced the three of them once again, her expression solemn. "The Shaper of Ages cast him into Khel-hârad, into the Land of the Dead, where his spirit remains to this day, beholden to the will of the Shaper."

Alysana nodded beside Yasha. "They say that the Holder's betrayal was so great that even his own brother, the Traveler, was forced from the Otherworld as punishment for the Holder's sins." The High Keeper turned to her, a look of surprise on her face. "Even in G'hen, these stories reach our ears," Alysana added.

"Then how might the Three help us get to the Shaper in the Otherworld?" Yasha asked.

The High Keeper paused as if searching for words and took a breath. "Imagine the Otherworld as having two doors, each with its own lock and key. The Holder of the Dead opens one lock, and the Shaper of Ages opens the second. Her key is held by your friend, of course," she said, alluding to Thornton's hammer. "And, just as the Blood of the Shaper must be used in conjunction with the Hammer of the Worldforge, so must the souls of the dead be used in conjunction with the Holder."

"So," Yasha started, "if we ask the Holder, he could get us into the Otherworld by using the dead?"

"*Ask* the Holder?" Sh'thanna scoffed, incredulous. "To help the Shaper?" The elder Athrani looked at her as if Yasha had suddenly grown wings.

Yasha was undeterred, though. "Yes," she said, crossing her arms.

Sh'thanna shook her head, turning away. After a brief silence, though, she looked back with narrowed eyes. "I will start by saying that there are a number of problems that would arise."

"Such as?" Yasha asked, a glimmer of hope in her eye.

"Well, for one," Sh'thanna began, "the Shaper of Ages, knowing that She could not trust the Holder with the secret of Her mortality, sealed him away beneath Do'baradai, where he sleeps to this day."

Yasha furrowed her brow as she tried to comprehend what she'd heard. "But I thought you said the Holder was in Khel-hârad, not asleep in Do'baradai."

"Both are correct," the High Keeper replied cryptically. Seeing the confusion that her answer gave, she elaborated. "The body of the Holder of the Dead lies in Do'baradai while his spirit inhabits the Land of the Dead, making him a captive in both places. Much like how the Shaper's spirit and body were separated when She gave Her Gift to the Athrani, anchoring Her physical form in this world. Or, at least, such was the plan," she added quietly.

"Then," Yasha said slowly, "we wake him up."

Sh'thanna winced at the words. "My dear," she reproached, "it is not that simple. You do not just 'wake up' a god."

"Why not?" Yasha asked. Behind her, she thought she heard Kethras laugh, but didn't bother to look. "You said yourself that his body is in Do'baradai. We just need to go there and find it."

Sh'thanna grimaced. "Because we don't know how," she said as she turned away.

The High Keeper's eyes were raised again to the tapestry behind the throne. Its borders were the oranges and reds of fire, surrounding a vast expanse of brown, which Yasha thought looked like sand dunes. There were splashes of green and blue throughout, and two great black pillars near the middle. At the top were the three figures—the Shaper, the Holder, and the Traveler, Yasha guessed.

Yasha was so engrossed in the scene that she was startled by the words that came next from the Keeper.

"The only ones who know the secrets of Do'baradai," she said quietly, "are the Three themselves and the Priests of the Holder, and to speak to them is to look death in the face."

Yasha was silent for a time while she mulled over the words. She was no closer to finding an answer when Kethras spoke up.

"Then we will go to Do'baradai," the Kienari said in his rough, low voice. "If waking the Three can give us hope, it is a chance we must take."

The look on the face of Sh'thanna told them she did not approve. "You put yourselves in great danger if you choose to walk that path," she said sternly. "There are some, even among my people, who would see them sleep forever and who will do anything to keep them at rest." She raised a finger in warning, adding, "And that is to say nothing of the dangers that will awaken along with the Holder."

Yasha felt something in the pit of her stomach, like a pebble being dropped down a well.

"We will be ready when the dangers come," Kethras asserted.

She just hoped she would land on something soft when they hit the bottom.

Chapter 27

Khadje Kholam

Awaken the Three

Sera

Sera looked at the general as if the last bit of his sanity had just gone up in smoke. When he had told her the plan, he had completely failed to mention the part where she would be used as collateral. She continued her hard stare, which had no effect on Tennech, as Djozen Yelto licked his lips.

"Now, that is interesting," said the fat man. He raised an eyebrow as he looked Sera up and down. "The next Shaper, you say? Tell me how."

Tennech stepped toward the gaudy throne. "As you can see from her eyes, this woman is Athrani," he said, to which Yelto nodded. "But one thing you do not know, one thing that I will tell you right now, is that the Shaper passes on her blood to any children she bears. And this one carries the blood of the Shaper inside of her."

Sera's hard stare intensified.

"But this one is not the Shaper," Yelto said. It was more of a statement and less of a question.

"Correct, O Great One," Tennech said with a flourish.

If Sera's gaze weren't so firmly locked on him, she thought her eyes would have rolled straight back into her skull.

"But her daughter will be."

"Will be?" Yelto echoed. "You are certain of this?"

"Without a doubt," Tennech said. "Seralith Edos can trace her heritage back all the way to the first Athrani. Her bloodline is ancient and powerful, and any children she bears will be the strongest to walk the earth."

"But how does that bring about the next Shaper?"

"By this one simple reason," Tennech answered as he held up a finger. "The Shaper's spirit has gone back into the Otherworld, meaning that the next daughter to be born to an Athrani mother of her blood will be her spirit reincarnated." He paused, no doubt for effect. "And, as a consequence, will possess her power."

Yelto blinked a few times from his throne, as though he were mentally chewing on the words and trying to digest their meaning. From his throne, he looked calmly at Sera, working his gaze over her like a paint-brush: up and down, head to toe. He inhaled sharply through his nostrils. Finally, he spoke.

"Yet one does not give away something so powerful for free." His eyes flicked back to Tennech. "So what is it that you are after, General Tennech?"

Aldis Tennech, once the general of all the armies of Gal'dorok, crossed his arms and smiled.

"I want an army," he said.

Once a general, Sera thought wryly, *always a general.*

Chapter 28

Ellenos,
Temple of the Shaper

Awaken the Three

Thornton

Thornton had the distinct feeling of familiarity as he woke to Yasha looking over him. She pulled her lips into a tight smile when he opened his eyes.

"I hope you got that out of your system," Yasha said softly, "because we have some traveling to do. There will be plenty of time for you to work it all out."

Thornton rubbed his temples as he sat up in the plush, expansive bed. He looked around the room—warmer and more vibrant than Sh'thanna's throne room, with rich wooden dressers and thick throw rugs accenting the floors—and some thoughts made their way into his head.

Dailus.

His father.

He grabbed handfuls of the silken bedsheets and squeezed as he felt the rage start bubbling up.

"Don't," Yasha said as she swatted his hand.

"Ow!" Thornton sucked air through his teeth as he pulled his hand back and shook it out. "What was that for?"

"You lost control down there," she answered quietly, taking a seat on the bed beside him. "Look . . . I know you've had a lot to digest over the last few days, but we really need to talk about what you are."

She paused, adding, "And what you're capable of."

Thornton looked at her blankly. Her red hair was loose around her shoulders, and the muted gray of her face made her green eyes stand out. They looked sharp and wild—just like her.

"I don't understand," he said. "Lost control?" He suddenly realized there was a blank spot in his memory, like someone had reached in and scooped it out; he didn't enjoy the feeling at all.

Yasha took a breath, apparently thinking. Before she could answer, though, Kethras spoke up. As usual, Thornton hadn't heard the Kienari come in.

"You nearly brought the prison down around us," Kethras answered through predatory teeth, "and Dailus."

The name was a whip crack to his skin, and Thornton winced at its mention.

"Don't say his name," he said through his teeth. "He doesn't deserve to live for what he's done. For what he's caused."

Kethras and Yasha traded uncomfortable glances as Thornton's words hung in the air.

Thornton narrowed his eyes as he looked at both of them. "What?" he asked flatly.

"You're not going to like this next part." Yasha grimaced.

"It doesn't matter if he likes it," came a voice from outside the room. Alysana, the G'henni woman who had accompanied Dailus thus far, stepped into the room. "It is necessary."

Her raven-black hair was pulled back in braids. Coupled with the soft leather armor she wore over a form-fitting dress, which had clearly seen a few battles, it made her look very much the part of a soldier. Her black leather boots came up just below her knees, with a dagger sheath in each. A long slit down the side of her dress allowed for ease of movement, and she slid across the floor with the grace of a dancer despite her battle regalia.

She was a far cry from the young barmaid he had met in Annoch, that much was certain. And just like that day back in Wern's tavern, Thornton found himself staring. A sharp nudge from Yasha pulled him back into the moment. He looked at her and then back to Alysana.

"For once," he said with agitation, "I'd like to stop waking up to surprises. Could someone tell me what's going on?"

"We're traveling to Do'baradai," Kethras answered. "With Alysana and Dailus, to awaken the Three. We may have found a way to bring back Miera . . . and your father."

***

Thornton was standing beside the bed now, and his hands were trembling. He clenched and unclenched his fists several times, and his brown eyes flashed with contempt.

"No," he scowled. "Not a chance. Out of the question."

"It wasn't a request," Alysana said as she crossed her arms. She shifted her hips slightly, and the short sword hanging from her belt caught Thornton's eye. "You have as much say in it as the half-eye does."

Thornton clenched his jaw as he started to see the G'henni woman for what she was: no longer a serving girl living in the shadow of her sister, Mordha, but a servant of the Shaper instead—and, by proxy, a servant of Sh'thanna. It was becoming clear to Thornton that the High Keeper had orchestrated this whole thing, from having Dailus sent over with Alysana to having them run into each other right before his "sentencing."

He had started to wonder how much more she was hiding behind the curtain, when Kethras stepped forward.

"I have spoken at length with Alysana and the High Keeper, and I agree," the Kienari said. "Dailus must accompany us to Do'baradai. He seems to know more than he is letting on, which means he must be watched closely, but also means that whatever he knows will most likely be the key to our success."

Kethras dwarfed the tall G'henni who stood next to him, and his fine, dark fur made even her pitch-black braids seem more bluish. "And besides," he went on, "I will be there to ensure he does not try anything that will get him killed . . . *early*."

Kethras's empty black eyes, like discarded coals, sent a chill down Thornton's spine. He was constantly grateful that the Kienari was on his side.

"He knows something we don't," Yasha said, "and refuses to tell us what. This is the only way to get it out of him."

Thornton started to pace around the well-furnished room. In keeping with the motif of the temple, the walls were a rich blue that almost seemed to glow and reminded him of how his hammer had reacted when it came in contact with the Anvil of the Worldforge in Annoch. A tinge of panic leapt through him as he realized his hammer wasn't right by his side, though the feeling immediately subsided when he saw it by the foot of his bed. Even at that distance, it seemed to instill a calming effect on him that he knew was deeper than any simple boyhood connection to a family heirloom. He walked over to it and gripped its age-worn handle, picking it up and examining it as he would the edge of a fire-forged sword. He looked deep into the intricate figures carved upon it, knowing now that they had been set there during creation itself by the Shaper, and he steeled himself.

"Fine," he relented. "Since it's clear I have no choice here, we might as well see what else we can get out of him." He placed the hammer back on the floor, resting the head on the ground and leaving it standing upright. "When do we leave?"

The others in the room seemed surprised by his reaction, as if they'd been sure he would've put up more of a fight. He thought he saw Kethras hiding some rope behind his back and peered at him suspiciously.

Alysana cleared her throat and looked at the others. "Whenever you are ready," she replied.

"As soon as possible," Thornton said firmly.

"Very well," Alysana said. "I will inform the High Keeper."

And with those words, the other three turned to leave.

"Just one question," Thornton said.

They all turned to look back at him.

"Where exactly is Do'baradai?"

The road to Do'baradai is treacherous and fraught with dangers;
what sleeps beneath, even more so.

—Khôl proverb

Chapter 29

Ellenos,
Temple of the Shaper

Awaken the Three

Thornton

Alysana was to be their guide on the journey to the City of Two Brothers, Do'baradai, and she was certainly qualified to be so. Having spent most of her young life in G'hen, living just a half day's journey from the Wastes of Khulakorum, she knew its secrets better than most. And, though she had left their protection when she was yet young, Alysana had insisted that she had spent enough time inside G'hen's walls to know what dangers awaited them outside—and in.

"We will travel south from Ellenos until we reach G'hen," Alysana announced. "From there, we can rest and resupply for our trek across the Wastes."

The Wastes, Thornton thought. *I don't like the sound of that.*

He tried to shake off the unpleasantness by watching the water below them as they made their way out of the First City. They were gliding along one of the many canals that crisscrossed the city like veins, on a small wooden boat with barely enough room to breathe.

"G'hen?" Kethras said to Alysana. The catlike Kienari was crouched near the rear of the boat, which held the five of them plus a helmsman whose sole job it was to ferry passengers from the heart of the city to the edge and back. "That is where you and your sister are from, if I'm not mistaken."

"You are not mistaken, Kienari," Alysana answered, a sly half smile on her lips. "Not much escapes you, I see. How is it that you came to know my sister?"

Kethras made a gurgled sound of laughter. "She knew mine," he answered simply. Nodding to the large knife that hung from Alysana's belt, he said, "And it looks like you did, as well."

Alysana gasped, while the sound of flowing water filled the silence that swept around them. She blinked a few times and pulled out the well-sharpened blade, offering it hilt-first to Kethras. "Then this belongs to you," she said in a voice scarcely above a whisper. "As does my life."

Kethras waved it off. "Keep both," he said. "I insist. My sister, Ynara, knew what she was doing when she left that knife with Mordha."

Thornton, perplexed, had been watching the scene unfold in silence. "Kethras," he asked, "what is she talking about?"

Alysana answered before the Kienari could. "When I was a little girl," she began, "I was very sick and was meant to travel from G'hen to Ellenos to see the High Keeper. To say it did not go as planned is to grossly understate how wrong it went, as the man who promised to take us to Ellenos had other, darker plans." She looked up at Thornton, and the young blacksmith could see the anger in her eyes at the retelling. "Pray that you never know what it is like to be made to do something against your will."

"Ynara heard the cries of Alysana and Mordha," Kethras interjected, "and made sure that the men who brought them about did not live to see another day."

Alysana considered the knife she held in her hands, its blade still sharp despite its age. "And she left us with this as a reminder," she said as she showed it to Thornton. "It is something I will never forget as long as I live—knife or no."

She slid it back into its sheath and nodded a silent thanks to Kethras.

"Touching," Dailus called out from the floor of the boat. He was lying on his side, his wrists tied together behind his back, and his arms were bound to his sides by thick ropes that ensured he would not be able to use any Shaping.

Alysana answered by kicking him in the ribs. "That is enough talking from you."

It was enough to keep him quiet for the rest of the trip.

***

Their boat glided past the powerfully carved houses and buildings of Ellenos as they traversed the canal that led to the edge of the city. Thornton had been studying the vast networks of waterways that covered the mountain-borne city and had been fascinated by their existence and purpose. On their way out, he had spoken with the helmsman, who had explained the layout of the canals: a great circle of water surrounded the city, which served as the main hub, with routes cutting through running north–south and east–west. In addition to these routes were hundreds of smaller ones that served as byways for all the other citizens to utilize; the main routes, terminating in the heart of the city at the Temple of the Shaper, were generally reserved for official crafts transporting troops or supplies, and were mostly kept clear. This meant that one could traverse the city by boat in a matter of hours, perhaps half the time it would otherwise take on foot.

Thornton felt a stiff breeze drifting past him as they floated on, and breathed in the sweet-smelling air of the First City. He had to admit: Ellenos was certainly well designed. And though it was far from anything he'd ever known in his small village of Highglade, it somehow made him feel at home.

As they approached the edge of the city, and the Wheel of Ellenos, Thornton squinted, seeing a deep purple banner waving atop a spear protruding from the ground. A smile spread over his face when he recognized the figure of Endar Half-Eye standing beside it.

"I hope you weren't thinking of leaving the city without saying a proper goodbye," Endar boomed. He was still a ways off, but his voice carried so well that it sounded as though he were standing in the middle of the boat.

Thornton stood up and waved. "I tried," he shouted, "but it looks like I can't shake you."

The big half-eye roared with laughter that whipped over the water.

Approaching the edge, the helmsman slowed the boat to a stop, and the party disembarked. Thornton was the first one off the boat, and he clasped the outstretched hand of the big man who commanded the whole of the Athrani Legion.

"The High Keeper tells me that you are off to Do'baradai," Endar said. His face and tone were serious.

"We are," answered Thornton.

"And him?" Endar asked, pointing his chin past Thornton at Dailus and eyeing him suspiciously.

"He's coming with us."

"Hm," the big man grunted. "Whose idea was that?"

"The High Keeper's," Alysana answered indignantly. She stepped forward with self-assurance, planting her legs firmly on the dock where Endar stood, looking him right in the eye.

The commander crossed his arms but did not answer; his frown did most of the talking.

"I don't like it either," Thornton replied, turning back to look at the tied-up half-eye who was still on his side in the boat. "But it seems that none of us have much choice in the matter."

Endar worked his palm over his face, rubbing his eyes in frustration. "If the High Keeper wills it," he said with closed eyes, "then so it shall be."

"So happy that you see it our way," Dailus said from the boat. His head bobbed up and down with the gentle movement of the water in the canal, overlooking the edge of the great Athrani city.

Alysana took an exasperated breath and moved to the half-eye captive to help him to his feet, off the boat, and onto the dock.

"Thornton," Endar said, grabbing his attention. "I've instructed my men to help you any way they can. They can accompany you as far south as Théas, but from there you will be on your own. I've left horses for each of you"—he glanced at Dailus—"though it appears I miscounted."

"We'll figure something out," Thornton replied, once again clasping the hand and forearm of the commander. "And thank you. Any help we can get will be much appreciated."

"It won't be easy," Endar warned. "You must understand this." He was looking Thornton right in the eye while he continued gripping his forearm. Endar's red-backed green eye, showing his half-human heritage, looked like a blazing sun that burned in the powerful stare of the man from Ellenos.

Thornton felt the gravity in his gaze and in his grip. He knew the commander of the legion would not say anything unless it was absolutely necessary, so he internalized the words and gave a nod that conveyed his understanding.

"He will have help," Kethras said from behind Thornton. The lithe Kienari looked as determined as his words were, standing there with more knives than limbs, making sure to indicate to Endar that Thornton was safe.

"Good," Endar replied. "I hope you find what you are looking for."

Thornton nodded his head. "I hope so too."

"Well, enough talk," Endar said gruffly as he let go of Thornton's gaze and arm. "The horses await you at the bottom of the wheel, along with as many men as I could spare. Now off with you," he said as he turned his back, "before I change my mind about letting that traitor go."

Alysana gathered up Dailus roughly, pushing him toward the great Wheel of Ellenos as they each took their place on the expansive platform that would take them to the base of the mountain.

From that height, overlooking the woods and plains below, Thornton could see for miles. *All of that road between us and Théas,* he thought, suddenly feeling the weight of the journey before them, *and it's not even halfway.*

The wheel groaned as it began the long descent down the mountain.

***

The distant Athrani city was not yet visible beyond the horizon far to the south; from Ellenos to Théas it was about three days' travel, and from Théas to G'hen it was three days more. The horses would let them make good time, and the armed escort would provide peace of mind.

But, looking back at Dailus once more, Thornton wondered just how much peace of mind he could truly have.

Better to wield power than to fear it.

—Khyth proverb

Chapter 30

Khala Val'ur

Awaken the Three

Duna

Duna gathered herself and marched forth. She pushed open the heavy door and stepped into the dimly lit interior that smelled faintly of granite and smoke. Standing in front of the orange glow of a fireplace, facing away from her, was a red-robed figure with white-gray hair who had his hands clasped behind his back. Duna watched the shadow that stretched out behind him, clawing at her near the entrance.

"Don't be afraid," the figure said. "I'm sure my men have told you all kinds of horror stories about me."

"I'm not afraid," Duna answered, almost sure that she meant it.

"Good."

Turning around to face her was the unwelcome sight of a Khyth of the Breaking: nebulous eyes, charred skin, and a palpable emanation of power that pushed her back like a gust of wind.

"I am Yetz," he said, "as you have no doubt surmised."

"Duna Cullain," she answered, gathering herself. "But you knew that already."

Yetz curled his lips in a smile. "I make it a point to be well informed. Many wars have been won with words just as easily as swords," he said. "And I will use whichever one suits my needs at the time." He kept his inscrutable eyes on her for a moment, and Duna could feel him sizing her up. "But before I tell you what I need from you, I have heard whispers that there is something you need from me."

Duna nodded.

"An army," she answered plainly.

The High Khyth smiled again.

***

Yetz led them through a series of hallways that seemed to go on forever, lit mostly by candles that barely kept the darkness at bay. The eerie silence that surrounded them only compounded the uncomfortable feeling that penetrated the stony walls of the High Khyth's spire. Their footsteps on the polished floor echoed throughout.

"I know that Tennech has fled," Yetz said from up ahead, "and that Durakas has died. And I know that means you have been put in the . . . unenviable position of taking orders from me now." His hollow voice filled the air between the hallways and seemed to come from all around. "But my work is far from done, and the Hand of the Black Dawn is still the Breaker's instrument—and, by extension, mine."

The two of them walked into a room that felt different to Duna: heavy, cold, and damp. It felt like a jail cell, but more open and less inviting. From farther inside she thought she could hear breathing, and it was doubtful that it was human. The sounds of chains moving over a stone floor rattled through the air, and Duna's composure left her; she was suddenly, and very sharply, afraid.

Before she could speak, though, Yetz reached out his hand toward the hallway they had just come from, and the sound of rippling flames made Duna turn her head. She watched incredulously as a stream of fire came pouring toward them, reckless and bright. She looked back at Yetz, whose face was expressionless.

Panic began to bubble inside of Duna as she remembered how the Khyth dealt with failure. The thought that she was being punished for Tennech's betrayal struck her like a bolt of lightning. She flailed in the darkness as she tried to avoid the flames.

But their heat never touched her.

The fear left her as quickly as the flames had appeared, snuffed out when she realized what Yetz was doing. He wasn't trying to execute her; he was pulling the fire from the candles like a rope, and using it to light the room. The High Khyth swirled his hands around swiftly, filling the room with fire and expelling the darkness inside by the light of hundreds of candles that lined the circular walls of the vast and empty chamber.

And there, shown by the light that flooded the room, was a massive pillar of scales and teeth that stared hungrily through Duna right where she stood. White, twisted horns topped a fearsome head that seemed to hang in the air, and the long, serpentine neck that rippled with subtle movement made what she was seeing unmistakable.

The Night Stalker, she thought. *The Shaper's Bane.*

"Are you familiar with the Gwarái?" Yetz asked coolly.

191

Awaken the Three

Duna caught her breath. She had seen two of them in the battle at Naknamu, but had never been close enough to appreciate just how terrifying they were. The one before her, with its great yellow eyes and endless black scales, did more than enough to help her understand why the Athrani had hunted them to extinction ages ago—*or so the world had been told*, she corrected.

She managed to compose herself before answering: "I only know of them in passing. Two of them marched under the general's banner in the Battle for the Tree."

"Good," Yetz replied. "Then you know what they are capable of."

"I do," Duna replied.

"Then use them for whatever purposes you may have. And now," he said, "we shall discuss what you owe me."

***

Duna exited the High Khyth's quarters, content in her moral victory.

When she had asked Yetz to help her fortify her army, she had honestly not expected him to capitulate. Yet he had done so—and more. Not only was he giving her more Khyth to bolster the Fist, but he would be giving her Gwarái as well.

Never mind what he was asking for in exchange. It would be worth it.

There was a good reason Durakas made me second-in-command, she thought with a smirk; she didn't often allow herself the luxury of pride.

As she rounded the corner to the barracks, though, she nearly ran over a messenger girl coming her way.

"Oh!" the girl exclaimed in a soft, husky voice. "General Cullain, I'm so sorry, please excuse me." She backed away, giving them both some room. "I'm so clumsy."

She had stopped short of running into her—barely—but that wasn't what caught Duna's attention. *She's too pretty to be a messenger*, she thought as she eyed the girl.

"Not at all," Duna said, shaking off the thought with a tight-lipped smile. "Were you looking for someone?"

"Yes, General," she nodded. "You."

Duna narrowed her eyes. "Is that so?"

She nodded again. "I'm to tell you that Master Khyth Kunas requests to speak with you. He is in his quarters, just outside the—"

"I know where his quarters are," Duna said, interrupting her. "I will find him. Thank you," she said curtly, nodding and walking away, but not before giving an appreciative glance at the messenger girl again.

She let her annoyance at being summoned start to burn off, as she knew that she would have to work closely with Kunas in the future. The least she could do was try to keep it under control.

***

"Ah," came the voice of Kunas from inside his quarters. "General Cullain. So glad to see you."

His door was open, and Duna could see him seated inside, appearing to be studying something. She didn't even break stride as she acknowledged him, walking right into the room as he stood.

"Kunas," she said with a disdainful nod. "That makes one of us." She didn't like him, and had no problem letting him know; he had always made her skin crawl. "I ran into your messenger girl," she added.

The Master Khyth nodded as he rose to greet her, closing his book and flashing a smile that looked like it took more effort than should have been necessary. "Excellent. How was your meeting with the High Khyth?"

"Good," she replied, caught slightly off guard. "He's agreed to give us the necessary troops. We may be marching with some more inexperienced Khyth, ones who have yet to undergo their Breaking, but their power will still be welcome. In fact," she said turning to look at him, "he's asked you to take one of them under your wing. Something about lines of succession?" she said with uncertainty.

"Ah," Kunas said, sounding pleased. "With D'kane gone, there is a void, one that I will be ascending to fill. He must have chosen my replacement."

Duna shrugged. "Anything to add to the fight against the Chovathi will be of use."

Kunas nodded in agreement. "They will not go down easily. Though they may not be as well trained as the remaining men of the Fist, they make up for it in numbers."

Duna paused at the mention of this fact. The size of the Chovathi force was something she hadn't yet fully considered. There would most likely be many more of them than there would be Thurians and Valurians combined—and even Sharians, if they were lucky; there was no way of telling how many Chovathi lay beneath the surface; but if they had emptied out Ghal Thurái as quickly as they had, it was a lot.

"But," she said quietly, "it is practically the Thurian way to be outnumbered."

And it was true: the Fist were the best that Ghal Thurái had to offer. They had historically been the best of the best. Yet such selectivity meant having fewer warriors in their ranks than they would have had by taking just anyone.

Their most recent defeat at the hands of the Athrani had been both moral and physical: the retreat of their general and the death of their commander. They would need to do more than just supplement their numbers with Gwarái and Khyth.

"How would you rate our chances of success?" Duna asked in a still-lowered voice.

The Master Khyth took a moment to consider. He looked out a window toward the barracks, where most of the men waited. A few of them were sparring, but most were sitting or standing around in idle conversation.

"Now?" he reflected. "Not good."

Duna mentally agreed.

"But," he continued, "I might have an idea that could possibly sway the pendulum of victory in our direction."

"I'm listening."

"More Chovathi."

The burst of laughter that escaped Duna's lips was both unbidden and unexpected. *"More* Chovathi?" she asked incredulously, a smile spreading across her face. "So the Khyth do have a sense of humor!"

She couldn't remember the last time she had smiled, let alone laughed. It made her forget her responsibilities, even if only for a brief moment. That was when she noticed that the Master Khyth wasn't laughing with her. Her smile faded and she furrowed her brow, perplexed. "You're serious," she said.

Kunas nodded, straightening his robes and clearing his throat. "I am," he said. The look he gave her told her that his pride had been injured.

"Explain," she said with narrowed eyes.

The Master Khyth got up and walked over to the door, pulling it closed behind him. "The Chovathi that occupy Ghal Thurái are not the only clan of Chovathi," he said. "While they may be most of them, they are not all of them."

"What are you saying?" Duna asked, arms crossed over her chest.

"I am saying we give them what they seek. The thing that all men crave, and the thing that ultimately destroys them."

Duna smiled.

Power.

Of course: it was a concept the Khyth would have been intimately familiar with.

"The Chovathi have been at war with Thurians for generations!" Her voice was still lowered, and came out as a conspiratorial whisper. "A simple offer of power over a rival clan will never sway them."

"They are the enemies of Ghal Thurái, yes," Kunas conceded quietly. "But do not even men fight amongst each other? Even Khyth? Even Athrani?"

Duna could only muster a thoughtful grunt. This Khyth was clever, she had to give him that. She wanted to see just how far that cleverness would take him.

"Then I suppose you have a plan," she said.

The Master Khyth, Kunas, smiled wickedly.

Chapter 31

Ellenos

Awaken the Three

Thornton

At the bottom of the Wheel of Ellenos, a dozen men on horseback waited. Thornton recognized one from the Battle for the Tree, but the rest were strangers. Regardless, they would be traveling together, so he walked up to the one he knew and reintroduced himself.

"Thornton Woods," he said as he extended his hand.

"I remember," the brown-on-brown-eyed Athrani said with a laugh. "Thuma, son of Úlin, second-in-command of the Athrani Legion." He clasped Thornton's hand with a firm grip and a smile. "I fought alongside your father."

Thornton flinched at the words but caught himself. He knew Thuma had meant well.

"You did?"

Thuma nodded. He was big, not quite as big as Endar but still a large man with a blond beard and hair. Strapped to his back was a great sword that Thornton thought was big enough to make any potential ambushers think twice about waylaying the riders.

"Then," Thornton answered, "it's good to have you with us."

Thuma grunted and looked out at the group of riders. "Endar tells me we're to accompany you to Théas."

"If you can take us that far," Thornton said, "we would be in your debt." He looked over the horses that Endar had picked out for them and smiled to himself when he saw Miera's old brown mare, Matilda, among them. Counting the horses and then the riders, he said, "But it looks like we're one horse shy."

Thuma looked at Thornton and company, glanced at the horses and then back. "Hmm. How about we leave the traitor behind?" he suggested with a grin.

Before Thornton could come up with an answer, Alysana interjected.

"He rides with us," she said from behind Thornton. "It will help me keep an eye on him." Walking up to join the two men, she added, "And if it becomes a burden, we can purchase a mount in Théas."

"Fine," Thuma grunted. "But he rides with *you*." Grabbing the reins, the bearded Athrani turned his horse around and pointed it south, motioning for the rest to follow.

Thornton walked over to a sturdy bay stallion that reminded him of Jericho, whispered a few calming words into its ear, and climbed into the saddle. Turning his head to find Yasha, he nodded at her.

She nodded back and started after the other riders.

Thornton watched her go, and felt the warmth fade from his face. He didn't like having to keep a secret from her any longer than he had to, and was determined to take her aside when the opportunity arose; he just hoped that it would come soon. Surrounded by Ellenian soldiers and an Athrani traitor was hardly desirable, but he hoped he might be able to steal her away for a few moments at some point along the way.

Just as he was about to follow, he felt a hand on his shoulder and turned to see Kethras looking him in the eyes. Even on horseback, Thornton had to look up to meet the gaze of the towering son of Kienar.

"We must be cautious," Kethras said in a voice just above a whisper. "Remember the Keeper's words: *There are those who would see them sleep forever.*"

Thornton knew Kethras was right; he felt it in his guts. "Keep your eyes open," he answered. "And I will, too."

The Kienari nodded, flashed a smile, and patted one of his daggers. "My steel will sing if it must."

"I don't doubt it."

Thornton looked around, as he again felt the presence of the woman that loomed like a shadow just beyond his grasp. In his heart he knew it was Miera trying to reach out to him, trying to tell him something, but at the moment he had no idea what he could do for her.

If she's trying to communicate, she's doing a terrible job.

He urged his mount onward behind Kethras, leaving Ellenos behind and setting out on the long road south to Théas.

***

They rode four abreast, with Thuma leading the way. Interspersed among their numbers were the other eleven men of the legion, who seemed to Thornton to be an excellent deterrent to any thieves who might catch a glimpse of them: they wore the purple and gold armor of the Athrani Legion, swords at their sides, and even their horses looked battle hardened. *I couldn't have picked a better escort if I'd tried,* Thornton mused.

Up ahead, Alysana and Dailus on their sturdy palomino seemed to be managing despite the awkward riding situation. Thornton edged his mount ahead to catch up.

Dailus was seated backward behind Alysana, looking miserable, with his arms tied to his side and no way to brace himself against the bouncing of the horse's trot. He was connected to Alysana by another rope, which the G'henni had wrapped around her chest. Thornton narrowed his eyes at the half-eye when he approached, hoping his misery was as deep as it looked.

"I'll be honest," Thornton said when he was even with them. "I didn't think I was going to see you again after Annoch."

Alysana turned her head and gave him a sly smile. "And I didn't think a young blacksmith could cause so much trouble."

Her deep olive eyes moved over Thornton like a wave, and he felt his cheeks flush a bit.

"It's not like I meant to," he riposted. "This hammer is more trouble than it's worth."

"I'm sure Aldryd would tell you it's worth much more than that."

She was right, of course. Whatever pains he'd suffered were nothing compared to what Miera was probably going through now at the hands of the Breaker, D'kane. *All the more reason to get to Do'baradai,* he thought grimly.

"I'm surprised Aldryd let you leave," Thornton admitted.

"It wasn't his choice," she retorted. "I knew that Mordha would be busy dealing with the increased watch around Annoch, and they knew that I owed a great debt to the Athrani people. It was an easy decision for me to volunteer to serve under the guard. And an even easier one for them to assign me to him," she said with a backward nod to Dailus.

Thornton was impressed. "It was really that important to you that you bring him to Ellenos?"

Alysana narrowed her eyes and looked at him. "No one does something like that to the people I care about without answering for it."

"I wish you'd stop talking about me like I wasn't here," said an exasperated Dailus.

Alysana threw back her elbow and caught him on the side of the head. "You don't have a part in this conversation, dead man," she said, turning her head so she had him in sight. "Remember: the only reason you're still breathing is because the High Keeper wills it."

Thornton saw the fire in Alysana's eyes and knew right then that she was perfect for the job she'd signed up for. He had a feeling she would see that Dailus paid his debt no matter the cost.

***

They were making good time by the end of the first day, and the twilit sky made for a pleasant backdrop as the Ellenians worked. When the sun had started to sink, Thuma had instructed his men to dismount and start making preparations for camp. They opened their saddlebags, pulling out supplies, with Thuma directing the rest of the riders in the effort. The big Athrani stood with his arms crossed as he watched his men, keeping his eyes on the surrounding area as well.

Alysana, who had wanted to get to their destination in a hurry, had seemed a little annoyed at the announcement. Thornton, on the other hand, had seen it as the perfect chance to have a talk with Yasha. All he needed was a moment alone to tell her the truth.

He saw the gray-robed Khyth standing off to the side, watching as the others did their work. *Now is as good a time as any*, he thought.

"Yasha," he said as he approached. "Can I talk to you?"

She turned her head and smiled at Thornton with her swirling green eyes. "Of course," she replied. "What's on your mind?"

"Not here," he answered. "Let's walk."

Thornton took her by the arm and helped her away from the camp as the commotion from the others filled the otherwise quiet evening air.

The countryside in this part of Derenar was mostly plains, which did not allow for much privacy. Making sure to keep the rest of the party in his sights, Thornton found a quiet spot far enough away where he was sure they could talk in confidence. He looked at Yasha, whose gray hood hung below her orange-red hair, and took a breath.

"Ynara told me something about you that you should know."

Yasha looked worried. "What is it?" she asked.

"It's about your father," he said. "She told me who he is."

Yasha's eyes grew wide with surprise. She blinked a few times, but said nothing.

Thornton went on, shakily. "And . . ." He searched for the words. "And I know him. I know your father." He felt a twinge of emotion start to bubble up inside him as he reached out for her, hesitant at first, then with more assurance as his breath found words. "I know him and I love him. Your father is Olson Woods, blacksmith of Highglade."

Yasha put a hand to her mouth, holding back a barely audible whimper. "Olson," she breathed. "So that makes you my . . . ," she said through her hand, "my . . ."

"Your brother," Thornton finished her thought, nodding.

Yasha covered her forehead with the palm of her hand, bracing herself as the concept soaked in. Thornton put out his hand to steady her, but she waved it off. "Just . . . Just give me a moment," she said.

She closed her eyes tightly and pressed the heels of her palms into them. Thornton was silent as she took it in, remembering how hard it had been when she told him that he was Khyth.

"I'm sorry I didn't tell you sooner," he said after a while, "but I knew I had to wait for the right time. This isn't something you can just throw at someone."

Yasha made no indication that she heard him. Thinking she just needed time, Thornton turned to go back to the camp.

"Tell me," Yasha said quietly. "Tell me about who he was."

Thornton paused. *Was.* The word stung. It still hadn't really set in. His father was gone, and he had never even gotten the chance to say goodbye—to *really* say goodbye. They had last parted ways in Annoch, before the Athrani Legion had made their march for the Tree, but that was supposed to have been until they saw each other again. Neither of them had had any way of knowing it would be so . . . so *permanent*.

His father had always been standoffish, but despite that, Thornton knew he had cared. He thought that if Olson had known about Yasha, he would have cared for her too.

And he knew he should say that to Yasha.

"There was a lot to him," he finally said. "He grew up around the forge, and spent his whole life learning how to be a great blacksmith. But he was more than just that; he was a good father. He looked out for me, and for Miera, and always had our best interests at heart. Everything he did, he did for us. It was never about him." He paused. "And I'm sure that he would have felt the same way about you."

Thornton could see Yasha's smile in the darkness.

"From the little time I spent around him," she said, "he seemed just the way you describe him."

But before Thornton could answer, Dailus's voice rang out.

"Stop!" the half-eye shouted from off in the distance. "You can't!"

Thornton spun around to look back at the camp, where the shout had come from.

"Watch me," growled Thuma. The big Athrani raised his sword, and swung.

A gift comes when you need it. A curse, when you do not.

—Khôl proverb

Chapter 32

Derenar, North of the Wastes

Awaken the Three

Rathma

Rathma was lost.

He had no idea where he was going, save for the fact that the Wastes were now behind him. He had unclasped his cloak hours ago and slung it over his shoulder to let his body breathe; the punishing sun was almost directly overhead, but the grasslands of Derenar made for much cooler climes than the deserts of Khulakorum. His dark red hair was tied up behind him, letting the rest of him cool off in turn.

He wasn't sure how far he would have to travel to find word of Jinda's whereabouts, but he knew that Farsteppers were rare outside of the Wastes, and the odds were good that someone would know something about a man matching his brother's description—and that's what he was by now: a man. Jinda had been younger when he left the tribes, but even Rathma had grown up in the intervening time, leaving the ignorance of boyhood far, far behind. Just as Rathma planned to do to the Wastes.

He planted his feet in the rough dirt trail and looked around, squinting to make the light more bearable. Behind him, directly south, was his desert home; and before him, leading north, was a trail going Holder knows where. It was clearly not a well-traveled path, although it appeared to have seen some recent use. Strange tracks, which looked as if they belonged to the biggest wolf he'd ever seen, led southward into the desert. Thanks to the relatively undisturbed topsoil of this region, the prints of the creature—*creatures?*—were well preserved. But when faced with the sands of the south, they became nothing more than a passing, forgotten mark on an endlessly shifting landscape.

"I guess north is as good a direction as any," he mumbled to himself. *Anything to get farther away from the Wastes.* Placing one foot in front of the other, he began to walk.

***

Many times the road split off, branching westward or opening eastward, but Rathma stayed the path. He reasoned that his brother might have thought the same thing, wanting nothing more than to distance himself from the warring tribes of the south. So he fastened his cloak and kept walking, step after step, slowly making his way along a path he hoped would lead him to something familiar.

By the time the weariness began to creep upon him, the sun had already started sinking. He had been walking long, and only now began to notice just how sore his legs had become. Knowing nothing of the geography of this land, though, he decided to press on. He would rather follow the path, and maybe stumble upon a city, than stop at night on a strange road with nothing else in sight.

But, as luck would have it, he would not have to walk much farther. For, up ahead, and barely distinguishable against the setting sun, were the outlines of something that made Rathma thankful that he was born a Farstepper.

"A cloak like that must be hiding something worth some money," he heard someone say, followed with the sound of sharpened metal slicing through the air.

Rathma didn't wait to count how many there were.

He took a breath, closed his eyes, and reached for the power that had been his since birth. But what was even more surprising to Rathma than how quickly he had been caught by these bandits was the fact that, when he attempted to beckon his power, he was met with nothing but empty silence.

The only sound he could offer was a disappointed "Huh."

Chapter 33

Ellenos

Awaken the Three

Lilyana

Ellenos at night was a completely different animal than it was during the day. It was also when the city turned its eyes away to let the dust that had been swept beneath the rug come out.

Lilyana and Coraline of Ellenos were two specks of such dust.

Am I dreaming? Lily thought.

It felt like a dream, but it was very real. It was real, she knew, because it was a memory she had long since tried to bury.

Bury, but never destroy.

For each time she would try, it would simply sprout again from the dark soil in her mind, bearing twisted, awful fruit that would rot and fall to the ground only to bury itself again and repeat the painful cycle.

Bloom, blossom, and die.

Over and over again.

"Lilyana," Coraline called from farther down the cobblestone street. "Listen to me."

Her mother wore a gown that matched Lily's dress: a soft, sky-blue affair with trails of white interlaced and a deep back that left little to the imagination. Yet Coraline's lithe, regal figure did wonders to the long-sleeved gown that only natural beauty could.

Young Lily scurried over. "I was listening, Mother," she lied.

Coraline gave her a look of doubt followed by a swift swat to the cheek, loving but stern. She pointed her finger at Lily and said, "None of that, young lady. I told you to follow closely. Now, do I have to hold your hand, or will you walk beside me like I asked?"

Lily gathered herself up and raised her chin. "I can walk myself," she insisted.

"Very well," her mother replied, still eyeing her warily. When she finally looked away, she pointed down the long road that led past the Temple of the Shaper. "That's where we will be going for the ball to-night. Do you remember what I told you?" She looked down to Lily for an answer as the two of them began to walk. A slit on the side of

Coraline's blue gown let her take long, smooth strides as she glided down the road as easily as a leaf on the breeze.

"Yes," Lily began. "Stay near you but out of the way. Make eye contact with anyone who speaks to me, and only speak when spoken to."

"And lastly?" Coraline asked, not looking back or breaking stride.

"Never let you out of my sight."

"So you were listening," she replied. Lily couldn't see it, but she could almost hear the smirk in her mother's words.

The looming blue outline of the Temple of the Shaper stood in the distance, silhouetted in the moonlight and painted by the torches that filled the streets. For a city this size, it was no surprise to see Ellenos so busy at night.

Still, Lily thought, *it's amazing.*

She had never been to the Temple, but had heard stories about it: that it was bigger on the inside than it was on the outside, and that it was filled with devout Athrani running this way and that, carrying out the will of the Shaper of Ages. Tonight would be her first time ever seeing the inside of the Temple, and it had only come at the end of unrelenting pleading with her mother—paid for in full by Lily's best behavior in months.

As they neared the guarded entrance to the Temple, her mother slowed her pace to come even with Lily, and reached down for her hand. Lily tried to pull away, but Coraline would have none of it.

"Stay close to me," her mother whispered.

They approached two strong-looking Athrani men who were dressed in fine purple clothing. Beneath the cloth, Lily could see the faint outline of armor. Each of them held a pike in his hands, and they tapped them on the ground once, in time, at the ladies' arrival.

"What have we here?" one asked as he peered down his nose at Lily.

"Lady Coraline and my daughter, Lilyana," her mother answered. "We are guests of the Tallister."

Before the guard could respond, they were surprised by the voice of an Athrani man who stepped forward from the shadows. He was tall and handsome, and looked older than Coraline by nearly twenty years. "Ah," he said. "My accompaniment has arrived."

He smiled warmly as he looked Coraline up and down, gently reaching out to take her gloved hand in his and placing a kiss on the surface of the white cloth.

"So good to see you again, Coraline," he said. "And this must be the daughter I've heard so much about."

Lily hid shyly behind her mother as the Tallister smiled down.

"It is," Coraline answered. "She promised she would be on her best behavior if I let her see the inside of the temple tonight."

The Tallister laughed as the guards parted to let them inside. "Well," he said as they walked inside, "let's hope those rules don't apply to you as well."

The hungry look in his eye as he looked at Coraline made Lily's stomach turn. If the whole night was going to be like this, she was going to have to work extra hard to stay in line.

The inside of the temple had better be worth it, she thought.

Chapter 34

Derenar, North of the Wastes

Awaken the Three

Rathma

"Well, look what we've got here." The words were in the language of the northerners and sounded too fancy to be spoken by bandits.

The man who'd spoken them had a voice that was smooth and low, and he looked as though he had a few years' experience of stopping people on this particular road. He walked over and yanked back the hood that hid Rathma's red hair.

"A Farstepper."

There were murmurs of excitement from most of the men—Rathma counted six—but one of them was looking at him with a puzzled expression.

"A what?" he asked. "You're not making sense, Evram."

Evram, the one who had pulled Rathma's hood off, was clearly in charge, despite the recusant tone of the other man. Though all six men wore dark tunics, Evram's was lined with elegant traces of silver thread, running up and down, which made it look like a gloomy lake catching the sun.

"A Farstepper, Denk. They're worth money. That's all you need to worry about."

Denk, a shorter man, shrank away at his leader's chastising.

Evram turned to Rathma, eying him closely, and Rathma got a better look at him in return. He had coal-black hair that was parted on the right, coming just below his jaw, with a neatly trimmed mustache that framed a patch of beard covering his chin. He had a devilish smile that aired arrogance, with something hiding behind his eyes that made Rathma uneasy.

"I know what you are," Evram said in a voice just above a whisper. His closed-lip smile reminded Rathma of a snake about to strike. "And what you are is worth money."

Rathma scowled. He needed to think fast, since he suddenly found himself unable to use the power he'd known since he was young. Fortunately, one of Evram's men did the thinking for him.

"I thought Farsteppers were special," said a voice from the back. "Able to move through the air and whatnot." He made a few gestures with his hands, slicing them around wildly.

"What's your point?" Evram cut back, not taking his eyes off Rathma.

"Well . . . I mean . . . why is he still here?"

Evram narrowed his eyes and pursed his lips in thought, lightly scratching the patch of hair on his chin.

Rathma didn't give him the chance to answer. "Your man is right," he said as he crossed his arms. "A Farstepper would never let himself be caught." He was keenly aware of the fact that all of his weapons were missing, and their absence felt heavier and heavier as the men closed in around him.

"But your hair and eyes say otherwise," Evram countered. "No man this side of the Otherworld has eyes like that." Turning to one of the others, he said, "Tie him up. We'll see what kind of price we can fetch for him in Théas."

Rathma felt several pairs of rough hands forcing him to his knees as his hands were bound behind his back. *Great*, he thought. *This again.*

"But what good is a Farstepper who can't farstep?" Rathma asked from his place on the ground. It was as much for his captors' benefit as for his own.

Evram had been walking back to the path, but Rathma's words stopped him fast. From over his shoulder, he answered coldly, "We'll see."

It was the last thing Rathma heard before a sharp blow to the back of his skull made the world go dark.

There are many paths to power.

Take as many as you can.

—High Khyth Anatoch IV

Chapter 35

Khala Val'ur

Awaken the Three

Kunas

Although it had been many years since Kunas had set foot in Khala Val'ur, the power that resonated within the city still stirred him.

After prying himself from the watchful eyes of Duna Cullain, he had made his way toward the surface again, winding his way through the black and cavernous walls of the Sunken City and eventually emerging beneath the star-flung canopy that overlooked Khala Val'ur. The city had been his home when he was a boy, but he'd never felt any real connection to it.

He had been sent off to Ghal Thurái shortly after his Breaking—he had been selected based on his potential, and the High Khyth at the time had seen fit to send him despite his youth—so the only memories he had of the city were of leaving it. He had proven himself as a Khyth apprentice in Khala Val'ur and as a Master Khyth in Ghal Thurái. The only thing left for him now was to pursue the title of High Khyth.

He allowed himself a smile at the thought.

It was not lost on him that D'kane, the Khyth who had been expected to take Yetz's place as High Khyth, was now rumored to be trapped in the Otherworld. That meant that he, Kunas, was now next in line to ascend to the position that was both envied and dangerous. With it would come political power and unparalleled influence, but it would also put a target on his back; no High Khyth had ever died of old age.

The Valurian sky was streaked with stars as Kunas made his way out of the northern pass of the mountains that surrounded Khala Val'ur. One thing that made the Sunken City so defensible was the two rings of mountains—one inner ring and one outer—that surrounded it, forcing any invading army through narrow passes to reach the city center. He stopped for a moment to admire it and the foresight his ancestors must have had when they designed it during the Shaping War. There was truly nothing like it in the world.

It was a pity that he would have to destroy it.

***

Even though he knew what to expect, Kunas was uneasy; Chovathi were anything but predictable. He also did not enjoy the fact that this one had told him to draw a blade across his own palm until it bled.

Is how find Ku-nas, the creature had said in its choking, gravelly voice. The way the Chovathi's tongue had run over his jagged teeth had made Kunas's skin crawl. But Kunas did as he was asked, well outside the protection of the walls of Khala Val'ur, and waited.

It had been at least an hour now by his count, and the creature had not yet made itself known. He didn't know how—or why—this Chovathi had found him shortly after the attack on Ghal Thurái, but the things Kunas had heard had intrigued him.

The Chovathi had told him that his clan intended to wipe out all the other clans, leaving them as the only remaining Chovathi in Gal'dorok. He'd said it would make them stronger, which Kunas had not understood; it seemed a paradox to him—killing off their own kind in order to strengthen themselves. But, then again, the Chovathi were as different from him as he was from humans.

He frowned, and waited.

***

The Master Khyth had nearly worn a path into the ground with his pacing about when he heard a guttural growl from the darkness followed by a rustling of leaves and snapping of twigs.

That must be him, Kunas thought. The impending sense of doom he felt told him that it was.

Even though Chovathi did not reproduce sexually—their mating rituals involved violent dismemberment and the regeneration of a new body—the races of men had seen fit to attribute male and female labels to them based on role and appearance. Male Chovathi were large and slow, rarely leaving their nests. Females were small, quick, and cunning, the hunters and scouts of their people. Therefore, most of the Chovathi that travelers came across, if they lived to tell about it, were small—nearly man-sized. And sure enough, when the hulking white creature emerged from the darkness, Kunas had forgotten just how large the males could be. He took an unconscious step back when he realized he had to tilt his head to look up at the creature before him. Once, when he was a boy, he had seen a bear while wandering far from Khala Val'ur on an errand for his master; this Chovathi could have eaten that bear in three quick bites.

"So," Kunas said as he wiped his bloody hand on his robes, "you found me again." He hoped his voice did not betray the fear that was surging through his body.

"Find blood. Follow blood." The creature labored over even the simplest of words, rarely speaking in complete sentences. In fact, this Chovathi was the only one that Kunas had ever seen with the ability to speak. The others he had seen had only communicated in shrill cries or low clicks. Nothing that had ever resembled a language—at least not a human one. But this one had done even more than that: he had named himself.

"Khaz follow blood easy," the creature growled.

Well, that is horrifying, Kunas thought. "Indeed," he replied, hoping the blood had only been a way for Khaz to find him and not an invitation to dine.

"What say of hunt?"

Kunas paused to digest the meaning of this question.

Most Chovathi concepts revolved around hunting because it took up such a large portion of their lives. If they were not killing each other, they were killing other creatures for food. But one thing that Kunas had quickly come to learn was that, despite Khaz's rudimentary usage of language, he was anything but stupid. Chovathi, Kunas had come to realize, were frighteningly intelligent. They possessed logic and reason, the ability to plan, and the capability to express a dizzying number of concepts. The concept he had just mentioned was Khaz's understanding of what Kunas was doing.

Ah, Kunas thought with sudden understanding. *He means the hunt of the other Chovathi clans.*

"We are interested in your help," he said. "We will empty out Ghal Thurái of the other Chovathi who occupy it, and your clan will rise to power."

Khaz made a noise like laughter. "Humans and Chovathi will struggle," he said as he spread his massive arms. "Will fight." He brought his hands together. "Will die." He squeezed his clawed hands together and looked right at Kunas, a wild and wicked grin splitting his twisted face.

"They will," he replied. "But you need to give them something to show that they can trust you." Even as he said the words, Kunas felt as if he were staring right into the eyes of a wolf. Khaz was hunched over to make eye contact with Kunas—yet another chilling reminder of the creature's intelligence. He dwarfed him like a full-grown man speaking to an infant. His ghastly white body was sharp and skeletal, and nothing like the smooth bodies of females. It was almost armor-like and clearly reflected his role as a warrior: the last line of defense in the nest, guarding the best-kept secret of the Chovathi.

"What Ku-nas need from Chovathi?" His eyes narrowed.

"When your clan has stabilized," he said, "you will follow me. Not the female called Duna."

Khaz snarled and looked away. Kunas couldn't tell if it was anger or something else. Chovathi behavior was not human behavior, Kunas knew; but the real question was, how deep did the well go?

"I know," Kunas began, "that you grow weary of living beneath the world, in the lonely and forgotten places of the earth."

"Truth," the Chovathi replied, still looking off in the distance.

Kunas suspected that there was more to these deceptively cunning creatures than they let on, and some of Khaz's actions had tipped him off that there might be much more lurking below the surface. He often appeared to be listening to things that were not there, as though he was the lone participant in an internal conflict.

"Then, if you follow me, I will give you and your clan the city of Ghal Thurái, your ancestral home."

Khaz finally looked back at Kunas. His face contorted, almost as if he were expending a great amount of mental effort. He looked away, eyes hollow, and loosed a rumbling growl.

"Ghal Thurái," the Chovathi repeated.

The words chilled Kunas to the bone, but Kunas managed a nod.

The twisted grin appeared again on the Chovathi's face, and Kunas couldn't help but feel like he was a rat serving a snake.

Better to serve the Chovathi snake, Kunas thought, *than the Khyth rat.*

Rats would eat their own if they were driven to, but the problem was that one could never tell if a rat was desperate enough to do so.

With the snake, it was not a question of desperation; it was a question of which rat it would eat—and when.

"Ku-nas will have help of Xua'al clan," Khaz finally growled.

With the help of Khaz and his clan, Kunas could finally push out Yetz as High Khyth and take Khala Val'ur as his own. And then he could simply exterminate the Chovathi as he saw fit, perhaps even keeping around some of the more useful ones, like Khaz.

"Good," the Master Khyth said with a smile, aiming to fill the bellies of the snakes so that one rat, and one rat alone, remained.

Chapter 36

Derenar,
On the Road to Théas

Awaken the Three

Kethras

Salt, iron, and fear bled together as Kethras heard the sound of sharp steel being drawn against leather. The hair on the back of his neck went stiff when he recognized what was happening.

The scent.

On its own, a scent is like a word: each can be uniquely identified and described, and has a meaning of its own; but when certain scents join together in certain ways, they take on a different meaning altogether. And the meaning that hung in the air now was one that Kethras knew.

He had smelled it on the Khyth that had ambushed Thornton and Miera on the road outside of Lusk. He had smelled it on Dailus in the temple of Annoch before the half-eye took the Hammer. He had smelled it just yesterday, when he ushered Thornton and Yasha into the Temple of the Shaper in Ellenos.

And now he smelled it on Thuma.

In a flash, he had his bow in hand with the drawstring taut, arrow at the ready.

Move.

Kethras had lived through enough battles to know to trust his instincts. So when Thuma came crashing toward him with that enormous sword of his, it was second nature to dive out of the way and fire off a warning shot, one that caught Thuma in the thigh.

His second instinct was to move toward the closest cover he could find. The wide open plains south of Ellenos—too far south of his forest home of Kienar—made that task difficult. He knelt low, baring his teeth in a reflexive show of ferocity, and backed away from Thuma. Even a seasoned Athrani warrior would have trouble spotting a Kienari cloaked in darkness.

Unconsciously, his fingers swept over the soft feathers of a second arrow before cradling it between his knuckles and nocking it in the span of a breath. He took aim at Thuma, exhaled, and fired, feeling the snap as his arrow sped through the air to its mark, burying itself deep in Thuma's shoulder with a thunk. The big man had twisted just enough to stave off a fatal hit, saving his own life but hampering his movement.

It will slow him down, Kethras thought, *but not by much*.

The guttural curse that Thuma let out confirmed Kethras's assessment as the Athrani snapped off the arrows at their shafts and threw them to the ground.

Not by much at all. "Thornton!" Kethras yelled, having lost sight of his friend. "We are betrayed!" He nocked another arrow, sweeping his eyes over the campsite and trying to determine just who was friend and who was foe. Were they all a part of it, or only a few?

There was no telling at this point.

The figures around him lit up with the reds and oranges of their body heat as his vision began to shift. Why Thuma had chosen twilight to attack a Kienari was beyond him, but Kethras welcomed the advantage.

Two blazing figures raced toward him, their swords a cool blue as they bled off residual heat from the day, and Kethras tightened his bowstring. Releasing the arrow, he struck the first one in the chest. The second one closed the gap quicker than Kethras expected, so he had no time to nock and fire; instead he grabbed an arrow from his quiver, sidestepping to the outside of the man's sword arm, and buried the arrow deep in the man's throat. He had already drawn his dagger when the man hit the ground in a frothy, gurgling death.

Stooping, Kethras gathered the arrows and looked around for other threats. He heard Thuma yell behind him, "Grab the boy and take the Hammer!"

Alysana drew her sword to square off against Thuma. *So she is still with us*, Kethras thought. *Perhaps we can survive this*.

The two warriors circled each other, neither wanting to take the first swing.

"You walk a foolish road, G'henni," Thuma warned, leveling his blade at her. Blood dripped from his shoulder, but he did not seem to notice, or care. "You should know better than anyone that the Three should remain undisturbed. There is a good reason we do not wake them."

"I know," Alysana answered. "But it is worth the risk!"

Thuma must have seen an opening; he brought his sword down on Alysana in a great, slow arc. She raised her sword to meet his, and the force of the strike took her to her knees. She did her best to keep her feet, but Thuma was too strong. He knocked her off balance, pushed her onto her back, and came at her again. Deftly, Alysana rolled out of the way, leaping up to catch him with a savage slice to the back as he stumbled by. It wasn't enough to kill, Kethras could see, but it had drawn blood. The rich iron smell clawed at his nostrils.

"The Shaper of Ages cannot stay trapped in the Otherworld forever," Alysana said. She adjusted her grip on the bastard sword she wielded, having taken it in two hands to compensate for the strength she lacked compared to the bigger man. Thuma turned around, shook out his head, and charged at her again.

As steel rang out against steel, Kethras grew increasingly alarmed that he could not find Thornton.

Where is he? he thought as he cursed in frustration.

His answer would not come as he was blinded by a sudden flash of light; Athrani fire filled the night sky like the sun.

Orange, red, and white flooded Kethras's eyes as he felt the heat of Shaping, heard the crackling as the fire fed on the air around them. Feeling the grass between his fingers as he knelt, Kethras backed away from the raging heat and let his other senses guide him. The air reeked of smoke and charred flesh. He could barely breathe through the maelstrom.

Coughing, he ventured to open his eyes again. They ached, and his vision was blurry. His pulse quickened when the battlefield came into focus again, and one figure was left standing.

Thuma, he thought, and a lump formed in his throat.

He looked closer.

No. Not Thuma . . .

His momentary relief at realizing the figure was Thornton was burnt away when he saw Yasha lying motionless at his feet. Her body was charred and smoking—just like everything else around them.

And, just like the flames, Thornton waned, wavered . . . and collapsed.

Chapter 37

Khala Val'ur

Awaken the Three

Duna

Duna had just lain down for sleep in the bunk in her quarters when she heard a soft knock at her door.

Kunas, she thought despondently as she opened her eyes. She groped for the lamp on her nightstand, lit it, and got up. Finding the robe that hung by her bedside, she pulled it on and walked toward the door.

Tying up her blonde hair and making herself somewhat presentable for whomever it might be, she cleared her throat. "Enter," she said loudly. *Either Kunas*, she thought, *or someone even more unwelcome.*

As the wooden door creaked open, she was pleasantly surprised to find that she was wrong. The messenger, Eowen, looking worn from his journey, stepped inside.

"General," he said with a deep bow.

Duna waved him off immediately. "Stop," she said, beckoning him inside. "Bowing makes me uncomfortable. Did you find my sister?"

"I did," Eowen answered, his smooth features lined by the lamplight's dancing shadows. "The queen is well, and asked after you."

Duna waved it away. She hadn't spoken to Lena in years, and after the way the two had last parted company, she was surprised that her sister would deign to speak her name at all. "Did she agree to help us?"

"She did, General. The Sharian fighting force—"Before he could finish the sentence, a second set of footsteps made their way into the room, along with an unwelcome face.

There he is, Duna thought.

"Ah," Kunas said, "I did not mean to interrupt. My apologies."

Duna gave him a look of contempt, one she knew came too easily when the Master Khyth was around. "I'm sure," she said with a sneer. Turning to Eowen, she dismissed him, saying, "I've heard what I needed to. If there is nothing more, you may return to your post."

The messenger began to bow, caught himself, backed away awkwardly to the door, and was gone.

"Kunas. To what do I owe the pleasure?" Duna asked as she shut the door behind them.

"I bring good news, General."

"Oh?" she asked, motioning him to sit at the small wooden table near the corner of her quarters. Though she was general now and could rightfully accept the quarters that Tennech had abandoned the moment he fled the forest of Kienar, she had not yet felt right occupying a house so close to High Khyth Yetz. Instead, she chose to stay in the visiting officers' quarters, which were at the top of the spiraling stairs that descended into Khala Val'ur, keeping her closer to the surface and farther away from the High Khyth.

She adjusted the burn of the lamp on the table so that its light filled the room. "Sit," she said, motioning at a chair. "Tell me what you know."

"I met with an emissary of the Xua'al clan," he said, making himself comfortable.

"And what did this emissary have to say?"

"First, that the Xua'al are willing to help us in the battle against the other Chovathi clans."

"Good," Duna said with a nod. "What else?"

"They want us to help cut down the numbers of all other Chovathi clans, leaving the Xua'al as the sole remaining clan."

Duna leaned back against her wooden chair, crossing her arms and taking the chair's front legs slightly off the ground. She narrowed her eyes and looked away, remaining silent for a moment while she thought.

Then she looked back at Kunas. "Are you suggesting that we back a Chovathi coup?" she asked with an arched eyebrow.

Kunas smiled a tight smile. "If you want to put a name to it, I suppose that's what it is," he said.

"So we'll be doing their dirty work," she said flatly.

"Perhaps," Kunas said, extending his pointer finger, "but the Xua'al will be indebted to us."

Duna looked away again and, pursing her lips, considered this for a moment. Certainly it would be better to be on good terms with one Chovathi clan than hostile with all of them. *And cutting down their numbers would surely be a good thing*, she thought.

She flicked her eyes back to the Master Khyth. "And you think this is a good idea?"

In the back of her mind she knew that Kunas's good ideas and her good ideas were not necessarily the same.

"Indeed I do," Kunas replied. The flickering light of the lamp made the Khyth's swirling eyes look like wildfire. But when Duna's expression didn't change, he leaned in. "The Chovathi are nothing like you think, General Cullain. They are intelligent creatures. They have thoughts, needs, and desires—just like we do. And, just like us, they have a longing for stability and order."

Duna chewed on this. She placed the front legs of her chair firmly back on the ground and stood up. "And you think that this alliance will put the odds in our favor?" she asked.

"I do."

"Then," she said, "I believe we can help each other."

Kunas stood as well, pushing back the small wooden chair he had been seated on and looking Duna in the eyes. "More than you know, General. The Chovathi can be a mighty ally if we let them."

Duna scoffed at this.

"I don't trust them, Kunas, but I do trust you to make the right decision," she lied.

"Your trust is well placed," he said with a bow of his head.

Knowing the Khyth couldn't see her expression, she said, "I'm sure it is," with a roll of her eyes. "I will tell Yetz that we plan to march on Ghal Thurái, and that the Chovathi will be among our ranks. I want you to take three of my captains to finalize this deal with the Chovathi. Can you do that for me?"

"Of course, General," he answered with a sweeping bow.

"And, Kunas," she added, eyeing him carefully, "I want to demonstrate to the Xua'al that trust goes both ways." She paused before saying, "I want the final word to come directly from their matriarch to you."

Kunas looked up at her from his bow, seeming genuinely shocked by this request. He probably was, but Duna could never tell.

"General," he began, hesitation in his voice, "the matriarch . . . well, she never leaves the nest."

"Very well," she said as she made for the door. "Then do it in the nest."

The Master Khyth looked stunned. "I . . . will see what I can do," he said.

"Good," Duna replied as she opened the door and nodded him out. "Dismissed."

Chapter 38

Derenar,
On the Road to Théas

Awaken the Three

Alysana

The night air smelled like smoke and molten steel. Alysana had trouble breathing as she regained consciousness and quickly realized why: she was pinned to the ground beneath something heavy and huge. She blinked a few times as the world came back into focus, and she found herself staring right into the eyes of Thuma. They were wide open, and they stared icily back.

A bolt of fear ran through her as she flashed back to the night that she and her sister were taken, helpless and alone, and far too many miles from home. That same feeling of powerlessness overwhelmed her now as she struggled to breathe, but the fear was soon replaced by horror at the realization that Thuma wasn't staring at her; he was dead on top of her.

She nearly choked as she took in the stench of death that permeated the air. Panic ran its fingers down her spine as she tried to heave off the corpse to no avail. The very real possibility of dying under him set her heart to pounding.

He's so heavy! she screamed to herself. It was the feeling of being grabbed from the dark, never knowing when or from where the killing blow might come; it stole the breath from her and threatened to never give it back.

But she wouldn't give up. Mordha wouldn't have.

Calm, she thought. *Be calm. Think.*

She stared back at Thuma's dead eyes and tried to figure out just how she could move him. Calculation trumped trepidation as she wrestled her thoughts back under her own control.

Okay. If I can tip him up . . .

Gritting her teeth and taking in what air she could, she planted her elbow into the ground and used it to prop up the massive body of Thuma just enough for her to roll out of the way before it fell back on top of her.

There. Free.

She pulled herself onto one knee, where she gulped in the air like a thirsty man drinks water. Chest heaving and still shedding panic, she stared at the aftermath. Bodies—everywhere.

And, as far as she could tell, she was the only survivor.

Mordha made battle sound so much more appealing than this, she thought wryly.

All throughout their lives, her older sister, Mordha, had made sure that Alysana had everything she needed. Even when they were little girls on their farm in G'hen, Mordha had looked out for her. When Alysana had taken sick and had to leave for the High Keeper in Ellenos, Mordha had absolutely insisted that she come along as well. When the Kienari (Ynara, she knew now) had freed them from the clutches of Ghaja Rus's men, Mordha had been the one to take the dagger that the Kienari offered, and to make sure that her little sister was safe. So when Mordha had volunteered for the guard of Annoch, Alysana had not been surprised, though she was sad that she would see less of her. But upon seeing the effect that her absence had on Alysana, Mordha had promised to make time for her, and it usually came in the form of friendly sparring.

What was it she said? "You have to learn to take care of yourself, because someday I might not be able to."

She was right.

Developing her skill with a sword had been part of learning how to take care of herself. It had come with its benefits too: Alysana's confidence grew along with her ability. The very first time she bested one of her superiors in a duel, Alysana knew that there was no obstacle she couldn't overcome.

But no matter how much Mordha insisted that battle would make her feel fulfilled, Alysana had certainly not been ready for her current situation, and this was not her idea of fulfillment.

She was in a state of shock as she looked around and saw no other movement. She remembered that there had been a blast of fire so intense that she was afraid the sun itself had crashed to earth. Looking down at Thuma, whose back faced the sky, she saw that his armor had melted and warped where the fire had hit.

This giant fool might be the reason I'm alive right now, she thought darkly. The heat had felt like standing inside a furnace, and Alysana was sure that no one else would have come out alive. But amid the armor-laden corpses of Thuma's men was an even more shocking sight. One that Alysana wasn't ready for, but one which could not be ignored either.

She focused first on the red hair that was somehow undamaged by the flames.

No, she thought. *Please no.*

The charred, naked body of Elyasha that lay on the ground was both beautiful and heartbreaking: the light gray tone of her skin melted into that gorgeous orange-red hair, as fire born from smoke. The young Khyth woman had spent so much of her life outside Khala Val'ur trying to hide herself, yet here she was now, the most breathtaking creature, lying bare among the ruins of these so-called beautiful Athrani.

Alysana somehow found the strength to take to her feet. Ambling toward the body of the young Khyth, whose robes had been incinerated, she dropped to her knees and hovered over her mouth in a desperate hope for breath.

"Come on, come on," she demanded quietly as she tore off a glove. She put the back of her dark hand right by Yasha's lips.

She waited. She listened.

"Breathe, damn you," she seethed.

Her demands were met, as she felt the faintest wisp of air against her skin, halting and slow.

Alive! she thought as her heart raced, and she wondered just how much of Yasha's charred body was from the fire and how much was from the Breaking. Yasha would need a healer if she were to have any chance of surviving, but that was a problem for after they got to Théas. For now, she just needed to stay alive.

Alysana was looking around for something to cover her with when the low, growling voice of the Kienari behind her nearly scared the life from her.

"I took a blanket from the campsite," he said. "It was far enough away that the flames did not affect it."

"Kethras!" Alysana shouted. "Stop doing that!"

She turned to glare at the towering black creature holding out a dark green wool blanket, his black eyes looking at her impassively. *He's impossible to read*, she thought. *He could be laughing, for all I know.*

"Forgive me," he said. "I'm not used to having to announce my presence everywhere I go." It sounded like complaining, but Alysana wasn't quite sure. "I will try to be louder."

Definitely complaining.

"It is fine," she said as she snatched the blanket from his hands and draped it over Elyasha. "Help me get her up. We have to get her to Théas and into the care of a healer." She looked over to the campsite. "Was there anything else useful? Any other survivors?"

"Three," Kethras answered, stretching out his long arm as he pointed to the camp. "Thornton, Dailus, and one of Thuma's men. I didn't catch his name. He was too busy screaming."

Her heart skipped a beat when he said Thornton's name, and she hoped Kethras had just as hard a time reading human emotions as she did Kienari ones.

"Good," she said, stone-faced. "I have some questions that I want answered. Can you get her somewhere safe?"

Kethras nodded silently and knelt to pick up Elyasha, while Alysana stood up and turned to the camp.

With the Kienari at her back, she could let her smile show now. There was one question in particular that she wanted answered, but that would have to wait. For now, there were other matters to attend to.

She took out her knife and started walking.

Chapter 39

Théas, City of a
Thousand Towers

Rathma

The city was wet with rain as Rathma was pulled through the streets behind Evram and his men. His cloak was soaked, his lower half splashed with mud, and he had never been so cold in his life. That, coupled with the fact that he was sure he was about to be sold as a slave—or worse—made him upset. And when he got upset, Kuu always told him, he got mouthy.

"Can't you cut my hands free? It's not like I can blend in here if I run." He waved his bound hands helplessly, as if making his case.

"You'll fetch a higher price if we don't have to break your legs," Evram said. "And I'd much rather have a heavier purse at the end of the day." He turned back to smile at Rathma. "Although the man we're going to see might pay top coin for you even if I sawed your legs off."

Plan B, Rathma thought bitterly.

They had entered Théas from the south earlier that day, when the rain from the night before was just starting to let up. Rathma gawked at the big buildings that were so close together that many of them looked like they ran right into each other. It was a big change from anything beyond the Wastes, that much was certain.

In the larger streets of Théas were laid stones that were smoothed out and held together by a gray substance that Rathma figured had been poured by the stonemasons. The streets were flat and easier to walk on than sand, but it felt unnatural. The multitude of horses that he saw pulling carts didn't seem to mind, though. The smaller streets were mostly dirt or cobblestone, but one thing was for sure: the city was huge. Rathma had never seen so many people this close together in one place before. It was as if someone had put all the tribes in one spot and started building on top of them. He wasn't sure how anyone could breathe like this, let alone live.

The street they now walked down had, in the distance, a huge white statue of a man on horseback clutching an enormous war hammer. Rathma wasn't sure who the man was supposed to be, but he looked like a Hedjetten or an emperor. The statue was surrounded by a great marble fountain with more water than Rathma had ever seen in one spot, and passers-by were tossing copper coins into it. A few children at the base were playfully copying the pose of the rider as some adults looked on. Rathma shook his head. *All that water and they just throw coins at it.*

"How much longer could we possibly walk?" he groaned. "Does this city ever end?"

"Stop whining. We're almost there," Evram said as he gave Rathma's rope a pull. "Through the alley."

As they rounded the corner from the main street, the dull roar of people was muted, and Rathma felt his sanity starting to return. He hadn't realized how loud the city was until it quieted down; it was like closing the door behind a roaring sandstorm: silent, sudden, welcome.

"Up there," Evram said, peering up to the second floor of a dark brick building. By a door in the alley was an imposing man with a sword at his side, arms crossed, who seemed to be looking for an excuse to run something through. As the party approached, the man's hand moved to the hilt.

"State your business or move along," he rumbled with a G'henni accent.

"We are here to see your employer." Evram smiled. "I believe I have something that will strike his interest."

The doorman looked at Rathma, eyeing his hair, his eyes, and his cloak. Rathma grinned and held up his rope-bound hands to draw attention away from the rest of him, but it only worked for a moment.

"Wait here," the doorman answered, and he disappeared inside, through the sturdy wooden door. A moment later he reemerged with the same gruff look on his face and grunted, "Upstairs and through the door."

"Thank you," Rathma said before being elbowed in the gut by Evram.

"Quiet," Evram seethed as he dragged him along. Rathma complied, waving silently at the doorman, who watched him and shook his head in bewilderment.

The wooden staircase that led to the second floor was well maintained, looking as fresh as if it had been built only the day before. The heavy footsteps of the half dozen men walking up it told Rathma that it was sturdy and solid, and could probably support five times that many men before it even started to creak. There were two more men guarding a door at the top—also G'henni—and the one on the right opened it without a sound. He gestured for them to go inside. After Rathma stepped in, he heard the door close behind him with the telltale clink of a metal bolt being closed, and saw the two men step in to guard the exit behind him.

They must really want to make sure we stay.

The inside was spacious and made of the same dark-stained wood that comprised the staircase, and smelled heavily of incense and wine. Several rugs covered the floor, but the walls were bare. At the opposite end of the long room was the figure of a man standing in front of a large window that overlooked the busy street. He had his hands clasped behind his back, and turned as he heard them come in. He was heavyset, and his clothes looked like they cost more than Rathma's village.

"Ah, Evram," the man said. "What have you brought for me now? My bodyguard insisted that I see you." His voice dripped with a G'henni accent, and his smile was adorned with gold teeth, for which Rathma thought he'd probably overpaid.

"Then he surely has an eye for the business, Magistrate," Evram answered. "I would watch out for him if I were you." He grinned. "May I sit?"

"Of course, of course," the magistrate replied as he gestured to one of several chairs. "Whichever one pleases you."

Watching these two talk is like seeing two snakes mate, Rathma thought as he pulled his hood farther over his eyes. *Yelto would love it.*

Evram took off his silver-lined cloak and hung it over the plush red chair closest to the dark G'henni man. He sat down, crossing one leg over the other, and cleared his throat. "What I have is a rare specimen," he said. "One that you will be hard pressed to find anywhere but the dunes of Khulakorum."

The man looked skeptically at Rathma, squinting to make him out in the dim room. "Surely, you don't mean—"

"I do," Evram said, holding up a hand before he could finish. Over his shoulder he said, "Denk, his hood."

Denk yanked back the hood covering Rathma's hair, and a low chuckle floated over from the other side of the room.

"Well, well," the man said. "This is a rare find indeed, Evram. You may have outdone yourself this time."

Evram raised one eyebrow. "High praise," he said with a smile. "Now let's talk coin, shall we?"

The magistrate took a seat by Evram, dismissed the two men at the door, and said, "Let's."

Rathma heard the door close again behind him and found himself wishing that Djozen Yelto had been able to carry out the execution in Khadje Kholam. And, for the first time in his life, he wished that he had the power of farstepping.

Never do in darkness what you would not do in light.

—G'henni proverb

Chapter 40

Derenar,
On the Road to Théas

Awaken the Three

Alysana

Alysana fumed.

Brandishing her knife, she stormed over to one of Thuma's surviving men. The Athrani was on his knees, tied up by Kethras, near one of the large tents that the legion had brought, his hands and feet bound together behind him.

"Who gave the order?" she demanded, grabbing a fistful of his long blond hair and pulling his head back to place her dagger at his throat. "Who gave it, and from how high up did it come?"

Now that she was closer she realized how young he looked—perhaps Thornton's age. She almost felt bad for treating him so roughly, but the scars on his arms and face told her that he had seen a few battles in his day. This was probably not his first time being threatened.

"You know I can't answer that," he said calmly, showing no sign of fear. The hint of a sneer betrayed his defiance.

Definitely not his first time, she thought.

All around them were the remnants of battle. Small fires still burned, feeding greedily on corpses and grass. The dead bodies of the men of the legion, armor melted to them like purple-and-gold caskets, lay still in repose. They were everywhere, the dead were, and Alysana had half a mind to keep them that way.

We'll leave them for the birds, she thought bitterly. She pushed the prisoner to the ground and the blade of her knife into its sheath. *It's more than they deserve.*

The Athrani, undaunted, looked right back at Alysana. "What difference would it make if I told you anyway?"

The look he gave her made her regret sheathing the knife so hastily. She turned her back to the prisoner and reached for it again, slowly this time, drawing it out with poise and conviction. They were beyond threats now.

Maybe we do bury them, she thought as she tightened her grip on the leather handle. *Starting with him.*

But her eyes went to the knife as she felt its balance, its weight. It was perfect—or as close to perfect as such a thing could be. With her back to the prisoner and her eye on the knife, she spoke to the darkness.

"Kethras," she said, "what can you tell me about this blade?"

She could almost feel the confusion on the captive Athrani's face. She knew the Kienari was watching, though, and she knew he could hear them; it didn't matter how far away he was. *The farther the better*, she thought. *More time for this one's imagination to run wild.*

A chill ran down Alysana's neck as she heard something stir in the darkness beyond, like leaves giving way to a breeze, barely more than a whisper.

And the whisper moved.

It approached like the silence after a storm: heavy, dark, and dreadful. Just like that night, all those years before. She caught his reflection in the gleam of her knife, and his hunter's smile almost made her heart stop.

There he is, she smiled to herself. When she needed him most.

"It is meant for carving," Kethras answered. "*Flesh.*" It came as a low growl, almost imperceptible, like distant thunder.

The Athrani blanched, his face matching the whiteness of the Kienari's sharp teeth—the only part of the dark hunter that was truly visible in the blackness.

"And you're sure it can do that?" Alysana asked, turning to face them.

Kethras's laugh—if one could call it that—sounded more threatening than mirthful. It was very much like the sound a man makes after his throat is cut.

"I am quite certain," he said. "The last time a Kienari used it, it spilled the blood of two smugglers from G'hen as easily as a man blinks."

Alysana watched the Athrani, who still hadn't turned his head to look at Kethras. *He doesn't need to look*, she thought. *He knows what a Kienari can do.*

"I'll ask you again," she said, stooping down to come even with the Athrani's eyes. "And I don't expect to repeat myself. Who gave the order?"

This time, her words got through and the soldier relented.

"It was Thuma. Commander Endar let it slip that the Highglader planned to awaken the Three, and it wasn't long before Thuma started recruiting riders to come along—or hunt you down if it came to that."

"Are there more?"

"Of course," he answered, almost incredulously. "We know about the dangers of the Holder and the Traveler, and"—he brought his voice to a whisper—"the Ghost."

Alysana scoffed. "The Ghost," she repeated. "I know of the Ghost."

"Then you should know of the dangers as well," said the Athrani, sitting up. "You of all people should know: if you awaken the Holder, you cannot stop what comes with him."

The words made Alysana bite down pensively on the edge of her blade.

"What does he mean?" Kethras, closer now, asked her from the dark.

Alysana crossed her arms and shifted her weight to one leg. "He means that the Three are tied together, and if we wake one, we empower the others." She looked up at Kethras and furrowed her brow.

"It is true," said the captive. "The Three retain great power still, even in slumber. And imagine the hatred that burns in the Traveler, punished by the Shaper for bringing unrest to the Otherworld . . . always just out of reach of the woman he loves. The woman he lost his life for."

"There is a good reason they are kept sleeping," Alysana confessed, turning to Kethras. "Aldryd would tell us the same: waking the Three is a move of desperation and must not be done thoughtlessly."

Kethras looked at her and then up at the sky. "Yet we have no choice."

Before she could answer, out of the corner of her eye Alysana saw something that made her stop. Earlier, they had placed Thornton and Yasha on the ground beside each other, covering them with light blankets to keep any burns they had from getting dirty. Now, those blankets were moving.

"Kethras!" she said, turning to the Kienari. "He's awake!"

She leapt to her feet in a run, with Kethras following close behind.

The two of them hurried to where Thornton and Yasha had been placed, surprised to see that the Highglader was conscious. He had a look of recognition in his eye when they approached.

"Where am I?" he asked.

"A safe place," said Alysana. "North of Théas."

Thornton looked around at the aftermath of the melee. "What happened?"

"We were making camp when Thuma turned on us and attacked." She looked more closely at him. "Do you not remember?"

Thornton shook his head. "Bits and pieces," he said. "I . . . I remember riding and talking to Yasha . . . and . . ." He gasped. "Yasha!" He looked around frantically for the girl and saw the damage the fire had done. "Is she . . . ?"

"She is alive," Alysana said quickly, "though in delicate condition. We have to get her to Théas as soon as she is stable."

Thunder rumbled in the distance.

"Then we should try to move them under cover. That is where the storm is coming from," Kethras remarked.

Alysana nodded and had stood to help when she heard Thornton speak.

"I'm just glad she's okay," the blacksmith said. "The last thing I remember was when the Athrani called those flames."

Alysana froze, turned, and gave him a long, wary look. "Thornton," she said slowly. "It wasn't the Athrani who called those flames."

He looked at her, confused.

"The one who called the flames," she went on, ". . . was you."

Chapter 41

The Wastes of Khulakorum

Awaken the Three

Kuu

Kuu and Sivulu made their way through the moonless night knowing that time was not on their side.

Though most of the Wastes was desert, the land was rocky and rugged in the north, near the border of Derenar, especially in the east, by the foothills of the Spears, the great mountain range that climbed its way northeast to the faraway reaches of Khala Val'ur. The terrain made the passage of time seem slow, the years marked by the erosion of the rocks themselves and the moving of dunes over the great, wide desert. So it was his gut, not the passing of the stars above, that was telling Kuu that they should hurry.

"How are we looking, Aurik?" Sivulu boomed as he and Kuu approached the meeting place.

The brothers were meeting up near the only real landmark in the area: a strange reddish rock formation jutting from the ground, sand-worn and broad, standing nearly three times as tall as a man. The features of the great rock were arced and smooth, vaguely resembling a giant man on horseback holding a weapon. In fact, people long before Kuu had insisted that it *was* a man, once, and had given it the name Ja'ad Shiddeq, which, in ancient Khôl, meant, "the rider who throws a spear at the heavens."

Ja'ad Shiddeq, "Rider's Rock" to Kuu and his brothers, marked a crossroads where one could travel all the way from K'har in the west, straight on to Menat in the east. To the south, past Yelto's stronghold in Khadje Kholam, even beyond the southern tribal city of R'haqa, lay the ancient city of Do'baradai. It had been a long, *long* time since anyone had lived there, Kuu knew. It wasn't worth going that far south to try to recruit anyone. As far as he knew, nothing lived there.

"Better than a day ago," came the reply from Aurik.

Older than his younger twin, Kaurik, by two minutes, Aurik was the more domineering of the two and had been waiting for them when they arrived at Rider's Rock. His shaggy, dark brown hair was longer than Kaurik's and was the only way that anyone but his brothers could tell them apart. He was lanky, like his younger brothers, but the three years he had on Kuu had made his deep green eyes seem like weathered gems set into his smooth brown skin. "The western tribes won't be swayed," he said. "Most of them are tired of paying tribute to Yelto, but they're more afraid of what Yelto can do if they were to turn against him. I spoke to five Hedjetti, and all but one of them turned me down: Hedjetten Djosa of the Ohmati."

Sivulu frowned and turned to the younger twin. "Any better news from the east?"

Kaurik—a spitting image of Aurik, but with short, messy hair—nodded. "A few Hedjetti from Menat said they would fight. All I had to say was 'Yelto,' and three of them promised their swords and those of their tribes: the Qozhen, Khuufi, and Elteri."

Sivulu nodded, and scratched at his dark beard. "The Elteri are good fighters, though few in number, and the Khuufi have a few Farsteppers among them. I suppose it's better than the 'none' we had before today . . . though we might need them sooner than we thought."

The twins looked at him with confusion. As an answer, Siv turned to Kuu. "Tell them what you told me."

"Yelto had a priest with him. I think they mean to awaken the Holder sooner than we thought."

Aurik hammered a fist against the big red rock that stood beside them, and Kaurik uttered a few choice words in Khôl.

"Then we shouldn't waste any more time planning," said Aurik with a shrug.

Sivulu didn't even pause for thought as he sliced a hand through the air. "Absolutely not. We've planned this for too long and invested too much to come up short now. Kuu," he said, turning, "you were there. What do you think?"

Kuu looked into the eyes of each of his brothers; they were all looking back at him expectantly. How it suddenly fell upon him to be the decision maker for the family was beyond him, but he took a breath, and the responsibility. "He has the Wolfblade," he said. "That's all that matters."

The words caught his brothers off guard, as the twins exchanged uncertain glances. They looked to Kuu to be their guide. "You saw it?" Kaurik asked. "How? Where?"

"He keeps it on a chain around his neck. The whole time we were his prisoners, he never took it off. It never left his sight."

"Well," Sivulu said, "at least we know where to look."

Kuu nodded. "And with a big enough distraction, I think we can take it from him."

"But what about the priests?" Aurik asked.

"They could have overpowered me and Rathma at any moment, but they didn't. They had more than a few chances, too." After a pause, he added, "I almost wondered if the stories were even true. I don't know if they're as powerful as they say."

The twins scoffed at this, and Aurik crossed his arms over his dark, bare chest. "Your own brothers can turn into wolves, yet you're skeptical of *their* power?" He looked at him as if Kuu's hair were on fire. "Wagering that the priests can't do what the stories say is as crazy as trusting Sivulu with a woman." His words were met with a shot to the shoulder from Siv.

"I'm not saying I don't believe the stories," Kuu retorted. "I just wonder what stopped them. It was even nighttime, the time that they're supposed to be strongest. But they didn't so much as raise a hand against us. It was almost like they were waiting for something . . . or something was holding them back."

Siv scratched his dark beard in thought. "Well, I don't like it either way. But if a few Priests of the Holder are all that stands between us," he said with a shrug, "I'd say it's a risk worth taking."

The twins grinned mischievously, and their green eyes shone with ambition. "I guess that settles it," Kaurik said. "When do we move?"

Sivulu looked up to the night sky, littered with stars and a waxing white moon. "The sooner the better," he replied. Looking back at his brothers, he said, "Aurik, you head back to K'har and gather the willing. Kaurik, I trust that you can rally the people of Menat—every one that we can count for our cause is a better chance of victory." He turned his head to Kuu, who was busy counting stars. "And I'll go south. We need the rest of the Wolfwalkers from R'haqa if we want to come out on top. Kuu, you'll need to do whatever you can from here. Rider's Rock will be the gathering place, and where we will make our initial movement to Khadje Kholam, and Djozen Yelto's fortress."

Kuu didn't move his eyes from the sky; he was too busy wondering whether or not this plan actually had a chance of succeeding. They had poured a lot of time and thought into it, it was true, but they'd also had Rathma to help them plan and to help rally more Farsteppers to their cause. When Djozen Yelto began his conquest of the tribes, the only thing more surprising than how fast he did it was that he was doing it at all. It was almost like the Hedjetti and their tribes had *wanted* to be conquered. Like they didn't value their freedom.

Maybe uniting the tribes under one banner is the answer, Kuu thought. But he would sooner die than see Yelto hoisting the crown.

His brother's voice snapped him back to the present.

"Kuu, did you hear me?" Sivulu's voice could carry when it needed to.

"Yes. Right." He looked back to the twins, already making their transformation to the lupine bodies that would carry them across the sands. "I'll just stay here then."

His oldest brother moved over to him.

"You did your part, Kuu," Sivulu replied. "And it was an important one. The information you gathered from inside Yelto's stronghold is just as important as any number of tribesmen fighting for us. And you took a big risk to do it, too." He placed a firm hand on Kuu's shoulder and squeezed. "You've made this old wolf proud."

Siv knelt down as he began his transformation.

Deep black fur erupted from his skin and blanketed him in a thick, dark coat. His fingers curled inward and became paws as his torso twisted, lurched, and changed; his mouth lengthened, filling out with fangs, and his limbs cracked and trembled as they broke and reformed. He was on his back as the change took over.

To an outside observer, it would have seemed an awful sight: a wolf writhing in pain, pawing at the air as it trembled. But to Kuu, it was a sight to behold. Siv was big enough as a man, but as a wolf, he had no equal. Watching him go from one imposing form to the other was like watching night turn into day. His muzzle, streaked with bits of gray, was nearly as high as Kuu's chest when he stood.

With a silent shudder, Siv finished the change and bared his jagged, razing teeth.

A smile, thought Kuu. *What a show-off.*

Sivulu hadn't made a sound, but Kuu knew that the transformation had been painful. That his brother could keep it in check, even smile, was a testament to his strength and his will. The only thing that remained of Sivulu the man was his eyes, gleaming green in the moonlight.

The telltale sign of a Wolfwalker, Kuu thought wryly. *Even the great Sivulu can't change that.*

As if in answer to his thoughts, Sivulu the wolf gave a graceful bow of his head, winked, and was gone. The whispers of lupine legs racing across the desert faded slowly into the night as the brothers began their journeys, each with his own task and direction.

Kuu pressed his back against the rock and slid to the ground.

Bringing his knees to his chest, he looked up at the night sky again, the domain of Ahmaan Ka, and said a silent prayer to Lash'kun Yho, even though he didn't believe that the old god was listening. Still, he hoped the Traveler was out there, somewhere, watching; if there was one person alive who knew what it meant to give up everything for a woman he loved, it was Lash'kun Yho.

And if there was another person alive who knew how much it hurt to lose her, it was Kuu Imha-khet.

Chapter 42

Haidan Shar

Awaken the Three

Benjin

Haidan Shar was a flurry of movement, and Benj had never seen it so busy. He was walking back to the Flats, nursing the bruises on his arm—Jahaz had let him off lightly—when his friend Shotes shouted for him. The chubby black-haired boy was coming from the stables, covered in filth, waving his hands frantically above his head.

"Benj, ith it true?" he asked. Shotes's missing front tooth turned his *s*'s to *th*'s and made the breath leaving his mouth whistle like a teapot. "Are we really going to war?"

Benj kept walking and simply nodded. His mind was on the horses, even though part of him knew he should be more concerned with the future of the Sharian army.

"When? Where? How thoon?" Shotes asked, with no pauses for breath.

"I don't know the details," Benj said dismissively, brushing past his friend and into the stables.

Benj hated war. He hated talking about war. He hated thinking about war. His mother had known that when she had offered him up as an armiger, but that didn't seem to matter to her.

Even though Benj had been born after his mother left her home city of Ghal Thurái, he felt as if he had grown up in the Mouth of the Deep just from her stories alone. She was always talking about the city, and saying how much pride the Thurians took in their army and how she had always wanted the same for him. But, while the Fist of Thurái was indeed legendary, Benj couldn't have cared less if he was part of something like that. He just wanted to tend horses.

"Ah, you're home!" came his mother Nessa's voice from behind him.

Benj turned around to see her hazel eyes sparkling in the midday sun, even though there was nothing to be sparkling about.

"I am. Jahaz cut me loose for the day to prepare," he said.

"*Captain* Jahaz," his mother corrected.

"Captain Jahaz," Benj mumbled. He knew better than to slip like that around her. She took such pride in the profession of arms. *Especially since, or because of, what happened.*

"And how are you going to prepare?" she asked, interrupting his thoughts and looking at him expectantly. "Grooming the horses won't teach you how to swing a sword."

"I know it won't," he answered curtly.

"Then why are you in here?" she replied, indicating the stables with her eyes.

Benj was moving the feed bag over to their biggest horse, Arrow, whose cream coat and charming demeanor made him the favorite. "Because."

It wasn't a good enough answer, but he couldn't think of a better one.

"That's not a reason," his mother said, moving closer. She looked upset now.

"I never wanted to be an armiger," he blurted out. The words spilled from him so fast that he barely realized he was saying them. His mother was next to him in an instant. She knelt down and grabbed him with her left hand, turning Benj to look her in the eyes. There was anger in them, but also compassion.

"I know you didn't, Benj," she said. Her hazel eyes wavered as they looked at his. "But it's the only hope you have for a good life. You know I would still be in Ghal Thurái if not for . . ."

"Stop it," Benj said angrily, recoiling from her hand. "I know." He crossed his arms and glared at his mother defiantly.

The sparkle returned to her eyes.

"I'm sorry," she said softly. "My days in the Fist are long gone. I gave up everything when I left Ghal Thurái . . ." She looked at him again. "Well, not everything," she said with a tight smile.

Here it comes, Benj thought. She was going to tell him the story—again—of how she had fled the Mouth for Haidan Shar in hopes of a better life for herself and, unknown to her at the time, the baby growing inside her. About the tales of the city's wealth that had spread throughout Gal'dorok. About the opportunity that awaited in the Gem of the

East, where even a disgraced warrior of the Fist could make something of herself.

But, instead of the story, all Benj got was a hand tousling his hair.

"Alright," she relented. "Tend to the horses." She stood up and made for the door. Stopping just shy of it, she added over her shoulder, "Do all the things tonight that Benj the boy would do, because, starting tomorrow, you'll have to be a man."

She walked out of the stables and shut the door behind her.

Chapter 43

Nest of the Xua'al

Awaken the Three

Zhala

Zhala was dimly aware of Khaz as he finished his meeting with the charred human—*Khyth*, she corrected. *Not human.*

She reached out for his mind to see what he was seeing, hear what he was hearing. The darkness of her cave faded as she opened an eye inside her broodling's mind, opening the floodgates of his senses as they came rushing in.

Khaz, she began, her words echoing in the male's mind, *tell me what you have learned.*

As matriarch of her clan, she was inexorably linked with the minds of her broodlings, who were more like extensions of her body than autonomous individuals; when they had been torn from her to make new Chovathi broodlings, their mental link remained. Now it was like moving an arm or breathing: she merely had to shift her focus, and the body part did her bidding. With this came all their thoughts and sensations, like two diverging channels of water suddenly joining to make a river, chaotic and strong.

She was the river.

Khaz's thoughts were chaotic, and he did not answer immediately. She tried again.

Khaz, she thought, *come home.* The thought made the male lurch. She was in his body now, and the sharp smell of blood clawed at her nostrils. She could see its cloud hanging in the air, see its trail leading back to the Khyth even as he retreated to Khala Val'ur. Even in the dark of night, blood was easy to follow; it was the strength of her people.

No, came the reply.

Khaz was moving through the rocky terrain close to their cave and was not about to stop for the sake of conversation. It was very much like him to do so.

Zhala smiled to herself. He was one of her favorites. She would never let him know, and she tried to keep the thought to herself, as she was afraid of the effect it would have on her other broodlings. His intelligence and willfulness had always struck her as particularly exceptional. Most broodlings were nothing more than mindless drones, happy to be inhabited by the mind of their matriarch when they needed it and content to go on clawing and slashing and eating and stalking when the matriarchs left.

But not Khaz. Khaz had a keen intelligence to him that had always fascinated Zhala. He had even been able to transcend the growls and clicks that most warriors used and had turned it into actual speech, guttural and rudimentary though it was.

Come home, she ordered again, feeling his hunger and knowing he would want to go hunting. *You are needed.*

She felt Khaz push back against her, feeling his hunger as her own. He was resisting.

No, he thought. *Want hunt. Need food.* He continued on his path away from the nest.

She had to admire his impetuousness. She could compel him to return, she knew, and he invariably would, but she decided to let him have his way. Letting the current of her consciousness split off from his, she began to slowly untangle their minds. Khaz's thoughts and senses gradually disappeared from her own, in the same way that the light retreats from the sky when dusk descends. Now she was left with only the darkness of her own thoughts as the sharp smell of blood left her nostrils. The comfort of her cave came back fully to her as she felt its coolness blanket her once again.

She was determined to wait for Khaz to return, and then she would reward him. He was the agent of her will, and he was setting her plan in motion to take back the cities and caves from the humans and the Khyth. Once again, it would be the Chovathi who would rule these lands, as they had done for generations before the humans discovered their own hidden power from the one they called the Breaker.

But once again the Chovathi would rule, and the Xua'al would be their emissaries.

They would rule because they were strong and because they were patient. They had sharpened their claws and toughened their hides, strengthened their jaws and deepened their minds. When the other clans had first decided to mount their attack on Ghal Thurái, Zhala had felt it—she was only dimly linked with the other clan matriarchs, but linked nonetheless—and she had known they would be weak.

They would need help, but the Xua'al were ready for this war. They were ready, and Zhala knew it.

The thought quickened her pulse, and she found herself wishing that she had compelled Khaz to come home this instant. But she quelled the thought, knowing the anticipation would make it even sweeter.

Tonight she would reward him well: she would let him make another broodling.

The anticipation of the pain from Khaz sinking his claws into her and rending her body was almost too much to bear. She needed it. She closed her eyes and reached out for another of her broodlings. She needed the distraction.

Hurry, Khaz, she found herself saying as her mind drifted off, as the sharp smell of blood came rushing in like rain.

Life is sacred. Taking a life, doubly so.

—Kienari proverb

Chapter 44

Derenar, Outside Théas

Alysana

Alysana was letting her frustration show, and Thornton didn't like it.

Their argument had started at dawn and had lasted most of the morning. They had all agreed to let the Athrani soldier bury his friends, but their calm discussion had grown heated when they brought up what to do with him when he finished.

"We can't just let him go," Alysana asserted in a harsh whisper. She turned her head to see if the blond Athrani man had heard her. Thornton was advocating for him to be spared, but she and Kethras saw things differently. "He will go back to Ellenos and send more riders after us. He is a liability."

Thornton narrowed his eyes at her words, but was cut off by Kethras before he could answer.

"She is right," the Kienari said calmly. "He is a danger to us all if he goes free."

Facing away from Thornton, Kethras was keeping an eye on the Athrani as he worked, idly fingering the hilt of his dagger.

"Then what if we take his horse from him?" Thornton asked in response. His arms were crossed and he wore a frown on his face that, from a few days of not shaving, was shaded with stubble. "Make him walk. It will take him days to get to Ellenos on foot."

"We don't know how long Yasha will need to stay in Théas to recover," Alysana shot back. They had taken one of the carts for transporting the tents and had laid Yasha in it—a quick and dirty solution to the problem of transporting her, but one that would work until they got her to the city and into the care she needed. Alysana glanced over at her, still asleep and wrapped in a blanket, then back again to Thornton. "It could be days, or weeks. But we can't risk more soldiers sympathetic to Thuma coming to look for us while she does."

"The faster we get her to Théas," Kethras insisted, "the better."

"I agree with you there," Thornton said. "But I disagree that we need to spill more blood to do it."

Kethras squared with Thornton and looked him in the eyes. "You are young, my friend, and have yet to learn that some things in this world cannot be solved with good intentions." His cold tone was coated with conviction, and he had the same serious expression as when he had first told Thornton that he had to leave his village of Highglade behind.

"Kethras is right," Alysana insisted. "It has to be done." Standing beside the Kienari, she glanced again to their prisoner, who was pushing another body into a shallow grave. "I will make sure he does not suffer."

Thornton's frown deepened; he hated the idea of passing a death sentence. As a blacksmith, his whole life had been about creation.

Until that awful day when he met the Khyth. After that, his eyes were opened to the horrors of the world, where it seemed killing and death were commonplace. He thought back to Ynara's words to him on that day: *These men are prepared to kill you. You must be prepared to do the same.*

They were right, he knew: if the Athrani soldier made it back to Ellenos to spread the word about what they were trying to do—trying to awaken the Three—there would be no telling how many more men would come storming after them. They were lucky enough to make it this far with only a dozen soldiers to fight off. Who knows how many more would oppose their cause?

Thornton watched the blond Athrani, who was probably no older than himself, digging and forming the last of the graves for his fellow soldiers. He was kneeling, arms outstretched, as he wove his Shaping into a burial site worthy of a warrior. Thuma, the biggest and bravest of them all, was the last to be put in the ground.

It was in that moment, of watching the power of Shaping flow through the world, that Thornton thought once again of Miera. *Anything that keeps us from waking the Three*, he thought, *keeps us from her. And I won't have that.*

And, as if the thought of her had summoned her somehow, Thornton realized that the familiar ghostly figure had appeared on the edge of his vision once again. He squinted as she almost came into focus and he could make out a woman in a white dress coming toward him. It was the clearest glance he'd had of her yet, and he thought that he heard her trying to speak, but just as she had appeared, she vanished.

Frustrated, he took a deep breath and scowled. He knew what he had to do; seeing Miera had all but confirmed it.

"Fine," he conceded. "I won't stop you. Just make it quick and be done with it."

Alysana nodded solemnly. She took out the dagger that once belonged to Ynara many years ago and walked deliberately after their captive.

Thornton looked away, not wanting to see the man's death. He turned south, toward Théas, watching the rising sun crest the Ilúvian plains to the east, and tried to clear his mind.

He had already endangered his own sister by somehow calling Athrani flames, and now his insistence on setting a prisoner free could have endangered Miera as well. His father was gone because of him, and an entire war had just been waged over the hammer he'd had since childhood.

I'm the liability, he thought sourly. *Not anyone else.*

By the time Alysana spoke the words "It is done," Thornton had already begun tying the horses together so they could lead all of them to Théas.

"Then let's go," he said coldly. He'd had enough of it. With a frustrated tug, he tied another knot.

He looked again at Kethras and Alysana. And then again to Yasha.

It was in that moment that Thornton knew something had to be done. With a heavy heart, he thought that he knew just what.

He narrowed his eyes as he looked again at the G'henni.

The hard part would be getting her alone.

Chapter 45

Ellenos,
Temple of the Shaper

Awaken the Three

Lilyana

Lilyana looked around the inside of the Temple of the Shaper as though seeing a sunrise for the first time.

"Momma, where are we?" she whispered absentmindedly. She hadn't called her mother "Momma" in years.

The handsome Athrani being escorted by Coraline chuckled. "Have you never seen the inside of the temple, my dear?"

Lily blushed and shook her head, having forgotten that there were other people around. The grand entrance to the temple was mostly empty, as the vast majority of guests were gathered in the adjacent ballroom, awaiting the arrival of High Keeper Sh'thanna. Lily looked to her mother, who gave her an expectant nod and a smile as if to say, *He's waiting for an answer.*

"I never have," Lily admitted meekly. "I've only ever seen it from the outside."

"In that case, please, follow me to the ballroom." His light blue eyes with a deep violet ring smiled along with him. "It's by far the most impressive part."

Lily barely heard him; she was too busy looking around the temple. Towering over the throngs of people was the blue marble walls of the vast interior, lit on this moonless night by torches that burned high above, bright and warm.

The inside was split into three parts: the entrance connecting to the throne room was in the middle; the ballroom was on the right; and on the left was a series of rooms for entertaining, dining, and many other things that Lily couldn't quite ascertain. As they walked to the ballroom, she looked down at the smoothly polished floor, which reflected almost perfectly, like the still waters of a lake.

"Come, Lily," her mother whispered harshly.

Realizing she had fallen behind, Lily hurried to catch up as they passed through a pair of huge wooden doors as tall as a house. Inside, the ballroom spilled out before her like a great marble field.

Colorful, courtly gowns filled Lily's vision as she looked around in wonder. There must have been two hundred people in the room, with enough space for them all to spread out their arms and spin. She had never imagined that the inside of something could be so spacious. But as her eyes floated over the crowd, they suddenly fell upon a woman who made everyone else look dull.

High Keeper Sh'thanna.

Coraline leaned down to whisper in her ear. "There she is," she said, indicating with her eyes. "Isn't she captivating?"

Lily could only nod in response. Even the light in the ballroom seemed fixated on the woman who had just cast the crowd into silence.

The High Keeper had sharp blue eyes surrounded by another blue ring, deep and engaging, and hair that draped her shoulders in perfectly elegant tendrils. Her elbow-length gloves were trimmed with silk and matched her long gold-and-white gown. Lily wondered if the Shaper of Ages Herself had had a hand in the woman's creation who was now descending a long staircase lined with pairs of soldiers. As the High Keeper passed, each soldier snapped to attention.

She walked slowly and gracefully, as though she knew that every eye in the room was on her.

Lily now understood why the people of Ellenos had chosen Sh'thanna to be the High Keeper at such a young age: she was like no one else.

When she turned to say so to her mother, though, she spied the only pair of eyes that were not on the High Keeper; and those eyes belonged to the Tallister, who was fixated on Coraline.

The High Keeper cleared her throat and addressed the room.

"Thank you, all of you, for coming," she said. Her voice carried well in the enormous ballroom, striking Lily as being both powerful and magnificent. "Tonight will be a night to remember. I hope it will soon have its place in Athrani history as being important not just for our people, but for the others with whom we share this world." She held her head high as she spoke, and Lily could see a flicker of emotion under the stern, regal mask the High Keeper wore. "Tonight is a night for hope, and for celebration. It has been many, many years since the Athrani split from humanity, and it has also been many generations since the end of the

Shaping War, when the Khyth rejected our common ancestry to embrace darkness instead."

The words made an uneasy murmur course through the crowd, as a mention of the Khyth was seldom followed by good news.

The High Keeper continued.

"Tonight, I have made the decision to send an envoy to the city of Khala Val'ur in order to forge a lasting peace between the Athrani and the Khyth." At this, the Tallister began to move toward the High Keeper. "And I have chosen the ambassador who shall lead our people to peace."

There were nods of approval and admiration, as well as a smattering of applause, when the Tallister stepped up to stand beside the High Keeper, waving his hand and smiling warmly.

"Thank you, High Keeper," he said, then turned to address the audience. "It is an honor to be chosen to represent our people, and I will do everything in my power to make sure this undertaking is a success. It will not be easy to repair a rift such as ours, but I will not be doing so alone. I will have help, and the High Keeper has allowed me to choose from our best and brightest." He paused, emphasizing the next point. "Even old wounds can be healed in time."

High Keeper Sh'thanna nodded gravely. "The Tallister speaks truly. Which is why tonight shall be about celebrating peace." She held out her hand, palm up, and swept it over the onlookers. "So, please, celebrate!" she said with a smile.

She clapped her hands twice, and a beautiful chorus of music burst forth from the orchestra, filling the air. The guests took their cue and began to pair off to start dancing.

The dull roar of conversation made the ballroom seem twice as full as it actually was, as the marble floors and walls made elegant echoes out of the sounds inside.

And amid all the hustle and bustle stood the Tallister.

He smiled and began walking. A few couples parted to make way for him as he walked toward Lily and her mother. When he reached them, he extended his hand to Coraline.

"Coraline," he said with a bow, "may I have this dance?"

Lily watched her mother cover her mouth in genuine amusement; she was smiling with not just her mouth but her eyes as well.

"You may," she answered as she placed her hand in his. "Lily," she said, "remember the rules."

Lily nodded at her mother and gave them a wary look. But her mother looked happy, so she covered it with a smile of her own.

As the two Athrani glided over the dance floor, Lily was surprised at how easily the Tallister moved. He was tall and refined, and his years of serving under the High Keeper had no doubt contributed to that. Yet, as handsome as he was, he was equally as graceful. And he seemed genuinely taken by Coraline.

Maybe something good will come of this, Lily thought. *Mother deserves it.*

What she saw next, though, made her reconsider.

She saw him lean in and whisper something to Coraline; the look of shock that came across her mother's face made Lily worried. Her mother looked at her with the same surprised look, and then back to the Tallister, as if considering some terrible possibility. The two of them had stopped dancing, and the waves of colors swirling by them from the other dancers made them look like two sparks that had been thrown from a roaring fire. The Tallister said something else that Lily couldn't hear, and Coraline forcefully let go of his hand. She slapped him and hurried toward Lily.

"Come, Lily," she said as she grabbed her by the hand. "We're leaving."

***

Back at their house, Coraline was frantic—and Lily didn't like it.

"Hurry, Lily, grab your things."

She was tearing through her chests and drawers in the house, gathering clothes of her own and stuffing them into a pack.

"Why, Mother? What's wrong?"

Her mother took a moment from her frenzied packing and looked Lily in the eye. "I don't want that man dictating our lives," she said. "Now do as I say."

Lily's heart was racing. She had never seen her mother like this before, but she knew how protective she could get. She just wished it hadn't been on such a beautiful night. Her mother looked so pretty in her dress.

"Here," Coraline said as she pressed a small, heavy pouch into Lily's hand. "Take this. If anything should happen to me, or we get separated, I want you to be able to take care of yourself."

"Momma, you're scaring me," Lily said. Her eyes had already started to water, and she felt herself breathing faster.

"Oh, sweetie," she said as she put down her pack. "Sweetie, I'm sorry." She slid over to where Lily was standing, and wrapped her arms around her. "I'm so sorry."

Lily felt warm tears welling up inside her eyes as her mother kissed her on the forehead.

Her mother, kneeling, looked her in the eye.

"You have to understand that I'll do anything to keep you safe," she said. "I don't want this life for you. I never have. I've always wanted more for you, more than I ever had when I was a girl, and I'll do anything to see that you get it."

Her mother's warm embrace flushed away the last of her tears as Lily tried to steady her breathing.

"Now," Coraline said gently, "can you do this one thing for me? Can you pack your things like I asked?"

Lily nodded hesitantly. "But where am I going?"

"You're finally going to meet your uncle Thaurson," Coraline said with a soft smile.

Chapter 46

Théas

Awaken the Three

Alysana

Alysana listened to the soft sound of the horse's hooves thumping in the dirt. It reminded her of home.

The small farm in G'hen that she'd left behind when she was still so young and fragile seemed so far away now. She had grown into a strong young woman, Mordha was always telling her, but there was a part of her that had never let go of that little G'henni girl. She glanced back at Dailus, who was still scowling from being tied to her and the horse, and reminded herself that she *was* a grown woman, with her own responsibilities now. And one of those responsibilities was lying unconscious in a cart pulled by Thornton's horse.

Alysana had seen Thornton call the flames that burned Elyasha, along with the men of the Athrani Legion, but she had not understood how he had done it. One thing she knew about the difference between Athrani Shaping and Khyth Breaking was that neither one could use the power of the other. But everything she'd seen told her that she had just seen a Khyth, Thornton, wield Athrani Shaping. It made her nervous being around him, the young man from Highglade, mostly because he had admitted that he had no control over his power.

If Aldryd were here, she thought, *he would know what to do.*

The old Athrani, Keeper of the Temple of the Shaper in Annoch, seemed to always have an answer. She sighed, coaxing her horse into a trot.

***

Evening had come upon them like a slow tide.

They were almost to Théas, and the great white city was spread out before them, like a long-forgotten dream. Alysana had only been there once before, during a supply run that her father had brought her on during the worst drought in G'henni history. The city was large, larger than Annoch, and spread out over a vast array of streets, roads, and buildings, with a dizzying number of people jammed inside its walls. The residents were mostly human: native Théans making up the majority of the population, with a smaller number of G'henni migrants among them who were looking for a change of scenery. There were also a good deal of Athrani scattered throughout the city, not nearly as many as could be found in Annoch or Ellenos; but this gave her hope that they would find a healer for Elyasha, or at least someone who could point them in the right direction.

She didn't know how tolerant the people of Théas would be of their two Khyth companions, but she was holding out hope. Turning back to Ellenos was out of the question, and Théas was the only city for days. They had no choice.

As they approached the edge of the city, Alysana looked at Kethras, who was growing increasingly nervous the closer they got. He was walking beside them, taking great strides with his impossibly long legs, and glancing around like a cornered animal. She decided to say something.

"Kethras," she began gently, "you . . . look like something is bothering you."

He looked at her as if she had helped remove a thorn from his hand. "Something is," he said.

Alysana looked at him expectantly. Taking the cue, Kethras went on.

"Stone, mostly," he said. He was nervously fingering the fletching of one of his arrows. "It makes me . . . uneasy. The way men use it—they seem to put it everywhere." He gestured at the walls as they approached, then looked back at her in defeat. "I don't know if I will ever get used to it."

Alysana nodded to show she understood. "Thornton told me that it has been a long time since you last ventured outside of your forest."

Kethras nodded.

"What worries you? Maybe we can do something to help."

The Kienari bared his teeth in an attempt at a smile. "The last time I came to a city of men unannounced, I had a knife put to my throat."

Alysana laughed. "I'm sorry," she said. "Mordha told me about it."

Annoch, where her sister had been standing guard and she had been waiting tables for Wern, had been Kethras's first real interaction with humans in who knows how long.

"Then you understand why I am nervous."

Thornton, now riding beside Alysana on the wide road that led into the city, said, "That makes two of us, but I'm mostly worried about how they'll react to seeing a Khyth."

To most of the party's surprise, Dailus spoke up as well. "You needn't concern yourself," he said, raising his rope-bound hands. "We are far enough from Ellenos that the reach of the High Keeper does not influence the citizens. Théas is a human city, first and foremost. Everyone else is seen as . . . extended house guests."

Alysana had not heard the half-eye say so much as a word since they made camp the previous night. She whirled around to give him an incredulous look and to say, "That is . . . actually quite useful. Thank you, Dailus."

She tried not to sound too thankful.

"Think nothing of it," he said through taut lips.

"Although," Thornton said, "I'm sure we do look unusual: a captive Athrani, two free Khyth, a Kienari, and a G'henni." He smiled at Alysana. "Good luck explaining that to the guards."

Alysana gave him a smirk in return. "Just let me do the talking, and we will be fine." Turning her head back to the Kienari, she said, "Kethras, do you feel comfortable enough to follow us into the city?"

Kethras nodded and looked at Thornton. "I go where he goes."

"Then I have an idea."

Chapter 47

Ellenos

Awaken the Three

Lilyana

They had been walking for days.

When they left the city of Ellenos—something Lily never thought she would do—it was under the cover of darkness. Her mother was doing her best to stay calm, but Lily could see through the act. She knew her mother better than she knew anyone, and the constant glances behind them, back toward the First City, let her know that everything was not all right.

Lily knew next to nothing about her uncle Thaurson, save for the fact that he left the city of Ellenos a long time ago because he looked too much like his human father, but that they were seeking him out now was more troubling than leaving the city to find him. "Please, Mother," she whispered, "can you tell me where we're going now?"

"It's better if I don't," was her answer. She was repeating herself now, as Lily had heard this same answer at least a half dozen times before.

They were in a densely wooded area with no clear path, and Lily was unsure of how her mother was so certain that they were headed in the right direction. But still the two of them pressed on, pushing branches and leaves out of the way as they moved ahead.

***

The night was still dark when they resurfaced somewhere outside the Talvin Forest, and Lily could see the hint of a city in the distance. She had been only loosely paying attention to where they were headed, and her underdeveloped sense of direction did her no favors. Both she and her mother wore black, and it had paid off a few times when she heard voices in the night, voices that her mother whispered belonged to the Tallister's men looking to bring them back. But this time, when the sound of voices and a fire came from up ahead, her mother did not shy away.

"Don't be afraid," she whispered without looking at Lily. "They may look rough, but these men will help us."

Lily grasped her mother's hand tightly as the two of them walked toward the firelight. Gathered around it, dirty from the road and looking as rough as her mother had warned, were five men in light leather armor. A few swords lay scattered about the slipshod camp, which consisted of nothing more than some sleeping rolls and a spit roasting meat over a fire.

"Are you Thaurson's men?" Cora asked.

The biggest of them, G'henni by the look of him, answered quickly. "Aye," he said. He was seated on a stump and chewing the last bit of meat from a chicken leg. Throwing the bone down and standing up to wipe his hands on his tunic, he asked, "Who might you be?"

"Coraline," her mother answered. "And my daughter, Lily."

"Well, Coraline," the G'henni replied, "my name is Tark. This here is Damazo"—he pointed to a light-skinned man probably from Théas—"my second-in-command. The other three are Agheer, Drausté, and Gorbun. They are a little rough around the edges, but there are no better smugglers in all of Derenar, and possibly Gal'dorok."

The three men nodded in turn as their names were spoken, but did not speak. They made Lily uncomfortable, and she found herself peeking out from behind her mother. Tark, apparently amused by the sight, laughed deeply.

"Nothing to fear, little girl. You are in good hands. Your uncle Thaurson would not have it any other way. He is a strong man who pays well, and a man like that is one that you would do well to keep happy."

The other men grumbled in agreement.

Still, Lily was unnerved by the sight of them. The rest of Derenar was only an idea to her, unfamiliar until now, and these men—these *human* men—who claimed to work for her uncle, were strange to her as well. There were not a lot of humans in Ellenos, and Lily's interaction with them had been minimal at best. She just didn't know how to read them.

If she had known how to, perhaps she never would have gone with them that night.

Come on, you bastards! Do you want to live forever?

—Reported last words of Araeas the Deathless, of Théas

Chapter 48

Théas

Awaken the Three

Alysana

The great city of Théas was, like almost all cities of its size, lined with a wall that separated the outskirts from the city proper. And, as Alysana's sister, Mordha, did for the city of Annoch, a number of humans were outside guarding the entrance to the City of a Thousand Towers. Though, unlike Annoch, there were no great gates to keep out intruders.

The northern entrance to the city was marked by two towering white walls that formed a corridor through which travelers could pass, ten horses wide. On either side of the walls, archers stood calmly surveying the land below them. And guarding the corridor were a number of well-armored guards variously armed with pikes, spears, and swords. The breastplates they wore were forest green with black on the sides and back—the colors of the Deathdancers of the Théan Brigade.

A mustachioed soldier approached them with an outstretched hand.

"Ho there," he said, eyeing Kethras suspiciously. "If you're here for the slave auction, you're a day early. And you'll need to make the proper filings with the city magistrate." The rope that Alysana had fastened around Kethras's neck had done the trick. Dailus, still tied up, opened his mouth to speak, but Alysana spoke over him.

"Yes, of course," she said, nodding at the guard and elbowing Dailus for silence. "Where can we find the magistrate?" She shot a look at Thornton, piled in back with Elyasha, which said, *Trust me*. Or so she hoped.

"In the city center, by the statue of Araeas the Deathless. Follow this road," he said, pointing with his entire hand, "until you reach the Fountains of Thenn. Turn right, and you will see the statue. The magistrate's office faces it. You can't miss it."

"Thank you," Alysana answered with a crisp salute, her right fist connecting with a creak as it struck the leather armor on her left shoulder.

The guard nodded. "Though your timing could have been better. I hear they have a Farstepper up for auction," he said, eyeing Kethras again. "Any other time and your bounties might fetch a higher price."

Alysana's eyes opened wide, but she did her best to mask her surprise.

"I will keep that in mind," she said.

And will most likely empty out my coin pouch in the process, she thought.

A captive Farstepper would be worth far more than she was as a guide through the Wastes.

The guard was wrong—their timing couldn't have been better.

Chapter 49

Haidan Shar

Awaken the Three

Benj

Nervousness soaked into the Flats like blood into a shirt. Benj could feel it in the air, see it on the faces of his friends. The poorest quarter in Haidan Shar was represented disproportionally in the number of men—and boys—that it would be sending to war, and each one of them wondered if he would be coming home again.

He was uncomfortable in his armor, consisting of little more than an armiger's leather breastplate and helmet, and was adjusting the sheath for his short sword when Shotes walked in. Shotes's older brother had been an armiger too, and Shotes was wearing his old armor. It looked ridiculous on him, like a pony wearing a saddle meant for a full-grown thoroughbred.

"Are you ready, Benj?" he asked shakily.

Benj shook his head.

"Me neither," the smaller boy answered with a sigh. His short sword hung loosely by his side in the worn brown leather scabbard that had clearly belonged to his brother as well, and possibly their father before them. He looked a mess, certainly not how someone about to go to war should look. It made Benj grimace. He tightened the strap on his helmet.

Shotes was only a year younger than he was, but even at eleven he still looked like a child. Benj was lucky enough to have started filling out, getting the height and weight that came with growing up, but he didn't let it fool him into thinking he was grown. He could see some of the other men of the Flats outside donning their own armor, and the difference was striking: how easy their gait and how stoic their faces. If any among them weren't ready or willing, they kept it hidden.

"Don't worry, Shotes," Benj said after a silence. "This is what armigers do. This is what we train for. Besides, we're lucky: some of the other boys our age don't have a captain to accompany them and will be going into battle on their own. Just think how scared some of them must be."

Shotes nodded and visibly relaxed. "I gueth you're right," he relented. "Sthill, it'th a little sthcary."

Benj agreed, and so did the butterflies in his stomach. They hadn't stopped fluttering around since his mother had told him he basically had to grow up overnight. It wasn't fair that a boy his age should have so much responsibility. Besides tending the stables and being an armiger, now he had to worry about going to war. It just wasn't fair. He had started to silently curse his mother for forcing him into all of this when, as if she had been summoned, her dawn-cast shadow made its way into the stables before him.

"There's nothing wrong with being scared, Shotes," Nessa said as she walked in. Her face was buried in the shadows that came from the rising sun behind her, their blurred edges bleeding into the soft orange light that formed her outline. She was carrying something with her, something wrapped in cloth. "Even I was scared the first time I went into battle. And every time after that. It's always in the back of your mind; you just have to choose whether or not to let it win."

Shotes's eyes went wide with amazement. "You?" he asked incredulously. "Were sthcared?"

Nessa laughed, though whether it was at the absurdity of the question or Shotes's lisp, Benj wasn't sure. "Of course I was," she said, stooping down to look the boys in the eye. "Everyone gets scared. Everyone. From Queen Lena to Captain Jahaz to even the Breaker of the Dawn— they all get scared."

Shotes mouthed a silent "wow," and Benj mentally agreed.

"But I've got something for you that might help," she went on. She placed the item she was carrying on the ground, wrapped in a rough off-white cloth that looked older than both of the boys, and started to unfold it. After three turns, the cloth revealed its contents: a polished silver bastard sword etched with indecipherable runes. It had a handle of black and a hilt of white. The colors of Khala Val'ur.

Benj stared at the sword, then looked up at his mother in amazement. "How did you get this?" he breathed. No regular soldier would have had a sword like this. This one was special. This one was *magic*.

"It's from . . . ," she began with a grimace, "that day."

Benj knew which one she meant.

"What day?" Shotes asked quietly.

Nessa looked at him and smiled.

"We were on a raid that had lasted almost a week," she said, starting the story that Benj had heard countless times before, "killing Chovathi left and right. But no matter how many we cut down, it seemed like two more rose up to take their place. We were being overrun, yet none of us would acknowledge it. They were closing in, and the sun was setting. It looked like it was going to be the last sunset we ever saw. Men were dying all around me, but I somehow managed to stand my ground. The Chovathi were unrelenting, and the last remaining man in my regiment fell dead beside me. I stared my own death in the face."

Shotes was wide-eyed. "Did you die?" he asked.

"No," Nessa laughed. "Because of one man," she said. "One man, and this sword." She held it up, and its perfectly edged blade caught the sunlight.

Benj watched as the blade gleamed as it moved. "What happened?" he asked in a hushed tone.

The look in his mother's eyes was distant, as though she was there again, reliving the memory. "He came in with a sword, this sword, which blazed like the morning, moving seamlessly through the sea of Chovathi, cutting through them like the sun cuts through fog. Dancing and turning, swinging and spinning. It was . . . It was the most beautiful thing I'd ever seen."

Benj knew there was pain behind the words. The pain of a survivor.

"When I saw what he was doing," she went on, "I had a sudden surge of hope, and bravery. I fought back, knowing deep in my heart that I had a chance of making it through; that the sunset I was seeing would not be my last; that I would make it home again to Ghal Thurái."

Benj looked down at the sword that she had placed on the ground. "And that's the sword he was using." It was more statement than question.

"It was," his mother replied. "He called it Glamrhys, which means 'foe cleaver' in old Valurian. And it certainly lived up to its name that day."

There was a brief moment of silence as Benj and Shotes took it in. The sword in front of them had been responsible for Nessa's survival, and there were no two ways about it. He had always heard the story, but his mother has never mentioned the sword.

If it hadn't been for this sword in front of him, this *very sword*, he wouldn't be here to appreciate it. He thought he heard something else from his mother, but he couldn't concentrate. He was too focused on the sword.

This was the sword that saved his mother. His head started to spin.

This was the sword that saved . . . him.

This sword . . .

This . . . sword . . .

"Benj," his mother said, a hint of concern in her voice, "come back to me."

He felt his shoulders being shaken.

He felt as if he was coming out of a trance. He blinked a few times to find that the sword, Glamrhys, had moved. It wasn't in front of him anymore. In fact, his mother wasn't, either. And the shadows had moved. The sun wasn't in the same position it had been in. How much time had he lost?

He took a deep breath, and his blurry eyes focused again on his mother. He shook his head, trying to focus. "I'm sorry," he started. The world blurred in and out. "I'm just nervous."

His mother looked at him skeptically, her eyes moving from him to the sword, and back.

"That's not nerves," she said. "That was a trance."

Benj looked at her, not knowing what to say.

"Don't worry, my love," she said in a soothing tone. "It's a good sign. Swords like these always choose their owners. And I think this one just chose you. Go on," she said, holding out the sword. "Take it."

Benj hesitated at first, unsure if he wanted to go into another trance again. But he trusted his mother, and the look on her face told him that it was okay. He reached out and grabbed the iron grip of Glamrhys. It was cold, colder than he thought it should have been; but right after his fingers wrapped around it, it started to warm up. He almost dropped it in surprise, but it felt too good to let go. Warm. Alive. Like it was a part of him.

It felt *strong*. And so did he.

"You have to promise me," Nessa said, "that you'll only use this if you have to. I don't want you needlessly charging into battle and endangering yourself unless the situation calls for it. Understand?"

She had a stern look on her face, the kind she would use when scolding him for being late or forgetting to close the stable door.

"I understand," Benj replied.

"Good. Now let's get you the sheath for that so we can make it official."

She stood up and made for the exit of the stables, and Benj followed right behind. If he was going to go into battle, at least he would be doing it with some added protection.

For once in his life, things were starting to go right.

Chapter 50

Théas

Awaken the Three

Alysana

Alysana was unprepared for the kind of attention that Kethras attracted. Drawn steel and threats she could deal with, but the silent gawks and gapes directed at the tall, strange creature made her uneasy. He was a legend come to life in the City of a Thousand Towers. Three times already they had been stopped and offered gold on the spot.

Surprisingly, no one batted an eye at Dailus being tied up; Alysana wasn't sure if it was because Kethras made him practically invisible, or because in Théas not even an Athrani was off limits. Whatever it was, she was relieved; there was no way she was setting the half-eye free.

"Surely you don't mean to keep me tied up the whole way to Do'baradai . . . do you?" Dailus asked. He had twisted his body around in the cart so he could face forward. "Even the Khyth wouldn't have treated me like this."

"You're right," Thornton snapped. "They would have treated you worse." He ended the sentence with a glare at Dailus that suggested he wished to test the theory.

"Fair enough," Dailus breathed as he turned back around.

***

Farther inside, Alysana was still leading Kethras by the rope she had fastened loosely to his neck. Thornton had had his hands bound for the sake of the guards on the wall, but Alysana had judged it harmless to let him free inside the city. None of them knew how the Théans would react to a Khyth being inside their city, but Thornton was his own man, and free, so Alysana had decided that was that.

In the cart, lying unconscious next to Dailus, was Elyasha. She was still wrapped in the blanket that Kethras had covered her in back at the camp, and Alysana knew they would have to fix that—fast.

She peered into the cart at the young Khyth woman, for any indication that she was recovering. Frowning, she did not like what she saw.

Thornton must have seen it too, because he spoke the words that Alysana was thinking.

"We need to get her taken care of." The worried look on his face gave weight to his words. Looking back up at Alysana, he said, "Let's find a room so we can stop parading Kethras around. It will make things go quicker."

"Agreed," Alysana answered. Thornton certainly had a point.

"I've had enough of being poked and prodded," Kethras growled, keeping his voice low. "A dark, locked room would be most welcome."

"Then that is what we will find," Alysana said, waving her hand at an old woman headed toward the gate. "Excuse me," she said. "Is there an inn on the way to the magistrate?"

The old woman's gray eyes smiled along with her lips as she answered. "Why yes, my dear. There's the Prancing Pony just ahead." Her smile faded, though, when she saw Thornton. "Although," she said, her voice lower now, "you may have better luck at the Broken Scabbard." She pointed farther away, bowed her head slightly, and scurried off toward the guards, giving a worried look over her shoulder as she did so.

Thornton was frowning as he looked at Alysana. "At least now we know how they feel about Khyth," he said.

Alysana grabbed him by the arm as she took the reins with her other hand, urging the horse forward in the direction that the woman had pointed. "There is nothing to be done about that," she said. "You are who you are and nothing will change that."

Thornton's silence didn't sit well with her, but she knew he was still struggling with who he was. *The poor boy has been through so much*, she thought. *It's a wonder he hasn't killed us all.*

***

It was a short walk to the Broken Scabbard through the streets of the City of a Thousand Towers—a city that lived up to its name, as far as Alysana could tell. It was a small inn, as she had expected, and that suited her just fine. They didn't need something expensive, and a cheaper place was more likely to have a rougher clientele, including the kind of people who would feel comfortable around the Khyth—and possibly a Kienari. Whatever the cost, though, she planned on recouping the losses after selling off the horses belonging to the legion. They were of good stock, and she knew the Théans would see as much.

"Wait with Yasha and the horses," she said to Thornton. "I will see about a room. Kethras," she said, "come with me in case I need to negotiate."

The Kienari nodded and bared his teeth in a grin.

The aged wooden door creaked open to a small and unwelcoming downstairs with a bar at the far end and a staircase leading upstairs. There were a few round, wooden tables occupied by the type of men one would expect to be drinking in a place like this, lit weakly by a half dozen candles lining the walls. Alysana looked around at the shoddy wooden interior, the sullen bartender, the unscrupulous characters drinking loudly, and decided it was perfect.

Walking up to the bartender, an older man with black hair, she asked, "How much for a room for me and a stable for twelve horses?"

"Twelve?" the bartender replied, putting away the glass he had been wiping down. He was looking at her, but didn't seem to notice Kethras.

"Twelve," Alysana confirmed.

The bartender narrowed his eyes and harrumphed. "Well, then. Two silvers'll get you a room, and two more'll get you food and care for your horses. Though you'll be taking up all o' my . . . stable . . ." His words trailed off as he noticed the Kienari for the first time. The color drained from his face, and his jaw went slack.

Trying to keep him focused, Alysana slammed down six silvers on the counter, bringing the man's wide eyes back to hers. "Then here's one for you for being so kind," she said, "and another for making sure we are not disturbed."

The bartender somehow managed to scoop the silvers off the counter and into his shaking hand. "M-My thanks," he said, then disappeared into a back room.

A moment later he reemerged with a dull bronze key. "Up the stairs and down the hall. Last door on the left." The color had still not returned to his face.

Alysana grabbed the key from him and gave a quick nod. "The horses are tied up out front."

The bartender turned his head slightly but kept his eyes on Alysana. "Paedrig!" he shouted. "Some stable work to be done, boy!"

Rapid footsteps made themselves known before the boy did; then a scrambling whirlwind of green eyes and red hair came tumbling out from the back. "'Course, Master Andor," he said hastily. "Right away." His eyes followed the rope leading from Alysana's hands to Kethras's neck, and gulped. "M'lady. H-How m-many need stabling?"

"Twelve."

"Oh. Ohh. Well, they're in g-good hands," Paedrig said with a clumsy bow.

"She knows they are," Master Andor said dismissively. "Else she wouldn't ha' come here. Now get out o' here. I'm not paying you for conversation."

Paedrig fumbled nervously with a key he'd pulled from his drab brown pants pocket and nodded, leaving through the front.

Alysana turned to Kethras and began to make her way to the stairs. "Now," she said, "to the room. We need to get Yasha taken care of."

Kethras nodded wearily. "Some rest would be nice," he said quietly.

The two of them walked up the stairs and down the hall, coming to a sturdy wooden door with a keyhole in it. Pushing in the key, Alysana turned it until she heard a click. She pushed the door open.

It was a small room, but she didn't care at this point. A bed was a bed, and she really couldn't have asked for more. She took the rope off Kethras's neck and put it in his hand.

"I am sorry I made you wear this," she said, but Kethras was already putting his hand up to stop her.

"No apology necessary, Alysana. It was a clever idea, and it worked." He glanced around the room as if looking for attackers. "It is dark in here," he said. "I like it."

Alysana smiled, and said, "Then enjoy it. I will go with Thornton to find a healer for Elyasha."

Kethras nodded at her as she exited the room, closing and locking the door behind her. If there was ever anyone who she felt confident would be fine on his own, it was Kethras.

She walked down the creaky wooden staircase and into the bar, where Master Andor was wiping down another glass and giving her a sour look. She paid him no mind and made for the door, intending to find Thornton and tell him the plan

Only there was no Thornton. The cart with Elyasha was gone too.

Alysana blinked, rubbed her eyes, and frowned.

It was going to be a long day.

Soldiers go to war; warriors return from it.

—Eder af'Thur, First Commander of the Fist of Ghal Thurái

Chapter 51

Khala Val'ur

Awaken the Three

Duna

Duna stood in the mouth of the Sunken City and pulled her fur cloak tighter. Winter's chill, which should have still been a few months off, was starting to set in.

One final round of inspections, she thought, flexing her fingers inside her wolfskin gloves, *and then we march.*

Khala Val'ur's pale morning light was thinly veiled by the fingers of fog that poured off of Gal'behem's peaks above. Duna looked out at her waiting army below, assembled at dawn and intent on her arrival. With a yawn, she breathed into her gloved hands and began her walk to the front through the crisp Valurian air.

Although she was no stranger to battle, Duna had never had to lead an army before; she had only led small companies or regiments during her time spent rising through the ranks. The principle of leading an army was the same as leading a company, though—albeit on a much grander scale. There was much less attention to tactics and more attention to strategy; it was something that Durakas had always excelled at, and something that she herself tended to struggle with.

But now that she was general, she had no choice: she must excel.

Out of necessity, Duna had appointed her own second-in-command: a young but promising captain, Aurin LaVince. He was walking toward her now, presumably having finished his own inspection of the troops.

"General," he said with a nod. He turned and called the massive columns of soldiers to attention.

All ready, Duna thought as she glanced up at the rising sun. Just as she had asked. *At least that part is going as planned.*

But as she looked around for the Gwarái that Yetz had promised her, with not a hint of them in sight, she knew the thought had come too soon.

"What now?" she grumbled aloud.

Puzzled and annoyed, she walked over to Aurin to find out why, on the day of their march to Haidan Shar, on the day they would need every advantage that they had—why not a trace of the beasts could be found.

"Captain LaVince," she said as she approached the young officer. "Where are the Gwarái?"

He looked at her and blinked a few times, as if trying to make sense of the question. "Pardon, General?"

Duna hated having to repeat herself; she hated being in the dark even more, though, so she did it anyway. "I asked where the Gwarái were," she said sternly.

Aurin furrowed his brow in confusion, as though he'd placed an order for an ale and been handed a wife instead. "I was told that you'd heard," he replied. "From High Khyth Yetz," he added, unhelpfully.

Duna, flummoxed, stood in silence while she processed the answer. Her eyes blinked enough times to have given their own response, but she decided that her mouth would work much better.

"I've heard nothing from Yetz," she finally said.

Silence. A soldier coughed.

"I don't understand," Aurin said, and he certainly looked like he meant it.

Great, Duna thought. *Here we stand, two confused officers in front of the entire Dorokian army about to embark on the most important march under its new commander.*

So far, this was not going well.

"He said something about having it brought in," Aurin offered.

Duna crossed her arms and frowned. "Walk with me, Captain," she said, nodding toward the rear of the congregation of soldiers. "And put the men at ease."

"Yes, General," he said, and motioned to the sergeant in front to let the men relax. The sergeant, in turn, gave a signal to the sergeants near him, who relayed the order to the rest of the army. The sound of thousands of armored soldiers shifting out of the position of attention sounded like a metal thunderstorm. Duna loved it.

"Tell me," she said as she began walking, making her way down the closest rank of soldiers, "what we are waiting on, and why."

Aurin scrambled to keep up with her, having already donned his platemail armor, making him slightly less mobile than the unarmored Duna. He certainly didn't look as warm.

"That's all I know, General. The Gwarái that High Khyth Yetz is having accompany us is being brought in. From Lash'Kargá."

Lash'Kargá, Duna thought. *That's odd. Why doesn't he just use*—But her thoughts were cut off by a faint noise, beginning like the distant beat of a drum and working its way closer to them. The noise resonated in her ears as she saw a shadow crest the peaks of the Great Serpent, engulfing her army like the night.

What the . . .

The great drum-beating continued as Duna watched the outline of what she knew to be a Gwarái slowly coming toward her. But what she was *seeing* and what she *knew* did nothing to reconcile the other, because the one thing that she knew for a fact was being blatantly contradicted by what was before her very eyes.

This Gwarái . . . had . . .

"Wings?" Aurin blurted out, pressing his helmet to his head in shock. "I didn't know they had bloody wings."

"Breaker's Hammer," Duna swore under her breath. "Neither did I."

Duna wouldn't have believed it if she hadn't been looking right at it.

Yet she was. And she *still* wasn't sure that she did.

The thing was dropping toward them, beating its great leathery wings to slow its descent, like the biggest blood bat she'd ever seen.

This Gwarái was at least half again as large as either of the two she'd seen at the Battle for the Tree. It had the familiar white horns, as well, though this one's were not curved; they jutted straight up, spiraling as they went, like the horns of an antelope. And they were at least as big as a claymore, maybe bigger. When the Gwarái finally reached the ground, Duna felt the earth beneath it tremble. Its ghastly yellow eyes scanned the troops as if it was looking for its next meal.

Duna had half a mind to order an attack, or even a retreat, when something caught her attention. There, seated in a leather saddle strapped on the creature's back, was a man in Kargan platemail, a deep copper brown that matched the sands which separated Lash'Kargá from the Wastes. And when the creature knelt down to rest beside the army, folding its great wings along its body, the rider stepped off. Removing the platemail helmet from his head was the legend himself: commander of the Lonely Guard of Lash'Kargá, and one of the few men said to have faced down a Farstepper and lived.

"Cortus Venn," Duna breathed, the perfect amount of amazement and respect in her voice, coupled with a tiny dash of incredulity. "Breaker's Hammer," she said again. The fact that the beating of the Gwarái's wings had stopped hadn't registered, so her voice carried much farther than she'd intended. Louder, she said, "You sure know how to make an entrance."

"I have to," Venn said, smiling, as he approached. "Why else would they put me in charge?"

Venn's thick brown hair, tied up behind his head, flowed into a great braided beard that hung down to his chest, decorated throughout with blood-red beads. As soon as he came into the light, and out of the Gwarái's shadow, Duna knew why he'd been placed in charge of the Lonely Guard: Cortus Venn was a Stoneborn.

There was no mistaking one this close up, even though she had never seen one in person. His skin was a smooth, milky white, the color of marble, and his veins and eyes were a murky gray. Duna had only heard stories about these men, elusive and near mythological as they were; and standing before her was a man who seemed to be no exception.

"Speaking of which," Venn said, clapping Aurin on the shoulder and not missing a beat, "I assume you're leading this army?"

There was silence as shock worked its way onto Aurin's face. He looked at Duna, confused, and then to Venn, who waited expectantly.

Duna drank in the moment just long enough to enjoy it. "No," she said as she suppressed a smile, her Thurian pride finally making its way to the surface. "I am." She reached out her hand in greeting. "Duna Cullain. General of Gal'dorok."

Venn looked surprised, but only for a moment. He sized her up, looking skeptically back and forth between Aurin and her. Finally locking eyes with Duna, he reached out and grabbed her waiting hand. "Cortus

Venn," he said with a firm shake. Then, grinning, he added, "But you already knew that."

"So you heard that," Duna said, returning the grin as they both let their hands drop. "We have one last inspection before we march," she said. "We'd be honored to have the commander of the Lonely Guard join us."

Venn nodded and looked out at the sea of troops.

"Looks like a fine bunch," he said after a while.

They all stood as one: the soldiers of the Fist, a small contingent of Khyth, and the remaining Valurian army. The black and white armor of Khala Val'ur and the white armor of the Fist meshed well into a uniform-looking army, Duna realized. Considering that they came from two different cities, it couldn't have worked much better even if they'd planned it.

She motioned for the commander to join her. "Please," she said, "this way."

Venn obliged.

The two of them, with Aurin in tow, walked along the edge of the soundly formed column of troops. Duna looked at their faces, not really seeing them but realizing the truth regardless: they were soldiers. And they were ready to die.

"It must have taken some coaxing," she said, turning to Venn, "to get you away from the Lonely Guard."

"Ah, they'll be fine," Venn said with a dismissive wave of his hand. "We're a lot like those Chovathi of yours: cut off a piece of us, and another will rise to take its place. We have to be replaceable," he said, eyeing a group of particularly young-looking soldiers. "Enough of us die out there at Death's Edge to make sure that we are."

Duna grimaced. She'd heard about what it was like in Lash'Kargá, that last bastion beyond the sands, and how they had to constantly push back the invading tribes to the south. But she'd never met anyone outside of Cavan Hullis who'd trained with the fabled fighting force. And here she was, keeping pace with their commander. She could almost feel the strength the man exuded, and was sure that her troops could feel it too.

"Well we are honored to have the great Cortus Venn here among our ranks," Duna said.

Venn waved it off. "Great men can only be called so after they die, when their whole lives are looked at." With a sidelong glance to Duna, he grinned wildly. "I don't plan to be great for quite some time."

And, for the first time in a while, Duna found herself laughing. "So be it," she said. She motioned for Aurin to have the men present their weapons as she walked the ranks. Steel hissed against leather as thousands were unsheathed. "How much did Yetz tell you when he sent for you?"

"Oh, not much," Venn replied. "He's stingy with information, that one. He told me that I would be riding this beast here"—he jerked his thumb toward the winged Gwarái—"and that I'd be reporting to the general." He smirked, adding, "He neglected to mention that the general was a woman."

Duna caught the friendliness in his tone. It was different from the tone that her old commander, Caladan Durakas, would use when speaking about women; though Durakas tolerated them and found them useful, he always seemed to think of women more as tools rather than people. This man, Duna could tell, was simply surprised to see a woman in such an enviable position of power. And, if she was honest with herself, so was Duna.

"Yetz is stingy indeed," Duna agreed. "He certainly didn't tell any of us that he'd begun breeding winged Gwarái."

"Ah," said Venn, a hint of amusement in his tone. "That's because *I* didn't tell *him*."

Duna stopped and looked at Venn, who was smiling that wild smile of his behind his bulky beard.

"You . . ." She blinked. ". . . what?"

"There are more secrets among the Lonely Guard than you're probably aware of," he said slyly. "Like how a Farstepper's power actually works, or how to bring a Gwarái back with wings after they die."

"How to . . . ," Duna stammered. "After they . . . ?"

"Die, yes," Venn nodded. "It's the only way we know of to get the winged ones."

Duna was dumbfounded. "That's amazing," she said. "How do you do it?"

Venn laughed. "Join the Guard and maybe I'll tell you."

She looked at him, considering. "Quite the offer," she admitted, "but I prefer leading over breeding."

"That so? Well, perhaps you haven't met the right man."

Duna smiled despite herself. "Fitting that we're out here checking equipment," she said with a smug glance at Venn. "Because you've got the wrong kind for me."

The confused look on the commander's face was the most beautiful thing Duna had seen so far, and she wanted to draw it out. Turning to Aurin, she said, "They are ready. We march."

Nodding to the sergeant in front of the entire formation, Aurin signaled for attention.

The city beneath the peaks of Gal'behem was large enough to hold nearly three times the number that it held today, but the path leading outside the mountain stronghold had to be traversed in a five-by-five line due to the narrow passages that surrounded it. The winged Gwarái and its rider would have no trouble getting out, however.

Duna turned to make her way to the front of the formation, preparing herself to lead her army, when she stopped and looked again at Venn, whose face still wore a look of shock.

"Close your mouth, Commander," she said. "At least your Gwarái will let you mount it."

Chapter 52

Théas

Awaken the Three

Thornton

The sturdy white stallion walked beside him, pulling the cart with Yasha inside, and Thornton reminded himself that she would be better off without him.

In fact, he thought as he looked back at her wrapped up in sleep, *she might have been better off never leaving Khala Val'ur.* The thought made him ill, and he pulled on the horse's bridle to quicken their pace to the healer. Everyone he'd asked had pointed him to the same person.

The city of Théas reminded him of Lusk with its wide streets and throngs of people, just on a much grander scale than he was used to. He looked up at the white buildings and houses as he passed, trying to discern what was what. *There must be a lot of money in the slave trade,* he thought darkly as he looked at the large, showy houses that dotted the streets. Some of them were the size of inns, and some of the inns looked big enough to house a village. He quietly realized how little of the world he had seen until he had ventured out on his own.

"Move aside," came a voice from up ahead. Before he could look to see where it was coming from, he was shoved roughly out of the way.

The shove triggered something inside Thornton as he suddenly found himself wanting nothing more than to break the bones of whomever had pushed him. The world around him shuddered and darkened as he felt himself losing control; it was the same feeling he'd had outside of Dailus's cell.

The same feeling he'd had before calling the flames that consumed Thuma.

The same feeling he'd had before burning Yasha . . .

The unpleasant memory snapped him back as he found himself staring into the dark eyes of a man with coal-black hair and a mustache. There were five others behind him wearing dark tunics, and more than a few of them had pulled out their knives.

"I'll say it again," the man growled. "Put down that hammer before someone gets hurt."

You have no idea, Thornton thought grimly. He looked at the hammer, which he didn't remember reaching for, and muttered, "Sorry." He slid the hammer back into its holder.

He had already hurt Yasha without intending to, and he was sure that if he lost control again, she might fall beyond the help of even the most skillful of healers. "It was my fault," he said as he raised his hands.

While the stranger dusted off his own silver-lined tunic, Thornton's eyes were suddenly drawn to the wolf-like brooch clasped near his neck. It was polished and worn, and something about it seemed familiar.

"You're damn right it was your fault," the stranger said, pushing past him. "Now out of my way. A guest of the magistrate shouldn't have to clear his own path."

Thornton turned to watch the men leave. All six of them walked as if they owned the world, with swarms of busy Théans simply moving out of their way. He looked back at Yasha, still barely breathing, and urged the horse forward. He needed to get her to a healer.

And then, when she woke up, he would tell her the plan.

***

The door to the windowless room creaked open as Thornton backed into it with his shoulder. Stepping through, he adjusted his grip on Yasha, who was cradled in his arms. *This should be the place*, he thought, while the faint smell of pine needles and smoke drifted over him.

A large crimson curtain hung in the back of the room, and the tables and floorboards looked old but well maintained. Books, vials of liquid, glass containers, and various metal implements were strewn about haphazardly with no logical order to be seen. *Either thieves were looking for something*, Thornton thought, *or the owner has never cleaned.*

A voice came from behind the curtain. "Is someone there?" it asked, sounding as though it belonged to a man old enough to have witnessed creation itself.

"Y-Yes," Thornton stammered. "I was told I could find Healer Silus here."

I just hope Yasha wakes up soon, he thought. *She'll understand.*

313

"That depends," came the muffled reply. "Who is asking?"

Thornton thought this an odd response, but answered anyway. "Thornton Woods." As an afterthought he added, "Of Highglade."

The thump of a wooden cane striking the old oak floorboards made its way toward Thornton, and the curtain pulled back, revealing a frail old man in a drab brown robe. Wild and wiry gray hair grew only on the sides of his head, standing up and out as if it were trying to escape. "Highglade, eh?" the old man asked. "Can't say I've heard of it."

"You wouldn't have," Thornton answered reflexively. "There's not much to it. Just a small village outside Lusk."

"Ah, Lusk. Of course," the old man said, hobbling closer. "There are some good healers in Lusk. Which is why I ask, Thornton of Highglade," he said, coming to a stop and leaning heavily on his cane, "what's a young man from north of Derenar doing all the way down here in Théas? Why come to old Silus, and not a healer in Lusk?"

Thornton grimaced and looked at the floor, partially out of shame but more to hide his eyes. "We were traveling when it happened. When I"—he caught himself—"when my sister was hurt."

"Your sister?" Silus echoed. By now, the old man was standing right next to Thornton. Yasha's face was uncovered, and Thornton was looking away, but he thought it strange that the old man wasn't trying to make eye contact with either of them. He felt relief, though, since their swirling eyes would have given them away immediately.

"That's right," Thornton replied. "She's been burned—badly—and I'm not sure how long she can hold out." He fixed his footing as his arms started to feel the weight of his burden, and he felt his patience wearing thin. "Can you help me?" he asked.

"I see they don't teach manners in Highglade." The old man frowned. With his cane, he pointed to a tall table, chest height, with a smooth maple finish. "Help your sister over there, and let's have a look at her."

Thornton carried Yasha to the table and set her down gently, unwrapping the blanket as much as his own modesty would allow. He watched as the old man hobbled over, cane thumping slowly, to the edge of the table. Silus held out his hands, palm down, a few inches away from Yasha's midsection.

The light that streamed out from the healer's hands should not have startled Thornton—most of the great healers were of Athrani blood, after all—but he breathed a gasp of shock nonetheless.

The old man cocked his head at this and looked in Thornton's direction. "Surprised to see an Athrani this far south?" he asked with a smile. "I haven't been here long, I suppose."

"No, it's not that," Thornton began. "It's just that . . . well . . . I didn't think you would help me." He was still looking at the ground, afraid to make eye contact with the old man and silently loathing the Khyth blood that ran through his veins.

"And why wouldn't I help you? After all, are we all not sons and daughters of the Shaper?" Silus replied. He was focused again on Yasha, holding his palms over her, with the faintest stream of white light flowing from his hands. His expression suddenly changed, though, from calm concentration to confused effort. The light from his hands was extinguished as he took a step back and placed a hand on his chin, cocking his head in thought.

"What is it?" Thornton asked. "Why are you stopping?"

"Your sister—is she from Highglade as well?"

The blanket was off her by now, and Yasha's body—and, consequently, her heritage—lay bare on the table. No man with any sense in his head could have mistaken her for anything else other than a Khyth of the Breaking. The earthy gray tones of her body that made her look like a burned-out fire were more than evident.

That was when Thornton finally ventured to make eye contact with Silus. Unlike all the other Athrani he'd ever met, though, Silus had eyes that were a single color: milky white, through and through.

That was exactly when it dawned on him.

He's blind! Thornton realized. *That's why he hasn't turned us away. Any other Athrani wouldn't have even let us past the door.* Like the water that had turned to steel below the Wheel of Ellenos, Thornton suddenly felt very heavy.

Do I tell him the truth and risk his turning us away?

He looked at the old Athrani who possibly harbored the same grudges against the Khyth that all men his age once did. There was a very good chance that if Thornton let slip the truth of who he was, Yasha might be denied what she so desperately needed.

Half-truths would have to do until he could make a better determination.

"Our father is from Highglade," Thornton finally said. "Why do you ask?"

"Because something is broken inside of her," the old man said. "Something I can't quite see, and something that is pushing back against me. Resisting. Something, I fear, that is the real cause of the damage to this young woman."

His cloudy white eyes looked at Thornton. "It's almost as if something inside of her is at war. Two halves of a whole." He gave Thornton a defeated smile of sympathy. "I'm afraid that it's nothing I can fix. I'm sorry."

The shock took a moment to register, but Thornton wasn't ready to accept it. "That's it?" he nearly shouted. "You're just going to leave her? Give up because something *inside of her* is *broken?*"

"Oh, I can fix the burns," Silus replied, waving his hands. "But if you intend on making her whole again, you're going to need help from someone with more power than I have. The energies of Khyth were never my specialty."

Thornton blinked a few times as a sly smile worked its way onto Silus's mouth.

"What?" the old man asked. "You think that because I can't see, I didn't know you two are Khyth?"

Thornton's jaw dropped.

"I'm blind, not stupid," Silus replied with a breathy chuckle. "I felt it the moment you walked in the door. But don't worry—a healer can't choose who he helps any more than a drop of rain can choose where it lands." He motioned for Thornton to come closer. "Now I just need an extra pair of hands. Place them on her stomach, please."

Thornton looked warily at the old man but did as he was asked. He walked over to his sister, pointing his gaze at the ceiling to keep her modesty intact, and used his peripheral vision to complete the task.

"Now hold them there," Silus said from behind him. "And don't move until I say. This will feel . . . strange."

Thornton felt a warm glow, like a budding fire, coming from behind him and saw the same light from earlier coming from the healer's hands. He felt a wave of calm wash over him, pulling him in and setting him at ease, while at the same time making the hairs on his neck stand up.

Back in Highglade with his father, maybe a year old, and there was a woman he didn't recognize.

Suddenly his arms went hot, as though he were holding them in the heat of a forge. He gnashed his teeth as everything inside of him made him want to pull his hands away.

Ellenos, with its wide canals and cloud-covered roads.

Beads of sweat formed on his face as his concentration waned, and he thought for a moment that he might faint.

Khala Val'ur and its dark, dismal depths.

But just as his eyes began to roll back into his head, the pain ceased. It was accompanied by the faint smell of something sweet and sharp, and a multitude of tiny, bright spots in his vision.

"There we are," Silus said. "You can let go now."

Thornton steadied himself and gasped in the air like a drowning victim. He held on to the table to keep from collapsing. The odd smell had receded, but the bright spots remained. He rubbed his eyes in an effort to get them to go away.

"Pain spots," Silus said.

Thornton crinkled his forehead inquisitively. "Huh?"

"The pain spots in your eyes. They'll be gone soon. It's a by-product of the healing. The same goes for the scent that comes with it. It's different for men and women, and even for humans and Athrani. Tell me," he said. "What did you smell? Sage? Blackroot?"

Thornton shook his head. "Nutmeg," he answered. "And vinegar."

This made Silus scratch his chin in thought. "Interesting. That means one of your parents—"

Before he could finish the thought, the door burst open, kicked in by the foot of an angry G'henni.

"Thornton Woods!" Alysana shouted, dragging a despondent Dailus behind her. "I want answers."

Without a word, Silus made a hasty retreat.

He sees more than he lets on, Thornton thought bitterly. He was still sorting through everything that had just happened while trying to think of what to say. He turned to face the storming G'henni and held out his hands to stop her.

But the look on Alysana's face turned from one of anger to surprise to disbelief as she peered past him.

On the table, holding a blanket to cover her breasts, Yasha sat up.

Chapter 53

Haidan Shar

Awaken the Three

Benjin

Today was not a day to worry about being late.

Benj could feel the heaviness that permeated all of Haidan Shar, and he wondered how many times his mother had felt it too. He reached down for Glamrhys at his side, running his fingers over the ancient leather sheath, and took a tiny bit of solace in it. He looked over at Shotes, in his ill-fitting armor, and couldn't help but smile. He was glad that his best friend was here.

The two of them were walking to the center of the city to meet their captains and the rest of the army. It wasn't the first time he'd done it, but it was the first time he'd done it for real.

This was war.

His heart jolted at the thought.

War.

They had always trained for this sort of thing—at least as long as he'd been an armiger—but they had never gathered to march to an actual battle.

Colors seemed sharper today, and smells seemed stronger. Benj could have sworn he felt something emanating from Glamrhys as he walked; and knowing there was more to the sword than just cold steel, that was probably the case. Today made everything inside him, everything around him, seem different.

"Armiger Benjin," Captain Jahaz called from the front of the formation. There was no anger in his voice. That almost scared Benj more than if there *had* been. "Fall in with the others. We captains are finishing up our inspections of the rest of the men, and then we will be off. Today is a big day."

That's an understatement, Benj thought, making sure he was thinking the words, not saying them aloud. "Yes, Captain Jahaz," he answered.

The troops in the city's center were facing the old, wooden stage that served mostly as the theater for the local mummers' troupe, but its official function was to elevate the queen when she addressed her people. Benj knew that's what they would be in for today.

Benj walked over to the file of armigers, arranged by height, and worked himself in right behind the tallest armiger, Amethyst. Older than Benj by only a year, she had hit her growth spurt two years before and had absolutely shot up. She used to line up near the end; now, the slender redhead was first in line.

"Taking your time, huh?" she whispered. She winked at him.

Benj blushed and jabbed her in the ribs with an elbow. "Shut up, Thyst," he said. "You think I'm worried about being late today?" He smiled smugly. "I said bye to the horses, finished my breakfast, hugged my mom—"

"You guyth hear that?" Shotes called out from behind them. "Benj loveth histh mom."

The chuckle from the rest of the armigers ruined their military bearing—Benj even saw a captain or two who had noticed it—but no one was going to say anything today. Morale was important, and there was no time where it was more important than on the edge of a battle.

"I love yours too, Shotes," Benj shot back, and the file erupted.

"Armigers!" a nearby captain shouted. "Bearing!"

Sometimes the need for one outweighed the other, though. It was a good lesson to learn as Benj tried to wipe the grin from his face. It took a few tries, but he got it.

Then, out of the corner of his eye, Benj spotted Captain Jahaz. He walked past them, toward the front of the formation. The armigers, being the most disciplined of the troops, were the left-most column of what amounted to a square of troops. In each column to the right of them was the rest of the army, also arranged by height from front to rear.

Jahaz kept going, walking right up onto the stage, where he promptly called the whole formation to attention. Hundreds of legs moved in unison, and all was still.

Haidan Shar's standing army was relatively small, mostly due to the fact that they preferred to hire outside mercenaries to fill their ranks, so Jahaz did not have to try hard to be heard.

"Sharians," he began. Benj felt proud watching his captain, the most senior of all the captains, address them. "Most of you are old enough to remember the last time we marched out together as an army. But," he said, looking over the faces in the crowd, "some of you are not. To those of you who do not remember it: don't worry—you will never forget this day as long as you live."

There was a collective chuckle of acknowledgment from most of the captains, and even some of the men beside Benj.

"And, as is tradition, I have invited the queen to say a few words before her best and strongest go off to battle."

With that, Jahaz stepped aside, and Benj's breath caught in his throat as he saw Queen Lena stride forward in the most magnificent platemail armor he'd ever seen. A sword was strapped diagonally across her back, almost as tall as she was, and Benj had no idea how she was moving so smoothly with it. She even looked graceful while armed to the teeth.

Then again, that was exactly why she was queen.

"Sharians," she began. "Mighty warriors!" She lifted her arms up in a V, and a cheer burst forth from all around. She reveled in it, soaking it in with a smile before letting it die down and speaking again. "Today, your mettle will be tested. You will find yourself facing an enemy that most of you have only trained for and only a few of you have actually faced. The Chovathi are a threat that our cousins to the west, the Thurians, have been fighting since before any of us were born." She swept her gaze across the troops, seeming to look at each one of them individually. "Take solace in that. Know that experience is on their side—and, by proxy, yours. Trust your training. Trust your captains. Follow your armigers. And, most importantly," she added with a grin, "follow your queen."

She grabbed the hilt of her massive sword with both hands and pulled it out of its sheath, swinging it in a circle around her head and then holding it out in front of her, its blade slanting upward toward the sun.

The entire army went berserk.

In that moment, behind the deafening cheers of bloodthirsty exuberance of the entire Sharian army, Benj was glad that no one was paying attention to the stiffening in his trousers.

"That is the greatest thing I have ever seen," he whispered to no one in particular.

He had no doubt that if he were dropped on the battlefield right in that moment, he could have killed every living Chovathi by himself.

War, he suddenly decided, wasn't so bad.

Chapter 54

Gal'dorok,
On the Khala-Shar Pass

Awaken the Three

Kunas

They had left at dawn, and the sun was now about halfway across the sky as Kunas looked back over the three captains. They were silent, save for some idle chatter between them, talking about the last time that any of them had seen combat (one had never), or their improved promotion odds now that General Tennech was out of the picture.

Their horses were moving at a comfortable pace, and they had managed to put a good bit of distance between themselves and the Sunken City. It was about a day's ride past Ghal Thurái, and another day to Haidan Shar, but they would not be going all the way to Haidan Shar.

"I'm just hoping to kill a few Chovathi and show General Cullain what I can do," said Captain Ohlez, a well-built, dark man who hailed from G'hen.

"Killing Chovathi soldiers ain't gonna get you a promotion," said Captain Jerol, a dark-haired native Thurian. "You need t'show y'can pick off their leaders."

"You're both wrong," the red-haired Valurian Captain Hunt said. "You have to show that you can lead if you want to make commander anytime soon."

Kunas rolled his eyes. He wasn't concerned with ideals such as leadership—although the murderous ambition of the other two men certain resonated with him.

"Quiet, all three of you," he snapped. "You would think that officers of your caliber would have gone on a diplomatic mission before and would know how to conduct yourselves."

Ohlez and Hunt looked indignant, and Jerol simply stared.

"If you're going to talk," he went on, turning forward again and keeping his eyes on the road, "talk strategy."

Jerol grunted. "Strategy?" he echoed. "How can we strategize if we don't know what we're up against?"

"And you call yourself an officer?" Kunas scoffed.

"Jerol is right," offered Captain Hunt. "We do need to have at least *some* idea of what we'll be facing before we can make any real decisions.

Troop strength, motivation, positions, natural and manmade defensive positions—all of those things and more need to be considered before adopting a strategy."

He sounded like he was quoting a war manual.

He probably is, thought Kunas, shooting a sidelong glance at the young Valurian. *He doesn't look experienced enough to have formed his own opinions about war.*

"Well, then, lucky for us we're scouting ahead, isn't it?" he said aloud.

He couldn't see it, but he could feel the captains rolling their eyes at him.

Now, where was that rendezvous point again?

Kunas scanned the foothills of the mountains as they rode along, shadows disappearing under the noonday sun.

There.

"Captains," he said loudly as he coaxed his horse to a gradual stop. "How are you at making camp?"

Captain Ohlez squinted up at the sun, and the other two exchanged puzzled looks.

"I don't understand," Hunt said. "We have at least a day and a half's ride left before Haidan Shar, and it's barely even noon. Why would we stop to make camp?"

"You didn't answer my question, Captain," Kunas said.

"Ahhhh," Hunt stammered. "All Academy cadets have to survive a week in the field during training, so," he shrugged, "passable?"

"Good," Kunas said as he looked around, indicating a small path that peeked out from behind some jagged rocks. "We will start there." He tapped his heels into his mount's ribs to head toward the pass.

***

It was a few hours past noon, and the four of them were seated around the small cook fire Hunt and Jerol had built, with Ohlez grilling some squirrels for them to eat.

Kunas looked down at the cut on his palm that he'd opened a few moments ago. He squeezed it, and a few drops of blood trickled out and landed on his robe. He hated that this was the best way to call the Chovathi, but he had no choice. If it worked, it worked.

While he knew they were close to the Xua'al nest, it was still alarming when the Chovathi got there so quickly. Smell alone wouldn't have alerted him of their presence; there had to be more to these creatures than that.

Kunas looked back to the fire. "I need you to be calm," he said to the captains as soon as he saw Khaz's lumbering frame come into view. The words didn't have the calming effect he'd thought they might, but the men were seasoned soldiers—two of them having seen combat—and the warning seemed to help. "Have you ever interacted with a Chovathi before?"

Captain Hunt, the youngest of the three, was the only one who shook his head.

"Then I need you to pay attention," Kunas said. "Close any open wounds you have now. If you can't, I would strongly advise that you go back to the road and stay there." He let the words sink in. "We're going to follow one of them into their nest."

Any sense of calm evaporated with the words.

Ohlez stood in surprise. "A nest?" he almost shrieked, trying his best to keep his voice steady. "Are you insane?"

The other two captains were frantically searching their own exposed limbs for any scratches or cuts they might have picked up on the ride out.

"It's the only way," Kunas replied. "And keep your voice down. While I'm quite certain that they can't smell fear, they certainly can hear it."

"You're doing an awful job of convincing me that it's a good idea," Ohlez said. "Why in the Breaker's name would we ever want to go into a Chovathi nest?"

Kunas sighed in exasperation. "If they're going to be our allies in this war, we have to show that both sides can be trusted. Besides, I've dealt with this one before. And I'm still here, aren't I?"

The three men did not look convinced.

By now, Jerol and Hunt had finished their self-inspections and seemed to be satisfied with the results.

"Fine," Hunt said, hand nervously holding the hilt of his sheathed longsword. "But you go first."

The other captains nodded in exuberant agreement.

Even Kunas was nervous at the prospect of going inside the nest. Though he had interacted with Khaz before, it had always been out in the open where he could run or call for help if things went sour. Going into the heart of a Chovathi nest to broker a deal was like walking into a pit of snakes and dangling a mouse in front of them.

Or, in this case, four mice.

"I will," he said flatly. "Just follow me, and don't make any sudden movements."

Khaz was nearly upon them now. He was an equally uneasy sight in the daytime, when the sun exposed all his hulking movements and angular features. His forelimbs reached the ground, and he used them like a second set of legs, knuckles pounding against the ground as he lumbered toward them.

He had seen Khaz at night, but in the daytime it was like shining a light on a nightmare. The creature's skin was lined with sharp, jagged ridges that had been invisible in the dark. They looked capable of doing some real damage if they were raked across flesh, he couldn't help thinking.

And they were about to go into a nest of these things.

"Kunas," Khaz growled as he approached. "You bring humans. Why?"

The Chovathi wasn't looking at them when he spoke. He had his head tilted in the air, as if listening to something far away.

Kunas swallowed the fear in his throat before he spoke. He had managed to control his emotions last time. It helped that he knew Khaz had a lot to gain by keeping him alive; he intended to keep it that way.

"Our leader, General Cullain, has asked that we speak to your matriarch. We want to discuss troop strength and our alliance with the Xua'al."

Right after Kunas uttered the word *matriarch*, Khaz turned his head to make eye contact with him—although "eye contact" was not entirely accurate, as the eyes of the male Chovathi looked more like sunken pits on his skeletal face. Kunas wasn't even sure that they were capable of sight. Regardless, they seemed to fulfill their purpose.

"Come to Chovathi nest?" Khaz growled. He had moved closer while Kunas had been talking, and was almost right on top of him. "Why?"

Kunas could feel the sharp inhalation of air as the male's cavernous nostrils did what they did best. He was sure that, as powerful as Khaz's sense of smell was, he was using it for *something* right now.

Maybe they could smell fear after all.

"We need to know that we can trust you," Kunas said, doing his best to remain calm. Ohlez and Hunt had backed away, but the stoic Jerol, with his Thurian blood, stood his ground. "And *you* need to know that you can trust us."

Khaz's forked tongue emerged from behind his jagged teeth and lightly grazed Kunas's face. Out of the corner of his eye, Kunas saw Jerol put his hand on his sword, but motioned for him to stop.

Khaz tilted his head again and seemed to be thinking. Finally, he turned back to Kunas and said, "Come."

Captains Hunt and Ohlez exhaled audibly, almost as if they'd forgotten how to breathe.

"See?" Kunas said, hiding the terror in his voice. "He agrees. Last chance to back out," he said as he started walking, not even bothering to look back.

When he heard three sets of footsteps behind him, he was secretly relieved. He wasn't sure that even he wanted to go into a Chovathi nest by himself; it would be a small comfort to have three Valurians accompany him inside.

Besides, he reminded himself with a mental shrug, if anything went wrong, he could always bring the whole mountain down on top of them, boulders and all.

Chapter 55

Théas

Awaken the Three

Thornton

Thin rays of sunlight intruded their way into the darkened room of the inn as Alysana continued to berate Thornton. It was very one-sided, and most of it was conveyed through shouting and frantic hand-waving.

"How could you even think that it was a good idea to leave us?" she seethed. "I do not give a damn how much of a danger you think you are—you do not abandon your friends."

Her hands were balled into fists, and she clenched her jaw so hard that Thornton swore he could hear her teeth grinding. He had never seen her angry. And he suddenly felt very small.

She was right, of course: he had abandoned them without considering the consequences. Even though he thought it was for the best, he had failed to consider the ramifications, the ones that would affect his friends and family.

"I just couldn't take it anymore. Any of it," he said in a calm voice. "I've been the single common factor in all this fighting and destruction and killing . . . and I thought that if I walked away it would all just . . . right itself."

Alysana crossed her arms and gave him a look dark enough to hide Kethras. "If that is truly what you thought, then you are a fool, Thornton Woods. A fool," she said with a huff. "A fire does not stop burning just because you turn your back on it."

Kethras had not said a word since they had returned from the healer, and Thornton did not have the courage to look the Kienari in the eye. Trying to leave without a word to any of them had been cowardly, and Thornton knew it. It felt like disappointing his father. But finally, after Alysana had ceased her shouting, Kethras stepped forward and drew a deep breath.

"You humans are much too short-sighted," he said in a quiet rumble. "You may have the best of intentions yet still bring about ruin and heartache in the end." He wore the darkness of the room like a cloak, and Thornton couldn't make out his expression, but he was certain he wouldn't have liked it. When he felt Kethras's hand on his shoulder, he flinched.

"But," he went on, "I cannot fault you for trying to make things better."

Thornton looked up to the tall Kienari, whose face was solemn and still. It reminded him of the great tree, Naknamu, and Thornton thought that "son of the forest" was a fitting moniker.

"It was stupid," Thornton admitted, and Alysana scoffed in agreement. "I should have thought it through."

Yasha, who had been sitting silently on one of the low-lying beds in the corner, looked up at Thornton and grimaced. "I can see why you did it, but the answer was right beside you this whole time," she said.

Thornton blinked a few times, trying to figure out what she meant.

She stood up and walked over to him. Taking his hand in hers, Yasha said, "*I* can teach you about what you are."

Her hands were soft, despite how the Breaking had ravaged her body. Whether it was out of revulsion for the power she represented or the thought of becoming something he hated, Thornton pulled away.

"That's the problem," he said. "I don't want to be what I am. I don't want to be a constant danger to people. And I don't want to have to become . . . something else . . ."

As his voice trailed off, Yasha sat there looking as if he'd slapped her across the face.

"I just want to go back to Highglade," he continued, "and do what I'm good at—blacksmithing. It's what my father raised me to do." He looked away, lowering his voice. "And the last time I checked, swinging a hammer at an anvil doesn't have to involve taking people's lives."

A silence followed as the tension in the room wrapped itself around each of them. Yasha turned her back to sit down.

"I'm sorry . . . ," Thornton began.

Yasha waved him off. "No. You're right. No one should have to be something they don't want to be." There was more than a hint of contempt in her voice.

In the palpable silence that followed, Kethras spoke: "Perhaps it would be best if we all got some sleep. We have been traveling long, and still have long to go. It appears that it is starting to wear on us."

Alysana was the first to agree. "Rest will do us all good," she said. She still had her arms crossed, but the look on her face had softened. "And we will need to be alert tomorrow."

Thornton was already thinking about a bed when he turned and looked back at the G'henni. "Alert? For what?"

"We have to make sure that we are getting the best deal," she said with a sly grin.

Chapter 56

Khadje Kholam

Awaken the Three

Sera

Sera had only been there one night and she already hated waking up in the heat of the Wastes. She sat up in her barely comfortable bed and wiped the sweat from her face, pulling her hair back to try to cool off. It was still early, but evidently the sun was already high enough to make an oven out of her quarters.

The two Thurians, Hullis and Dhrostain, had been permitted inside the walls, but their lower-ranking status as captains did not see them invited as guests into Yelto's inner compound, which was rather extensive, much to Sera's surprise.

When the four of them had come in, Sera had half expected the Wastes to be made up of nothing more than some loosely scattered tents over sand dunes. What she saw was something else entirely: Khadje Kholam was a city in its own right, boasting a multitude of people and buildings that dominated the landscape. Row upon row of houses and shops seemed to have sprung up from the desert itself, as if each were a seed that had been sown by the wind. The result was a bustling colony in the heart of the desert.

Yelto's compound was more or less the center point of the city, and the arid lands around it were littered with huts and buildings made from hardened mud and stone. In each of those buildings lived all manner of people: goat herders, horse tamers, leather workers, spear and sword makers. Each of them served a purpose in the tribe, and all of them looked as though they could handle themselves in a fight. *It's surprising that they were so easily conquered*, Sera mused. She worked out a kink in her neck and turned her head.

Tennech, who sat with his back to her, staring out a small window in their room, did not turn to look at her, but Sera knew he had been waiting for her to wake up. She took a long look before speaking.

"Those things you said about my daughter becoming the next Shaper . . . ," she began.

Tennech waved her off. "I told Djozen Yelto what he needed to hear. I will have my army, and you will have a claim to rule the tribes, and possibly even Khala Val'ur, if events unfold in our favor."

Of course, she thought. *Aldis Tennech always has a plan.*

"Yes . . . yes, of course," she stammered. *He did not become general by accident, after all*, came the afterthought.

Tennech turned and fixed his eyes on her.

"We are close, Sera," he said. "And if he cannot help us, we will have to take matters into our own hands. But, for now, do what you need to do to make yourself presentable," he said as he stood. "Djozen Yelto has invited us to break our fast with him."

***

The Djozen's dining hall was every bit as impressive as Sera had expected it to be, and for that reason alone she refused to be impressed by it. It was filled with all manner of things that surely existed as a blatant show of wealth. There were gems of every color inlaid into the brickwork, candleholders made of silver, small statues made of bronze; there was even a rug that looked to be embroidered with gold. She was certain that if gold could be made into a serving girl, Yelto would have it done.

The high ceilings of the spacious room had transoms at the very top of the walls that let in just enough of the soft morning light. Tapestries hung all around, and a long wooden table bearing a white tablecloth with silver trays was fixed in the middle of the room.

At its head, of course, sat Yelto.

"Ah, General Tennech. Do come in."

A serving girl was pouring the last of a bottle of wine into the Djozen's goblet as the fat man made a beckoning motion for them to join him.

"We are honored, Djozen Yelto," Tennech replied. He held his arm out for Sera to precede him to their seats, which were positioned opposite each other and next to the head of the table, where Yelto sat. The old general waited for Sera to be seated, then did so himself. He cleared his throat and looked at Yelto. "I'm told that you have some things you would like to discuss," he said.

"Indeed," Yelto replied. He clapped his hands thrice, and the doors to the dining hall opened. "But we should not do it on empty stomachs."

Awaken the Three

Into the dining room poured at least a dozen girls with serving trays topped with food and drink, moving flawlessly as if they were performing the opening scene of some well-rehearsed dance. Silver flashed as it caught the light, and the servants whirled past each other and over to the table, carrying their fare as easily as if it were an extension of their bodies. Candles were placed and lit, drinks were poured, and cutlery was disseminated all in a dizzying, deliberate performance. *He even uses meals as a chance to show off,* Sera thought.

When the dance was done and the last candle lit, the largest array of food that Sera had seen in recent memory had been laid out before them.

Looking down the rows of tall white candles, Sera was surprised by the amount of meat she saw, as well as being perplexed by some of the fruits that were laid out. A few of them she recognized, but most were foreign to her—no doubt native to these lands south of Gal'dorok. She was staring hard at a bowl of odd-looking brown fruit when their host took notice.

"I see that the lady has good taste." Yelto smiled. "The fruit of the ykesha plant is sweet and delicious, and always in season. It is one of the most prized foods in this region." Motioning to the bowl, he urged, "Try it."

Sera stifled a grimace and reached out to grab a piece of the fruit, which fit nicely into her palm. Its skin was rough, and she saw a line that went all the way around, implying that the outside was a husk. She looked up expectantly at the Djozen, who nodded his head in encouragement. She worked her finger under the husk to peel it off. Beneath it was a fleshy pink orb covered in hundreds of small red seeds that were buried into its flesh like fleas. She stared at it with a mixture of horror and curiosity.

"It's quite good," Yelto said. "Don't be shy."

She held her breath and raised the orb to her mouth, hesitating before sinking her teeth into it. Sweet juice filled her mouth, as relieving as it was delicious. Yelto was right: it was quite good. She swallowed, eyeing the fat man and deciding that she was not surprised that he had good taste in food. She placed the rest onto her plate and looked to Tennech expectantly.

The general raised an eyebrow and peered down the table at a plate of what appeared to be an entire goat, head and all, cooked to brown perfection.

"I'll stick to the more, er, traditional fare," he said with a nod. A serving girl hurried over and cut off a piece, then placed it on his plate. Picking up a knife and fork, Tennech cut into it. "Now, Djozen Yelto, may I ask what you would like to discuss?"

The garish Djozen did not bother with a knife or fork. He used his hands to feed himself a piece of meat torn off of a small, cooked bird. "First, you must understand," he said through a mouthful, "that we have no true armies among the tribes. Our warriors are many, and skilled, but they do not fight for a common cause. Most of the time they are making war with each other." He swallowed, and washed it down with a long sip of wine. Tearing off another piece of meat with his hands, he bit off a portion of it. "Which is fine—until you try to get them to do anything."

Sera and the general exchanged wary glances but helped themselves to the collection of food while Yelto talked, piling it onto their plates and sampling the fruits and meats that the servant girls had brought over.

Tennech was finishing the bit of goat when he acknowledged Yelto. "I have a great deal of experience in leading troops," he said, putting down the knife. He reached over to take a sip from his wine. "It's not an easy business."

"Indeed it is not," Yelto said as he wiped his hands on a cloth. "Which is why I think we can help each other."

The general put down his wine and regarded Yelto. "I'm listening," he said.

"What if I told you that I have been waiting for years for you to come along?"

"I would say that I'm sorry you've had to wait so long." Tennech chuckled. "But it surprises me that there is no one like me among your people already."

"Not someone *like* you, General," Yelto corrected. "You in particular."

The general furrowed his brow. "I'm not sure I follow."

"Someone told me that a Dagger would arrive on the backs of two black pillars. That this Dagger would bring with it the Seed of the First City and would deliver this Seed for a price. And," he added, "that his army would scale the mountain to victory."

Tennech tugged on the end of his graying mustache and stared at Yelto, hard. "I would say, then, that this sounds like someone I would very much like to meet."

At these words, Yelto pushed his chair back and stood up. "Excellent," he said. "Because she very much wants to meet you too."

Chapter 57

Gal'dorok,
Outside Haidan Shar

Awaken the Three

Benjin

The army had been marching for a day, but it felt to Benjin like weeks. He'd gone on plenty of marches before, but never any this long; most of the ones he'd been on had lasted a few hours, limited to the outskirts of Haidan Shar. Now, they were far beyond the border of their once-sleepy fishing town.

"How much longer, do you think?" he whispered to Thyst, hoping that the footsteps of the army would prevent any words from reaching the captains leading the formation.

"I don't know, but we have to stop for rest soon," she answered. Adding, "Don't we?"

"No," boomed Captain Jahaz without turning around. "We don't. We march until we're where we need to be."

Benj felt his cheeks flush with embarrassment. He hated to look weak in front of his captain.

Fortunately, Thyst disagreed with Jahaz.

"That seems stupid," she said flatly, taking the heat off of Benj and placing it on herself instead.

This time, Captain Jahaz did turn to look at them.

"Does it now?" he asked. The chainmail coif that he wore over his plated armor allowed him to turn his head just enough to glare at the pair of them. "And I suppose you'd handle it differently if you were queen?"

"I would," Thyst replied. "What's the point of getting somewhere fast if you're exhausted? What if we have to fight right away? Everyone will be thinking about wanting to rest instead of focusing on the battle at hand. Sure, we get there on time, but at what cost?"

Benj could scarcely believe his ears. He gaped at the girl in front of him, barely able to keep his feet moving in time with the rest of the army.

"She makes a damn good point," laughed one of the captains beside Jahaz. The lead captain turned his head to look at him instead.

"Quiet, Zheyo. I don't need you questioning tactics we've used for generations," Jahaz said. Adding, in a sharper tone, "This isn't battle school anymore."

Zheyo chuckled but didn't retort.

Maybe Thyst had the right idea. Maybe it *was* a good thing to question tactics. "That's how we've always done it" didn't seem like a very good reason to keep doing something.

Benj kept that thought to himself. He was just an armiger, for now. Maybe someday, when he proved himself worthy of a commission to be an officer, he could question things, but he had no intention of rocking that boat any sooner than it needed to be rocked.

Thyst clearly saw things differently.

"I think it's perfectly valid," she objected, putting more than a hint of authority in her voice.

Then, to Benj's horror, Captain Jahaz called the entire army to a halt then and there.

So this is how my friend dies, he thought. *Executed in public.*

He suddenly felt the urge to kiss her. Maybe he would die a virgin, but that didn't mean both of them had to.

"What is the meaning of this, Captain?" said Queen Lena from up ahead.

She was striding toward them, massive sword strapped to her back, with its edge trailing above the ground.

"It appears we have some dissenters," Jahaz replied. "Go ahead," he said, turning to Thyst. "Tell her."

Benj couldn't see Thyst's face, but he guessed it was frozen in fear. She wasn't saying anything.

"Go on," Zheyo said. "It's a fine idea."

Thyst stepped out of formation and, with perfect discipline, marched up to the queen and saluted.

"Your Grace," she said. "I questioned the tactic of marching straight there instead of stopping to rest along the way. And I—"

The queen cut her off. "Questioning orders?" she asked. "My orders? You walk a dangerous path, young armiger."

The two of them were standing in front of the army, and Benj had the best view out of anyone. He was right there, and could see every movement and every facial expression. He thought it was curious, then, that the queen didn't look angry.

She looked impressed.

"Tell me," the queen went on, "why you think we should alter our course. And tell me what you would have us do."

"I would have us stop for the night," Thyst said, gesturing to the encroaching dusk. "We have enough men to stand watch with no problem. Have them sleep in shifts. The rest of the army can get the rest they need and be fresh tomorrow when we arrive."

Queen Lena, much to Benj's surprise, smiled.

"I think that's a fine idea. What did you say your name was, young armiger?"

"Thyst—I mean, Amethyst. Your Grace. Amethyst Al'miera."

"Well then, Amethyst, who is your captain?"

"Captain Zheyo," she replied, pointing at him.

The queen shot a look at the now-smiling captain. "Of course. That makes sense. Well," she said, looking back at Thyst. "You and Captain Zheyo are invited to dine with me tonight. And any guests that you see fit to invite. Now," she said, turning to Jahaz, "I believe we have a camp to make."

Jahaz acknowledged her with a salute and barked orders to his men.

This was not at all how Benj had thought the night was going to go.

Chapter 58

Théas

Awaken the Three

Rathma

Rathma sat huddled in the corner of the huge stone cell, convinced that his life could not get any worse. He gagged again at the overwhelming stench of human waste and turned to Yozna, one of the other captives, and asked through the thin cloth of his shemagh, "How can you stand the smell?"

The underground prison they had been transported to was dark and cold, and filled to capacity. There must have been at least fifty other people—all set to be sold at auction. Men in their position cared nothing for hygiene.

"You get used to it," the thin G'henni said with a shrug.

That's how I'll know I've hit rock bottom, Rathma thought. *When the smell of shit doesn't make me sick anymore.*

Yozna had been the only one to acknowledge him when Rathma had been thrown in, and by now the two had managed to trade life stories. The big G'henni had been a well-to-do farmer once, before his youngest daughter fell gravely ill. To pay for her treatment, and for an escort for her into Ellenos, he was forced to start selling off his land. When the debtors came around, though, he found the expenses to be much greater than he had anticipated. He began selling off more and more land to satisfy the debtors, but gradually found himself with no more land to sell. And, with no land to farm for money or food, he had nowhere else to turn; he found himself in chains before the last of his crops were even harvested. Yet he was satisfied in the knowledge that his two daughters were safe, and that his youngest daughter survived.

Rathma admired the man—but he still stank.

They were crammed into a cell with a dozen other men, chains around their wrists, and had simply been told to wait. Wait for what, Rathma knew, but wait for how long was another matter.

"Alef has been in here for a week," Yozna said, nodding to an older man with lighter skin, who looked like he was from up north. "He says he is used to the smell."

Rathma frowned. "I hope it never comes to that." Thinking aloud, he added, "This is the first time in my life I've been held somewhere and not been able to get out. I don't like it."

Yozna laughed, a booming guffaw that shook the walls. "No one does," he said. He leaned nonchalantly against the solid stone of the prison wall, looking less like a slave and more like a man waiting for a drink order. "Do you think we picked this life?"

Rathma looked around the cell to the faces of the other men. They were old, young, dark skinned, light skinned, and somewhere in between. The one thing each of them shared, though—the one thing they all had in common—was the look of defeat on their faces. It couldn't be wiped off, no matter how strong the cloth or how fervent the effort.

"That's not what I meant," Rathma grumbled. He stood up and shook out his shemagh, greatly missing the cloak that Evram had taken. "I just meant that I've always had options before. Always been free to . . ." He waved his hands around vaguely. ". . . go where I want."

Yozna looked down his nose and raised an eyebrow. "Then perhaps you should not have gotten yourself caught," he said.

Rathma glared at the G'henni out of the corner of his eye. "For the last time," he rumbled, "I didn't see them coming."

Yozna chuckled and put his hand on Rathma's shoulder. "Do not be angry at the past," he said. "It is too late to change it. The future is far more worthwhile. There is still time to fix that."

The unmistakable sound of boots on stone, accompanied by a ringing chorus of chains, made Rathma think that he would need to focus on the future sooner than he'd anticipated. He leaned out and peered past the thick iron bars of the cell, down the long corridor that had been suddenly flooded with torchlight. He squinted at the two distant figures. Knowing that nothing good was going to come from that direction, Rathma sank a little when they got closer.

A big Théan man with a ring of keys walked in front of the magistrate. There were five cells, each at capacity, and Rathma wondered just how two men were going to keep all the other slaves under control.

"I am Luzo," the Théan said, "your commander. And you belong to me." There was a low murmur from the slaves, and Luzo glared at them through squinted eyes, daring someone to challenge him; his strong jaw and thickly stubbled face suggested that he was more than capable of backing up any threat he made. "But that's not the reason that you should fear me."

The low chatter from the slaves came to a stop when a man in light-colored robes stepped forward.

"This is Caelus," Luzo said to the silence. "An Athrani." He looked around the cells, as if the word should've had some meaning to all those who heard it. "Do all of you know what an Athrani is?"

There were many nods, but no one said a word.

Rathma, puzzled as to what would make everyone fall so deathly quiet, said, "I don't."

Luzo looked in Rathma's direction, snorted, then looked back to Caelus. "Show him," he said, and he took several steps away from the Athrani.

If Rathma hadn't seen it with his own two eyes, he would have thought that it was another of his grandfather's stories. But right there, in the depths of the near-lightless prison, he saw a man pull fire out of thin air.

Caelus the Athrani held his hands out in front of him, palms facing the ceiling. With a stirring motion, he reached out to grab something; and, as if it were listening, the air grabbed back, catching fire with twin flames that sparked to life from the darkness. Rathma jumped as he watched the flames follow direction, floating above Caelus's hands as he moved them through the air, two tame birds of impossibly bright plumage. Around and around they swirled in a dance of light and heat, showing no signs of dimming or dying, floating like phantom embers in a light-soaked prison. They flared up and shrank down a few times, seeming to grow with every cycle, until the last flare brought them together as a single conflagration. Then Caelus clapped his hands together. The explosion of flame filled the prison in a sudden, scorching surge.

Then it was gone.

The men in the prison remained silent, and Rathma was sure that his gaping was audible.

"That," Luzo said, "is an Athrani, and that is what they can do. So if you value your life or simply dislike having your flesh burnt off, I suggest you do what we say. And that is why you should fear me." He rattled a length of chain and glared up and down the corridor of the prison. "Any questions?"

The profound silence matched Rathma's confusion. *How could he do that?* he wondered. *That shouldn't be possible. Those flames were real! With someone like him on our side, we might stand a chance against Yelto . . .*

His cell door swung open.

Luzo looked inside and yelled, "Now get moving! There's money to be made!"

Chapter 59

Théas

Awaken the Three

Alysana

Alysana awoke before everyone else, more out of habit and less out of obligation.

During her sentry training in Annoch, she had always been up earlier than the others because she liked to have the advantage. It gave her a head start on the day, and she found that it presented a psychological edge as well: everyone else would struggle to catch up to her, and it made them see her as the one who was always looking back at them. That suited her just fine. She was willing to work extra hard to make sure she got what she wanted.

She still had to find her way to the magistrate in order to get the necessary paperwork for the slave auction, but that was not what was on her mind at present. Instead, she was thinking about how close Thornton had come to leaving them. She had always thought of him as trustworthy and loyal before this. Now, she wasn't sure how to think of him. As she slipped through the door and closed it gently behind her, she shook her head to rid it of the thoughts. *One day at a time*, she told herself.

***

Théas was covered with a thin morning fog that poured into the streets, wrapping up the buildings and people in its pale embrace. It was not so thick as to conceal everything around it, but for someone like Alysana who was not familiar with the city, it may as well have been. She ended up relying on the directions of several Théans despite not having far to go. Finally, after more walking than it should have taken, the building she was looking for was within view.

There were only a few hours left before the auction started, and she would have to hurry if she had any hope of bidding on the Farstepper that would supposedly be making an appearance. And, in order to participate in the auction, she had to bring something to the table as well. She didn't like doing it, but it was necessary. Shoving Dailus inside, she hoped that things would work themselves out. She had not discussed it with anyone else, but as far as she saw things, Dailus was hers to bargain away as she deemed necessary—and this was necessary. He was their best and only bargaining chip. If everything went as planned, she would simply buy him back at the end of the auction.

The doorman downstairs had instructed her to go up to see the magistrate. When she opened the door to his office, he was standing with his back to her. When he turned to greet her, the blood froze in her veins.

It had been nearly fifteen years, but Alysana would never forget that face; it was etched into her memory along with its cold, calculating eyes and the chill of deceit.

She knew this man.

"A fellow G'henni!" he said with enthusiasm. "I am always pleased to see my people on the right end of this business." He made a quick and graceful bow. "I am the magistrate, as you no doubt have gathered. Your humble servant, Ghaja Rus."

Hearing the name again made Alysana's blood boil. She knew she should say something, but no words would form on her tongue. The most she could do was nod, as the rest of her strength went toward keeping her composure—and resisting the temptation to leap across the room and slit his throat.

"A quiet one," Rus added after the prolonged silence. "A rare trait among our people, but one that is not without its merits. Come," he said, waving her in. "Let me see what you've brought."

Here, Alysana at least had the presence of mind to push Dailus forward. The half-eye's hands were still bound in order to incapacitate his Shaping, and there was a gag in his mouth. To prevent him from saying something that would jeopardize the operation, Alysana had him drugged on top of all that, making the Athrani sway more than willow branches in the breeze.

Ghaja Rus approached Dailus and circled him, looking him up and down the way a winemaker would look at a vine of grapes. He made a few grunts of approval, as well as a few "hmm"s of curiosity. He picked up Dailus's arm and let it drop to his side. He measured the thickness of his legs. He pushed him to test his balance, which almost ended poorly. Finally, he stared into his eyes.

"I have to admit," Rus said after a long while, "we do not get many Athrani, and the ones that we do get do not fetch a very high price. They tend to shy away from labor, and often the risk of flight is too high for the investment." He felt Dailus's arm again. Turning to Alysana, he said, "But this one looks like no stranger to a day's work. I suppose we can work something out. How does fifteen coppers sound?"

"Twenty," Alysana countered automatically.

"Silent but for when it matters," Ghaja Rus said with a smile. "Very well, twenty coppers. My man downstairs will give you what you are owed." He went over to an oaken desk in the corner of the room and pulled out a piece of parchment. On it he scrawled the sale price; then he dripped a bit of red wax onto the paper, pressing his seal into it to make it official. "This will get you your payment and grant you entrance to the auction," he said as he walked back. "Do not lose it. I am not fond of making more work for myself."

Alysana nodded curtly and took the piece of paper, turning to leave.

"I do have one question," Rus said before she could leave.

Alysana froze in her tracks, not wanting to take her eyes off the door that would take her outside and away from this wretched excuse for a man. She felt him coming closer, could hear his breathing as he approached—like listening to a wolf stalking a deer in the forest.

The brief thought that Rus had recognized her flickered through her mind. Without her consciously making it do so, Alysana's right hand began to creep toward her dagger. She could feel her fingers on the hilt. Rus was close enough now that a quick, fluid movement would have been enough to plunge the blade into his neck, erasing decades of torment in a single, bloody act of revenge.

One swift move. That's all it would take . . .

"It is rare that I see such a pretty face around here. Especially one that reminds me of my home in G'hen." He had snaked his way in front of Alysana and now stood between her and escape. With a bow, slow and refined, he extended his hand to her. "Will I see your face again? Apart from the auction, of course."

Her hand relaxed, moving subtly off of the dagger and into his open, waiting palm. She nodded, and felt his fingers wrap around her like a constrictor feeling out its prey. Cringing, she closed her eyes as she felt his lips touch the back of her hand.

"In that case, it was a pleasure doing business with you, O silent stranger. I hope it will be the first of many pleasures," Rus said in a sensual whisper, letting her hand drop to her side.

Alysana, deciding that the silent approach was working so far, did not offer a response. She was also afraid that the bile creeping up her throat might give away her revulsion by loosing itself over Rus's finely finished floor. Instead, she kept quiet.

With a look of mysterious indifference, she left the way she'd come in.

***

She managed to make it a whole three steps onto the streets of Théas before emptying the contents of her stomach onto the hard gray stone. Wiping her mouth, she stared up at the office of the magistrate. Opportunities like this did not just present themselves every day, but when they did, one tended to do everything possible to take advantage.

Suddenly Alysana felt very good about all the training that Mordha had made her go through. She smiled as she stared down at the dagger that had made its way into her life all those years ago, and knew that, finally, it would serve the purpose she had always known it would.

Waking up early has once again paid off, she thought with a wry smile.

Turning, she walked through the thickening fog, down the streets of Théas, and toward the inn. There was much to do and much to plan. It was not every day that the chance for revenge fell into her lap.

Chapter 60

Nest of the Xua'al

Awaken the Three

Kunas

The moment that the four of them stepped into the cave, the smell hit.

"Breaker's balls," choked Captain Hunt as he covered his face with his hand. "What is that?"

It was like being splashed in the face with sulfur, and Kunas nearly gagged.

"Chovathi," Ohlez said, his words muffled by a cloth shemagh he'd put over his mouth and nose. "Awful things. Don't bathe much."

Kunas wasn't sure that hygiene had anything to do with the over-powering stench that filled the cave; he thought it had more to do with how many Chovathi were gathered inside. Before he could voice his opinion, though, their guide growled at them from up ahead.

"Quiet," Khaz said. "No talk. Follow."

Though the sunlight waned outside, being inside the cave made it seem as if night had fallen hours ago. It was as dark as a Gwarái's scales, and Khaz was leading them deeper into the heart of the nest, only stopping when they lagged behind. Once, Captain Hunt had mumbled something about not wanting to be there, and Khaz had rumbled a second warning about being quiet. The rest of the way was spent in silence.

Khaz

Zhala had been in his mind ever since they'd set foot in the cave, and he could feel her distrust of the humans. The two of them had been conversing back and forth in his mind, and he had found himself having to quiet the humans at least twice now. He couldn't pay attention to them and Zhala at the same time, and it would just be easier to make them be quiet.

I do not like them being here, Khaz, his matriarch said. *The nest is sacred. No one from the outside has ever seen it—never should see it.*

Need to show trust, Khaz retorted, *and humans can help us.*

He felt Zhala agree, but the feeling of her discomfort did not change. There were still strangers in her home, and she was unlikely to change her opinion of them anytime soon. So he kept walking, kept moving toward the center of their cave where the heart of the brood lay.

Theirs, the Xua'al, was large by most standards: Zhala, their brood matriarch, controlled the six broodmothers, who in turn controlled hundreds of broodlings beneath them, warriors and scouts alike. It was the broodmothers that were the real strength of the Chovathi race: they were the ones who could be torn limb from limb to make new, viable Chovathi whenever they were needed. Any other Chovathi created from the sundered limbs of another would not live more than a day—long enough to be useful in escaping combat, but they would simply wither and return to the earth before long. It was the Chovathi born of the broodmothers that had lives of their own. So, while warriors like Khaz had their roles, it was the broodmothers that helped the clan thrive and the matriarch who kept them alive. Neither he nor Zhala knew if the humans knew that, but he did share his matriarch's concern for the clan just from letting them in. But if it came down to it, Khaz knew that the secret he held inside of him would keep his clan safe, or at least ensure their survival. As long as one of them remained, the Xua'al would live on.

Yet, as they walked into the expansive heart at the center of their cave, he only felt Zhala's unease grow. Each of them could sense that there was danger, but there was simply no way to tell where it was coming from—or when.

Kunas

The deeper in they got, the stronger the smell became; it seemed to thrive in the darkness somehow. Hunt had already stopped to retch twice on the way in, and was now doubled over to share some of the contents of his stomach with the cave's floor. Ohlez had tightened his shemagh again, and both Jerol and Kunas had tied cloths to their faces to try to block the smell.

"I can't take this anymore," a frustrated Hunt said as he wiped his mouth.

"Then do something about it," said Jerol, motioning to the cloth that hung down below his armor. "You've got a knife."

"I'd rather plunge it into my neck at this point," Hunt said, doing his best not to choke again.

Khaz was a good deal ahead of them, and Kunas wondered why he wasn't immediately chastising them for talking again.

Then he saw it.

The Chovathi had stopped at the end of a corridor ahead of them, his outline barely visible in the darkness of the cave. On either side of him were stalagmites jutting up from the floor, getting taller as they moved away. As Kunas got closer, he could see that there were stalactites on the ceiling high above that did the same. It was almost as if they were a set of giant jaws, large enough to swallow an entire army of men in a single bite. He paused to consider that that was just what it might have been, and he stopped walking as a hollow feeling grew inside of him. The firm hand of Captain Ohlez broke him out of his trance.

"The faster we get there," the G'henni said, "the faster we can leave."

Kunas couldn't argue with the logic. He didn't like being around the Chovathi any more than he had to, especially enclosed in a cave with no easy exit. He walked on to join their Chovathi guide, standing on a ledge that jutted out from the cave wall, opening into a vast, rocky chamber.

The chamber was dimly lit by phosphorescent plants, giving off an eerie blue glow and allowing Kunas to see around. Looking up, he suddenly wished that were not the case, because nothing could have prepared him for the sight before him when he stepped into the heart of the nest.

For there, on the far wall of the cave, was an *impossibly* huge Chovathi.

A Chovathi that seemed to be growing out of the rock itself.

Chapter 61

Théas

Awaken the Three

Alysana

The men were led in chains and defeat.

Alysana watched the rows of ragged, tired individuals as they were prodded and forced into the center of the market square. They walked in a line, with their hands clapped in iron shackles, but their feet free. Arranged with the taller and stronger men toward the front and the weaker and shorter men toward the rear, they numbered in the dozens and looked to come from just about every background. Alysana's eyes widened when, toward the back of the line, she saw that there were children in chains as well. She knew beyond a shadow of a doubt that the men who had captured these children were the same ones who had tried to take her and her sister all those years ago, thanks to Ghaja Rus.

Her rage rose at the thought. From the corner of her eye she saw Thornton scowl, undoubtedly feeling the same.

Under his breath the blacksmith muttered, "The sooner we can get out of here, the better."

They had decided, back at the inn, that Thornton would be the one to accompany her to the auction. Ghaja Rus had seen her face and would recognize her if he was in attendance. It would be highly unusual for her to bid on the slave that she'd sold, she reasoned, but not surprising at all for a Khyth to want to walk away with an Athrani prize, even if that prize was a half-eye.

"I do not like this any more than you do," she conceded. "But that Farstepper will be beyond useful to us where we are going."

While they waited for the slaves to finish shuffling into place, Alysana looked around at the City of a Thousand Towers and grudgingly admitted that she was impressed. The market area of Théas was massive, and the city seemed to have been built around it; white, towering buildings crowded together like naked trees in a forest of stone.

The brickwork in the market area was exquisite, with repeating diamond patterns on the ground that drew the eye and clearly delineated this part of the city from the rest. Like an ornate throne room, it was apparent that this was the gem in the crown of Théas. A massive slab of limestone was the centerpiece of the market area, which had stairs carved into its sides, making it look like a stage. The more she studied it, though, the more Alysana realized exactly what it was. *Little surprise*, she thought with a frown: Théan prosperity was built on the backs of slaves.

The auction area was just one part of the sprawling marketplace, yet it was the center in every sense. The shops and surrounding buildings formed a circle around it that was wide enough for a few hundred people to crowd into. Access to the auction area was made by one of five avenues: the first, to the north, was where the slaves had come from; the second entrance was by way of a wide alley that came from the east, eventually leading to the eastern gate of the city; the remaining three entrances led west, southwest, and south.

As Alysana looked up and down the faces of the men and boys who had been herded in, she saw none of the telltale signs of a Farstepper: red hair and red eyes, the hallmark of men born with a power that few understood. She turned to Thornton and whispered, "If he's here, I don't see him."

Thornton squinted, scanning the crowd of slaves. "Maybe he's in the back," he mumbled absently.

The slaves had lined up behind the limestone stage, standing precisely in five rows of ten columns, neatly equaling the width of the stage itself. *Military precision*, Alysana noted. *No doubt for the benefit of the buyers to show they can take orders.*

As the crowd of a few hundred settled down, Alysana touched the coins in her purse that she had made from selling off the horses earlier—a necessity if they had any hope of purchasing the Farstepper. But as she scanned the faces of the slaves one more time, she realized there was another thing missing: Dailus.

"Our first specimen," came a voice from the front corner of the stage, that of a tall, thin man in fine clothing, "is a raider from the frozen lands of Hjorl." Standing by the auctioneer was a thick G'henni whom Alysana recognized as Rus's doorman. "We will begin the bidding at one silver piece."

In the center of the stage stood a tall, handsome man in worn leather armor and furs. Alysana gaped as she found herself thinking, *This man is a slave?* He was well muscled and surprisingly good looking. He had a chiseled jaw, and his light hair and skin, along with the blood he shared with the people of Hjorl, meant that he was as hard and tough as a block of solid ice.

The surprise on her face must have shown more than she realized, and she was startled by the smooth, deep voice of the man beside her. "They always start with the best ones first," he said. She turned her head to see an older man in a fur-trimmed velvet cloak over a dark shirt with golden embroidery. His white hair retained only the slightest whispers of the black that it clearly once had. "By the time they get to the smaller ones, the weaker ones, the men who can afford them are among the few still bidding." With a hint of disdain he added, "Only the most desperate of men would pay for a child."

Alysana smiled a thin smile and turned her head to face the man. "What makes you think I didn't already know that?" she asked coyly.

"Well, for one, I've never seen you before," he said as he smiled at her. "And I would definitely remember seeing you." He bowed and took her hand in his, kissing it softly as he looked her in the eye. "Connus, at your service."

"Alysana," she answered with a flush. Looking at him, she could tell he had been handsome in his youth, with his dark eyebrows framing a pair of piercing brown eyes that bored deeply into her own. She felt her knees tremble a bit as his charm caught her off guard and drew her in; she had never been happier that her dark G'henni features hid her blushing so well. "Pleased to meet you." She quickly slipped her hand from his and turned away before any further damage was done.

"One silver piece," Connus said loudly, raising a finger in the air but still looking at Alysana.

"We have one silver," replied the auctioneer, as he acknowledged him with a nod.

Connus leaned over to her. "This one must have been caught in a border clash," he said, nodding to the slave on the auction block. "The Hjoruns rarely make their way this far south. They content themselves to raiding Ellenos, or even Annoch, but mostly stay to the Kvenni tundra north of Derenar."

"Two silvers," said a man from deeper in the crowd. The auctioneer echoed his call.

"Three," said another.

"Four," said Connus. And to Alysana, he said, "Life in the north makes them hardy and unyielding. Most of them are bred as warriors and hunters, and they know their way around skinning an animal. Very useful protecting a caravan or"—he lowered his voice—"as assassins."

Alysana stiffened and looked at the cold, blue eyes of the man on the auction block. He seemed indifferent, as if he cared little that he was being bid on, or even who won. *Unyielding indeed*, she thought.

"Five," said one of the previous bidders. He looked dark and unscrupulous, and Alysana wouldn't have been surprised if he intended to use the northerner as a hired blade.

A few of them went back and forth, with more men dropping out when the bidding reached ten silver pieces. It slowed to a trickle, and eventually the old man beside her, Connus, made the winning bid of eighteen pieces of silver. He seemed pleased, and expressed as much in a grunt of satisfaction.

"Well worth the price," Connus said as he leaned over to her again. His deep voice sent a pleasant shiver down Alysana's spine. She smiled thinly and felt her purse again. They had gotten a good deal on the horses: three gold pieces for all nine. The other three horses they had kept for the ride through the Wastes. *If eighteen silvers is what it takes to win the best of the lot*, she thought, *I should have enough to buy back Dailus.*

But the auction continued, longer and longer, with no sign of the Athrani half-eye or the Farstepper. She began to grow nervous when the number of slaves dwindled to a handful and there was no sign of either of the prizes, prizes she thought would have surely come toward the front.

Maybe they keep them in a separate waiting area, she thought with uncertainty.

"You haven't bid yet," Connus said to her, interrupting her thoughts. "Are you waiting for something in particular?" Looking at her dress and eyeing her purse slyly, he added, "These have all been good choices. I doubt you're waiting for the end to see the cheaper ones."

Alysana shifted uncomfortably and kept her eyes on the auction block. "Perhaps," she said stiffly. "I heard there was a Farstepper."

"Ahh," Connus said knowingly as he tapped his temple. "Then you will certainly want to stay 'til the very end."

"Oh? What comes then?"

Connus simply smiled and turned his attention back to the stage. "You'll see, if you're lucky."

Alysana turned to Thornton, who had been silent for most of the auction, and gave him a puzzled look.

"Don't look at me," he said. "You're the one who's from here."

"I am not *from here*," she corrected. "And I do not think I would be so quick to claim it if I was."

As the bidding died down and most of the crowd dispersed, Alysana looked around. Despite what Connus had said, about the men who would wait for the end being the poorer and desperate, what she saw intrigued her. Most of the men left in the crowd, about a dozen, wore fine clothes and had been some of the more active bidders.

"Connus," she said, getting the attention of the older man.

"Yes, my dear?" he asked in his smooth baritone.

"I thought you said only the most desperate men would remain."

"I said only the most desperate would pay for a child." He nodded at the G'henni man, who had caught his eye. The G'henni nodded back as the last slave, a young boy born a slave according to the auctioneer, was sold off. The G'henni stepped off the stage and approached Connus, bowing slightly.

"Connus, yours is always a welcome face at the auction."

"Yuta, I trust Magistrate Rus is well," Connus responded, nodding in return.

"He is, and he requests that you join him for the private auction afterward."

"Of course. You know I can never turn one down."

Alysana was surprised at the exchange, but more surprising was when Yuta turned to her and said, "And he would very much like to see you there as well, my lady."

Chapter 62

Gal'dorok,
Outside Haidan Shar

Awaken the Three

Benjin

"Come in," said Queen Lena from inside her tent. Benj couldn't remember the last time he'd felt so nervous.

"Go on," Jahaz whispered, urging him toward the tent. "She means you."

Benj turned to look at Thyst, who was wearing the same simple clothes she'd had on under her leather armiger battle armor. They were all dressed plainly tonight, and it almost seemed odd to be going to see the queen dressed as such. But when the two of them stepped forward and opened the flaps to the spacious tent, Benj felt a sense of relief to see that the queen was dressed equally informally. She wore a dress in the colors of Haidan Shar—blue with white frills—that, while remaining plain and unadorned, still looked elegant on her.

And then he looked inside.

He had not expected luxury like this in the wilds of Gal'dorok. Glancing around, Benj realized that these hastily made and entirely mobile quarters were larger than his entire home back in the Flats; there was enough room to fit fifty men inside, comfortably.

"Thith ith amathing," Shotes whispered from behind.

Benj smiled. He had to agree: it *was* amazing.

There was a brazier in the middle with a crackling fire, big enough to fill the tent with warmth; there was an enormous bed with opulent covers; a table with maps and various papers strewn about; and a long dining table, with chairs and place settings all meticulously arranged.

Benj had never seen anything like it; he'd never even realized something like this was possible. Since he'd never been invited to dine with the queen before, he'd never had any reason to picture how she dined. He could only imagine what the dining hall in her castle looked like.

"Ah," Queen Lena said, standing by the fire and warming her hands. With a smile and a turn of her head to Thyst she added, "So you do know how to follow orders."

The captains behind her chuckled.

"Yes, Your Grace." Thyst blushed.

"Please," the queen said, beckoning them inside, "come in. You're letting all the warm air out."

Benj and Thyst did as they were asked, with Shotes and the three captains following them in.

"Tonight, you will dine with me," the queen said. "While I do not tolerate the questioning of orders, I can appreciate the questioning of tradition, especially when it comes to military practice."

Zheyo, the last to step in, cleared his throat. "I suppose that is my fault, Your Grace. The girl most certainly learned it from me."

"And why," the queen asked with a smile, "does that not surprise me?"

"You are who you train with," Zheyo replied with a polite shrug.

Queen Lena laughed at this. "Indeed. Now, there will be plenty of time to talk while we eat. There's no reason we can't do both."

The queen moved from her place by the fire and walked toward the table, where one of her accompanying servants pulled out the chair for her.

"Please sit," she said to them, motioning to the empty chairs. They each did as they were asked, armigers sitting next to their captains, with the queen at the head of the table. "I've waited long enough for food today," she said with a hint of exhaustion.

With those words, the servants around them lifted the silver domes atop the serving platters to reveal a feast that made Benj's stomach growl. Steam rose from the meats and vegetables that were spread over the table, and Benj swore that the Shaper Herself would have dined like this too. The sounds of cutting meat and the clanking of cutlery soon filled the tent.

Queen Lena was cutting into a piece of quail on her plate when Jahaz spoke up.

"Your Grace," he began, "while we are on the topic of questioning things, if I may be so bold . . ." He looked at her expectantly. When she nodded, he continued: "Is there a reason we departed before your uncle returned?"

Queen Lena put down her fork, looked at him, and smiled. "While the men that Connus seeks to acquire from Théas will certainly prove useful, I did not judge them to be so critical as to wait for them to arrive. I don't believe that they would turn the tide of this battle, but that may not be the case in future ordeals."

Jahaz, seeming satisfied with that answer, smiled and bowed his head. "Thank you for indulging me, Your Grace."

The queen waved him off, her mouth already full with another bite of her quail.

Benj smiled to himself. He liked her; she didn't seem so intimidating here. In fact, he would hasten to call her friendly—although he would never say that out loud.

"As for you, young lady," the queen said, pointing her fork at Thyst, "I'd like to hear some more about what's rattling around in that head of yours."

Thyst beamed and sat up straighter. "Really?"

"Really. It's part of why I asked you here tonight."

Thyst looked at Zheyo for permission, much to his and Benj's surprise, but the captain nodded, as if to say, *Obviously.*

"Well, Your Grace," Thyst began, "I've studied the practices of the Athrani Legion, and I think they have some merit to them."

"Such as?"

"Such as the idea of granting citizenship to those who volunteer for the army."

Queen Lena swallowed her bite and looked at the captains at the table, who each gave a contemplative shrug.

"It's not a terrible idea," said Jahaz.

"We already employ hirelings and mercenaries," said Shotes's captain, Ardwynn. She glanced at the other captains as she added, "At least it would command some sort of loyalty from them besides cold, hard coin."

Queen Lena seemed to be considering this. "It certainly has its merits," she admitted. "I'll think about it. Thank you, Amethyst."

"Of course, Your Grace," Thyst said with a bow of her head.

"But the most important question I have for all of you tonight," the queen said after a healthy drink from her wine goblet, "is this." She let the silence fill the room so that only the crackling of the fire could be heard. "Do we come away from this battle allowing any Chovathi to live at all?"

She placed down her goblet and looked at them all expectantly.

Their answers, like the sun at night, were simply nowhere to be found.

Chapter 63

The Wastes of Khulakorum

Awaken the Three

Sivulu

Yelto's stronghold was now in view, and Sivulu, sprinting swiftly ahead on his four legs, signaled the men to a halt. Changing back into his human form, he turned to address them, and could spot immediately the ones who were not used to being around a Wolfwalker: they averted their eyes from him as though his power was unnerving. But Sivulu knew that another aspect of him was making them equally uncomfortable, as a light desert breeze swept over his naked body.

Wolfwalkers, who spent a good part of their lives wearing nothing but the fur on their bodies, were not bothered by nudity the way some of the other tribes were. And for those who lived, worked, or traded with Wolfwalkers, the naked human form was not such a shocking thing. There were some, however, who regarded bare flesh as sacred and intimate, only to be revealed to a lover in the heat of passion. Sivulu did not understand such a mentality and was not bothered by a few men looking away uncomfortably; he would be back in his second skin soon enough. He smiled to himself and addressed the multitude.

"You all know why we are here and what we aim to accomplish," he said loudly, sweeping his gaze over the mighty collection of men. They were hundreds in number, warriors through and through. He hoped it would be enough. "Thanks to intelligence gathered by my brother, Kuu, we now know where Yelto keeps his prison. We also know that it is well guarded. But lastly, and most importantly, we know where Yelto keeps the Wolfblade."

The men were silent, but a few dozen of them gave knowing nods.

"Hedjetti," Sivulu called out. "To me."

At his beckoning, four large men from four different tribes stepped forward and approached him. As the Hedjetti of their respective tribes, each man had earned a place of respect by displaying traits of strength, ferocity, and leadership. Each tribe handled it differently, but all of them shared one thing in common: the old Hedjetti all died by the hands of the new ones. Therefore, each of them knew what it meant to take a life, and each of them respected death. They knew that their deaths would come too, perhaps in battle or at the hands of a new Hedjetten. But each of these experiences had chiseled them into formidable warriors, warriors that Sivulu knew would be indispensable in the battle for the Wolfblade. And the Hedjetti that stood before him now—from the tribes of the Ohmati, Qozhen, Khuufi, and Elteri—were four of the best.

They gathered around him in a semicircle as he went over the plan one more time.

"Jotun and Garus, you will lead the assault on the western wall with the Qozhen and Elteri. Hroth and Uzma, you take the east with the Kuufi and Ohmati."

Each man nodded as his tribe was named.

"The Wolfwalkers," Siv went on, "will divide themselves between the two forces to fight our way to the center of the stronghold. There, I will use this"—he held up the leather pouch around his neck, which held the key that Kuu had stolen—"to make my way inside."

Hroth of the Ohmati stepped forward. "My men have heard that a Priest of the Holder fights for Yelto," he said. The tall Hedjetten wore his dark, braided hair in rows that hung past his shoulders. On the ends of several of the braids were white beads, one for each kill he had made in defense of his tribe. Sivulu counted at least twenty.

"Your men have heard right," Siv answered with a frown.

"Then this will be a bloodbath," Hroth said darkly.

"Perhaps. But our aim is not to kill them off. Our aim is to get inside."

"And then?" asked Jotun of the Elteri. His scalp and face were bald, making the red streaks of war paint that much more grotesque.

"Leave that to me," Sivulu replied.

The answer seemed to satisfy the Hedjetten, but Sivulu wasn't worried about appeasing him. He looked to his left, where the sun was completing its journey across the sky of the Traveler and giving way to the night sky of the Holder. An assault under His watchful eye would have been considered suicide if not for the endgame that Sivulu had in sight.

He turned his eyes back to the stronghold of Djozen Yelto, where the Mother of Wolves waited. She was the key, he knew, to setting Sivulu's people free once and for all.

Do'baradai, Yelto, and the Holder all waited. He hoped they would not have to wait too long.

Chapter 64

Théas

Rathma

The three of them were marched, single file, into a spacious and well-decorated room, the likes of which Rathma had only seen in Djozen Yelto's stronghold in Khadje Kholam. If his bearings were right, they were still underground, and the lack of windows certainly seemed to reinforce that notion.

At the center of the empty room, standing waist-high, was a platform of marble, with eight thin pillars spaced evenly about its circumference. Ten men could comfortably stand shoulder to shoulder across its diameter, and Rathma figured it to be the platform on which they would be displayed. *Better than the prison cell,* he thought dourly.

Alongside Rathma stood two other men who had been set aside during the initial gathering of prisoners. One of them had been in the cell that Rathma had been kept in: Habrak the Stoneborn, whose people were as reclusive as they were powerful. Rathma had never heard of them, but the whispers of the other men in the cell told him that the Stoneborn were revered as mighty warriors, with none being their equal. The other one Rathma didn't know, but if he and Habrak were any indication, he was probably not to be trifled with. A glance at the heavy wrist and ankle manacles was enough to confirm his suspicion.

"Alright," said Luzo. "Listen up, you maggots. This is where you prove your worth. For one reason or another, you've been selected above the others to have some sort of . . . intrinsic value. And that value translates to more coin for us." He paused, grinning. "And we like coin."

There was a rumbling of laughter from the guards behind him.

"So that means, be on your best behavior. Or"—he glanced back to Caelus the Athrani—"you'll have to answer to him."

Rathma didn't know exactly how he would have to answer, but he didn't want to find out.

Just then, from a corridor off to the side, echoed the voice of the man called Ghaja Rus. ". . . are sure that you'll be pleased at the selection we have for you. My men have combed the lands, far and wide, to find the best and most valuable individuals for your approval."

His voice was coming closer, and it sounded like he was being followed by at least a half dozen people, if the echoes of their footfalls were to be trusted.

Ghaja Rus, the man who was more snake than human, had apparently found some people willing to pay a little extra for the most dangerous of beasts—man.

But, as the footsteps came closer and their owners trickled into the room, Rathma's heart nearly stopped in his chest when he saw what stepped in.

"In here?" a female voice asked. "I was not expecting something so extravagant."

The rest of the world faded from view as a tall, dark-haired woman with skin of deep chestnut and lips of scarlet wandered in, eyes hiding behind thick lashes that looked too long to be real. The dress she wore, snow white and formfitting, kept no secrets about what was hidden beneath.

Cold embrace of the Holder, Rathma swore. *She's amazing.* He was certain that the rest of the room could hear his heart thudding against his chest.

"The lady has fine taste," Rus crooned.

I bet she does, Rathma thought. He was barely conscious of anyone else in the room when the low growling of Luzo snapped him back.

"Remember what I told you," the Théan rumbled, pressing the wood of his cudgel into the small of Rathma's back. His voice was barely above a whisper, but somehow it still shook Rathma like the growl of a desert wolf. He could feel the man's breath on the back of his neck.

Ghaja Rus continued to direct them inside. "Right this way," he said with a smile and a bow as the last of the patrons filed into the room. There were only a handful of them, but each was dressed like he or she could buy the city of Théas and still have gold to spare. Most of them looked old enough to be one of Rathma's grandparents, including an olive-skinned woman near the back whose silver hair matched her low-cut dress. If she hadn't been so elegantly dressed, Rathma would have thought that she had also come from beyond the Wastes. She had a sharp air of indignation that suggested that she was too good for the room and was losing money just by standing in it.

"I expect this lot to be better than the last pile of garbage you tried to peddle to us, Rus," she said in a confident lilt—and, Rathma noted, a hint of a Khôl accent.

"Yes of course, Lady Elana," Rus answered with a bow. "I assure you that you will be pleased."

By now the three slaves had been isolated on the circular stage, with Luzo lurking behind them. Rathma felt the eyes of the room fall upon him.

"Ladies and gentlemen," Rus belted out with bravado, "I present to you the auction to end all auctions. The finest spoils that Derenar and Gal'dorok have to offer—and beyond."

A hush fell over the well-dressed patrons as they did their best to not look impressed. Rathma's eyes were still on the dark-haired woman near the back, who looked as surprised as if she'd just seen a ghost.

"Our first item," Rus continued, "was brought to us from the fields of Dal'amir. A Stoneborn, whose people are as unbreakable as the rocks from which they take their name. Luzo, show them," he said as he nodded to the Théan.

From behind him, Rathma heard the sound of steel hissing against leather—a sword coming free—and he looked to his right, where Habrak was standing. As Luzo swung the well-sharpened blade right for Habrak's neck, Rathma let out a shout of warning; but by the time the yell left his lips, the blade had found its mark. The blow was strong enough to slice his head clean off, biting through bone and flying through flesh like a breeze in an orchard.

Or at least it should have been. The blade caught in Habrak's neck like an ax in a tree stump, and Rathma had to blink his eyes a few times to make sure he wasn't seeing things.

"The Stoneborn," Rus said loudly, "make excellent soldiers due to their . . . unique physiology."

Habrak reached up and pulled the sword out of his neck as if he were picking off a hangnail.

"They do not bleed like we do, and their tolerance for pain is unparalleled."

Rathma stared, jaw agape, at a man who looked perfectly human, save for his gray eyes. "What are you?" he whispered.

Habrak merely grinned.

"Five silver pieces," came the first bid. It was Lady Elana, standing rigid and proud.

"Six," came an immediate counter from an older man standing next to her, streaks of black in his graying hair and beard.

Ghaja Rus smiled as the two of them went back and forth, squabbling over the seemingly unkillable soldier standing before them.

A third man chimed in, gaunt but refined, and raised the price by a staggering amount. Each of them topped the others until the man with the black and gray hair finally won out, a smug smile gracing his face.

"Habrak the Stoneborn goes to Connus for two gold pieces," Rus announced. "And I'm sure he will use him well."

Knowing laughter spread among the patrons, as well as from Luzo. Rathma shifted in his chains uncomfortably.

"Next up," Rus continued, "is a specimen from Ellenos."

When hushed murmurs of excitement permeated the air, Rathma looked over to the man he didn't recognize, wearing night-black robes, and watched as he stepped forward.

"No doubt many of you are familiar with the power of the Athrani," Rus went on. "This one is a half-eye: born of an Athrani father and a human mother, with all the power of the Athrani"—he turned to address the crowd—"and all the stubbornness of a human."

There was reserved laughter from the patrons at this joke, though Rathma did not grasp the humor.

"May we examine him?" Lady Elana asked.

"Yes, of course," said Rus, stepping out of the way with a flourish.

A number of them approached the marble circle, eyes fixed on the one they called "half-eye."

It's like they're looking at a piece of meat, Rathma though incredulously. They poked and prodded, taking his chin in their hands and squeezing, looking at his teeth and his muscle tone, his hair and his eyes.

"So he can Shape?" asked one of the men.

"He can," Rus replied.

"And we are supposed to just take your word for it?" Lady Elana quipped, much to the delight of the other patrons.

"My word is worth more than the Stoneborn and the half-eye combined," Rus retorted. Apparently Lady Elana had ruffled his feathers. "But for you, my lady, and for the sake of the man you represent, I shall offer proof."

With a nod to Luzo, Rus had the shackles removed from the half-eye. The black-robed Athrani stood there looking confused for a moment before Rus said, "Go on then, show them a little something."

Before Rathma could blink, the Athrani had turned the marble pillars around them into liquid water with no more effort than it took to exhale. The splash from the spontaneous waterfalls drenched everyone as it fell, loud and heavy, and made its way off the platform. Gasps filled the room as Luzo scrambled to clamp the shackles on the half-eye again, but the performance had its intended effect.

"Ten silver pieces," said Connus, dripping wet.

"Twelve," countered Elana, who was wringing out her hair.

"Sixteen," came a silky voice from behind them. Rathma's eyes immediately went to the young, dark-haired woman who was tying her hair back, and he found himself unsurprised that such a lovely voice had come from so entrancing a source. He tried to control his gaze when he noticed her wet dress.

"Eighteen," said Connus, who was promptly elbowed in the ribs by the lovely young newcomer.

"Two gold pieces," she said, and stared defiantly at Connus.

"Four," said Lady Elana.

Rathma could see that the young woman was thinking about it. She looked down at her purse.

"Whatever you have in there," Lady Elana said, "I assure you that I have more."

The young woman's shoulders sagged in apparent defeat. She looked up to the half-eye and back to her purse—and then, inexplicably, at Rathma. He could feel the red in his cheeks as they burned with embarrassment. He quickly looked at the floor.

Rus waited a few beats before awarding the Athrani to Lady Elana.

She nodded her approval to the young woman. "A wise decision," she said under her breath. Turning to the Athrani, she smiled and said, "Have my men escort him out and ready a horse. He'll do just fine."

"And now," Rus boomed, "our final item for the day. A treasure from beyond the Wastes, an ancient legend come to life. Some say that they are descended from the Traveler himself, imbued with the power to walk in and out of the Otherworld at will. A being so elusive that, rumor has it, they can only be killed by one of their own. Ladies and gentlemen, I present to you . . . *a Farstepper.*"

Rathma had been prepared for many things, but silence was not among them. He was suddenly very conscious of his red eyes, and felt the flush on his cheeks that no doubt matched his hair. But it would not last long, as he was suddenly pulled back to the present by the demanding voice of Lady Elana.

"Horseshit," she said, to the amusement of everyone around her. "The Athrani was one thing, Rus, but I will not accept this man as a Farstepper just based on your word." She stepped forward, close enough to look Rathma right in the eye. "If this one has the blood of the Traveler in him, I would see it for myself."

For the first time since he'd come to Théas, Rathma saw both Luzo and Ghaja Rus looking uncomfortable.

"Ah, well, you see," stammered Rus. "He . . ."

"The iron on his wrists is the only thing keeping him here," Luzo said sternly from behind Rathma.

"Well, I'm not paying so much as a silver until I see what he's worth," said Elana.

Luzo looked haltingly at Ghaja Rus, who gulped audibly.

"I suppose there's no harm in letting him loose. He can't go far." Rus glanced around the room, which was encased entirely in brick.

There were no windows, and nowhere for Rathma to escape to even if he could—which Rus didn't know was a possibility. But as Rathma felt the iron shackles drop from his wrists, their sudden lightness was in stark contrast to the heaviness of the absence of his power. No matter how hard he wanted it, how hard he tried, he couldn't move through the air as he'd done since he was a boy. He was stuck fast to this wet marble platform, next to a man called "half-eye"—a man who had been openly mocked and derided by the very people who had just paid an exorbitant fee to own him.

Rathma trembled with rage and impotence. He did everything but move.

"Show them," Luzo growled. "Use your power."

The blow to his back from the Théan barely even registered.

Through his teeth, Rathma protested. "I can't," he seethed.

Luzo's cudgel struck him on the back of the head, forcing him to his knees.

"I said show them!" he shouted.

Rathma ground his teeth sharply as he wanted nothing more than to blink away, instantly envisioning jumping behind Luzo and slitting his throat.

But nothing came. Nothing but the blunt end of Luzo's cudgel again and tears of frustration.

"I, uh, assure you," Rus stammered, "that he is a Farstepper. He was procured from a most reliable source."

Murmurs of discontent spread throughout the small crowd of patrons, who started to disperse after the lack of an impressive display that they no doubt had expected.

"I don't know how you did the eyes, Rus," Lady Elana scoffed as she turned to leave. "But let me know when you get a real Farstepper."

Connus, along with the rest of the bidders, seemed equally disappointed, and he and the others made their way to the corridor and out of sight.

Everyone, that is, except for the black-haired woman.

"I'll take him off your hands at cost," she said. Her words were confident, as though she was doing them a favor.

Rus looked at Rathma with a mixture of rage and disappointment. For a moment, Rathma tensed as he thought the G'henni was going to take Luzo's cudgel and beat him to death. But when the beating did not come, Rathma relaxed.

"Very well," Rus replied. "Two gold pieces for the Farstepper." His words were empty, as was his smile.

"He is worth half that," she countered, "and you know it. One gold piece and I will remove this shame from your sight."

It worked.

"For one as lovely as you," Rus replied, "it is almost too rich a price." He waved his hand dismissively at the Théan. "Luzo, give the lady her winnings."

With a nod, Luzo loosened the shackles on Rathma, handing them over, along with the keys, to the black-haired woman.

"Thank you, Luzo," she said, grabbing Rathma's arm. "Come with me."

***

When the light of the Théan moon finally found its way to their faces, Rathma and his new owner had left Ghaja Rus and Luzo far behind.

So it came as nothing short of surprise to Rathma when the black-haired woman said, "You are mine now, Farstepper. My name is Alysana, and we have much to discuss."

Rathma blinked, mouth agape.

"Now," she went on. "What can you tell me of Do'baradai?"

Chapter 65

Nest of the Xua'al

Awaken the Three

Kunas

The ledge of rock they were standing on jutted out from the cavern behind them, big enough for eight men to stand on. It was nearly a third of the way up the wall, with about twenty feet of nothing below them. But the thing that made him the most nervous was what the ledge faced.

Kunas wasn't sure if the Chovathi matriarch was growing out of the rock or if the rock was slowly swallowing her into itself. Across from them was another cave wall, huge, maybe a hundred feet high, which looked more like a mural than a cave: out of it came a white, twisted face twice as big as a man, with fragmented arms reaching out in either direction, slowly blending into the rock. Veins lined the arms, but Kunas wasn't sure what they carried; he didn't think there was any way it could be blood.

It was like looking at someone floating on her back in a pool: partially submerged, yet somehow also a part of the water.

The creature itself was enormous. He had no idea that Chovathi even got that big—she was perhaps seventy feet tall—and he wondered if it had to do with her place in the rock.

She was certainly not normal. And the last thing he expected her to do was speak. So when she said, "Come forward, Kunas," all he could do was blink and stare.

The words echoed throughout the cave and, for the moment, were the only sound. Finally, Captain Hunt asked in a small voice, barely above a whisper, "How in the Khel does she know your name?"

Kunas tried to say, *I don't know*, but the only thing that worked on his body were his eyes, which moved over the surface of the gargantuan rock-borne creature in the same way that water moved over a riverbed. He observed the mammoth limbs and the horrific face that jutted out of the rock like a nightmare. He looked at the huge clawed hands, half sunken into the rock and seemingly immobile, just like the rest of the . . . *thing*. And, lastly, he looked at the eyes.

As if the craggy horror before him weren't already unnerving enough, the eyes in its head were another thing entirely. They bulged and darted about like the eyes of a dreamer, neither focused nor predictable, changing seamlessly in color from white to red to black; there was no way to tell what they were looking at, or what they were seeing, for that matter.

Kunas finally found his legs and stepped forward to the ledge, footsteps echoing in the blue-hued interior.

"I am Kunas," he managed to choke out. "Of Ghal Thurái."

He was probing the rocks around them for weakness in case he had to bring them down on everyone, but something about them felt strange.

"I know you are," the creature said. Her voice was not at all like Kunas had expected a Chovathi to sound; it was titanic and hollow, like a windstorm. "Khaz has told me."

Kunas glanced at the Chovathi beside him, who was looking, stone-faced, at the matriarch.

"And what else has he told you?" Kunas managed to ask.

"He has told me," the great Chovathi said, "that you seek an agreement."

"I do."

The chamber rumbled, and Kunas suddenly realized that the creature was laughing. It was a deep, menacing laugh that made him consider bringing down the mountain regardless.

"And what can a creature like you offer Zhala, matriarch of the Xua'al?"

Now it was Kunas's turn to laugh.

"I think you underestimate me," he said. "And you underestimate the Khyth. I have the ear of the most powerful general in Gal'dorok and the trust of the most feared Khyth in the land. If we can reach an agreement, and if your Chovathi will fight with us, we will crush your enemies together. And then you will have *my* ear."

The ever-moving eyes of the matriarch seemed to pause for a moment; whether it was Kunas's eyes playing tricks on him or the giant creature was actually looking at him, he wasn't sure. But when she spoke again, it was certainly to address him.

"Then you will have the help of the Xua'al. I will give you our numbers and my gratitude."

Kunas thought about asking what good her gratitude would do him when she was trapped in the rocks here, but he thought better of it. Something told him that he wouldn't like the answer.

"Done," he said.

"But first," she said slowly, "a blood pact."

Kunas raised his eyebrows in surprise. He wasn't expecting that request. "Ah," he said, pausing. "Whose blood?" He wasn't exactly in a position to bargain.

Hunt and Ohlez drew their swords.

But before he could say anything more, the hairs on his neck stood up, and he realized that Khaz was behind him. He could hear the lumbering warrior's breathing, and suddenly the wound on his hand felt like a burning knife being dragged across his skin.

He could have sworn that he remembered closing up the cut.

Didn't he?

He felt Khaz's hand on his shoulder.

Kunas reached out again and thought about bringing down the rocks on top of them. This time he meant it.

But something dark and awful made sure he would never do that again.

Whatever it was, it was powerful.

And whatever it was, brought pain. And . . . something else.

Chapter 66

Khadje Kholam

Sera

Yelto led Sera and Tennech down a long corridor made of smooth stone that looked like it had come fresh from the quarry. Their footsteps echoed through the bare, hollow hall, and the torch Yelto was holding popped crisply as it burned.

Halfway down the hall, the big Khôl pressed his palm against a lighter section of the wall, and the stones slid heavily away. They made a scraping sound as they retracted into the wall, leaving a doorway where moments before had been impassable stone.

"I find it useful," Yelto said as he turned back to look at them, "to keep my most precious possessions well hidden. Everything else is on display."

"Most wise," Tennech said with a slow nod.

"Besides," Yelto added as he ducked his head to descend the stairs beyond the doorway, "what better place than a prison to keep someone valuable?"

Sera followed Tennech, who was right behind Yelto, down a spiraling staircase made of the same pale stone of which the hallway was comprised. Echoes were muted in the cramped space, and the torch that the Djozen carried suddenly came in handy. She wondered what kind of person was important enough to lock away yet worthless enough to be treated like a prisoner. *A strange mixture*, she thought. She had a suspicion that she was about to see for herself.

The air around them seemed to relax, as it suddenly felt lighter and less stifling. Moments ago it had felt to her like walking in front of an oven, but as they descended it became increasingly cooler.

From one of his pockets, Yelto produced a ring full of brass and silver keys. They clinked together as he grasped one of them upright, leaving the others to slide to the bottom and rock gently as they tapped against each other. He approached a sturdy wooden door and fit the key in the lock, turning it with ease and pushing the door back.

"We have a few of these to go through," Yelto said, "so I apologize. But I assure you, it is worth having the extra security."

Two soldiers stood on the other side of the door, and Sera wondered just how often they saw the sun. They nodded at the three of them and continued on through. The jingle of Yelto's keys preceded the opening of another large door, this one mostly iron, with another pair of guards waiting on the inside.

"Now I'm intrigued," Tennech said as he followed Yelto through. "This is certainly a lot to go through."

"When one is gifted power," Yelto answered without looking back, "one tends to protect it."

Tennech raised an eyebrow and looked at Sera. Sera shrugged.

The three made their way to a door that was guarded this time by five guards, bigger than any of the ones by the other doors—and armed to the teeth. The biggest one, in the center, said something in Khôl which Yelto immediately answered. *A challenge and response*, Sera realized.

As one, the guards lowered their weapons and stepped out of the way. The biggest guard put a plain silver key into the lock on the heavy iron door. It made a satisfying thud as the lock opened. He pulled on a circular handle and the door groaned open.

Sera peered inside, but it did her no good; whatever was behind this door was sitting in a darkness blacker than even the deepest recesses of Khala Val'ur.

A female voice croaked its way through the void.

"It has been a long time since you have come to visit me, keeper of my prison."

"Indeed it has," Yelto called into the dark. "Indeed it has. And I've brought guests." He held up his torch, casting its light farther into the cell and illuminating the source of his pride, the thing that he was so careful about locking away.

In the middle of the well-guarded cell sat a woman, silver haired and thin, her hands folded patiently at her side as though she had been waiting for them this whole time. Sera was surprised to see that the light of the torch did not fully illuminate her figure; instead, it passed right through her as if she were made of glass.

As if she was . . . a ghost.

"Daughter, son, step into the light," the woman said. She was hidden mostly in shadows, and her ethereal visage flickered with the torchlight.

Sera and Tennech, intrigued, did as she asked, and a courtly smile fluttered across her lips. "The Dagger and the Seed," she said. "I've been expecting you."

"The Dagger?" Tennech asked defiantly. "How is it that you know that name?" His voice was steady, but Sera heard the momentary waver in it, which she recognized as fear. "I have never been beyond the Wastes, yet you speak as if you know me."

"I do know you, Aldis Tennech." The woman smiled again, and Sera saw a fierceness behind her sharp green eyes that reminded her of a wolf. "I am the one who goes between," she answered. "Some call me the Ghost of the Morning; to others I am Mother to Wolves. But all you need to know, Dagger, is that I am called Asha Imha-khet, and I have seen what lies beyond this world and more. I have seen its beginning and I know of its end. And you, Dagger of Derenar, still have a part to play."

"Explain yourself," Tennech demanded as he took a step closer to the ghostly woman. "I have no patience for riddles."

"Then I suggest you wait and see what comes to pass, though you will not have to wait long. For, rising with the sun, are the forces that shall bring ruin to Khadje Kholam, united by the Key and strengthening the Seed."

With these words, she turned her icy stare to Sera.

"And you—" she began, but was cut off by a guard bursting into the room.

"Djozen," he said between rapid breaths. "The tribes are here (*gasp*). They are led (*gasp*) by the Wolfwalker (*gasp*) Sivulu."

Yelto clutched the blade that hung from his neck. "Then the time has come, just as the Ghost foresaw, General," he said as he turned to Tennech. "Now you prove your worth."

There are two sides to every story, and the victor can tell both.

—Khyth proverb

Chapter 67

Gal'dorok

Awaken the Three

Duna

Duna had not anticipated how absolutely unnerving it would be to march beneath a winged Gwarái, and she felt herself flinch with nearly every flap of its wings. She couldn't see Cortus Venn from where she was, but she was sure the man was grinning.

Part of her knew that if she figured out the secret to breeding the winged Gwarái, she would be able to march anywhere at any time, and to mobilize even quicker. She had a sudden vision of hundreds of her troops aboard the winged terrors, sent out across the whole of Gal'dorok, and beyond. The thought made her smile. She did enjoy success.

She turned to see LaVince marching beside her, looking equally in awe of the giant black serpent with devil wings. He was squinting in the evening light, and his silence over the last few miles probably meant that he had simply been staring the whole time instead of paying attention to the troops.

"LaVince!" Duna snapped, grabbing the attention of the young captain. "Eyes on the road."

"Sorry, General," he said in his surprisingly professional manner. "I just didn't know they came like that." He shook his head uncomfortably. "Until a few weeks ago, I didn't even know they existed at all."

"None of us did," Duna answered. She recalled the two Gwarái that Hullis and Dhrostain had ridden into battle in Kienar, and had no real knowledge of where they came from or how they were made. But Cortus Venn certainly did. Now it was her turn to look up and squint.

***

They had marched for nearly a day, and the sun was beginning to set. Venn had set his huge Gwarái down ahead of the army and was waiting patiently for them to catch up.

Must be nice, Duna mused, *to be able to drop in wherever you please and not have to deal with the smell of the stables.*

She walked her horse over to him as he sat, grinning, on the back of the beast.

"It really is a marvelous view from up there," Venn said to her, nodding to the sky. He patted the creature's saddle and smiled.

"Oh, I'm sure it is," Duna said. She got down from her horse and started to walk toward the Stoneborn and his mount.

"Would you like to see it sometime?" Venn asked. Duna didn't think it was possible, but his grin actually got wider. "I can pull some strings."

"I'm sure that's what you tell all the women, but I'm not interested," Duna said with a grin of her own.

Venn let out a laugh that filled the canyon they'd stopped in. "I like you, General Cullain. You can dish out as much as you can take." He jumped down from the Gwarái to stand eye to eye with her. "Now where are these captains we're waiting on?"

It was a good question; the three of them should have been waiting for them when they got there.

"I'm not sure," she said absentmindedly. "They should be here by now."

She scanned the horizon to the east toward Haidan Shar, still about a day's ride away, then looked back west. No sign of them. She frowned.

Then she felt the earth move . . .

. . . rumble . . .

. . . and split.

In an instant, Chovathi poured forth from the broken cracks in the earth like smoke from a fire, and Duna thought that she was seeing her death.

The creatures clawed their way out of the chasm, white, enormous, and fierce. They were certainly bigger than any of the Chovathi she had seen in all her raids with the Fist, and bigger than any she'd ever thought were possible. They didn't even look like the same *species*. These Chovathi were angular and sharp. Their hulking bodies had huge arms that reached all the way to the ground when they walked, giving them a stooped appearance as they lumbered along. They pounded their knuckles into the earth below, propelling themselves forward on fearful forearms. And there were scores of them too—far too many to count, possibly even outnumbering the Fist's own men.

Awaken the Three

Duna could hardly move. She had no idea how many of her own soldiers had probably soiled themselves already. Cortus Venn's Gwarái had apparently not liked what he was seeing either and had taken to the sky. Cortus was left below, shaking his fist and yelling at the insubordinate beast, commanding him to land. Under any other circumstances Duna would have laughed, but she still found herself frozen in shock, and what she saw next stole her attention and made her rub her eyes in disbelief.

There, riding on the back of one of the Chovathi emerging from the crack in the ground, was Kunas, Master Khyth of Ghal Thurái.

And here she had thought that Cortus Venn knew how to make an entrance.

Chapter 68

Khadje Kholam

Awaken the Three

Tennech

Aldis Tennech walked out of the stifling grasp of the underground and found himself embraced by the waiting arms of evening. He closed his eyes and took a breath.

Ah, he thought with a smile, *there she is.*

Like the smell that came before rain, the air tonight was thick with a familiar sensation. It was one that he knew and one that he welcomed.

War.

She was coming.

***

"Give me the lay of the land," Tennech said.

"You've seen most of it," Djozen Yelto replied. He gestured to the walls of the stronghold that separated them from the desert outside. "There is not much to the defense of Khadje Kholam."

Spoken like a man who has never commanded troops, Tennech thought wryly. "Let me clarify," he said, turning to face him. "Do you have archers? Light infantry? Heavy infantry?" He glanced around the compound. "Where are the weak points? Where are they most likely to come from? Where can we defend most easily?"

Djozen Yelto looked as if he had just eaten poison. "Ah," he started. Turning his head, he shouted for his guards. When two dark, stocky men reported and dropped to a knee, Yelto barked, "The general has questions. Answer them," and turned to walk away, seeming to have suddenly become preoccupied by something else entirely.

***

After gleaning from the guards what intelligence he could, Tennech finally had a feeling for what he was up against and how he could best defend the stronghold in response. The endgame, he knew, was to defend the prison that lay below; everything else was disposable.

The holding cell of the Ghost of the Morning was the single best-defended space this side of the Wastes, and Yelto had made no secret about it. Tennech didn't know why this woman was so important, and he didn't care. The "why" was inconsequential; it was the "how" that concerned him.

To address that concern was a matter of threes; he always looked at it like lighting a fire.

First, came the posturing and planning, like gathering fuel for the fire: tedious but necessary.

The land around them was mostly flat desert, offering no substantial advantage to either side: the defenders could clearly see them coming, but the invaders knew exactly what they were walking into. Therefore, setting a perimeter defense would be paramount.

To do this, they would line the walls with archers to pick off the first wave. Then, below the walls, they would position the light infantry to repel any invaders who made it over. It was a fairly straightforward structural defense, a strategy that Tennech had studied and excelled at during his time at the Valurian military academy. But from what he gathered from the guards, whose Khôl accents were still strong, there were an undetermined number of invaders they kept calling "beast-men." He wasn't sure what it meant, but the guards spoke of them with reverent fear.

Strategy could only take them so far, Tennech knew. He hoped preparation would trump terror.

After gathering fuel for the fire, then, came the next step: arranging the fuel and getting it ready to burn. This consisted of establishing orders and a chain of command.

Tennech quickly identified troop leaders: Hullis plus three on the walls and Dhrostain plus one inside. The six were given overarching orders and a general strategy, and would pass along any relevant commands to their troops. They were to be the relay for any real-time orders that had to be passed as well. And, as such, they would also be held accountable for any failures; Tennech made sure this last point was driven home. When he was sure that all of them understood, he sent them on their way.

Next—last—came his favorite part. When all was said and done, when the pieces had all been placed and the battlefield set, there was only one thing left to do: set it ablaze.

Smiling, he turned west to watch the sun dip below the horizon and to listen to the far-off echoes of approaching footsteps. He knew what was coming, and the feeling in the air gripped him even tighter.

Strategy and planning were merely a tired preamble: a mindless gathering of tinder for the spark, hardly enjoyable. There was no flourish to it. Everything was rigid and moved along predetermined lines.

But the execution—oh, the execution!—now *that* was a thing of beauty. It was where the spark met fuel and caught fire, becoming wholly unpredictable. It was where skin met steel; where blood, sweat, and bone sang out; where lives were lost and chaos reigned. For, no matter how carefully laid the tinder or how expert the spark, the flame paid it no mind; it simply burned what it wanted.

So when the first of the invaders crested the horizon with the largest pack of wolves that Tennech had ever seen, he looked to Sera and grinned. He knew this blaze would be particularly bright.

There was fuel enough to burn for days. There would be flame enough to pale the stars and darken the skies with its ashes.

And upon those ashes Aldis Tennech would build his empire.

Chapter 69

Théas

Awaken the Three

Thornton

"Tell them what you told me," Alysana demanded.

They were all gathered in the small, dark room at the Broken Scabbard, and Thornton was feeling cramped. He looked at the cloaked stranger standing before him, and a feeling of familiarity washed over him. The man had features that Thornton thought he recognized but couldn't quite place. It put him on edge.

"You'll have to narrow it down." The stranger grinned. His accent was thick with Khôl, which made his words drip like syrup off his tongue.

"Then start with all of it, Farstepper," Alysana answered darkly, uttering the last word like an epithet.

"Please," he said, holding up a hand and hanging his head. "I am hardly a Farstepper." His words were laced with regret. "I just have the body of one. Call me Rathma."

"Very well," relented Alysana. "Rathma. Tell us what you know."

Rathma simply shrugged. "The Wolfwalkers, along with some of the tribes, seek to overthrow Djozen Yelto and free their mother."

Yasha asked, "What's that got to do with us?"

Rathma looked at her and smiled slyly. "I don't know."

"Don't be coy," said Alysana. "Tell them their mother's name."

He sighed and said casually, "They call her the Ghost of the Morning."

There was a brief silence as a realization blanketed the room.

The Ghost of the Morning. Thornton knew that name. "One of the Three," he said.

Rathma looked at him in surprise. "What does a northerner know of the Three?" he asked, red eyes narrowed in suspicion.

"He knows what I told him," said Alysana. "And he knows of the dangers."

"The only danger is Djozen Yelto getting his way," Rathma replied dismissively. "Which is why the tribes move now. The freedom of the Ghost is worth any price."

Thornton, stepping forward, said, "Rathma, maybe you can help us. We seek the help of the Traveler and the Holder."

Rathma laughed. "No you don't."

Thornton was taken aback. "Ah. Yes. We do," he said haltingly.

"You don't know what you're asking," Rathma replied. "You do not want to wake the Holder."

"So we've been told," Yasha remarked.

"You're right," Thornton shot back. "We don't want to—we *need* to."

Rathma looked confused. "What could you need to be desperate enough to wake the Holder?" he asked.

"A way in," Kethras said in a low growl.

In the dim light, the Kienari was barely more than a shadow towering over the rest of them, but suddenly Thornton was reminded that he was more than just a shadow; he was a force to be reckoned with. Darkness upon darkness he stood, seeming to dare the Farstepper to flinch.

Thornton broke the tension. "We need the help of the Traveler to get to Khel-hârad," he insisted. "And the help of the Holder to get to the Otherworld."

Rathma looked to Thornton more confused than a man who had just been commanded to fly. "You do not want to wake the Holder," he repeated.

"You keep saying that," Thornton said, looking nervously at his companions. "Why not?"

"Because," Rathma answered, "it is said that, when he awakens, with him will come his army—and the Days of the Dark."

There was an uncomfortable silence as the ominous words hung in the air.

"The Days of the . . . ," Thornton began.

"Which is why," Rathma went on, ignoring him, "the Ghost must be set free. She and the Traveler are the only ones who have any hope of stopping him. But now," he added with a hint of frustration, "her spirit is imprisoned by Djozen Yelto."

Thornton and Alysana looked at each other.

"Is there any way to get into the Otherworld without using the Holder?" Alysana asked.

Rathma shrugged. "That is a question for the Three; I do not know the answer. But my guess is no."

Thornton rubbed his eyes in frustration. "Then what choice do we have?" He looked around the room for an answer.

"None," Kethras conceded. "But we are no closer to waking one of them than we are to waking the Three. We must go forth as planned."

Rathma looked at each of their faces. "I do not understand your reasons, but if you know what you know and are still willing to risk the dangers . . ." Nodding, he said, "I will help."

"Thank you—" Thornton began, but Rathma cut him off by holding up his hand.

"But there is a problem."

Thornton groaned. "What is it?"

"All spirits, including the Three, require a Vessel: an earthly body that they are tied to."

Yasha furrowed her brow. "Why is that a problem?" she asked.

"Normally it would not be, but when Djozen Yelto took control of the Wolfblade, he severed their ties to their original Vessels. It is how he has imprisoned the Ghost, and how he plans to control the Holder as well."

Yasha looked at Thornton and then back to Rathma. "What if we find a new Vessel?" she asked. "Could we stop him from doing that?"

"Perhaps," Rathma said, considering. "But if the Traveler were awakened, he would surely be able to get you into Khel-hârad."

Khel-hârad. Land of the Dead.

Thornton knew it was their best chance of making their way toward the Otherworld and figuring out how to free Miera. It was also the stinging reminder of his father's fate. He clenched and unclenched his fist.

While the way to the Otherworld was seemingly closed to them without the Holder, perhaps there was a "back door" that would allow them to make it through.

Kethras must have reached the same conclusion. "Then that is where we must start," he said firmly. "We need to find a Vessel for the Traveler."

They all seemed to be in agreement.

Which is why it seemed odd to Thornton that Rathma looked so down.

"Then you are in luck," he said, sounding almost defeated. "If we can find someone to perform the ritual, I know of a candidate."

"Oh?" Alysana asked, surprised. "Who?"

Rathma's lips formed a thin smile. "Me."

Chapter 70

Khadje Kholam

Awaken the Three

Sivulu

The Hedjetti had their orders, and they were spread out according to where they were to end up in the assault. Looking over the horde of troops, Sivulu saw that the wolves—his people—were divided up evenly and ready for battle. Not a single Wolfwalker was left on two legs. Even he had taken to his lupine form to begin the assault, allowing him greater mobility and speed.

And a great set of fangs, he thought as he ran his tongue over his canines.

He took a final look back over the gathered force, then steadied his great green eyes on the compound. Turning his head to the sky, he let out a howl, fearsome and strong, to signify the start of the attack. It was soon joined by the haunting voices of the other wolves, and Sivulu thought he actually saw Yelto's compound shudder in terror. He wouldn't have blamed it; the howls were heralds of death. The Hedjetti behind him rallied their men forward, beginning their swift advancement on the stone compound.

The stars above them winked to life one by one as they approached, and the first of the defenders' arrows hissed sharply into the sand.

"Forward!" came the cry from Hroth, who led the wave of warriors breaking off to the east. "There is more to fear than the sting of steel!"

Sivulu watched the two forces break away as they began to surround the compound. The dust they kicked up as they charged served to obscure their numbers a little better in the dark, but he was sure that advantage would be short-lived. He also knew that breaching the wall would come at a steep price.

From inside the wall, he heard a strong voice barking orders. He couldn't quite make out the commands, but the sharpness and urgency behind them were, he knew, born from battle.

He had split off with the force to the east and was nearly upon the outer wall. A few of the Ohmati had brought ropes and grappling hooks and were hurling them up at the wall to start their climb amid a hail of arrows. When one of them fell, another fearless warrior was there to take his place.

War was not an easy language, but these men spoke it fluently.

Tennech

The wailing of wolves penetrated the sky as Tennech tightened his verbal grip on his men. "Dhrostain," he shouted to the captain on the wall, "get them in line!"

"Yes, General!" He turned to address the archers around him. "No hesitation! No mercy! These men are here to kill you. Let's not make it easy!"

Tennech could sense that the wolves had a profoundly demoralizing effect on the men under his command. The chilling howls that filled the air shook even him, the man who could look High Khyth Yetz in the eye and not back down.

He had to get control of his men now, or he might lose them entirely. He turned to Sera, who had been watching silently, and nodded. "Now is the time," he said, and she turned without answering.

She knew what she had to do. They had to play their one advantage now or risk losing the battle entirely.

Or, more accurately, their two advantages.

Tennech watched her open the great gates that held back the Gwarái, and he smiled. The fire was about to catch.

Chapter 71

Théas

Awaken the Three

Thornton

The smell of pine hit Thornton's nostrils as he opened the door to Silus's shop, and it reminded him of home. The fir trees in Highglade were abundant enough to soak the air with their scent, and on a clear summer day you could smell it for miles. They were only ever overpowered by the smoke from Olson's forge, and even that was seen as a welcome respite.

Despite the heavy smell of herbs and incense that hung in the air now, Thornton could pick out pine like a beggar could a gold coin in a pile of coppers, and the look on Yasha's face told him that she smelled it too.

"It's called soap, old man," she whispered as she crinkled her nose. Behind her, Rathma chuckled to himself as Thornton shot his sister a disapproving look.

"Silus," he announced as he brushed past her. "It's Thornton. From earlier. I have a . . . favor to ask."

He heard the old man rummaging around near the rear of the shop. They had perhaps caught him napping.

"Ah yes, Thornton. The young Khyth boy," he answered, emerging from behind the crimson curtain with a head full of unkempt gray hair. "Of course."

Thornton flinched at the words. "Ah, just Thornton, if you please."

Silus waved it off. "So what is it, *just* Thornton? How can I help you?"

Rathma stepped forward. He crossed his arms defiantly, and his red eyes gleamed with determination. "We need to know if you have any experience preparing Vessels."

Silus tilted his head at the new voice and frowned. "Planning on raising the dead, are we?"

"Something like that."

"You don't know what you're asking."

Steeling his jaw, the Farstepper said, "That's what I told them."

Thornton nudged him.

"We need your help."

The old man thumped his cane on the wooden floor as he moved toward them, shaking his head. "For one, there is a reason they are called Vessels: like a captain takes over a ship, whatever being is invoked takes control of the body."

Rathma seemed to hesitate. "We can deal with that."

". . . Permanently."

Rathma blinked hard. Thornton turned to protest, but he held out a hand before he could speak. "What else?"

"There must be a guide. Someone to accompany the spirit of the Vessel to their destination. To secure the anchor and complete the ritual."

"We have that covered," Yasha asserted, nodding at Thornton. "What else?"

"'What else?'" the old man echoed. "As if I'm asking you for ingredients for bread! What else," he breathed incredulously.

"Just tell us," Rathma demanded.

Silus shot him a dirty look that, despite his blindness, conveyed his agitation perfectly well. "*What else*," he said mockingly, "is that you need a god."

They were silent. Yasha and Thornton traded defeated glances.

"So if we don't have a god—" Yasha began.

"Then I'm afraid I can't help you," Silas said, cutting her off, as he shook his head and started to walk away. Turning back to them for a moment, he added, "You could use an artifact touched by the gods themselves. But," he said as he chuckled, "good luck getting one of those; there are only a handful in the world."

Thornton, stupefied, let his mouth hang open.

"So," Silus went on, reaching up to pull back the curtain, "you see why it's so difficult to prepare a Vessel. Now, if you'll excuse me—"

"Thornton has the Hammer of the Worldforge," Yasha blurted out.

It was enough to make Silus stop in his tracks and drop his cane to the floor with a loud thump. He was completely still, as if the words themselves held power. As if he dared not anger them by moving, or breathing.

Finally, in a whisper, the old Athrani asked, "How?"

Thornton approached him. Reaching over his own shoulder for his hammer, he laid it on a nearby table and took Silus's hand. "I don't know. But feel for yourself."

He helped the old man over to where his hammer lay, and guided his palm down the grooves of the white-ash handle, just as he himself had done so many times before. Silus traced the shallow carvings that had been put there by the Shaper Herself when She forged the world from the void. He moved his hand to the solid black head that was always inexplicably warm despite being made from cold, hard steel.

Thornton could see that tears had welled up in the old man's eyes.

"*I* know, Thornton," Silus said quietly. "*I* know how. It's the only thing that makes sense, and it is what makes you the perfect anchor for the Vessel." He took his hand off the Hammer and turned toward Thornton. When he did, Thornton had the sudden feeling that he was standing in front of a charging bull, and his feet were frozen where he stood. He felt the weight of something rushing toward him: something that had gone missing yet had always been there. Something he had always known but had somehow forgotten; a childhood memory that had been lost for years and suddenly found.

What he found was the answer to why he held the Hammer, why he could carry it despite his Khyth blood. It was the answer to why his father had wound up alive inside D'kane's prison instead of dead somewhere outside of it.

It was the answer to why he could call flames from nothing. Just like . . .

"It appears," Silus said, "that your father kept more than one secret from you two . . ."

Thornton held his breath, knowing what was coming.

". . . about the Athrani blood that flowed through his veins . . ."

Poor Yasha.

". . . and yours."

She certainly was getting good at fainting.

Chapter 72

Gal'dorok, Outside the Nest of the Xua'al

Awaken the Three

Duna

Duna had not known what to expect before she saw Kunas barreling toward her on the back of a Chovathi, but that certainly wasn't it. The Chovathi came to a stop a few feet in front of her, stooped down, and let Kunas step off.

Something about him seemed . . . different.

"General Cullain," he said, his voice still carrying the same hollow timbre that all Khyth of the Breaking had, but it was changed somehow—bigger. "I hope you are ready for war."

She was, and she knew it. By the looks of it, so was Kunas, and all the Xua'al he'd brought along with him. She wasn't sure how many Chovathi clans waited beneath the mountain fortress of Ghal Thurái, but if the Xua'al's numbers were any indication, there were a *lot*. Duna was suddenly relieved that the Sharians had agreed to join them.

"I am ready, Master Khyth," she answered, not sure why she felt the need to be so formal with him. "And I see that your deal was a success," she said as she swept her gaze over the Chovathi that had rumbled forth from the earth, seeming to come out of the rock itself.

"More than you know," he answered.

Cryptic. Typical.

The Chovathi were calm now, standing around in the way that human soldiers would do as they readied for inspection. The realization caught her by surprise as a shiver ran through her: what Kunas had said before about Chovathi being intelligent was true. Perhaps they had been underestimating these creatures for generations now. She was suddenly relieved that they had agreed to help each other—and that they would be eliminating a huge number of Chovathi soon after.

If they are really as intelligent and organized as this—

Her thoughts were interrupted by a screech from the Gwarái, still airborne above them.

"Damned beast!" Cortus Venn shouted from nearby. "Get down here!"

The Gwarái screeched again, and Venn turned his head in the direction the creature was looking.

"Ah," the Stoneborn said, turning to Duna with a grin. "Looks like we have company."

Duna turned to see where Venn was looking.

Marching in from the east, from the shores of the Tashkar Sea, was the Sharian army, led by none other than her own flesh and blood, Queen Lena Cullain.

And when the first arrows from the Sharian army started to fall, Duna thought for sure that her sister had come to put an end to what she had started all those years before.

Chapter 73

Théas

Awaken the Three

Alysana

Kethras had been pacing the length of the room for quite some time now, and it was making Alysana nervous; he looked like a hunter stalking prey.

"Kethras," she said softly, "can you stop that?"

His eyes met hers, but he did not stop his pacing. "Stop what?" His padded footfalls scarcely made any noise in the dark, cramped room.

"The moving back and forth. It is . . . unsettling."

Kethras, seeming to suddenly become aware of his behavior, came to a stop and dipped his head. "Ah," he said, "I apologize. It was mindless wandering; I relinquish the reins to my body when my mind is otherwise occupied."

Alysana knew what he meant: during her training, she often found herself idly playing with the dagger she'd been given, as a way of letting her mind drift off. It was soothing to her. She felt her hand moving toward it now, as her thoughts began to stray. Then the realization caught her like a sudden splash of cold water: the three of them had been gone for quite some time. Should she be worried? Just as she started to say something about it to Kethras, the Kienari's ears perked up.

"I hear them," he announced. "They have returned."

***

Elyasha looked woozy but awake. Thornton looked a little pale as he sat gripping his hammer. Rathma, on the other hand, looked as stoic as ever.

What had happened at the Healer's?

"Did you find out what you needed to?" Alysana asked.

Rathma nodded gravely. "He told us what we can expect." With a nod to Thornton, he added, "And a little more."

The words didn't seem to register to Thornton, who was idly tracing the grooves carved into his hammer's handle.

"When do we begin preparation?"

"Now," Rathma answered. "Silus has already started."

"So he is able to prepare a Vessel after all?"

"Yes."

Alysana noticed that the Farstepper's answers were short and abrupt. He had volunteered to be a Vessel, but she wondered if something Silus had said was making him have second thoughts. She walked over to him and sat down.

"Is something bothering you, Rathma?" she asked.

For the first time since they had met, Rathma looked at her—really looked at her. His expression was one of relief, as though she had offered to shoulder a burden that he had been carrying for years.

"Yes."

Alysana shifted uncomfortably. She hesitated and then sat down next to Rathma, lightly touching his shoulder. "What is wrong?"

"I thought I would be ready," he confessed. "After my brother left, I was taught that the responsibility would fall to me, but that always seemed like a far-off concept—like dying or . . . marriage." The last word caught in his throat as he averted his gaze. He coughed, and continued: "I never thought I would actually need to become a Vessel. It was never supposed to be me. It was supposed to be my brother, Jinda."

Alysana's jaw hung open. She looked at the red hair and eyes that all Farsteppers shared and wondered how she hadn't seen it sooner. In retrospect, it seemed so obvious.

"Jinda? You brother . . . is Jinda?" she stammered.

"Yes. You know him?"

Alysana blinked away her surprise and nodded.

"He is the eldest. Our bloodline, my mother always told us, can be traced back to the Traveler himself. Even our family name, Yhun, means 'son of Yho.' Whether or not we actually *are* is not for me to say . . ." Looking down at his hands, he spoke as if his mind were a thousand miles away. "I never thought about why he left until tonight."

Alysana was at a loss for words. She wanted to say that Jinda must have had a good reason for leaving, or that it was all for the best, but she wasn't sure even she believed either one of those things. Before she could gather her words, though, there was a knock on their door. Alysana stood up and opened it. Facing her was none other than the old Athrani healer, Silus.

"We are ready," he said. His face was solemn, and Alysana was sure that if he could have seen, he would have been looking right at Rathma.

Rathma stood up and forced a smile. "Then let's get this over with," he said. "I have a body to surrender."

Chapter 74

Derenar

Awaken the Three

Lilyana

The G'henni called Tark had been leading them each night using nothing but the light of the stars and his so-called impeccable sense of direction to guide them. They never took anything that resembled a well-traveled road, so Lily thought it actually *must* have been impeccable. She was impressed with his ability to keep them pointed in the right direction—wherever that direction was.

He kept assuring her and her mother that they would be reaching their destination soon, but that had been at least two nights ago. Lily was beginning to wonder just how loyal these men were to her uncle.

"Mother," Lily quietly said as she tugged on her mother's long sleeve, "do you know where they're taking us?" She was seated atop a young stallion that Tark had let her ride, and her mother was walking beside her.

Coraline looked up at Lily and smiled. "I've told you, young lady: to your uncle. He's going to meet us near the border of Gal'dorok. It's a long journey."

Lily saw her mother smiling with her lips, but her eyes did not appear to share the sentiment. That made Lily nervous. She looked up at the moon, which had gotten fuller in the past few days, and frowned.

***

They were getting close to the border, according to Tark. The landscape had certainly changed. Far off in the distance, illuminated by the moon, Lily saw the tops of mountains that she could only assume were the peaks of Gal'behem, the Great Serpent. It was hard to distinguish the peaks from the clouds; the orange glow of campfires that dotted their sides was the only way Lily could be sure she wasn't looking at an approaching storm.

"What are those fires?" Lily asked, pointing.

"Tough to say," Gorbun said from behind her. His voice was not nearly as gruff as Lily had expected; his short, dirty blond hair made the stocky man seem approachable, but the way his eyes darted back and forth as if he was looking for something made her uneasy. "Could be patrols from Khala Val'ur. Could be fighters from Ghal Thurái out 'unting Chovathi."

Chovathi, Lily thought. It was the first time she'd heard the word, and it sounded scary. "Wh-What are Chovathi?" she asked.

A laugh came from the tall, dark Agheer, half G'henni by birth. "Something to be feared," he answered. He had tied back his black hair, and Lily could see the seriousness on his face. "They enjoy the taste of flesh, and they see well at night. Open flame keeps them at bay—usually." He added the last word almost as an afterthought and looked right at Lily when he said it.

"Quit screwing around, you two," said Damazo from in front of them. "You're scaring the girl."

"Good," retorted Gorbun. "She's right to be afraid of the Chovathi. They'll eat 'er alive if they catch 'er alone."

Lily wasn't sure how much of that was true, but she didn't want to risk finding out. For the first time since they had found her and her mother, she actually found herself being thankful that these men were with them.

Agheer drew in closer to whisper to Lily: "He's right." And the serious look on his face made her shiver. "I fought one once, a long time ago." Raising his arm, he pulled back his sleeve to reveal thick off-brown scars that ran the length of his forearm. "Left me with this. Claw marks."

Lily's eyes went wide as she looked at the scars. They were jagged and wide, and none of the thick black hair on the half G'henni's forearm were present, making them easily distinguishable even at night. *No wonder he wears long sleeves*, Lily thought. Her eyes darted back to Agheer's.

"How did you get away?"

Gorbun laughed from up ahead. "'e did what any smart man would do: 'e ran."

Agheer smiled sheepishly and nodded. "Though, to be fair, so did Gorbun. But"—he raised his voice at the blond man—"remind me whose turn it was on watch."

Gorbun waved his hand dismissively. "It's not my fault that Drausté makes such good roasted pork. My eyes were as 'eavy as my belly."

Lily heard him pat his stomach, with a laugh.

Agheer nodded in confirmation. "He does make good pork."

Lily found herself cracking a smile. Maybe these men weren't so bad after all. At least Agheer seemed nice.

***

Looking ahead, Lily could see the tops of the mountains beginning to turn orange as dawn crept its way toward them. If previous nights were any indication, they would be stopping soon. Tark always had them seek shelter during the day while one man stood watch, rotating in and out to get a few hours of sleep. But, in a rocky outcropping up ahead at the foothills of the mountains, Lily was surprised to see a caravan. There were a few covered wagons, a number of horses, and at least a half dozen people. It was still early, and the remains of a campfire were still smoldering. One man was hunched over it and looked to be putting it out.

"Ho there," Tark called out. He was ahead of the group, with Agheer, Gorbun, and Damazo in the rear.

A burly man with brown hair and a thick beard looked up, shaded his eyes with his hand, and smiled. Standing up, he started walking toward them. "Tark!" he shouted. "Took you long enough!" He was grinning from ear to ear when he approached. His eyes immediately went to Coraline.

"Cora! It's really you. It's been so long," he said wistfully. Shifting his eyes over to Lily, he added with a laugh, "Too long it seems. She's gotten big!"

Coraline walked over and gave the man a hug. "So have you," she said as they embraced. "It's good to see you again, Thaurson."

"You as well." Thaurson's eyes glimmered as he looked at Lily, smiling. "And *you*," he said. Though Lily was still seated atop her horse, Thaurson was even with her eyes. He was tall and broad, and strong by the looks of it. But when he reached out to take her hand and gave it a kiss, Lily was surprised by how gentle he was. "You were only a baby when I left Ellenos." Turning to Cora, he said, "She looks like Mother."

"I know," Cora answered with a smile.

Thaurson turned his head to shout at the caravan: "Morgan! Come meet your niece!"

From one of the wagons peeked out the head of a rosy-cheeked brunette. "This is the first time I'm hearing about a niece," she shouted back. Gathering the length of her white dress covered by a green apron, she shuffled over to them. She was tall for a woman, but standing next to Thaurson, the couple looked normal. Lily thought that if these two had any children, they were bound to be giants.

"Morgan," Thaurson said, pointing to Lily, "this is Lilyana."

Lily giggled as he used her full name. "No one calls me Lilyana unless I'm in trouble. My friends call me Lily."

"Well," Morgan said as she smiled, "pleased to meet you, Lily."

Thaurson was looking back at the caravan, covering his eyes with his hand, as though he was searching for something. "Where is that boy?" he asked.

"Sleeping in the wagon," Morgan answered. "It's nearly dawn, though. I'll go wake him."

As she walked off, Tark and Thaurson shook hands, laughing like old friends. Lily saw Thaurson pass him a small cloth pouch, which she thought was most likely the smugglers' payment for escorting her mother and her. Tark shook his head, though, and muttered something about the job not being done. Thaurson's face darkened a bit at the words and he looked away. Looking back at Tark, he nodded his understanding and put the coin pouch away.

Just then, a young boy about Lily's age came racing up to them. He had brown hair and looked like a younger version of Thaurson. Lily got excited when he came closer, as she realized this could be her cousin. She'd never had a cousin before!

"There he is," Thaurson said as the boy raced over to him and was picked up in the big hands of his father. "Son, I want you to meet your cousin, Lily."

Thaurson held up the boy so that he was even with Lily while she was seated in the saddle. He giggled and shook her hand.

"Lily, this is your cousin, Olson Woods."

Hope is a powerful thing. That is why its destruction is the most powerful of all.

—High Khyth Anatoch IV

Chapter 75

Khadje Kholam

Awaken the Three

Tennech

The wolves came with the fury of a storm and the fierceness of a fire. There were not many of them, but that didn't matter; they tore through men like a tide, unstoppable, unyielding. Tennech watched his two captains, Hullis and Dhrostain, shout orders to the men under them, trying to quell the chaos.

Tennech, the Dagger of Derenar, smiled. He lived for moments like these. The archers on the wall had done a lackluster job of defending the compound against the invading army, and he wasn't surprised. From the looks of Yelto, it had been a long time since they had needed to fend off invaders.

Crashing over the rough-hewn stone came the fierce, rugged men of the tribes, swords and daggers in hand. They were olive skinned and strong, covered in scars and wounds that were undoubtedly the product of a lifetime of battles. He noticed that a few of them had an unusual hair color that somehow did not look out of place against their black-haired tribesmen: red. *Farsteppers*, Tennech thought with a frown. He knew the Otherworld had been closed and that the source of their power would have been cut off, but it did nothing to ease his mind. They were still deadly. They swept over the wall, yelling and frenzied.

"Sera," he said calmly over his shoulder, "I hope you're ready."

His answer came in the form of a groaning iron door and a rumbling pair of growls behind him. *Just in time*, he thought. The talons of the Gwarái struck the stone of the compound floor as they walked, high pitched and hollow, and Tennech remembered just how much damage those talons could do when properly employed. And though there were no Shapers here to feed their bloodlust, he knew they would be as savage as these wolves seemed to be—if not more so.

When the first wave of warriors dropped below the wall, Tennech learned just how savage two cornered Gwarái could be.

Sivulu

Sivulu came from the east with the men of the Kuufi and Ohmati. The walls surrounding the compound were solid and tall, and the only way through them was *over*. He narrowed his lupine eyes as he surveyed the wall, maybe eighteen feet high. The heavy gray rock that made up the wall had not been smoothed out when it was placed, making hand- and footholds for any thief brave enough to scale the wall—or for any wolf crazy enough to try. Khuufi and Ohmati warriors flooded past him, brandishing steel. Occasionally, one would catch an arrow somewhere on his body. Sometimes they would flinch; mostly they just kept running. It made Sivulu shiver with pride.

He hunched down low, eyeing the wall one more time, and sprang forward.

Tennech

It had been a long time since Tennech had drawn his sword in battle, but his old friend was there at his side as if he'd never put it down. A general usually had the luxury of commanding his troops to do the fighting for him, but Tennech was never one to shy away from a fight, especially one as exciting as this. He locked eyes with an encroaching tribesman and could almost feel the fury coursing through him. The warrior wore his hair in long braids, tipped with white beads too many to count. Shirtless and scarred, he was pulling his sword out of the midsection of one of Yelto's guards. He grinned at Tennech, yelled something in Khôl, and ambled toward him amid the sea of bloody chaos.

"Come get yours then, young pup," Tennech growled. He flexed his fingers around the hilt of his sword and readied himself.

War had come.

She was here, and Tennech knew of only one way to greet her.

Awaken the Three

Sivulu

Sivulu felt the craggy walls between the pads on his feet as he pressed against them, digging deep, pulling with every ounce of strength in his formidable lupine body. He defied gravity as he leapt, surging upward, cresting the wall as if the feat itself were effortless. On his way up, he flew past two surprised guards who watched his impossibly high arc that brought him well over the height of the wall. Their shock at his sudden appearance gave them no time to react as Sivulu crashed into them on his way back down into gravity's capricious clutches.

In wolf form, time seemed to slow for Sivulu; he was lighter, faster, stronger. He moved more gracefully, more fluidly. His jaws found the throat of one of the guards he'd landed on, and his teeth sank into the man's flesh as effortlessly as if he were closing his eyes. Mouth wet with the copper taste of blood, Siv found the exposed flesh of the second guard as quickly as he'd found the first. A chance and his ground were two things that the man never stood.

Siv peered over the edge of the wall to see Hroth pulling his sword from the stomach of another fallen guard. He saw the Hedjetten make eye contact with an older man standing in the center of the swirling storm of swords like an oak tree. He heard him utter an elegant curse that called into question the man's heritage, mental capacity, and sexual ability all in one. He'd never seen Hroth so energized. Which was why, when the aging man in platemail sank his sword deep into the decorated warrior of the Ohmati, Sivulu nearly swallowed his own tongue.

Tennech

The tribesman came at him like a whirlwind. He'd picked up the curved sword from the guard he felled and, brandishing a blade in both hands, looked like a silver storm of light and sound, yelling and spinning and slashing at the air.

"All wind and no lightning!" Tennech shouted at him. "Let's see what you're made of."

Tennech watched the man's movements. They were quick but undisciplined, strong but unfocused.

He'd seen it before when he was at the military academy in Khala Val'ur: strong men who relied on nothing but the fact that they were larger than the others, putting the full force of their weight behind their swings and relying on brute force to get the job done. Tennech, falling neatly in the middle of the distribution of size among the warrior men, had learned to rely on his wit as well as his strength to come out on top. Over the years, as he packed on muscle on top of skill, he saw the two begin to blend together seamlessly.

A man whom the other cadets called Behem after the mountain itself, was pitted against Tennech in a duel one day. Smaller by almost half his body weight, Tennech knew there was no way he was going to come out on top in a purely physical battle.

And, as the braid-wearing tribesman surged forward, Tennech relived the duel in his mind.

Behem had come at him with both swords raised high, his right arm trailing his left, and Tennech had his sword raised to block the blows; but at the last second, Tennech slipped out of the way and let the massive warrior's momentum carry him forward and off balance, bringing the butt of his hilt down on the warrior's head, stunning him. He stepped back to avoid a follow-up slash from the stunned man. Gliding backward, Tennech gracefully parried two more blows from the big man and countered with a slash of his own. Of course, they had been using wooden swords, but the bruising they left was very real—and the blood that came from the Khôl warrior before him was real as well. Like the blackness that came between blinks, the difference between what was real and what was memory was indistinguishable to Tennech, but it didn't matter; his body knew what to do after years of training. He shifted his weight from his back foot to his front, thrust forward cleanly with his sword hand, and found the weakness in the flesh that all warriors wear. He felt the resistance when his blade bit bone, and heard the groan that all dying men share.

He pulled his blade back, wet with fresh blood, and it reminded him of his first blade, Glamrhys—the blade he had given to his first love, all those years before.

The love that had spent the night with him, beneath that starry Thurian sky.

The love that he had promised his life to.

The love that he had killed for.

The love that had left him.

All those years before.

Nessa . . .

Nessa. He had loved her, once.

The memories hit him like a flood, and as the man before him collapsed onto the dusty earth below, Tennech found himself unable to move.

He looked at the tribesman, reality and memory winking in and out like two sides of a spinning top.

His face was numb; his body, unresponsive. And when the streaking black wolf made its way to him in a flash, he almost didn't see it.

He felt the jaws and teeth, though, and he had no defense against them as they closed around his throat. He did not try to fight it.

Death for the Dagger of Derenar was just like his life: apathetic, cold, savage—and alone.

Chapter 76

Théas

Rathma

Silus led them to the door of his shop, and Rathma could feel the heat spilling off of a fire inside. He peered around the old Athrani, surprised to see that the ever-present curtain had been drawn back to reveal a much larger shop than he had imagined. Past the tables and shelves filled with every conceivable remedy was a vast, empty space whose purpose was unclear, but it was one that Rathma could guess.

"Go on in," Silus said as he waved them inside. "Everything is ready."

There was still the smell of pine that made Rathma crinkle his nose, but it was overtaken by the smoky smell of ash and flame—and the feeling of power. This particular power was one that he had known since boyhood, yet it was somehow different: like seeing the face of an old friend many years later, knowing that it had changed, but still recognizing it on the surface. A chill ran through his body as he stepped into the shop just behind Thornton. It was only to be the two of them tonight: Vessel and Anchor.

Thornton looked back at him, his swirling brown eyes deep with seriousness and concern. "Are you sure you're ready?" he asked.

It didn't matter, Rathma knew, but he wasn't going to tell Thornton that. "Yes," he said with a grim nod. "I was born for this."

The answer seemed to satisfy the blacksmith, who gave him a small, encouraging smile, then turned and continued farther inside.

Rathma let the tingle of power flow over him as he welcomed back his old friend, content in the knowledge that he would be surrendering himself to it completely soon enough.

Silus led the two of them back past the curtain, which had been parted down the middle and tied back with gold-colored rope as thick as a man's forearm. The rear of the shop, heretofore concealed by the curtain, dropped downward to reveal a great room that had been hollowed out of the earth itself, stone floors abruptly replacing the wooden ones of the front of the shop. The top of a ladder peeked over the edge of the floor, and Silus surprised them by deftly maneuvering his way down it. Rathma still had trouble reconciling the man's blindness.

Standing at the top of the ladder and looking down, Rathma could see that the room carved out below him was larger than he'd initially guessed. It looked like it was being used as a storage facility, or at least part of it was, as the room itself was massive.

Climbing down the ladder, easily twenty feet to the bottom, Rathma finally got a look at the cavernous space around him that was comprised of little more than cold stone. There were shelves with wooden crates full of Holder knows what, but those only went back a few rows into the otherwise empty room. Behind them was a trail of red wax candles, two of them every few feet, providing a path to the back—where, illuminated only by the candlelight, stood the figure of Silus with his arms outstretched.

The healer was facing the rear of the room that felt more like a cave, and Rathma noticed something painted on the wall before them. As he approached, it became apparent what it was: a large mural, paint still fresh, of the Traveler, Lash'kun Yho.

Rathma knew it was the Traveler because of how the god was described in the legends his people told; and once again he found himself questioning the old Athrani's blindness, as the figure painted on the wall resembled Rathma almost to a tee. He had long red hair, with the sun-darkened skin that the tribes were known for. He was garbed in a dark cloak, resembling Rathma's own, and was flanked by two smaller paintings: to his left, a wolf; to his right, a skull.

"At least there's no mistaking who we are calling," Rathma muttered.

"There must not be," Silus said without turning to face him. "Thornton, the Hammer." He pointed to his right, to a gray stone pillar that rose only a few feet high, with a smooth, flat top. "Place it handle-up."

Thornton nodded, placing the black head of the hammer atop the pedestal to let the white-ash handle point to the ceiling of the great room.

"And Rathma," Silus said, pointing to a spot directly in front of the mural, "stand here."

Rathma complied, feeling the tug of power more strongly than he could ever recall.

If the Traveler knew he was being called, he certainly showed it as Rathma moved into place.

Silus began a chant the words of which Rathma did not immediately recognize—until he listened closer.

> *Lash'kun, Lash'kun, Lash'kun Yho*
>
> *Dobrak mahn ihmantu cho*
>
> *Mith te'kunde ah'man'o*
>
> *Lash'kun, Lash'kun, Lash'kun Yho*

Without warning, the room erupted with light as the candles behind and around them suddenly flared, burning away all other shadows save one—Rathma's—which fell directly on the mural of the Traveler. Rathma felt the hair on his arms raise as a surge of power leapt through him.

The paint that made up the mural began to bubble, distorting the figure of the Traveler as his face began to droop, looking like flesh-colored tears running down the wall. Rathma felt his own body begin to heat up, and he suddenly found himself unable to move as he filled with power. To his right was the bright blue glow of Thornton's hammer.

Silus continued his chant.

. . . Dobrak mahn ihmantu cho . . .

The blue glow from Thornton's hammer intensified, leaping and engulfing Rathma.

. . . Mith te'kunde ah'man'o . . .

And a pain more intense than any he had ever known racked his entire body. He had the sensation of being pulled apart in every direction, as if his skin had decided to flee his bones. He opened his mouth to cry out in pain but found himself unable to. And, with a snap like a cord breaking, the world went black.

Thornton

Rathma collapsed in a heap after the blue light from the Hammer of the Worldforge engulfed him. But then, as if nothing had happened, he stood up. Stretching as though he had woken up from a long sleep, he turned to face Thornton.

"So," he said with a twinkle in his red eyes, "I understand you are after the Shaper."

Chapter 77

Gal'dorok

Awaken the Three

Duna

Arrows came down like iron rain, sticking into the hides of the huge Chovathi around them and taking some Valurians with them as well. Kunas, a look of madness in his eyes, whirled around to face the Sharians, screaming, "What are they doing?" at the top of his lungs. He was practically frothing.

Duna didn't have an answer, but she had a guess: her sister, Lena, probably thought that these Chovathi were the enemy; any rational person would. But if the Sharians kept trying to kill the Chovathi, while killing her army as collateral damage . . .

She had to get them to stop before this whole thing exploded.

"Kunas," she said, "they think we're being attacked. What can you do to stop them?"

"Destroy them," he answered entirely too seriously.

"No! We need them." She surveyed the land and thought about the possibilities. "Can you raise a wall? Maybe something to slow them down while I find Queen Lena."

Kunas's eyes bulged, and he looked like he was trying to contain his rage—or perhaps his power. "You would spare those who attack us?"

Another volley of arrows came down. A few dozen Chovathi shrieked in pain, and half that many more fell to the ground dead. Her men did not fare much better.

Kunas was staring death at the approaching Sharians.

"They think they're helping," Duna snapped. "Now give me that wall or I'll find another Khyth who will."

Kunas still did not make eye contact with her and seemed to be having his own internal struggle about how to stop the Sharians.

"Very well," he finally conceded.

He held his arms out and raised his hands. The sleeves of his robe fell away from his arms, revealing the cracked skin that signified a Khyth of the Breaking.

Duna was never ready for the feeling she got when the Khyth used their Breaking: it was like having the warmth sucked out of a room; it never felt good.

Power, redirected. Refocused.

It chilled her, and she would never be comfortable with it.

The Master Khyth was bent slightly backward, and his arms were stretched out in a semicircle, as if he was holding up a great, invisible weight on his chest. He was drawing a great deal of power for this, Duna could tell. He clenched his fists . . . and the earth trembled.

There was a deafening crack as immeasurable tons of rocks were cleaved in two. From the center of the battlefield, between Duna's army and the Sharians, the earth split, with the fissure quickly making its way across the entire length of the Sharian's front line.

Kunas thrust his fists forward, and the earth groaned again. Where it had split, on the Sharian side, a wall of earth began to rise up.

Only Duna realized that it wasn't actually rising up at all—it was being peeled back. Kunas wasn't summoning a wall; he was paring back the surface of the earth to *move* one instead.

Very clever, Duna admired. By peeling back the earth, he was forcing the Sharians to retreat; if he had just *raised* a wall between them, they might simply have walked around it. This tactic forced them back, though, which gave her more time to get to their army and tell them to stand down.

For now, the volleys of arrows had ceased. Duna seized the opportunity.

"Eowen," she called to her messenger, "come with me. They know you, and that should get us the ear of the queen."

The blond messenger nodded and maneuvered his horse beside hers.

She looked at Kunas. "Good work," she said flatly as she gave her horse a tap with her heels. "Listen for my signal to lower the wall."

The Master Khyth did not answer her; he was still steeped in concentration, bending the earth to his will.

The wall continued to rise, slowly, as Duna and Eowen set off for its edge. They would have to be quick if they hoped to find the queen and convince her to back down—because the *real* enemy still waited beyond.

***

Duna couldn't recall how many years it had been since she and her sister had been together—and, frankly, she didn't care to. When they had last parted ways, it had not been on the best of terms. She wondered if Lena still thought about it.

She supposed she would find out soon.

"Follow my lead," she said to Eowen. Pulling out a piece of white cloth from beneath her armor, she wrapped it around her hand and raised it above her head as they approached the edge of the wall. She wouldn't risk being shot at, even though—or perhaps, because—her sister was the leader of the troops.

Eowen nodded and did the same.

Their horses rounded the edge of the wall, and the entirety of the Sharian army came into view. Duna grimaced. She hadn't been this close to her sister in years, and she hadn't thought about *that day* until recently. The sour taste still lingered in her mouth.

It had never mattered to Duna that the rule of Haidan Shar passed to the strongest instead of the firstborn. Duna had never seen physical strength as important; she relied on her wits to finish battles. Lena, on the other hand, preferred to do things the old-fashioned way: by rolling up her sleeves and taking a swing at whatever was in her way.

And the last time they were together, Duna had been in her way—at least, that's how Lena had seen it. It was why Lena had her exiled.

"Ho there!" came a voice from up ahead. It was a man on horseback coming to greet them.

"You're from the Dorokian army," he said, pulling his horse to a stop. He was a dark-featured man—not dark enough to be G'henni, but perhaps one of his parents had been. "Eowen, isn't it?" he asked as he recognized Duna's messenger. "What brings you here?"

"Correct, Captain Jahaz," Eowen replied with a slight bow from atop his saddle. "We've come with a message for the queen."

"What message?"

Duna addressed the captain: "That your army is attacking the wrong enemy."

Captain Jahaz looked at her for a long moment, studying her features. He looked at her hair and her eyes and her armor. "You must be the sister that she's spoken of," he finally answered.

"I am."

The captain nodded. "Then follow me."

***

When they got close, there was no mistaking her, despite the years that had passed in the interim.

"Duna," her sister said. "You haven't changed."

The words had a bitter aftertaste as Duna swallowed them. Lena *had* changed—but, somehow, for the better. She still had the same flowing blonde hair that she'd had in her youth, and the sharp green eyes that Duna had always envied. While Duna's own eyes seemed to be set too far apart, Lena's were spaced flawlessly; where Duna's forehead seemed just too large for her own head, Lena's was perfect. In short, Lena was everything that Duna was not.

Including reckless.

"Neither have you," she answered. "Still running headlong into battles that you have no reason to fight, I see."

"No reason?" Lena echoed. "Your army was under attack from the Chovathi. You should be thanking me—just like you should thank me for sparing your life that day," she added sharply. "I could have had you killed—*should* have had you killed—for murdering Allyn."

Duna laughed. "Allyn?"

So, she did still think about it. She was too angry to do anything with the thought, though.

"Allyn," Duna went on, "was going to get rid of you the second you became useless to him." Her hand went to the sheath of the dagger that she'd held on to ever since that night. She wanted to throw the proof in Lena's face right now. "You never were good at assessing a situation, were you? You've always just lowered your head and charged forward. Well, this time you got the wrong people killed."

Her hand shook as she unclasped the sheath.

But before she could bring it out, her sister exploded at her.

"*People?*" Lena shouted. "We were killing Chovathi!"

Duna's hand moved away from the dagger again. Now was not the time; she had to control this situation first.

"Just listen to me for once, Lena!" Duna snapped. She squared herself against her younger sister; they were at least equals on horseback. "That's what we're trying to tell you: we're not under attack. We're being helped."

Now it was Lena's turn to laugh. "*Helped?*" she asked incredulously. "Being helped by the Chovathi? I always knew that you were weak, but I never knew that you were crazy too."

"Listen. We've brokered a deal with one of their clans who seek to consolidate power. In exchange for helping them, they will help us by killing off the other clans."

The queen was silent for a moment. She eyed Duna, then the wall, and then her army.

"There seems to be no downside," she said. With a look back at her sister, she went on: "And while I may not have your gift for strategy, I do know this: when a deal seems too good to be true, that's because it is."

Duna shrugged. "We'll worry about that after we retake my city."

Lena sighed and shook her head. "Fine. If there's one thing I remember about you it's that you won't let go when you've got something in your grasp . . ." She tapped the crown on her head. "With one exception."

The tone was soft, but the words were a dagger.

"Just tell me," she added, adjusting herself in the saddle, "where to swing this sword."

At those words, Duna gave a loud whistle . . .

. . . and the wall began to tremble. The colossal structure began its recession back to its original place in the ground, shedding boulders and dirt like a drawbridge made of the earth itself. It groaned to a stop, and the landscape was once again clear.

"Right there," Duna said, pointing.

The two armies were once again face to face, but neither of them was focused on the other. Instead, when the dust had settled, their singular objective was where Duna's finger pointed.

There, in the clutches of the waiting Chovathi, were the peaks of the captive city of Ghal Thurái.

Chapter 78

Théas

Awaken the Three

Thornton

Everything was the same about the Farstepper Rathma, but somehow it all had changed. On the surface, he still looked the same as the young man from beyond the Wastes, but there was something about him, something intangible, that Thornton couldn't quite place. He had seen it before, when Miera had gone into the Otherworld and been overtaken by the Shaper of Ages. There was still some of her left, but a god requires room—among other things. He approached with caution.

"I'm trying to get to the Otherworld," Thornton said. "Can you help?"

"I can," said Rathma—although Thornton knew that he was no longer truly Rathma, he was Lash'kun Yho, the Traveler. "For a price."

Not surprising; the High Keeper of Ellenos had warned them that their passage into the Otherworld via the Land of the Dead would come at a cost; now it was just a matter of finding out how great.

"Of course," Thornton said offhandedly. "What is your price, Traveler?" He used the god's title in hopes of sounding competent.

"We will discuss that when the time comes. But first there is the matter of traveling to Khel-hârad. Do you know the dangers?"

Thornton was unprepared for the question. "Uh," he stammered, "I do . . . not."

The Traveler smiled. "Allow me to educate you," he said. He was using Rathma's voice, but his intonation was different. It was like listening to his father hammer steel using a borrowed hammer: the sound and cadence were right, yet somehow everything else was so very wrong. "Only the dead may enter Khel-hârad, with few exceptions. This is not for the protection of those inside Khel-hârad—it is for the protection of those trying to enter."

Thornton thought back to his time in the Otherworld and shivered. It was a cold and hollow place. He could only imagine what Khel-hârad, the Land of the Dead, would be like.

"Once you enter," the Traveler continued, "you will be changed forever." There was a pause as he obviously meant the words to sink in.

"How do we get there?" Thornton asked, waving it off; some things were worth the cost. "And once we're there, how do we cross into the Otherworld?"

"Eager, aren't we?" the Traveler asked with a grin that made Thornton's grimace turn into a frown. "I will take care of the 'how.' All you need to worry about is the 'what.' As in, what happens when we get there."

Thornton nodded. He looked over to Silus, who had been silent during the exchange. "Silus," he began, getting the old Athrani's attention, "will you tell my friends that I'm leaving?"

A nod of understanding came from the old healer, and Thornton felt a bit of relief. At least his friends would know that they had succeeded in this. He felt a twinge of guilt at leaving Yasha again, but he reasoned that she had spent her entire life without having a brother; now that he was gone, nothing would have changed.

"Well," Thornton began, feigning confidence again, "we should get moving then. Khel-hârad waits."

The words brought out that smile from the Traveler again. Thornton was sure that if Silus could've seen, he would have said something. But the facts were that the old Athrani *was* blind, the Traveler was their only way of getting into Khel-hârad, and Miera was still trapped in the Otherworld. All these things added up to one simple fact: he had to go, and had to agree to the Traveler's price.

"Indeed," the Traveler said. "Come. Take my hand."

He reached out, beckoning Thornton to come closer.

Thornton did as he was asked, grasping the wind-worn palm of the man from Khulakorum, feeling warmth followed by a jarring cold flash through him. He had felt this sensation only once before: when he had crossed into the Otherworld.

There was no turning back.

The stone and wood of Silus's shop melted away like wax, rushing at him suddenly, reminding him that he was dealing with a power much greater than any he had ever wielded—even greater than the Hammer of the Worldforge.

Awaken the Three

He had taken a head-first dive into a pool of unknown depth, and there was a very real possibility that he would strike the bottom.

And when the crisp coldness of Khel-hârad hit him, he realized just what the bottom felt like.

Chapter 79

Khadje Kholam

Awaken the Three

Sivulu

The copper taste of blood was still fresh in Sivulu's mouth as he turned to find the entrance to Djozen Yelto's inner compound, where he knew they were keeping Asha Imha-khet. Hroth of the Ohmati had fallen, but his men fought on, and there would be a new Hedjetten chosen after the battle. All around him men continued to fall, Farstepper and Khôl alike, but the chaos would not keep Sivulu from his goal.

At least that is what he told himself before he saw the giant black creatures defending the inner gates. They were bigger than anything he had ever seen, and he was sure that each of their forelimbs could have smashed through the stone of Yelto's compound with only the slightest bit of effort. One of them let out a mighty cry that made Sivulu wince and paw at his ears. As a wolf, his senses were staggeringly sharper than when he was a human, and he had never lamented that fact until now.

"Uzma," he shouted to the remaining Hedjetten from the Kuufi tribe, his voice gnarled by his lupine vocal cords, "get rid of those things! Refocus until they are taken down! Beyond them lies the prize."

Uzma nodded and turned to bark orders at his men. The tribesmen still poured over the walls in great numbers, only being slowed by the stubborn swords and arrows of Yelto's rapidly depleting army.

Sivulu watched the twin black pillars as they spewed death before them, pinning men to the ground and tearing them in half with barely a shred of effort. Their long necks were topped with horned heads that gored and skewered with ease, and their mouths were caverns of daggers that made even steel look flimsy. Five Kuufi had rushed them at once only to meet a swift and bloody end. The fifth warrior had caught the tip of one of the creature's horns, driven deep into his ribcage and straight out his back, and was tossed unceremoniously over the wall.

This was proving to be difficult, yet they had to get past them in order to free the Ghost.

At least that is what he thought before the streaking figure of Kuu came careening through the legs of both creatures, heedless of danger, racing right toward the gates of the inner compound of Djozen Yelto.

Chapter 80

Khel-hârad

Awaken the Three

Thornton

The air was cool, and Khel-hârad stretched into infinity.

All around them were shifting shades, and it was difficult for Thornton to tell what was real and what was simply his mind playing tricks on him—or if the two were one and the same. He felt the strange tingling down his spine that he had felt during his brief stay in the Otherworld and knew that he was standing in its twin: a remnant of creation, another plane of existence.

Just as the Shaper ruled the Otherworld, so did the Holder rule the Land of the Dead. He was in here somewhere, waiting—waiting to be anchored to a Vessel in the same way that the Traveler had been. The thought made Thornton shudder.

He knew the Traveler would be able to get him to the threshold of the Otherworld to find Miera, but he didn't know how he could get in. He felt the weight of his hammer, still strapped to his back, and wondered if it might still be the key. The Hammer of the Worldforge had, along with the power of the Shaper, sealed the Otherworld. Perhaps it could unseal it. Regardless, the Traveler was the one in control now.

Thornton looked at the body of Rathma, now inhabited by a god. The god smiled.

"Getting in to Khel-hârad," he said, "is the easy part."

He began to walk, motioning for Thornton to follow.

"Everything that follows is a bit more . . . difficult."

***

Khel-hârad was unlike anything Thornton had ever imagined, and the intransitive nature of the world was making his head hurt.

For being called the Land of the Dead, Khel-hârad felt very much alive: everywhere Thornton looked there were jutting mountains and rolling hills, teeming forests and dying deserts. But the one thing that made him uneasy—and the one thing that truly made him realize the scale of this place—was that, no matter how far he could see, he never saw a horizon. Everything just . . . kept . . . *going*.

Even in Derenar, the land had an end. Once, when he was a boy, his father had taken him east to the Tashkar Sea, where he had looked out onto the water and had been sure that it went on forever. But even the water came to an end, somewhere out there on the horizon, where it looked like the world just stopped.

Nothing like that existed in this place; there was never an end in sight. Thornton couldn't wrap his mind around it, and after a while he had given up trying.

***

"It was you mortals that made it this way, you know," the Traveler said.

Thornton closed his eyes and rubbed his temples. "What way?"

"Like this," the Traveler said, indicating the scenery with a grand wave of his hand. The two of them had been walking for quite some time, but had not spoken. "The trees and the light and the life. All of your dead were the ones that brought life here, ironically. When this place was first created, it was barren and empty."

With a humorless laugh, he added, "I should know."

The path that they trod was lined with grass and strangely colored flowers. In fact, Thornton had noticed that everything in this place was almost like an imitation of things that existed in Derenar. There were trees, but they had oddly colored leaves or unusually shaped branches; there were plants, but he recognized none of them; there was a sky, but something about it seemed . . . off.

"What happened that changed it?" Thornton asked.

"When the first of your dead came here," the Traveler responded, "all that they had were their spirits, but within those spirits lived sparks of power. Some of the dead clung to the lives they were forced from, refusing to let go, thus bringing a bit of the world of the living with them. Whenever that would happen," he said with a dramatic snap of his fingers, "the power manifested itself in creation."

Thornton felt a breeze blow by, warm yet chilling, as if it was a breeze that did not quite understand what being a breeze meant.

"All of this is because of the spirits of the dead?" Thornton asked. He looked to his right, to a great forest that stretched out before them, curving away from them like a waterfall made of trees. There was a river in the middle that snaked away as well, never seeming to get any thinner despite flowing into the distance. The sky above was a strange shade of blue, and the few, sparse clouds that he saw never seemed to move.

It all just . . . kept . . . going! Thornton had to rub his eyes when his mind started trying to make sense of it: the scale, the impossible perspectives—it made him dizzy, and he had to look away, focusing back on the path in front of them.

"No one spirit was responsible for what you see here," the Traveler went on. "It is the collective longing of countless generations, brought into being by the very ones who left the shadows of themselves behind in your world."

Thornton knew all about having to let go of something that he'd never intended to leave. "They were torn from their lives," Thornton said absently, "so they tried to bring their lives with them."

He had said the words aloud but had not really meant to—only, now, it all made sense to him. He knew why this place was the way that it was.

When he looked at the strange representations of everything around him, he felt as though he was trying to remember a dream after just being awakened. In the dream, everything would have seemed so crisp and clear and real; but when he awoke and tried to remember what he'd been dreaming, it always came out twisted and distant: faces were blurred, words were indistinct, colors were uncertain. It was like reaching for a hand just beyond his grasp.

This world, he now realized, was just that: a dead man's dream of a life once lost.

Thornton looked again over the forest that stretched out into forever, and frowned.

He had no intention of being stuck in someone else's dream any longer than he had to be.

The Traveler kept walking, and Thornton Woods followed closely behind.

Chapter 81

Gal'dorok,
Outside Ghal Thurái

Awaken the Three

Duna

The armies, led by their respective commanders, marched as one toward Ghal Thurái. By habit, they were still separated: Duna marched the Thurians and Valurians; Kunas, the Chovathi; and Lena was directing the Sharians. Cortus Venn, high above them all, was still riding on that *thing* that almost made Duna as uncomfortable as the Chovathi did.

But all of them were at the front of their armies—*the* army—highly visible and in control.

Like any good commander should be, Duna thought with a hint of self-assurance.

The fact was that she had a dizzying number of self-doubts about her ability to lead at all. She had tried not to let them get to her, pushing them down to drown them in self-confidence, but they would always resurface in the form of the malicious uncertainty that she should by no means be leading these armies.

And maybe I shouldn't be, came the latest thought. *All I've commanded is a retreat from the forest of Kienar. Maybe Lena would be better suited to lead.*

She looked over to her sister, who was riding to her right. Queen Lena, outfitted in her platemail, with that oversized sword strapped to her back, looked poised and confident—regal, even—as they marched toward the Mouth of the Deep. And, as a monarch, she should have been so. None of those things surprised Duna. But one thing did stick.

As a monarch.

The fragmented thought resonated in Duna's mind.

Her sister *was* a monarch. And, as a monarch she was, by definition, not a military officer. And the fact remained that Duna was no subject of Haidan Shar.

Huh.

She gave her sister a casual, sidelong glance.

In fact, she thought, *as the highest-ranking military officer in all of Gal'dorok, I'm actually in charge of* her.

The thought was so absurd that she didn't even try to stop the laugh that came forth—and it was loud enough to get her sister's attention.

"What?" Lena asked suspiciously, peering at her from atop her mount. "Care to share?"

"Oh, I was just reminding myself that I'm the highest-ranking officer in Gal'dorok."

"Yes, you are. Congratulations." She clasped her hands and shook them in mock celebration. "So what?"

"So," Duna replied, "that means that I'm in charge of the armies of Gal'dorok—which, as of today, includes Haidan Shar."

Lena narrowed her eyes.

"And you are part of the Sharian army. Therefore—"

Lena cut her off. "I'm not taking orders from you," she said flatly.

Duna smiled. She would try not to get under her sister's skin too much. After all, it was a historic occasion: for the first time since the Shaping War, all the armies of Gal'dorok would be marching under one banner, united in one cause.

In the past, Haidan Shar had been the lone holdout, refusing to send troops to support the military conquests of their neighbors in Ghal Thurái and Khala Val'ur, who were really only loosely associated anyway—until Duna had ascended to the rank of general, that is.

Now they were all hers to command.

And command, she would.

"All things considered," she said to Lena, "once we approach the Mouth, it's very important that you listen to me. I know those mountains and hills; I know the rocks and crevices. I'll know where the Chovathi will be defending."

Lena looked at her uneasily, and Duna realized it was the first time the topic of the Chovathi had been broached since the merging of the two armies.

"You really think they'll be that organized?" Lena asked.

Kunas, who Duna had almost forgotten was there, spoke up. "Assuredly," he said. His rasping, hollow voice took her by surprise. "The Chovathi are nothing like you humans think. They are cunning, they are patient—and they are strong."

Duna didn't like the way that Kunas had said *you humans*, but she let it go, giving him no more than a suspicious glance from her place beside him.

"It is their cunning that worries me," Lena said. She was looking at the Chovathi that were marching under their banner. "What assurances have you of your new allies' loyalty?"

Duna had to agree. What if they *were* walking into a trap? It was more than just possible; it was probable: What better way to secure the Chovathi's place in Ghal Thurài, their ancestral home, than to wipe out the armies of Gal'dorok? The thought made her shiver.

Maybe Lena had been right to start attacking the Chovathi upon arrival . . .

Kunas answered, interrupting her train of thought. "Ghal Thurài is my city," he began. "It is my home. I will defend it at all costs. And that includes"—he held up his palm to reveal a large gash across it—"making a blood pact with the Xua'al."

Duna looked at the cut, obviously recent, and then to Kunas. She didn't know what a blood pact with the Chovathi entailed, but she certainly wanted no part of it.

"What have you done?" she asked.

"What was necessary," Kunas replied, fixing his eyes on the road ahead. "When we have fought our way inside, you will see. But you have my word that the Xua'al clan means to slaughter the other Chovathi tribes, and nothing more."

Duna adjusted her position in the saddle. *I suppose that is as good an assurance as any*, she thought.

Then again, how much did she trust the word of Kunas?

Most of the ride after that was spent in silence.

***

"We are close," the Master Khyth said as they approached, his gaze fixed on the path ahead.

Duna raised her eyes to the city she had called home for most of her life. Now it was only a shell of what it once was: a city that had taken her in, the exiled daughter of a king, and raised her to be the woman that she was. It was a city that she loved. A city that was now in ruins.

Her anger burned as hot as the fires on the night of its occupation.

"We are here to take it back," she said, turning to her sister. "My men know the city best. A head-on assault through the entrance will only bottleneck us. We will be more successful if we spread out."

Lena had already donned her platemail helmet. If she hadn't looked like a warrior before, she certainly did now. "Then what do you suggest?" The words echoed behind the metal of her bevor.

"There are five entrances: the main entrance at the Mouth," she said as she pointed to the ravaged marble columns that once stood so proud, "and four subentrances on the edge of the mountain." She indicated four passageways that would not have been obvious unless one knew where to look.

Lena looked at Duna, hesitated, then relented. "Fine. But I will choose who goes where."

Duna considered this. "Fine," she shot back.

"The Xua'al will storm the two western subentrances." She looked over at Kunas, de facto leader of the Chovathi forces, who nodded his assent.

Lena went on: "The warriors of the Fist of Thurái should take the two eastern subentrances; the Fist are the best trained and have the best knowledge of the land, and will prove to be most effective in uncertain terrain. The remaining soldiers of Khala Val'ur will provide assistance as needed."

"That will work," said Duna.

"Finally, my men will storm the front. Yes, we will face the most resistance, but it will be on level ground, where we will not have to worry about navigating uneven and unfamiliar terrain. We don't know how deep in the Chovathi will be, and we're prepared to go looking for them."

Awaken the Three

Duna thought about this. Her sister was right, but to enter the Mouth alone, even with their numbers, would be nothing short of insanity. "You want your men to storm the gates head on?" she asked. "By yourself?"

Lena had a grin on her face that told Duna that she had planned for this.

"Not by ourselves," she said, turning her eyes to the sky, where Cortus Venn still circled on his Gwarái. "We'll send in an emissary."

Duna followed her gaze to the airborne creature that could blot out the sun if it were in the right place. She thought about the Stoneborn, Venn, whose power she had only heard about through secrets and whispers. She had to admit: he would make one hell of an emissary.

"Then we'll begin the division of troops at once," Duna said. She turned her head to the sky and cupped both of her hands to her mouth. "Venn!" she shouted. "Feel like knocking on the front door?"

The booming laughter that came from the commander of the Lonely Guard was answer enough.

"Then it's settled," Duna said—and just in time.

No sooner had the words left her mouth than the gates to the Mouth of the Deep swung wide open. More Chovathi than Duna had ever seen in her entire life—more than she had ever known *existed*—began to flood from the entrance.

"Well," Lena said, drawing out her enormous longsword and giving her mount's ribs a pair of kicks, "at least we won't have to look long."

Duna was silent.

In that moment, all of the self-doubt that she had managed to suppress, all of the apprehension and insecurities that she thought she'd locked away, all the questions about her leadership and her competency—all the negative things that she could possibly hold inside—came bursting forth from her mind like a flood.

A flood of fear. A flood of doubt.

A flood made of white-tipped claws and jagged teeth.

Chapter 82

Khadje Kholam

Awaken the Three

Dailus

Dailus woke up with a headache that clawed at the back of his eyes.

He was lying on his back against a stone floor, and he could feel cold metal on his wrists and ankles, which were spread out and stretched with no slack in the chain. He could only move his head, barely, and he did his best to look around.

The room he was in was cool and dark, which told him that he must be underground. The ceiling above him was circular and wide, and the only light in the room came from a half dozen red candles arranged around him in a circle. He didn't take it to be a good sign, but not much these days actually was.

It had been an exhausting ride from Théas—there had been plenty of urgency when Lady Elana had shouted orders at her guards in a guttural, foreign tongue—and Dailus was relieved when they had finally stopped. He'd had enough of being tossed around on horseback to last him a lifetime. But, as soon as they crossed into the Wastes, his escorts had seen fit to render him unconscious. He really wished that people would stop doing that.

He had never been this far south before, and the lack of moisture in the air was starting to get to him. He decided to bear with it and hoped he adjusted to it quickly. Although, after being sold as a slave in that humiliating auction the other day, he wasn't sure how long he would be staying in one spot—or how long he would be alive, for that matter.

Just as his mind started to wander, he heard footsteps behind him. They approached him and stopped, just beyond his vision.

"Lady Elana has done well," rasped a voice in an accent, slow and strong. "You will make a fine Vessel."

Dailus didn't know what a Vessel was, but he didn't like the sound of it.

"What does that mean?" he asked, and the footsteps began again. In front of him walked a man dressed in a dark blue robe with a white border.

"It means you have been chosen," the man said. Although, when Dailus got a better look at him, he would not have called him a man: he looked more like a skeleton, as the skin from his neck on up was missing, and his unblinking eyes stared hauntingly on.

Dailus swallowed the sick that crept up his throat.

"Chosen?" he choked. "For what?"

"You will see," came the ominous answer. "But for now, be silent. The Vessel must be cleansed before the Holder of the Dead may enter."

"Cleansed? What . . . ," Dailus began to ask. Then he saw the gleam of a knife that the man had pulled from his robe. He couldn't make out many details, but he saw the iron carving of a howling wolf gracing the handle.

"Silence," the man said as he knelt down. He held out the tip of the knife to one of the candles and watched as the flame licked at the edge of the blade. "May Ahmaan Ka find this body suitable."

"No," pleaded Dailus limply, but he knew it was useless.

The man's unblinking eyes shifted to Dailus as he brought the blade to the top of his forehead. "We are all equal in the sight of the Holder."

Dailus felt the blade glide across his skin; it was incredibly sharp, and nearly painless. The only indication he had that it had bit into his flesh was the warm oozing of blood that he felt on his face.

He looked up, trembling at the skinless, skeletal face before him. The horrific realization came forth slower than the blood: that face would soon be his, too.

A scream escaped his lips when he felt his own skin peel back, and he swore he saw the lidless man smile.

Chapter 83

Khadje Kholam

Awaken the Three

Kuu

Kuu knew that he had to act fast. His padded feet pounded against the desert floor as he raced toward Yelto's compound. He heard his brother yelling after him, but it didn't stop him. *Wait behind?* he scoffed. *Not a chance.*

The walls of the fortress were high and broad, but that didn't matter. The gate was open, and Kuu was small enough in his fox form to steal his way inside.

But directly inside waited the robed figure of a Priest of the Holder, standing right in his path and staring him down.

"I see you've returned, boy," the priest hissed, drawing himself up to his full height and gripping his staff in his hands. The sounds of battle exploded around them as swords bit into armor and blood spilled on the ground. "But you're too late: the Holder is being awakened as we speak. His dominion over this world is drawing near."

"Then let me pass," Kuu said with confidence—he hoped.

"And allow you to free the Ghost?" the priest scoffed. "Never." His ghastly eyes were narrowed in contempt.

Kuu was undeterred. "It was worth a shot," he said. Backing up, he began the transformation back into his human form. If he was going to fight, he would do it in the body that was more capable.

His vulpine form was quick, yes, but it didn't hold a candle to how deft and maneuverable his human form was—not to mention how good it was with a sword. As his bones cracked, split, and reformed, he looked around for a weapon he could use. The sounds of clattering steel rang in the air as Yelto's men clashed with the tribesmen. On the ground, next to the body of an old man in platemail, was the perfect blade. He dashed over to it as the last of his fur receded, naked flesh his only armor, and picked it up.

Facing the priest again, he held the sword out in a readied stance. "Then I guess I'll have to go through you," he said defiantly.

The priest's exposed facial muscles contorted into what Kuu assumed was a grin. "You are welcome to try," came the hissed reply.

Raising his staff in the air, the priest brought it back down, smashing the end of it on the ground with a resounding crack.

And all around him, Kuu felt the earth shake.

He had heard of their power, and had hoped for his entire life that he would never find out if the stories were true. But when he saw the first of the bodies shudder back to life and stand up, he knew right then that the stories were not just stories.

"The Holder has given us a gift," the priest said with an air of self-importance. "You should count yourself as privileged to witness it firsthand."

Kuu frowned. He didn't feel privileged. If anything, he felt afraid. But despite that, he held fast. Shifting his attention to one of the reanimated bodies that shambled toward him, blood still oozing from an open neck wound that had felled the original owner, he turned to face the thing. He wasn't quite sure what power drove the body now, and he was determined not to dwell on it; the only thing that mattered to him now was how to stop it.

"Thanks, I guess," Kuu said indignantly.

The body of the man—one of the Kuufi, he could see—was slow and clumsy, walking like a drunkard after a long night in the taverns. The eyes were glazed over with death, and Kuu wondered if the thing was even using its eyes to navigate at all, or if it was simply being compelled by whatever power had brought it back to life. As it closed in on him, Kuu knew that it probably didn't make a difference. He readied his sword.

The creature hobbled nearer.

Kuu flexed his knees, going into a fighting stance. And then, quicker than he could blink, the creature was toppled by a huge, green-eyed wolf.

The terrible din they made as the two of them crashed to the ground sounded to Kuu like the end of the world.

"I told you to stay put," Sivulu growled, sinking his fangs into the thing's neck and tearing out the throat. He bit again and shook his head savagely, severing muscle and sinew, and dropping the head from its former body. The big wolf looked up and narrowed his eyes. "You're going to get yourself killed."

Awaken the Three

Kuu shrugged this off as he turned to face another encroaching corpse, swinging his sword above him and gracefully relieving the creature of its head by way of his own biting steel. "We'll see," he said, turning to engage another. They were rising up all around them, and the priest was just standing there, grinning that skeletal grin. Kuu wondered if he was even expending any strength.

"No, Kuu," Sivulu shot back, pouncing on another corpse and driving the thing to the ground. "Your brothers and I can handle it. You weren't built for this."

The words made him wince, a blow he couldn't deflect. "Siv," he countered angrily, "I can handle myself."

As if to prove his claim, he took down another two corpses that had gotten closer, slicing his sword through their throats as easily as he would butter bread. A third one, though, had caught him by surprise from behind. By the time Kuu saw it, the thing had already raised its curved sword and was bringing the blade down on him. He turned to parry the blow but was forced to his knees by the surprising strength of the creature.

Ka's breath! he swore to himself. *How are they so strong?*

Before the thing could do any more damage, Sivulu knocked it off balance, bringing it to the ground in a howling crash of livened steel.

"Then prove it," his older brother said, glowering at him from atop the fallen body. "There's still time to free her."

Kuu used the hilt of the sword to help him stand up, growling with frustration as two more creatures approached. "What are you saying?" he asked his brother.

"I'm saying I will handle the priest," Siv answered. "You need to go after the Ghost. She is our last hope if Yelto succeeds in waking the Holder." He looked Kuu in the eyes. "You can get farther inside than any of us; they won't be looking for a fox. You can free her."

Kuu growled in frustration. His brother was right, but he didn't want to leave him. They were outnumbered, and the numbers were only growing further and further against them. He looked at Sivulu as the huge wolf lunged at the throat of another of the priest's puppets.

"Go!" Sivulu growled. "You are wasting time!"

Kuu swung his sword at the neck of another approaching corpse and watched the thing drop to the ground. He felt his bones breaking apart and fusing back together as his body changed. He hated doing it, but his sense of duty overrode his sense of comfort.

"And you," he said as he turned and headed toward the entrance to Yelto's chambers, "are the same old Siv."

If what the priest was saying was true—and Kuu didn't doubt that it was—their lives were all in danger. Yelto was waking the Holder. But there was still hope as long as the Ghost was with them.

Chapter 84

Derenar

Lilyana

Lily awoke to the sounds of an argument. The words were low and whispered, but they pierced the air nonetheless.

"He knows me, and he knows my face. He'll never stop looking," came the first voice.

"I can keep you safe," said the second. "I know of a small village, far out of the way. Come with us. I can protect you."

"No," said the first. "I am not important. She is. And he doesn't know her."

That was when Lily realized they were talking about her. She rolled over to wake her mother but found that she was alone. She pushed back the thick blanket that had kept her warm all night and climbed off the end of the wagon. Standing by the embers of a dying fire were her mother and her uncle Thaurson. She wiped the sleep from her eyes. In her grogginess, she hadn't even recognized their voices.

Her mother was the first to notice that they were no longer alone, turning to her with a look of concern on her face. "Oh, Lily," she said, kneeling down and spreading her arms. "Did we wake you?"

Lily nodded and walked over to give her mother a hug.

"I am so sorry, my darling. It isn't safe yet. But I have a plan that will protect you."

Lily looked expectantly at her mother.

"Your uncle knows someone who can take good care of you," Cora said.

Thaurson nodded. "He's a good man. Still a little young, but he means well. And he can be trusted."

"Where is he?" Lily asked.

Her mother and her uncle looked at each other. Looking back at Lily with a smile, Thaurson said, "We'll take you to him."

Chapter 85

Ghal Thurái

Awaken the Three

Benjin

This is it, Benj thought. *This is war.*

It was the thing that he'd trained for most of his life; yet, as scores of Chovathi poured from the mouth of Ghal Thurái, he suddenly felt very much like a boy who'd been thrust into battle.

In other words: exactly what he was.

Only minutes before, he'd been a confident armiger, attendant to Captain Jahaz, and even a friend of the queen.

Now, he was just another child.

Thyst was beside him, readying an arrow to nock on her bowstring.

"This is insane, right?" she asked. She pulled back on the arrow but seemed to be lost as to where to fire it. At this point, there were entirely too many targets. "They can't really expect us to fight all of those things . . . can they?"

"I-I think they can," Benj stammered. "And I think we have to."

There had been a brief moment of chaos when the creatures had first emerged; everyone in the army had expected the Chovathi to be waiting for them in the depths of the Mouth. What they had not expected them to do was to leave the protection of the mountain city's walls. This change in expectations had caused a commotion through most of the army, made even worse by something that happened immediately afterward.

Every now and again, on their march up, Benj had caught glimpses of a man riding on the great winged Gwarái's back. And when the Chovathi started emerging from Ghal Thurái, the surprise must have caused the man to fall off, and the gasps of surprise from the men around him told him that the ending would not be pretty. Benj stared in horror as he watched the man that was now hurtling toward the ground.

But the longer he watched the man falling, the more Benj realized something: he hadn't fallen at all—he had jumped!

"Look out below, you bastards!" the man yelled, roaring with laughter. His arms were spread wide, and he was holding swords in both hands, chest and head thrust toward the ground in a controlled free fall toward the largest concentration of Chovathi, clustered right by the entrance to the city.

In fact, not only had he jumped, but he was actually *aiming*!

"Thyst! Are you seeing this?" Benj asked, not taking his eyes off the earth-bound maniac.

"Yeah," she said in a near-whisper. "Is he . . . ?"

"Aiming," Benj said incredulously. "Yeah."

Even Captain Jahaz had stopped for a moment to watch the spectacle. "He's gone mad," the captain breathed. "Not like it matters now."

And then, as if to prove them wrong, mere seconds before he hit the ground, the man twisted deftly in the air so that his back was facing the ground, swords in the air, like a well-armed boulder about to hit home.

Then he collided with the ground so hard that all of Ghal Thurái shook.

"Breaker's balls!" Jahaz swore.

A massive plume of dust rose up so high that Benj thought he'd just seen the end of the world. He closed his eyes reflexively, as if he expected to feel the death that would inevitably hit him, probably in the form of a rockslide or a crater that would open up and swallow him.

But when neither of those things came, he opened one eye and looked at the spot where the man had crashed into the world: the entrance to the Mouth. The dust was still rising, but there looked to be a huge pile of . . . something where the man had hit.

"Venn, you absolute madman," Benj heard a woman say. It was General Cullain, the queen's sister.

Benj looked again at the pile. He squinted, trying to make out just what it was. Then he realized: it was a pile of Chovathi bodies.

And out of the center of it, clawing his way to the top, was Cortus Venn.

"How . . . ," Jahaz began. "How is he still alive?"

General Cullain laughed from up ahead. "You wouldn't believe me if I told you." Turning to Queen Lena, she said, "Well, now that he's made his entrance, what's say we make ours?"

The queen smiled at her. She was holding her greatsword in one hand. At those words, she thrust it forward and yelled, "For Gal'dorok!"

The entirety of the army—Sharian, Thurian, and Valurian—shouted at the top of their lungs. It was enough to make Benj want to cover his ears; he didn't feel much like shouting. But, after seeing what the man called Venn had just done, and knowing that he was on their side, he definitely felt like fighting.

He would follow *him* just about anywhere.

"Come and get it, you bottom-dwelling whoresons!" Venn shouted, loud enough for Benj to hear, as he brandished his two swords around him in a whirl of blades. He was cutting through Chovathi seamlessly as if he'd been doing it his whole life. Benj's jaw dropped. Was he going to take on the whole army by himself?

"Save some for us, Venn!" shouted General Cullain. She and her army had split off and were making their way away from the main gate where Venn had crash-landed. Queen Lena, on the other hand, was motioning her army forward.

They would be charging the main gate, Benj knew.

He felt the leather sheath by his side, where the sword his mother had given him was hanging.

Glamrhys, she'd called it. He felt that he would need it. He hoped it wouldn't be soon.

Duna

"That Venn is something else," Duna said with awe. If she hadn't seen it with her own two eyes, she wouldn't have believed that he could survive a fall from the winged Gwarái, several hundreds of feet in the air.

But he'd done just that, and it was incredible.

"I'm just glad he's on our side," Captain LaVince said from beside her. He was commanding one of the three battalions that had split off from the main body of the army, with Captains Jerol and Ohlez leading the remaining two. The three of them together would be heading into the subentrances of Ghal Thurái.

"I think he's his own side," Duna said. "But at this point it doesn't even matter; he's killing Chovathi by the dozens. I don't even know if they can do anything to stop him."

She watched again in awe as the Stoneborn slashed his way through a crowd of the lumbering white beasts that still poured from the Mouth. She shook her head and collected her thoughts.

Turning to her men, she put her thoughts into words.

"Now," she shouted, "we do it how we planned it! Battalion one, take the eastern-most tunnel; battalion two, the western-most. Battalion three, lend your strength as needed; you will watch the backs of the others and make sure they are not caught unaware by unaccounted-for Chovathi. Does everyone understand the plan?"

The battalions and their respective commanders slammed their swords against their shields twice in acknowledgment.

"Then let's take back Ghal Thurái!" she shouted, raising her sword into the air.

The army cheered in response. Music to her ears.

She turned to Kunas beside her, in charge of the Chovathi contingent. "Now will you tell me," she began, barely audible over the cheers, "what we have to find once we're inside?"

He wasn't looking at her. Instead, he was looking over his hulking white troops. "Leave that to us."

Again with that you versus us, she thought with a frown. *What happened in that nest?*

"Very well," she answered. "A lot of people are counting on you."

Kunas looked at her, his swirling eyes a vortex of fury.

"And all of them are expendable," he answered. Wordlessly, he turned his horse and headed for the two middle tunnels that formed subentrances to the Mouth, followed silently by the monstrous Xua'al warriors behind him.

The Sharians had already begun their ascent to Ghal Thurái, moments away from clashing with the Chovathi that had come forth from the mountain fortress. And, though the Sharians would certainly be the ones to start the conflict, Duna had a feeling that the Xua'al would be the ones to end it.

Chapter 86

Border of Gal'dorok
and Derenar

Awaken the Three

Lilyana

They had been riding for a few hours now, and Lily was incredibly sore. She couldn't remember ever riding a horse before, although her mother swore up and down that she had. One thing was for sure, though: she hated it. If she ever had a choice between walking or riding, she vowed that she would walk.

"We're nearly there," said Thaurson. He was in the lead, seated atop a great stallion that looked very well suited for his weight. "We can dismount and walk the rest of the way."

Lily's relief at those words was palpable.

Gorbun was behind her, and he seemed to sense it.

"Don't like ridin'?" he leaned in to ask.

Lily shook her head.

"Me neither, truth be told. But Thaurson loves it. Probably because it means he doesn't 'ave to carry all that weight of 'is around."

Lily looked at her massive uncle and giggled.

"What's so funny, you two?" Thaurson asked.

"Nothing," Lily said, beaming at Gorbun.

"Then follow me," he said, taking his horse by the reins. "They're out on patrol today, away from the city. They know me and they've had dealings with Gorbun. Just remember what I told you."

Lily nodded.

But instead of moving on, Thaurson kept looking at her. He looked back over his shoulder, as if considering something, then let his horse's reins fall from his hands.

He walked over to Lily, knelt down, and put his hand on her shoulder.

"I want to hear you say it again," he said.

Lily's lip quivered a bit. "My mother loves me very much," she said to him. "And she is doing this to protect both of us."

"That's right," he said, and stood back up. "Now follow me and do as you're told."

***

They had walked into an area that was not quite woods and not quite mountains. Off in the distance, Lily saw a group of soldiers on horseback.

"Is that them?" she asked, and was hushed immediately by Thaurson.

"Gorbun, flag them down," he said.

The blond man nodded and walked out in front, approaching the riders who were still a good ways off. The riders saw him waving and changed their course to intercept him. When they got closer, Lily could see that most of them were still young.

One of them nodded at the two men with her. "Gorbun," he said, a thin man with dark hair and the beginnings of a mustache. "Still doing runs?"

Gorbun nodded. "Found this one outside Lusk," he said, pointing his thumb over his shoulder at Lily. "Thought she might fetch a good price."

The dark-haired man dismounted and went over to look at her. Lily fought the urge to hold on to her uncle's leg. *Be strong*, she reminded herself.

The man knelt down to look at her, inspecting her eyes and her face. "Athrani," he said, seeming pleased.

"Aye," answered Gorbun.

The man looked up at him. "It's unusual," he said, "but not unheard of." Turning his head back to the other riders, he said, "We just had one come in the other day. An envoy from Ellenos. The Tallister. What was his name?"

Another rider, pale and blond, said, "Yota, I think."

"No, that's not it," said the dark-haired man. Then, snapping his fingers, he said, "Yetz! His name is Yetz." He looked pleased at remembering this information, and looked back at Lily. "So you won't be the first of your kind in Khala Val'ur. Maybe one day you'll get to meet him. Who knows," he said, standing up. "But slaves and ambassadors don't usually mix. Anyways," he said, turning to Gorbun, "she's a good find. We'll take her. I'm in need of a protégé."

He reached into the leather pouch that was tied to his waist and dug out a pair of coins, tossing them to Gorbun. "For your trouble," he said. "Fine work as always. You too, Thaurson," he said, nodding at Lily's uncle. "And I'll take her horse as well."

Thaurson just gave him a nod.

"Now," the man said, looking Lily's way once more. "What do they call you?"

Lily looked at him and then back to her uncle, who shook his head.

"I . . . don't have a name," she said meekly.

"Hmm. Well, that's no good," said the man. He eyed her keenly, and Lily thought that he was staring straight through her. "We have to call you *something*."

One of the riders behind him piped up: "Captain Tennech, what about that gal from Ghal Thurái you're always going on about?"

The dark-haired man looked at Lily and cocked his head, then looked back to the blond rider. "You know, Lieutenant," he said, "that might actually fit." Turning to go, he motioned for Lily to follow and pointed to Ruen, the young brown horse she'd come in on. "Can you ride that thing?"

She nodded.

"Good. Then get on. And welcome to Gal'dorok, *Seralith*."

Chapter 87

Ghal Thurái

Awaken the Three

Duna

It wasn't easy to lead an army that was split into three parts, especially underground, but Duna had no choice.

She had always known General Tennech to be the kind of general to wade into battle along with his troops, even if only to shout directions at them, such as telling them to back off or to press the attack. She looked to follow his example now, as she knew that he was probably the greatest military mind alive.

Their army had met some Chovathi resistance at the entrance to the tunnel, but not nearly as much as she had imagined, which most likely meant that the bulk of the forces was concentrated near the entrance to the Mouth. She thought of the long staircase that descended deeper into Ghal Thurái, and how treacherous it would be trying to fight one's way down it. And, for the first time in a long time, she thought about the welfare of her sister.

She just hoped that Kunas was upholding his end of the bargain as well.

Kunas

She is in here, the voice said to him. It was driving him onward, urging him forward, deeper into the reaches of Ghal Thurái.

At first, he'd thought he had gone mad. But then, when the Xua'al matriarch had used the blood pact to open his mind and senses to what she was seeing and feeling, he embraced it; if madness was this intoxicating, he welcomed it gladly.

Where? Kunas asked. *How far?*

There was a momentary silence as he could feel Zhala probing the deepness with her mind. Despite being a half day's walk away, the Xua'al matriarch had no problem extending her consciousness into the cave through the use of her broodlings.

Not far, she replied.

Just as she said that, Kunas felt the mountain around them tremble.

What was that? he asked.

This place resists my presence, came the answer. *There is great power here.*

Kunas felt his need for self-preservation drive him to leave, but Zhala put a stop to it.

Continue, she said in a stern tone. *My power is limited, and so is our time.*

"Oh, wonderful," Kunas said out loud. He wasn't sure if Zhala couldn't hear him, or if she was simply ignoring the sarcasm. Either way, she was silent and Kunas found himself pleased.

"What wonder-ful?" Khaz asked from behind them.

The Xua'al foot soldiers were carving their way through the tunnel in one of the subentrances to Ghal Thurái, meeting firmer and firmer resistance as they went deeper. Zhala was right: the matriarch was here, and she may have been redirecting the bulk of her soldiers to rally to her protection. It was like they had hit a wall of Chovathi, a wall that pushed back no matter how hard it was attacked.

"Nothing, Khaz. Push on," Kunas replied. He was not used to combat in such limited confines as the inside of a mountain, and he found himself unable to effectively use his Breaking without crushing his own army as well.

Khaz gave a grunt of acknowledgment as he hurled himself at a crowd of oncoming Chovathi scouts.

Chovathi-on-Chovathi combat, Kunas noted, was an interesting dance to behold. Since the only way to properly kill a Chovathi was by removing the head, there was a great deal of posturing involved. If an errant fang or claw managed to sever a limb, that limb would be used to regrow an entirely new body.

The bulk of this army, though, was made up of scouts, much smaller than the warriors who made up the Xua'al army. And, as such, they were outmatched in hand-to-hand combat. The larger warriors simply picked them up and tore their heads from their bodies, thus ensuring their death. The carcasses were tossed aside, plunging into the cavernous stone of the mountain.

Yet a Chovathi army that did not rely on its strength of numbers and the ability to replenish its ranks was no army at all. So it seemed that, for every scout they killed, another one would rise up to take its place, which is why the Xua'al army's progress into the depths of the mountain fortress had suddenly stalled.

As Kunas opened up a chasm in the ground to swallow a number of encroaching troops, he thought, *This is useless. We could fight them all day and not get anywhere.*

Yes, Zhala replied in his mind. *Which is why you must leave my broodlings to fight the battle—you are the one who can win the war.*

He dropped a boulder from high above them, crushing some enemy soldiers but taking a few of his with it.

How? asked Kunas.

By going to the source, Zhala replied. And just then a light appeared at the edge of his vision, red and flickering like a flame. *I have found it,* she said, and Kunas realized what he was seeing: it was the outline of the Chovathi matriarch, deep within the stone. Somehow, Zhala was able to pinpoint her presence and "paint" it for him. No matter where he turned his head, the flickering red outline was there; even when he looked away completely, he could "see" her in the back of his mind.

You are useful, he admitted.

I am much more than that, Zhala answered, her powerful voice echoing inside him. *Now go. I can mask my presence, but not for long.*

Kunas took a look at the rocky walls that stood before him, and listened to the sounds of Chovathi bodies being torn apart. He let the surging creatures flow around him; they seemed oblivious to his being there at all. He decided not to waste the opportunity, so he moved forward, farther into the Mouth of the Deep, trudging ahead toward the burning, pulsing light of the Chovathi matriarch—the one constant in a churning sea of enemies.

Duna

Suddenly and perplexingly, the Chovathi army had retreated back into the walls of Ghal Thurái. The most unnerving thing about the retreat, though, was how synchronized it had been—as if they had all received the call for retreat at precisely the same moment, despite Duna's hearing nothing at all that would have been such an indicator.

Even Captain LaVince looked perplexed.

"They seem to be retreating, General," he said, wiping off his blade after pulling it from a nearby Chovathi's neck.

"So I see," said Duna as she watched them go. Only moments before, they had all felt the mountain tremble, and she was worried that Kunas might be trying to bring down the whole thing in one grand act of destruction. But, much to her relief, it had seemed to be nothing more than a tremor, and the mountain remained intact. "I hesitate to follow them," she said, adding, "It could very well be a trap."

LaVince gave a grunt. "A retreat deeper into the Mouth seems like it would protect them," he conceded. "But we also might be able to tighten the noose around them as well—choke the life out of them while they are weak." He turned to Duna. "But it's your army, General. We await your command."

She could hear the snarling retreat of the Chovathi as the sounds of battle around them began to quiet. She wondered exactly why they were retreating; was it to reinforce another part of their army? To protect something? Was it a planned escape? And if they were to follow them deeper into the mountain, did the Chovathi have some way of bringing it all down upon their heads?

She had no idea how willing the Chovathi were to destroy their ancestral home in order to defeat their enemies, and she wasn't willing to risk that being the case.

"We should fall back," she said at last. "I don't like it, whatever this retreat is. We can regroup outside and reinforce the Sharian army. Perhaps they are the reason these creatures are doing what they are doing."

"As you command," LaVince said to her. He then signaled his sergeants to begin the extraction of troops outside the mountain tunnels.

While Duna had experience fighting Chovathi, she had never seen them on this big a scale before, and certainly not this well organized.

She hoped she was making the right decision.

Benjin

The Sharian army had fought its way through a slew of the fearsome white creatures, and had just about reached Cortus Venn, who was still madly chopping down Chovathi like a farmer harvesting wheat.

"Who wants more?" he shouted maniacally as the creatures continued to surround him; but as fast as he could cut them down, they seemed to be reappearing from the depths of Ghal Thurái.

From up ahead, Queen Lena was swinging her giant sword in terrifying arcs, taking the heads off of two or three Chovathi at a time. Benj almost stopped just to watch her work, but he knew his duty lay in supporting Captain Jahaz, who would never let him hear the end of it if anything slipped by him.

Things seemed to have come to a deadlock, though: their own army was not pushing farther in, and the Chovathi numbers did not seem to be dwindling. Which was why, without any apparent cause or signal, when the Chovathi army started a perfectly synchronized retreat back into the mountain, Benj was overjoyed. He watched them as they turned tail and ran.

He started celebrating.

"Thyst!" he yelled to his friend, who had already picked off a few fleeing Chovathi with her bow. "They're running!"

Thyst smiled at him, looking as though she would be taking the credit for sparking the retreat. Yet, when Benj looked over to their leader and saw the look on Queen Lena's face, he was surprised to see that it was not one of relief, it was one of puzzlement.

Captain Jahaz must have noticed it too. "Your Grace," he said, sheathing his sword, "something troubles you."

"I do not understand why they flee," she answered. She sheathed her mammoth sword and watched as the white tide receded into the depths of Ghal Thurái. "And I do not like it." Standing with her arms crossed over her armored chest, she surveyed the area. She looked up at the winged creature that was still circling them, as if to make sure that they were covered in all directions.

"What do you see, Your Grace?" Captain Jahaz asked.

"Weakness," she answered plainly. "We have them in our grip, and now we must squeeze."

Jahaz nodded, and signaled for the troops to follow the retreating Chovathi.

Benj had always seen the queen as strong, and this act only strengthened his opinion. He didn't care about the whispers that spread among the troops that she was the less tactically minded one in her family; what he was seeing now—the pursuit of a fleeing enemy in order to ensure victory—spoke of strength to him.

His chest swelled with pride, and he knew, then and there, that he would follow his queen anywhere—even to his own death.

Eternity, in the truest sense of the word, can be neither comprehended nor explained; for, in order to do these things, one must experience it first.

—Lash'kun Yho, the Traveler

Chapter 88

Khel-hârad

Thornton

The more they walked, the more that *time* became a foreign concept to Thornton. He'd always heard of the idea of eternity, but he'd always thought it just a figure of speech—some way to explain waiting a long time or being married to someone. He'd never thought eternity might be an actual thing, yet here, in the Land of the Dead, he wondered if time even existed at all. He wasn't sure if he had been here for a day, a year, or a lifetime. In fact, if he were somehow transported back to the room in Silus the Healer's, he was convinced that no time would have passed at all.

It was the same feeling he got in the Otherworld: the sense that these places were somehow beyond time, beyond any sense of the word, just existing in a moment, forever.

The thought, like the scenery, made his head spin. The Traveler must have noticed, because he had stopped walking. He turned around to look at Thornton.

"Don't worry. We don't have much farther to go," the god said.

Thornton answered with a nod.

"Are you feeling alright?"

"My head," Thornton said with a surprising amount of effort.

"I told you," the Traveler said with a chuckle. "This place has that effect on the living. Be glad that you're uncomfortable—it means you're still mortal."

Thornton grimaced an acknowledgment. "It doesn't mean that I have to like it," he said.

"True," the Traveler replied. "But should you find yourself lost, you'll want to remember what it feels like, that feeling."

"If I get lost?" Thornton asked, puzzled.

"Yes," the Traveler said, starting off again. "If we get separated somehow."

Thornton tried to follow but found that his legs didn't work.

"What do you mean? What could separate us in here?"

The Traveler was silent as he walked on; Thornton didn't like it one bit.

**

They had passed over deserts, grasslands, jungle, and even a frozen wasteland. Thornton had stopped keeping track of all the different climates they'd gone through and decided instead to focus on something more useful: trying to figure out what he was going to say to Miera when he saw her again.

He knew she would probably be upset with him, going against her wishes like this. After all, it was she who had sealed the Otherworld. Granted, she had done it in an ill-conceived attempt at self-sacrifice, saving herself so that the rest of the world could live; but if what Ynara, the Binder of Worlds, had said was true, then he would just have to deal with Miera being angry with him. He knew in his heart that he was doing the right thing.

But it still didn't make the prospect of facing an angry Miera any easier.

**

They were trudging now through a desert of some sort, but one whose rolling dunes with snow-capped mountains beyond seemed entirely foreign to Thornton. He wondered which people were responsible for this place. Then it dawned on him: he could probably ask the Traveler. If anyone might know, it would be him.

"Traveler," Thornton said, catching the god's attention.

"Yes?" he asked, not breaking stride. The sand made whispered crunching sounds beneath his sandaled feet.

"You said that every spirit in here was responsible for this place's appearance . . ."

"And you're wondering who would have made such a place as this?"

"Y-Yes," Thornton replied.

"My people," the Traveler answered. Turning his head to look at Thornton, he added, "Those from beyond the Wastes."

Thornton stopped. He certainly hadn't expected that answer. "Your people are the Tribes of the Sun?"

"That's what they call us now, is it?" the Traveler asked with an amused chuckle. "The Tribes of the Sun." He had come to a stop in front of Thornton and seemed to be trying out the words on his tongue. "Interesting. Although it makes sense: my power waxes during the daytime and my brother's wanes. Though why they chose to group all of them together confuses me. But," he said, turning to face Thornton, "to answer your question: yes. They are my people. Or they were. I'm not sure anymore . . . Time and relationships are so . . . foreign to me now."

Thornton was silent but intrigued. He wondered what else the ousted god would tell him.

"Your brother—that's the one they call the Holder, right?"

The Traveler looked away; Thornton must have hit a nerve.

"Ahmaan Ka. Yes. That's right." His voice was distant. "He was my brother. Once."

Thornton didn't feel like asking him what he meant by that. Instead, he listened, hoping that the god would continue. He did.

"But he betrayed me," he said, fury burning behind his wild red eyes. "He took the woman I loved, and he forced himself on her. He defiled her, debased her. That beautiful, perfect woman—gone."

Thornton could see that his fist was clenched and trembling. He'd seen the wrath of one god already; he wasn't sure that he wanted to see another's. So, trying to sound understanding, he asked, "What happened?"

The Traveler looked at him, and the fury seemed to subside. "The damage was already done," he said. "And it's how I know that the gods of creation have a sense of humor: the woman I love would go on to have exactly what she could never choose between," he said. "Twins."

Thornton was silent.

After a moment, the Traveler spoke again.

"It's why they call her the Mother of Wolves, and it's also why her children are called Sons of the Traveler—because both of those things are true," he said. He turned away. "Those born with the gift of farstepping are my children. And those known as Wolfwalkers are the sons of my brother, Ahmaan Ka." He paused and took a breath. When he spoke again, his voice seemed calmer, more controlled. "But she loved them both because that's the kind of person that Asha Imha-khet was. And it's why I can't stand to see her imprisoned for one moment longer. Now come," he said, starting off once again. "We're nearly there."

***

They had come to the edge of the infinite desert that seemed to have taken a lifetime to cross. The Traveler had been silent the rest of the way, and Thornton wasn't about to change that. As the sand had gradually given way to grass and dirt, Thornton had started to feel something; he wasn't exactly sure what it was, but it was strange. Powerful. Beckoning.

He hoped it was Miera. Because if it wasn't, he wasn't sure he would like what it was.

And that was when he saw it: the figure he'd seen over and over again during his journey. It was the woman of his visions, only she was so much clearer now than she had been any other time he'd seen her before. She was wearing white, just as she had all those times before, only this time he was able to see her hair.

It was silver.

Silver from roots to ends. Silver—and not at all like Miera's.

This wasn't Miera; this was . . . someone else.

Guardian, she said, her voice echoing in his mind, *do not lose your way. Yours is a difficult path, fraught with danger, but it is necessary. I am sorry. I have tried to warn you many times before this, but I could never reach you.*

Thornton looked at her in wide-eyed disbelief. He wasn't sure how to answer. "Who are you?" he finally asked.

I am the One Who Goes Between, she answered, *but that is not important. What is important is that you remember why you are here, and for whom. Never, ever lose sight of that.*

"I don't understand," he started to say, but before he could she was gone.

Thornton looked around for her, sure that she would come back, but she was nowhere to be found.

"We're here," said the Traveler from up ahead.

Thornton, still dazed from the apparition, shook his head and walked toward the Traveler.

"Place your hammer there, on the ground," the god said as he pointed to an unremarkable piece of green grass growing on the edge of the desert. Looking ahead, Thornton was surprised to see that the air in front of them was wavy and strange, the way it would get on a hot day.

Thornton did as he was commanded but looked around, confused.

"Is this it?" he asked, placing his hammer handle-up. "The entrance to the Otherworld?"

"It is," said the Traveler. His voice was steady. Calm. Almost regretful.

"How do I get through?" he asked.

"You don't," the Traveler answered as he moved toward the Hammer. "We aren't here for you."

Before Thornton could react, the god grasped the Hammer of the Worldforge with both hands, raising it high into the air and bringing it down in a furious, powerful arc. It slammed into the ground and bathed the air around them in its glorious blue glow. He did it a second time, and Thornton heard something crack.

"What are you doing?" Thornton asked, but he got no answer. Just a look from the red-eyed god whose face was masked in pain.

A third time, the Traveler drove the Hammer into the ground, and again Thornton heard something crack. Up ahead, he saw what he could only think was a tear in reality itself.

The Traveler was unrelenting in his actions and continued to smash the black steel head of Thornton's hammer deep into the ground of Khel-hârad.

And finally, when Thornton thought that the world itself would pull apart, the Traveler stopped.

And a familiar voice that Thornton had never expected to hear reached his ears.

"You have done well, Lash'kun Yho, and for that I am grateful. When I am finished, I will give you what you were promised."

It was a deep voice, hollow and scorched, and as empty as Khel-hârad was immense.

The Traveler turned to Thornton, pain and longing filling his eyes, and his whispered apology of "I am so sorry" was the second-to-last thing that Thornton had expected.

The last thing Thornton expected was the one thing standing before him right now: the once-Khyth and now-Breaker, D'kane.

Chapter 89

Khadje Kholam

Awaken the Three

Kuu

The inside of Yelto's compound was utter chaos, and the men who were supposed to be guarding it were trying to get a look at the battle outside. And, as much as he hated to admit it, his brother had been right: none of them so much as batted an eye at the diminutive gray fox, whose padded feet sped through the stony halls. He was likely to make it a good way in without having to change back and fight his way through.

At least that's what he thought.

He didn't count on being recognized, though.

"Hey," said a guard who looked a lot dumber than he apparently was, "you're that wolfwalker." The man was already drawing his sword when Kuu ran toward him.

"Don't know what you're talking about," Kuu said as he leapt into the air and began to change back. He had the advantage of being quicker—much quicker—than the guard was, and intended to use it. By the time he collided with the guard, he had changed back almost completely, striking the man in the chest with his feet. His weight and momentum brought them both tumbling down, and the tenuous grip that the guard had on his sword caused it to clatter to the ground when they hit.

Kuu saw his chance and took it. Reaching for the sword and grabbing it by the hilt, he brought it up, igniting terror in the man's eyes. He hesitated, then drove it down into the man's throat.

He didn't enjoy killing; in fact, he would have preferred not to have to do it at all, but he was left with little time and even less choice. He had to get to the Ghost if they had any hope of surviving.

As the man's body went limp, Kuu heard the familiar sound of metallic keys falling onto a stone floor, and he realized that the man he'd just killed was also a jailer. Those keys would get him where he needed to go, but it was not going to be easy; he couldn't just walk in.

Or could he?

He looked at the armor of the man in front of him. It was a little large for him, but the only one who would pay attention to that was the one wearing it.

Kuu looked around to make sure no one was watching and started unhooking the guard's armor.

***

Swinging the key ring around on his finger and whistling, Kuu tried to act as nonchalant as possible. If he looked like he belonged, he reasoned, he could get deeper inside the jail with minimal resistance. And, for the most part, he was right.

The only problem he ran into was when he came to a huge, metallic door guarded by five men. They all had their eyes on Kuu as he approached.

"Password," said the biggest one.

Kuu kept walking but didn't answer.

"Password," the guard repeated.

Kuu had to think. He was unlikely to guess the right word, and there was no way he was going to be able to take on these five men; they were enormous and well armed. Even with his three brothers there with him, he would have had trouble taking them on.

Brothers.

That gave him an idea.

"Djozen Yelto has awakened the Holder," he said. "He requires the Ghost of the Morning as a tribute."

The men stood there as if digesting the information. They looked at each other uncertainly.

"Well?" Kuu said, doing his best to look impatient.

"Where is the Djozen?" asked the big guard, with a mixture of skepticism and confusion.

"He was overseeing the ceremony," Kuu answered.

"In the temple?" another guard asked helpfully.

"Yes," Kuu said with a nod of assurance. "The temple."

The biggest guard didn't look convinced. "We aren't supposed to let her out. The Djozen said so himself."

"Well," Kuu countered, "the Holder told the Djozen to bring her. I was there; I heard him say it myself."

There were acceding murmurs from the guards, and the big one seemed to be leaning toward opening the door. His hand moved to the silver key on his belt. Then he stopped.

It's been a good run, Kuu thought. If he couldn't talk himself out of this, he knew there was no way he was getting past them—and he had to get past them.

He could feel his palms begin to sweat as he thought about which man he should try to kill first. Maybe if he moved quickly enough, the others wouldn't realize what was happening.

Kuu inched his hand closer to the hilt of his sword.

"What did he sound like?" the big guard asked in hushed reverence.

Kuu stopped. He wasn't prepared for that question. "The Holder?" he asked, regaining his mental balance.

"Yes. What . . . what was his voice like?"

Kuu's face darkened. The answer to this question, unfortunately, he knew.

"It was like hearing a dream. A dream where you are being chased. Where you are falling and your whole body is hurtling toward the ground," he said. "He sounded like terror, like fear . . . like death."

If the big man wasn't convinced before, he certainly was now. He took the key off his belt and placed it in the lock, turning it with a thud as the bolt opened. A tug on a circular metal ring was all it took to open the door where, inside, sat their only hope of salvation.

"You are too late," came a voice from inside.

And Kuu's heart sank.

Dailus

Ahmaan Ka flexed his fingers.

It was the little things, now, that brought him joy. He had been without a body for so long that he'd forgotten what it was like to have one.

510

This one was full of sensations and an energy that hummed inside of it, but it was also full of dull aches and unwelcome pain. He was mortal again—mortal, with the power of a god.

To his right was one of his priests—the one who had performed the ritual to let him enter his new Vessel—and the fat one who called himself Djozen. He turned to them and said, "Well done, my servants."

The priest fell to his knees before him. "I hope that this body pleases you, O Holder."

Noting that the fat one stayed standing, Ka replied, "It does."

He could feel the power inside himself, and he knew it was the power of the Shaper—the same power that had purged him from the Otherworld and forced him into Khel-hârad. He smiled to himself, knowing that he now wielded a part of it. Yes, this body did please him.

"However," said the priest, looking up at him from his knees, "we are still under siege."

"Not for long," the Holder said, gesturing for him to rise. "Where is the Ghost?"

"She remains in her prison," the priest replied.

"Then I shall see her myself. I want to see the look on her face when she knows that she has lost."

The priest nodded and smiled a skeletal smile.

Asha Imha-khet.

It would be good to see her again after all these years—and even better to see her in pain.

Chapter 90

Ghal Thurái

Awaken the Three

Kunas

The deeper Kunas went, the more he thought about abandoning his course altogether. But every time that thought would pop up in his mind, he would feel Zhala's presence and she would snuff it out like a candle. She was compelling him to move forward, to pursue the matriarch deep in Ghal Thurái, against his will. Only her will was *becoming* his will. He was no longer safe in his own thoughts; he had a permanent houseguest— and the houseguest was quickly becoming the owner.

This deep underground, the bowels of the Mouth of the Deep were quiet and cold. Kunas could hear the distant drip of water somewhere up ahead, the only occasional break in the silence. The muted sounds of battle droned on behind him like the memory of a fading thought: he knew it was there, but it meant nothing to him. His compulsion, his urge, his need, drove him deeper, away from the distractions of the world.

Although some part of him knew that it wasn't *his* to begin with.

But it was becoming his.

He felt the power behind her thoughts—and the power before him, in the matriarch—and smiled.

Duna

The army had gathered outside the subentrances to Ghal Thurái and accounted for their losses. They were minor, but Duna reminded herself that her troops were not replaceable like the Chovathi were. She noted that the Xua'al had not felt the need to retreat like she had, and wondered if she had indeed made the right decision. She thought that maybe they had been able to sense danger, the way that some animals seem to be able to predict a natural disaster. Either way, the fact that she would be reinforcing her sister's army made the decision to call for the retreat that much easier to digest.

Captain LaVince approached.

"General," he said, "our forces have all made their way back to the surface. We are ready to storm the gates."

Duna nodded. "Then we move."

514

LaVince, behind her, signaled the departure, and they once again moved as a single force toward the entrance of Ghal Thurái.

Just as they rounded the ridge that gave them a view of the front gates, still a good distance away, they caught the tail end of the Sharian army doing exactly what Duna had feared they would do: descending into the Mouth of the Deep to pursue the Chovathi scourge.

Kunas

Deeper he moved—so deep that there were no longer steps that the Thurians had carved into the rock of their underground city. In the heart of the earth, Kunas found himself surrounded by the naturally occurring caverns and rock formations that were prevalent this deep down. There was a coolness to the air that was unlike the chill of Khala Val'ur; it was different somehow, devoid of substance. It was an emptiness that spread its arms and worked its way into the rock around him.

And in that emptiness, a fire burned.

He was close.

Like the beating heart of a man which gives life, so was the Chovathi matriarch the heart of Ghal Thurái, encased in the rock that surrounded all of them. Her presence flowed through the mountain and beyond, reaching out like tree roots and slowly becoming one with whatever she touched.

He knew that, since she had bonded with these walls only recently, she would not be as deeply ingrained as Zhala was in her nest. He knew this because Zhala had told him; he now knew many things thanks to her: she was showering him with new knowledge, new sensations, new dreams. It was almost overwhelming at times, like trying to drink from a rushing river, but Kunas was thirsty and had no desire to stop.

He loved the feeling that the power brought him. Vaguely he recalled his own Breaking, when he had opened himself up to the power of the Otherworld, its conduit and repository for nigh-unimaginable power— power, and pain. The pain that every Khyth experiences after their Breaking, paid as a price for power. Yet, the moment he had embraced Zhala, the pain had stopped.

Awaken the Three

He had not protested.

He continued down, toward the burning heart of the Chovathi.

***

You are close, Zhala said.

I know, Kunas answered. It was like stepping into a stream and being pulled by the current. *What do I do when I find it?*

I will show you, Zhala replied. *Do not fear.*

And he did not. He simply followed and obeyed.

***

The more he followed the fire, the more he understood the fundamental nature of the Chovathi. The thoughts came unbidden to him as he let Zhala in more and more.

They were living beings, the Chovathi, but they were more like a fungus or a parasite than an animal; it was one of the reasons they were able to divide and reproduce the way they did: it was easy for a spore to make copies of itself. The sweet, delicious knowledge she imparted to him was like honey on his lips, and he didn't want it to stop. So he didn't try. She was filling him up, and he embraced it.

He walked on, drinking in the power.

He saw flashes of the other broodlings that were inside the mountain. Flashes of the Xua'al. Flashes of the others. Flashes of . . .

Flashes . . .

They were . . .

Yes, came the affirmation from Zhala.

. . . the same.

Now you see, she said in a soothing and motherly tone. *They are all my children.*

The room that Kunas stepped into was enormously tall, just like the one that Zhala occupied in the nest of the Xua'al. But instead of the matriarch he expected to find, it was nothing but blank, jagged stone.

Home, Kunas found himself saying.

Home, Zhala agreed.

Kunas approached the wall and reached out his hand, pressing the tips of his fingers into the cold stone. He reached into his pocket to find his dagger—the one he had used in order to call Khaz, the one he had raked across his palm to make the blood oath with Zhala. He took it once again and raised it to his hand. He felt the cold steel against his skin and slowly dragged it across.

His actions were no longer his own, he realized, and it was like staring at his reflection in a pond. He felt nothing. He was detached from himself, from his body. He did not feel the pain of the dagger when it drew his blood—he had Zhala to thank for that—and he smiled a distant smile of appreciation, like a drunkard who has found another flagon of wine.

Put your hand to the stone, she said, even though he knew she didn't need to. He would have done it anyway. But she was letting him know that he still had some semblance of control, of choice. She was so kind. So giving. So . . . loving.

Kunas pressed his hand against the wall, and he felt the warmth as his blood began to seep into it.

Home, Zhala repeated as her essence flowed into the walls of Ghal Thurái, into its ancient and familiar corpse that was being slowly brought back to life.

Kunas could feel her joy at being reunited. It was the only way to start anew, to merge the blood of men with the stone of earth and the will of the Chovathi. To make something more, something greater.

Something new.

But this is not the end for you, she said to him.

Visions of Khala Val'ur flooded his mind, of Haidan Shar. Of Théas. Of other cities whose names and faces he did not know. Yet he knew what awaited them; this was only the beginning. He smiled. He was so grateful to be a part of Zhala's brood. She would guide him. She would protect him. She would love him.

And as the walls of Ghal Thurái came crashing down around the ant-like humans who infested it, he felt the suffocating blackness as it embraced him, just as Zhala had promised she would do.

Home, he thought with a smile.

And he felt pain no more.

Benjin

The pounding in Benj's head was unbearable, and everything around him was dark. He couldn't move. It felt like a mountain had been dropped on him.

He tried to breathe, and was terrified to find that he couldn't.

And then he realized: it was because he didn't need to.

A thousand sensations came flooding in all at once.

He felt . . . blood? Skin? He felt the earth. And he felt Glamrhys next to him, that burning light of salvation that comforted him now.

He heard a voice and felt the weight shift on top of him. Something was tearing away at the rocks and rubble that lay on top of him.

"Boy,"—he now heard the voice clearly—"are you alright?"

He knew the voice, but wasn't sure how.

He saw sunlight peek through and saw a hand reach down and grab his own. He was pulled up, gently, and looked into the gray eyes of someone he knew.

Venn, they had called him. Cortus Venn.

The Stoneborn.

Benj looked up at the man who regarded him coolly.

A smile cracked his lips. "That's the blade of a Stoneborn, boy," he said.

Benj looked down and saw the glowing metal that he held in his hands and lifted it up to look at it, confused, and then looked at Venn, who placed a hand on his shoulder.

"I'm sorry you had to find out this way, but there is much to tell you."

The sound of hoofbeats approached from behind them, but Benj didn't turn to see who it was.

A voice called out to them—a woman's voice.

"Venn," she said, "what happened? I . . . I saw—"

"Yes," he said, cutting her off. "I'm sorry, Duna, but your city is lost."

There was silence.

She added softly, "Then so is the army of Haidan Shar."

Venn took his hand off Benj's shoulder and nodded grimly.

"But why? How?"

"I can't say for certain, but I know that the Chovathi matriarch is behind it."

"There is no way anything could have—"

"Survived?" Venn said, cutting her off. "No, and I'm afraid that was the point. It was what she intended all along, only I didn't realize it until it was too late. She has consolidated her strength, drawing it all into herself, with the weight of Ghal Thurái. But she is there, buried under the rock, gathering her strength and spreading, seeping into the stone and shaping it to her will. She has returned to the heart of the Chovathi, where they were first formed, to finish what she started."

Duna was silent again as she looked out over the rubble. The once-mighty mountain had collapsed onto itself, filling the cavernous spaces, Benj somehow knew, with rock and stone and earth. Now all that was left was a mound, a gravesite for the city that humans had only briefly managed to reclaim from the Chovathi.

A reclamation that had literally come crashing down.

"Is there anything we can do to stop it?" Duna finally asked.

Venn crossed his arms and shifted his weight to one leg. "We're going to need more Stoneborn—a lot more," he answered.

Duna looked at him, her expression blank. "And how do we do that?"

Venn smiled.

"I'll show you."

Chapter 91

Khadje Kholam

Kuu

"I don't understand," Kuu said. He couldn't make out anything in the darkness of the cell, and he was straining to see inside.

"The Holder has been awakened," came the voice. "You are too late—*we* are too late."

"But too late for what?" Kuu asked, stepping inside and pulling the door shut. When he turned around and his eyes adjusted, he almost wished they hadn't.

"To stop the coming dark," the voice said. Before him, flickering like candlelight, was the visage of a woman dressed in white, whose silver hair and sharp green eyes told Kuu exactly who she was.

"Mother," he said with a degree of reverence. The one they called the mother of his people was standing before him, with only a few feet of space separating them. He hadn't expected to actually make it this far, but from the tone in her voice, it might not have mattered. "You know this for sure?"

"Yes, Kuu, I do," she said. "I have seen it. I knew it the moment that the Holder filled his Vessel. He has the Wolfblade, and he is coming for me. We are lost."

"No," Kuu said reflexively. They had all been planning and orchestrating this for so long; he was not about to abandon hope now. "There has to be something we can do," he said. "Anything is better than nothing."

The Ghost was silent for what felt like an eternity.

"There is one thing," she finally said, hesitance lining her voice. "And it cannot be undone."

"Then do it."

The Ghost stepped forward, and for the first time Kuu noticed how stunningly beautiful she was, even in the darkness of her cell. It was no surprise that not one but two gods had fought over her. He found himself willing to do anything she asked of him. When her hand reached out for his cheek and he felt the cold of her embrace, his thoughts were drowned in a flood of sensations.

He felt warm and cold all at once, like standing too close to a fire on a frigid night.

He felt his knees start to shake, and bile crept up his throat.

He wavered, staggered, and fell.

And then the world went black.

Sivulu

There was no end to the attackers.

For every one he killed, it seemed another rose to take its place, thanks to the malignant powers of the Priest of the Holder. He was beginning to tire.

Behind him, the battle still raged. And, although the wolfwalkers and their allies were mighty warriors, there was simply no turning some tides. He began to feel that a retreat was not only prudent but necessary. He hoped Kuu was able to make it to the Ghost.

That was when he saw it: a gray streak that burst from Yelto's palace and into the light.

Kuu! He'd made it!

He felt a surge of energy and hope as his brother ran free.

But that hope turned to dismay when he realized the truth: Kuu was alone.

There was no Ghost to be seen.

So this is it then, Sivulu thought. *We've lost.* He watched the soldiers closing in as the minuscule form of his brother charged past him, out of the compound, and headed straight for the dunes of the Wastes of Khulakorum.

He didn't intend for his last thoughts of his brother to be ones of disappointment, but the cold blade that slid past his ribs ensured that they were. A strong hand brought him to the ground and rolled him onto his back, where he stared into the eyes of a brown-haired woman. Her multicolored eyes, haunting and sharp, were filled with hatred—and tears.

"I will not make you suffer," she said through a clenched jaw, "because you did not make him. But Aldis Tennech was the father I never had, and you robbed me of that, forever."

With every heartbeat, Sivulu could feel the blood pumping out of him and onto the desert floor; the feeling of defeat was too great. If the Holder had been awakened and the Ghost was gone, what was the point?

He let go of his lupine form. If he was to die, he wanted to die as a man.

The woman before him watched him change, but her rage did not subside.

"If you seek mercy from me," she said, her sword hand trembling, "you will not receive it."

"No," Sivulu protested weakly. He could heal himself, he knew, but his world was crumbling around him. Everything they had fought for—everything they had died for—was coming undone. "Let it never be said that Sivulu Imha-khet begged for mercy."

Gathering herself up to her full height, the woman grasped her sword with both hands, pointing it down at Sivulu's chest, poised to drive it through his heart.

"And let it never be said that Lilyana Coros ever gave it," she said as she drove the blade down with all of her strength.

There was cold, there was pain.

There was darkness . . .

There was nothing.

Chapter 92

Khel-hârad

Thornton

Thornton could barely think, let alone move. He wasn't sure if he would be able to use Breaking in Khel-hârad—not that he knew how to consciously summon it anyway.

He cursed himself for not listening to Yasha when he had the chance.

"Ah," D'kane said as he looked his way, voice quaking with power. "The *boy* from Highglade. How thoughtful of you to deliver to me the Hammer." He reached out toward the Traveler, who was still holding it. "Traveler," he said without taking his eyes off Thornton, "my prize."

The god known as the Traveler held the ancient Hammer of the Worldforge in his trembling hands, bowing his head in reverence to the recently ascended Breaker of the Dawn.

"Of course, my master," he said, and he bent down on one knee.

And then, his rumbling voice an octave lower, he added, "Come and get it."

The wild red eyes of the Traveler snapped open, and he lunged at D'kane with blazing speed.

D'kane, the Breaker, could only stare as the Hammer of the Worldforge came at him like the unstoppable force that it was. The Traveler was impossibly quick—so quick that Thornton had barely realized that he'd moved at all.

But D'kane was quicker. He sidestepped the blow and raised his hands, clenching his fists as if drawing in power. Unimaginable power.

"Stop this foolishness, Traveler," D'kane snarled. His eyes burned with unending hatred and scorn. "You were banished once—don't think I won't do it a second time."

And, all around him, Thornton could feel a massive surge, like the sudden influx of winter that makes the world slow to a frozen crawl. He braced himself for the terrible and vengeful explosion of strength that D'kane was about to release upon the two of them.

So when the Traveler merely stood there, smiling, Thornton thought that the wandering god had lost his mind.

"You forget yourself, Breaker," the Traveler said as he edged closer to D'kane. "And you forget the limits of your power."

The Traveler made a fist, and Thornton heard a distant thundering crack, like the top of a mountain had just been cleaved off. And then a *true* winter's chill draped its arms around them all—and squeezed.

D'kane dropped to his knees and cried out in agony as the sudden and terrible cold enveloped them, its howling winds accompanied by the biting and stinging of a ferocious, unbearable frost.

"Or maybe," the Traveler said as he approached, looking coolly at his tightly balled fist, "you never knew them at all."

He flexed his fist again and the Breaker howled.

"We had a deal!" D'kane screamed, fighting to get out the words amid the whipping and whirling winds.

"And I broke it," the Traveler said with a hint of amusement. "Ironic, isn't it—*Breaker?*" He flexed again and the Breaker cried out.

"You will never awaken the Ghost without my help," D'kane said through clenched teeth.

"Ah," the Traveler said, raising the Hammer, "we will see about that."

Forged by the Shaper Herself before the dawn of creation, the Hammer of the Worldforge had been the only thing that could free the Breaker from His chains—and it was also the only thing able to defeat the ancient god. And, just as D'kane had done to the previous Breaker of the Dawn, the Traveler held out the Hammer now, menacingly, while Khel-hârad was blanketed by his cold and icy power.

But, much to Thornton's surprise, the Traveler did not move to strike the Breaker.

Instead, he turned to him.

"And now comes your part," he said. "You must do this thing, Thornton, for I cannot."

The wretched winds of winter swirled around them as Thornton blinked at the Traveler in disbelief. Frost bit his cheeks and stung his eyes.

He couldn't bring himself to move; all he could do was stare. "Thornton!" the Traveler snapped, and the god had his attention. "Come! Take the Hammer. It is the only way."

Thornton didn't understand, but that had never stopped him before.

"What do I need to do?" he asked as he approached the Hammer—and the Breaker.

"You want to free your friend, don't you?" the Traveler asked.

Thornton nodded.

"And you are prepared to give anything to do it?"

For that last part, Thornton had not been prepared. He balked at the word *anything*.

But, after the briefest of thoughts, he nodded again.

"Then take the Hammer," the Traveler said, "and strike him down." He was pointing a wind-whipped finger at D'kane, still writhing on the ground in agony.

"No!" cried the Breaker. He thrashed in the grip of the Traveler's summoned frost.

But Thornton, as he had done for more than half his life, wrapped his hands around the worn wood of the Hammer—*his* hammer, his strength—and succumbed.

It was familiar, warm. He let the power course through him.

"Yes," Thornton said.

D'kane held himself steady and looked him in the eye.

"Your father couldn't stop me," D'kane wheezed. "And neither will you."

Father.

In that moment, the memory and the sadness of his own father's death washed over him anew. It crashed down on him with a fierceness strong enough to peel the cold from his soul and replace it with a fire: a furious, burning rage, unending in intensity, undying, untamed.

He didn't need it to come—but he let it.

He knew what he had to do.

Jaw clenched in rage, he held the Hammer up toward the Breaker, just as he'd seen D'kane do before he drained the ancient god of all of His power. He summoned all of his strength. He focused.

And the Hammer glowed blue.

D'kane's eyes snapped open.

"No!" the god hissed. "You cannot—you must not! Draining me will not bring your father back, and it will not destroy me either!"

Thornton felt the power starting to move.

"Don't listen to him," the Traveler warned.

Thornton felt a sudden jolt surge through him like lightning, and he knew that nothing D'kane could say would change his mind, and he doubted that he could have stopped it if it had. The Hammer's glow was a burning sun, and even the frost around them began to recede; there was no going back.

"But you *must* listen," D'kane said weakly. "For there must always be a Breaker."

The power was screaming into Thornton now. It felt like standing in front of a burning forge, with all the intensity of a thunderstorm. Thornton's anger mixed with his hatred for D'kane; he drew on the sorrow of his father's death and the anger he'd felt when he learned that the world was cold. Uncaring. Empty.

Through the aching and the burning power that he siphoned, Thornton clenched his teeth and gathered enough focus to speak.

"Just like you destroyed the Breaker," Thornton growled, "this will destroy you."

But, through the reckoning and the blue, D'kane looked up at him—and smiled.

"I didn't destroy Him, boy," he said with a smile that almost made Thornton drop the Hammer. "He cannot be destroyed. He is the universe, He is creation."

There was another crack that filled the air, and the two of them were hurled violently apart. Thornton, flying backward, was blasted backward so hard that if he had needed breath in this place, it would have all but left him.

As he landed, he felt the last of D'kane's strength flowing into the Hammer, and onward to him.

D'kane, the Breaker, shuddered, lying limply on the ground. Beaten, but not destroyed.

He struggled to sit up, and looked at Thornton. "I could never destroy the Breaker, boy," D'kane said weakly. "I merely replaced Him."

And, with a look that chilled Thornton to the bone, he pointed a charred, wilted finger, and whispered, "And now you will, too."

The words hung in the air like a lover's kiss: unforgettable and world-stopping. It was only then that Thornton realized that D'kane, Master Khyth of Khala Val'ur, was right. As his desiccated form sank below the frozen ground of Khel-hârad, Thornton suddenly felt a jarring and uneasy presence beginning to fill his mind. It was like watching the sun being swallowed by the moon, casting the world into that looming and heavy darkness that comes with the unstoppable and the unexplained.

It was a power he had felt when he had first called upon Breaking, a strength that filled him almost to the point of bursting.

It was a cloak, a candle, an old friend.

It was the power of his hammer, but somehow much, much more.

And, from the recesses of his mind, that power spoke.

We are one now . . . , it said, the words echoing deeply and hauntingly in his mind.

. . . Breaker.

Epilogue

Swift fox feet found their way across the sand, leaving the chaotic corpse of Khadje Kholam far behind. The Holder's grip was far too tight; there was no stopping what was to come. He had his Vessel and he had his army. Even if neither of those things had come to pass, he would still have accomplished his goal, for he still had the one thing that could have prevented all of this, and the one thing that had been his gift to the woman he loved—if he was indeed even capable of love. And Yelto had mocked her with it by keeping it just out of her reach.

The Wolfblade.

That simple piece of steel that was forged with a single drop of blood from both the Holder and the Ghost to bond them together as a symbol of their promise. It was the only thing she could think of to stop him, and she knew of only one way to get his attention: she would have to bring him to her.

As the wind-whipped dunes of the Waste spread out before her, Asha Imha-khet raised her eyes toward Do'baradai, the city that held the Holder's tomb—and, inside it, the Vessel he had once called his own.

The sun was sinking, and the Ghost hoped it would not be forever.

For, now, the Days of the Dark were upon them.

Glossary

Ahmaan Ka: twin brother to **Lash'kun Yho**, he is also called the Holder of the Dead, or simply the Holder. His domain is the night.

Aldis Tennech: a human general of Khala Val'ur, he once comm................ anded all the armies of Gal'dorok until he fled to the Wastes with his second-in-command, **Sera**.

Aldryd: an aged Athrani residing in Annoch, where he holds the title of Keeper. He resides in the Temple of the Shaper.

Alysana: a G'henni woman, younger sister to the second-in-command of the Guard of Annoch, **Mordha**. She was ordered by Annoch's keeper, **Aldryd**, to watch after the traitorous half-eye **Dailus**.

Annoch: The capital city of Derenar, it is also called the City of the Forge and is home to Athrani and humans alike. Inside its walls lies the Temple of the Shaper. A person from Annoch is called an Annochian, and their army's colors are scarlet and gray.

Anvil of the Worldforge: used by the Shaper of Ages, along with the Hammer of the Worldforge, to create the world. It can be found in the Temple of the Shaper in Annoch.

Asha Imha-khet: a mortal woman who long ago captured the attention of the Traveler and the Holder. She is also called the Ghost of the Morning.

Athrani: a people who worship the Shaper of Ages and are known for their power to transmute matter, called Shaping. Their distinctive multicolored eyes allow them to be easily distinguished from humans.

Athrani Legion: a collection of soldiers who march under the banner of Ellenos, comprised mostly of Athrani and half-eyes.

Aurik: twin brother to **Kaurik** and older brother to **Kuu**. He is a Wolfwalker.

Benjin: a young boy from Haidan Shar, he is armiger to **Captain Jahaz**. His nickname is **Benj**.

Binder of Worlds: one of the creators of the world, along with the Shaper of Ages and the Breaker of the Dawn. She is the guardian of the two worlds and helped to imprison the Breaker in his chains.

Breaker of the Dawn: One of the creators of the world, along with the Shaper of Ages and the Binder of Worlds. He was imprisoned by the Shaper ages ago and continues to be a thorn in Her side. His followers, the Hand of the Black Dawn, sought to free him from his prison in the Otherworld.

Breaking (power): Gifted by the Breaker and wielded by Khyth, it allows the user to move or reshape matter, but not to change its essence. It can be learned by anyone and is not limited to those born of Khyth blood. (See also **the Breaking**.)

the Breaking: a ritual undergone by Khyth apprentices that serves to increase their ability to wield the power of the Otherworld. The ritual is often fatal, scarring the Khyth for life and leaving their skin looking burnt and cracked.

Caelus: an Athrani in the service of **Luzo** the Théan who helps keep the Théan slaves in line by using his Shaping.

Caladan Durakas: former commander of the Fist of Ghal Thurái, he was killed at the Battle for the Tree.

Cavan Hullis: a captain from Ghal Thurái known for his gift for strategy.

Chovathi: a race of subsurface-dwelling creatures who formerly inhabited Ghal Thurái. They are pale and carnivorous and can only be killed by removing the head.

Cortus Venn: commander of the famed Lonely Guard of Lash'Kargá, he commands an elite unit responsible for the safety of Lash'Kargá—Death's Edge—by driving away invaders from the Wastes.

Dailus: an Athrani half-eye from Ellenos who meets and befriends **Olson Woods**. He betrayed **Thornton** and stole the Hammer of the Worldforge, intending to surrender it to Khala Val'ur.

Derenar: a large region encompassing many human and Athrani cities. It is bordered to the east by the region of Gal'dorok and to the south by the Wastes of Khulakorum.

Djozen: the title for the ruler of a number of tribes.

Djozen Yelto: a Khôl who currently leads two of the three tribes and seeks to unite all three under his rule.

Do'baradai: an ancient city far to the south of Khadje Kholam, it is said to be the resting place of the Three. Its name means "the two brothers" in Khôl.

Duna Cullain: former second-in-command of the Fist of Ghal Thurái and subordinate to Commander **Caladan Durakas**, she assumed the rank of general when her commander was killed and **General Tennech** fled.

Ellenos: also called the First City, it is home to the Athrani and is their capital city and the seat of their government. A person from Ellenos is called an Ellenian, and their army's colors are purple and gold.

Elyasha: called **Yasha** by her friends, she is a Khyth of the Breaking who is the daughter of **Olson Woods** and sister to **Thornton**. She was a former apprentice to **D'kane**.

Endar: an Athrani half-eye who ascended to the rank of commander of the Athrani Legion.

Eowen: a messenger under **Duna Cullain**'s employ.

Evram: leader of a group of bandits who have dealings with the slave trade in Théas.

Farryn Dhrostain: a short, fierce captain from Ghal Thurái.

Farstepper: a rare breed of humans possessing the ability to move from one point to another by traveling through the Otherworld. They come from beyond the Wastes of Khulakorum and are known for their skills as warriors and assassins.

Fist of Ghal Thurái: a greatly feared and respected army out of Ghal Thurái, it was most recently led by **Caladan Durakas**. Alternatively referred to as the Fist of Thurái, or simply the Fist.

Gal'behem: the mountain range that surrounds Khala Val'ur in Gal'dorok. Its name means "the great serpent."

Gal'dorok: A large region encompassing many human and Khyth cities. It is bordered on the east by the Tashkar Sea, to the west by the region of Derenar, and to the south by the Wastes of Khulakorum. Its name means "great pinnacle."

Ghaja Rus: a G'henni who made his fortune from the slave trade. He had former dealings with Khala Val'ur through General **Aldis Tennech**.

Ghal Thurái: also called the Mouth of the Deep, it is a Khyth city built into a mountain. A person from Ghal Thurái is called a Thurian, and their army's colors are copper and white.

G'hen: A city that borders the Wastes of Khulakorum. Its people are known for their dark skin. A person from G'hen is called a G'henni.

Ghost of the Morning: see **Asha Imha-khet**.

Gwarái: An ancient beast created by the Breaker of the Dawn in order to hunt down the Athrani. They feed on the blood of Shapers and can be used to absorb their powers. They were believed to be hunted to extinction during the Shaping War.

Haidan Shar: A city east of Ghal Thurái, also called the Gem of the East, it is a prosperous city that has grown from a once-simple fishing village. A person from Haidan Shar is called a Sharian, and their army's colors are blue and white.

half-eye: A derogatory title given to one born to an Athrani father and a human mother. One of their eyes appears human, while the other appears Athrani (with a second ring of color behind the first). They are capable of Shaping.

Hammer of the Worldforge: an ancient artifact that the Shaper of Ages used to create the world, along with the Anvil of the Worldforge. Collectively they are referred to as the Pieces of the Worldforge.

Hand of the Black Dawn: The name of those who serve the Breaker of the Dawn and seek to free Him. They are led by Khyth, but humans are drawn to them as well. They operate primarily out of Khala Val'ur.

Hedjetti: the title for the ruler of one tribe. The singular form is *Hedjetten*.

Highglade: a village to the east of Lusk whose claim to fame is **Olson Woods**, a blacksmith of great renown. A person from Highglade is called a Highglader.

the Holder: see **Ahmaan Ka**.

Jahaz: a captain in the Sharian army.

Jinda Yhun: Captain of the Guard of Annoch. He is a Farstepper from beyond the Wastes.

Kaurik: twin brother to **Aurik** and older brother to **Kuu**. He is a Wolfwalker.

Keeper: A title given to an Athrani who is charged with the protection of the Temple of the Shaper found in their city. There is one Keeper for every temple, and there is typically one temple in any given city where Athrani are found.

Kethras: a Kienari male, brother to **Ynara** and son of **the Mother**.

Khadje Kholam: a city situated near the northern end of the Wastes of Khulakorum, it is a large tribal city and the current seat of the ruler of several tribes, **Djozen Yelto**. To its west is K'har, and to its east is Menat.

Khala Val'ur: also called the Sunken City, it is the capital city of the Khyth, as well as the capital city of Gal'dorok. A person from Khala Val'ur is called a Valurian, and their army's colors are black and white.

K'har: a tribal city to the west of Khadje Kholam. One of the tribes in the area is the Ohmati.

Khaz: a male Chovathi warrior of the Xua'al clan.

Khel-hârad: the Land of the Dead, whose keeper is the Holder of the Dead.

Khôl: the language spoken in Khadje Kholam and some of the tribal cities nearby. It is also used as a term for someone from Khadje Kholam.

Khyth (title): one who has undergone the ritual of the Breaking in order to gain access to the power of the Otherworld. Above this title exist Master Khyth and High Khyth.

Khyth (people): a people who worship the Breaker of the Dawn and are known for their power to move and manipulate matter, called Breaking. Their eyes resemble smoke and are inherited by their offspring.

Kienar: a small forest near the Talvin Forest that is home to the Kienari.

Kienari: Creatures of stealth and mystery, much taller than humans, who call the forest of Kienar home. They are often described as cat-like, with fine black fur and tails. Their night vision is exceptional and uses heat rather than light to locate their prey. They are master marksmen and feel at home in the trees.

Awaken the Three

Kunas: Master Khyth of Ghal Thurái, he was sent to the city shortly after his Breaking. He is next in line after **Yetz** and **D'kane** to ascend to the position of High Khyth.

Kuu: the youngest of four brothers, he is a Wolfwalker who is still mastering his power. He is able to transform into a gray desert fox.

Lash'Kargá: a southeastern city of Gal'dorok that sits on the edge of the Wastes of Khulakorum. It is nicknamed Death's Edge.

Lash'kun Yho: twin brother to Ahmaan Ka, he is also called the Traveler. His domain is the day.

Lilyana: **Lily** to her mother, she is a young Athrani girl from Ellenos.

Lusk: a human town on the edge of the Talvin forest that has recently become a hub of trade in Derenar.

Luzo: commander of the slaves of Théas. He is a brutish man whose sole duty is to keep the slaves in line.

Menat: a tribal city to the east of Khadje Kholam. A few tribes inhabiting the area are the Qozhen, Khuufi, and Elteri.

Miera Mi'an: a young woman from Highglade who has known **Thornton** since they were young. She never knew her mother and was raised by her father. She was revealed to be, unbeknownst to her, the reincarnation of the goddess the Shaper of Ages.

Mordha: a G'henni woman who is part of the city guard of Annoch. She is second-in-command to **Jinda Yhun** and older sister to **Alysana**.

the Mother: often called the First Kienari, and the Binder of Worlds, she is one of the three gods of creation, and mother to **Kethras** and **Ynara** (see **Kienari**). She was killed by **D'kane** in the Battle for the Tree and was replaced as Binder of Worlds by her daughter, **Ynara**.

Olson Woods: a highly skilled blacksmith from Highglade and father to **Thornton Woods** and **Elyasha**. He was killed by **D'kane** in the Otherworld.

the Otherworld: an ethereal place of power that exists parallel to—and beyond—this world. It is where the Breaker of the Dawn was imprisoned and where the Athrani and Khyth draw their power.

Pieces of the Worldforge: the Hammer of the Worldforge and the Anvil of the Worldforge. Both were used by the Shaper of Ages when creating the world.

Rathma: a Farstepper from Khadje Kholam and younger brother of **Jinda Yhun**.

R'haqa: a tribal city south of Khadje Kholam and north of Do'baradai.

Seralith Edos: an Athrani woman from Ellenos who left the Athrani city for Khala Val'ur, she serves **General Aldis Tennech**.

Shaper of Ages: one of the creators of the world, along with the Breaker of the Dawn and the Binder of Worlds. She gave up her power to the Athrani so they might defend themselves against the Khyth, who were empowered by the Breaker. Her most recent reincarnation was the Highglader **Miera Mi'an**.

Shaping: gifted by the Shaper and wielded by the Athrani, it is the ability to transmute matter into any form imaginable. Only those who are of Athrani blood can Shape.

Shaping War: a long-finished but not forgotten war between the Athrani and Khyth, which served to drive a permanent wedge between the two races. It has been a continuing source of hatred for both of them.

Sh'thanna: the female Athrani Keeper of the Temple of the Shaper in Ellenos. She is friends with **Aldryd**.

Sivulu: the oldest of four brothers, he looks out for **Aurik**, **Kaurik**, and **Kuu**. He is a Wolfwalker of great renown.

the Spears: a mountainous region in the east of the Wastes of Khulakorum. Its peaks run north–northeast into the mountains of Gal'behem, the Great Serpent.

Théas: also called the City of a Thousand Towers, it is situated halfway between Ellenos and G'hen. Its fighting forces are known as the Deathdancers. A person from Théas is called a Théan, and their army's colors are forest green and black.

Thornton Woods: a young blacksmith from Highglade, son of **Olson Woods** and brother to **Elyasha**.

the Three: the collective name for the Traveler, the Holder of the Dead, and the Ghost of the Morning. They sleep in Do'baradai, where, the stories say, they await their reawakening.

Thuma: second-in-command of the Athrani Legion, he is a large Athrani man with a blond beard and brown eyes.

the Traveler: see **Lash'kun Yho**.

the Wastes of Khulakorum: a desert region far to the south known for producing Farsteppers. Most of the region is referred to by outsiders as "beyond the Wastes."

Wolfblade: an ancient weapon infused with the blood of the Ghost and the Holder, and that binds them together. Djozen Yelto has it in his possession.

Wolfwalker: a human who is able to transform into a wolf by the use of an ancient power. Stronger Wolfwalkers are able to transform into larger, monstrous wolves; less powerful Wolfwalkers can only muster the form of smaller canine animals, such as foxes.

Ynara: a Kienari female, sister to **Kethras** and daughter of **the Mother**. She ascended to the role of Binder of Worlds when her mother was killed.

Zhala: brood matriarch of the Xua'al Chovathi clan, she has six subordinate broodmothers, one of whom controls the male **Khaz**.

Acknowledgments

They say that it takes a village to raise a child. Well, the book that you hold in your hands is the result of the efforts of such a village—my friends and family. There were so many moving parts in it beyond just my fingers on a keyboard that I hardly even know where to start.

When in doubt, though, I always thank the strongest woman I know. Thank you, Mom. Without your love for me, as well as for C. S. Lewis and J. R. R. Tolkien, I never would have developed into the fantasy writer and the man that I am today. I owe you everything, and then some.

Thank you, Dad, for your unwavering support and your words of wisdom, and for never letting me quit; Matt, for being my sounding board, my voice of reason, and the best friend a guy could ask for; Sara, for your love and encouragement, and for reminding me that nothing worth having ever comes easy.

To all my beta readers: Damon Heard, Jack Pryor, Chantel Green, Willem VanZeben, Tom LaMantia, Chris Tatalone, Stephanie Marwan, Amanda Mackey, Lauren Walker, Pat Flaherty, Jessica Santacrose, Jen Thurman, Jenny Boyle, Liz Yokum, Ricardo Presas, Nathan Muller, Dale Myers, and Shawn Olphin. This book would not be where it is without your selfless help.

To every single person that ever said anything good about *Gift of the Shaper*, you keep me going. Let me say that again, with emphasis: you keep me going. Thank you for your belief in me and for your support of me, by which I am constantly humbled and moved. I love writing, but nothing prepared me for how much I would enjoy other people loving my writing.

To my editor, Earl, who did such an amazing job with the first book that I had to have him on board with the second. To my publicist, Susan Schwartzman, who saw the story in a combat veteran-turned-author and knew that the world needed to hear it. To Dan at Indigo River, who gave me the chance to become a published author—a chance that I will never forget.

Thank you, one and all, you incredible village.

𝔄bout the 𝔄uthor

David "D. L." Jennings is a fourteen-year veteran of the United States Air Force, having deployed eleven times in support of US Air Force Special Operations. His debut novel, *Gift of the Shaper*, won the 2018 Beverly Hills Book Award for Best Fantasy and was a runner-up for the 2018 Best Book Award.

When he is not reading or writing epic fantasy, he enjoys traveling, listening to '90s punk, and watching Ohio State football.

CPSIA information can be obtained
at www.ICGtesting.com
Printed in the USA
LVHW042111310720
662090LV00004B/490